# INFINITY BORN

## Douglas E. Richards

Paragon Press

# PART 1
## The Rod of God

# 1

It was nearing seven in the morning and President Dillon Mattison was still reeling, three hours after having been awakened from a sound sleep and hastily ushered deep into the earth.

Years earlier the President's Emergency Operations Center, built in the 1940s under the East Wing of the White House to withstand a nuclear attack, had been replaced by the bunker he was now in. This one was below the West Wing, and so fortified and deep that it made the other seem soft and shallow by comparison, as well as containing substantially upgraded communications and computer systems.

What had been *PEOC*, the President's Emergency Operations Center, was now *DUCC*, the Deep Underground Command Center.

During his mad dash to get here, swept along by a whitewater river of Secret Service agents, Mattison had decided that the name DUCC couldn't be more appropriate, although it needed to be spelled a different way—D-U-C-K, not D-U-C-C. And spoken more emphatically. DUCK!

Because that was what he was really doing here. He was *ducking*. And it was beginning to really irk him.

Yes, there had been a horrendous mass casualty event that had taken the world by surprise, at least those who weren't still sleeping in blissful ignorance. But he needed to be out front on this, on television. He needed to be presenting a face of calm. He needed to reassure, to grieve, to publicly provide condolences on behalf of a traumatized nation to friends and families of those tragically lost.

The last thing he needed was to be trapped in a glorified conference room as if he were in personal danger, sniveling like a child frightened of an act of nature that had happened thousands of miles away and that couldn't possibly be a threat to him.

When the Secret Service had insisted that he remain where he was until they were dead certain this was a natural event, and not an attack, he had agreed. But this had been in the beginning of the crisis and by now they should be certain. He would give them thirty more minutes, out of respect, before he demanded to return to the surface.

Lou Nevins, Mattison's Chief of Staff, sat beside him at the ridiculously elongated conference table, listening to a report coming through the comm in his ear, his face looking bleaker by the second. "We have an update on casualties," he said to the gathering, which consisted of five flesh-and-blood humans on the president's National Security Council and numerous others desperately gathering intel and joining or leaving the proceedings as virtual attendees, popping in and out of the Command Center in 3D glory, nearly indistinguishable from the real thing.

Everyone was juggling conversation and a frenzy of activities, but stopped in their tracks to listen to the Chief of Staff's update.

"The original estimates were three thousand dead," said Nevins, looking sick to his stomach. "But this has risen pretty dramatically. We're probably looking at closer to five thousand."

The meeting participants all looked as though they had been punched in the gut. The president visibly cringed and then shook his head in horror. Five thousand! The biggest loss since 9/11.

Even as he thought it, Mattison's political instincts seized on the best possible spin to put on the situation. *Today at three-thirty a.m. Eastern Standard Time*, he would say during his address to the nation, *a terrible tragedy occurred.*

He would ignore the fact that the Secret Service had kept him in his underground prison for so long that his entire audience would already know this.

*A meteor struck the city of Turlock, California,* he would continue, *with devastating effect.*

He would go on to describe the terrible tragedy further, explain that its toll of lives was heavier even than on 9/11, and make it clear that no words could express his or the nation's sense of loss. *Although this is of little comfort right now,* he would add, *we can take some solace from the fact that this was an act of nature and not one of terror.*

He wouldn't have to spell it out further. The casualties may have been greater than those on 9/11, but at least this was a one-off event, not the prologue to a war against terrorism with no end in sight. In this case, the event would at least mark the *end* of the dying rather than the beginning. This would do little to salve the country's immediate emotional wounds, but at least he could put the tragedy in the most positive context possible.

It didn't help that Turlock, California, had become a shining example of the best of America. Of the future of America. When the US tech sector had grown too big for Silicon Valley, and Silicon Valley real estate had become too pricey to house non-millionaire employees, Turlock had beckoned. A hundred miles due east of the famous tech mecca, and a hundred times less expensive, it was the perfect place to spawn the son of Silicon Valley. Five years earlier the migration had begun, and Turlock farmers sitting on huge tracts of land had cashed in big.

Construction was rapid and never-ending as tech companies raced to Turlock—a city the press had begun calling New Silicon Valley, or NSV. Fortunately, the meteor had struck one of the less dense sections of the burgeoning city, and after midnight when the corporate headquarters affected were unoccupied. If it had struck during business hours the number of casualties would have skyrocketed. This, at least, had been a blessing.

Unfortunately, a spate of apartments and condos had sprung up near enough the strike to be in the blast zone. Anything and everything within a little over a half mile of the meteor's point of impact had been destroyed, forming a circle of death over three miles around that was still filled with raging fires.

During 9/11 any number of people had burned to death, or had been forced to jump to their deaths to be free of the blistering heat. In the case of Turlock, many times this number had been burned alive, flash-fried, vaporized. Bile rose in the president's throat as images of helpless victims dying in this way flashed across his mind's eye.

Surely this was the most horrible of all ways to go.

The impact crater was centered on what had once been Quantum Sensor Technologies, a relatively small two-story building that had been in place for just over two years. Next to it had stood the headquarters of Cambridge Nanosystems, which had been a gleaming twenty-story glass structure. Along with these two, five other tech companies had built corporate headquarters of various sizes within the blast radius, and all seven had been flattened and incinerated.

As New Silicon Valley, Turlock had become one of the most concentrated centers of brainpower, innovation, and outside-the-box thinking in the world. It wasn't as if tech geniuses were any more deserving of life than grocery clerks, but the blow to the economy and America's technological competitiveness would be significant.

President Mattison was vaguely aware that Lou Nevins had continued speaking, giving the reason for the increased fatality estimates and describing the progress being made by first responders, called in from neighboring cities as well as the military, which Mattison had ordered deployed within minutes of reaching the Command Center.

Those flooding onto the scene had their hands more than full battling the raging fires and finding and tending to survivors. While no one could have possibly survived within the extended circle that was still in flames, a shock wave had swept through structures up to nine miles distant from the center of the strike, including additional apartment and condo complexes, causing hundreds, or even thousands, of injuries.

Mattison's attention had drifted off, but it returned abruptly as the virtual presence of his Secretary of Homeland Security, Jeff Brown, popped into the meeting across from him and interrupted Nevins in mid-sentence. "This situation just went from bad to worse," he announced gravely.

Brown paused for a moment to be sure he had everyone's full attention. When all eyes and ears were fixed firmly on him, he continued. "Early on there were indications that not everything about the Turlock incident was what it seemed. But before I shared these suspicions, I wanted to be certain, and do some additional digging."

The president swallowed hard. "*What* suspicions?" he demanded, realizing that Brown had, indeed, been absent from the proceedings for long stretches over the past three hours. Now he knew why.

"Half an hour after the strike," replied the Secretary of DHS, "one of my experts, a professor at the University of Arizona named Cathy McGowen, told me that her analysis of satellite footage of the crater footprint suggested it wasn't created by a meteor. At least not a natural one."

The vice president, Pattie Hammond Blask, was seated to Mattison's left, and was in no mood for riddles. "What the hell does that mean?" she demanded. "We've all seen the footage. And we've all seen it compared to aerial footage of past meteor events. It looked exactly like those."

"I'm not an expert," replied Brown, "but my understanding is that Dr. McGowen determined that the center of the crater was deeper than it should have been. Based on the ratio of the crater's depth to its radius, she concluded that the meteor had to be shaped more like an arrow than a ball. Since then I've awakened hundreds of people in DHS and beyond, and I've confirmed that she was right—and much more."

The Command Center was as silent as a tomb as they awaited the rest of Brown's report. Given the stunned expressions on the faces of Andrew Havens, Secretary of Defense, and General Eric Faust, Chairman of the Joint Chiefs, Mattison was convinced the two military experts knew *exactly* where Brown was going with this.

"Based on Dr. McGowen's calculations of the shape, velocity, and angle of impact of the meteor," continued the Secretary of DHS, "my experts were able to go back into infrared satellite footage and get a still of the object."

He touched a tablet computer and an image filled an eight-foot-tall touchscreen monitor against one wall of the Command Center's conference room. While not perfect, the image was surprisingly sharp, and had been placed next to images of known objects such as trees and buildings so viewers could get a sense of its size.

"Is that a telephone pole?" whispered Secretary of State Chris Best in disbelief.

Brown gestured to Eric Faust. "Do you want to field this one, General?" he said.

"It's a rod built for a kinetic attack," said a seething Chairman of the Joint Chiefs through clenched teeth. He visibly fought to calm himself so he could continue. "Built to be dropped from orbit. Nicknamed *the rod of God*. You don't need an active weapon or explosives to get nuclear bomb level results."

"That's exactly right," said the Secretary of Defense, nodding in grim agreement. "The total kinetic energy an object picks up by being in motion is half of its mass times its velocity squared. So a tenfold increase in an object's velocity increases the energy it carries a *hundredfold*. If this object is stopped dead in its tracks, all of this energy is released." Andrew Havens frowned deeply. "Pick up a bullet and throw it at someone and it barely registers. But if this same tiny bullet is going fast enough, we all know how much damage it can do, how much force it can impart."

"Speed kills," said General Faust, picking up the baton. "It's nearly impossible to overstate its power. Darth Vader wouldn't need a *Death Star* to destroy the Earth—or any explosives for that matter. He'd just need to put a single star cruiser on autopilot and ram it into the planet at a tenth of the speed of light. That would be *more* than enough to do the trick. If Vader had ever figured that one out, he would have put a lot of Death Star contractors out of work."

Mattison's eyes widened. He had never considered just how much of a force amplifier raw speed was. If the Earth really could be destroyed by a single ship moving fast enough, humanity would be totally helpless to defend itself against a spacefaring alien civilization. He would never watch another space movie in quite the same way again.

"In 1908," continued the general, "a meteor leveled over seven hundred square miles of dense wilderness near the Tunguska River in Russia. In total, the damn thing knocked down eighty million trees. *Eighty million*. And it was smaller than a high school football stadium."

"The use of kinetic weapons dropped from orbit is illegal by treaty, of course," explained Andrew Havens. "But that doesn't mean our military hasn't studied the shit out of the concept. So has every other military, for that matter."

Brown gestured to the image on the monitor, ready to resume his presentation. "We've analyzed its composition, shape, and weight. It's absolutely textbook for a kinetic round. The concept is simple. Just drop something from orbit, with no explosive payload necessary and very little guidance—assuming you've calculated correctly. As Secretary Best noted, the most effective shape is basically a stream-lined, tapered telephone pole made of tungsten. This metal is very tough and has a melting point four times higher than steel. And this shape is hard to detect and cuts through the air nicely, increasing its velocity at impact."

He paused to let this sink in. "The experts DHS contacted esti-mate that this glorified telephone pole hit the ground between Mach ten and Mach eleven."

"What is that in miles per hour?" asked Pattie Hammond Blask.

"About eight thousand," replied Brown. "Which is a little over two miles per *second*," he added to give further perspective. "This is more than twice the velocity of a rifle shot."

"Only this rifle round is made of tungsten and weighs tens of thousands of pounds," noted the president.

Brown nodded grimly. "My people estimate the energy released on impact was the equivalent of thirty thousand pounds of TNT."

This was a mind-blowing figure, but Mattison had seen the devas-tation with his own eyes and had no doubt that it was accurate.

So this had been an act of war, after all. The Secret Service had *not* been overly cautious. If more of these flying tungsten telephone poles were poised to drop, being deep under the White House was much preferred to being inside of it.

The president gritted his teeth. "It goes without saying that we need to know who is behind this," he insisted. "Immediately! And we need to know if more of these things might be raining down on us. This information is of the highest possible priority," he added unnecessarily.

Brown nodded. "Which is why I didn't spend time reporting this finding two hours ago. Instead, I galvanized my organization to find these answers."

"Are you saying you have them?" asked the president.

"Yes," replied the Secretary of Homeland Security. "With very high confidence. I'll walk you through what we've found, but let me give you the bottom line before I do. First, we're confident that there is only one of these, thank God. And second, this attack wasn't instituted by Islamic radicals or an adversarial nation-state. It was launched by a single American civilian."

He paused, almost as if for dramatic effect. "To be more specific, it was launched by Isaac Jordan. From the *Eureka*, the flagship of his R-Drive fleet."

Mattison's jaw dropped open, and his wasn't the only one. "Isaac Jordan?" he said, shaking his head slowly. "Impossible! I don't believe it."

"I understand why you might say that," said Brown. "But once you see the evidence I've gathered, I'm sure you'll change your mind."

# 2

President Dillon Mattison could only absorb so many shocks to his system, and after learning that the meteor strike on Turlock was really an attack, the idea that Isaac Jordan might be responsible was one shock too many.

There was no way Jordan was behind this. He didn't care how much evidence Jeff Brown thought he had gathered.

Isaac Jordan was a legend, admired around the globe. His personal wealth was greater than that of most nations. He was a superstar entrepreneur, scientist, and world-changer who had become a bigger celebrity than Stephen Hawking, Bill Gates, Steve Jobs, Mark Zuckerberg, or Elon Musk before him.

There wasn't a person on the planet who didn't know his story.

Born last in a family of seven children, his father had deserted them soon after his arrival, leaving his mother to raise a family she couldn't possibly afford. Largely responsible for himself since the day he learned to walk, Jordan had worked at odd jobs to earn money for food, and was largely absent from school.

Fortunately for him, he possessed a once-in-a-generation genius, and lived in an era in which he could pirate digital copies of expensive textbooks. He became a self-taught polymath, his genius unconstrained by narrow college majors or PhD programs, free to roam, to explore whatever interested him across numerous disciplines. Chemistry, math, physics, biology, computer science, sociology—he dived deep into each with unparalleled zeal.

He made millions starting and selling mundane companies by the time he was twenty-five, and then took a year off from business to change the face of physics as profoundly as Newton or Einstein had before him.

For years the concept of an electromagnetic drive that would revolutionize space travel had captured the imaginations of crackpots. Even a few legitimate scientists—including a NASA group tasked with exploring exotic concepts for future propulsion—had detected slight amounts of propulsion being generated by such a device, dubbed the EmDrive. Still, the majority of those in the physics community were convinced this was nothing more than experimental error and that anyone who believed otherwise was a self-delusional idiot.

There was good reason for this dismissal. The EmDrive flew in the face of accepted physics—the *only* flying most believed it would ever do. Since the days of Newton, it was clear that for every action you needed an equal and opposite reaction. You could move an electric car on Earth without the need for propellant, true, but only because the car had the *road* to push back against, providing forward movement.

But in space, with nothing to push against, if you wanted to drive a rocket or a spacecraft forward, you had to shoot something out of its back end. Nothing in space could be propelled without propellant. Period. End of story.

Only those behind the EmDrive claimed the device could achieve propulsion in a vacuum without expelling *anything*, without the need for heavy fuel that weighed down spacecraft and made travel to Mars and beyond prohibitively costly and time consuming. The drive was a truncated cone, narrower at one end than the other, and totally enclosed. It created force by bouncing electromagnetic radiation back and forth inside of it—in this case, microwaves.

Believing this strategy could work was as ridiculous as believing you could get your car to move forward by sitting inside of it and bouncing ping pong balls against the dash. It was utterly absurd.

But the data stubbornly continued to show that this is exactly what was happening. That this reactionless drive had somehow found a loophole in the laws of nature.

Isaac Jordan, high school dropout, decided to take the data at face value and see where this would lead him. Einstein had done the exact same thing a century earlier. At that time, data seemed to indicate that the speed of light was exactly the same no matter how fast its source was moving toward or away from an observer. Instead of decrying this result as impossible, Einstein decided to determine what the laws of physics would have to be for it to be true. What he found—that as objects approach light speed their time slows relative to unmoving objects, their mass increases, and their length decreases—at first ridiculed by many, was later proved to be true in every instance, and had totally upended physics.

At the age of twenty-six, Isaac Jordan managed to do nothing less. By assuming the EmDrive effect was real rather than a hoax, he was able to completely rewrite the laws of physics. His work was utterly revolutionary. Disruptive. Profound.

Jordan should have been a lock to receive a Nobel Prize, but the fact that he didn't even have a high-school diploma weighed against him. Einstein had been a lowly patent clerk when he had done his seminal work, but he, at least, had earned a PhD, and his Nobel Prize wasn't awarded until fifteen years after he had developed his theory of relativity, and not even for this contribution.

But even so, even without a formal education, Jordan's contributions were so unparalleled the Nobel committee couldn't *possibly* deny him his due. Couldn't, at least, unless he committed an unpardonable sin, which he managed to do with breathtaking speed.

Instead of going forward as an academic purist to develop his theories further—the kind of academic purist the committee liked to reward—he had shown himself to be a ruthless capitalist. He had wasted no time in patenting numerous applications for his theoretical discovery, leaving the ivory tower realm of science to exploit them commercially, forming yet another company, Space Treasure Industries, or STI.

His theories allowed him to perfect a Reactionless-Drive design that put the fledgling EmDrive to shame. He rapidly built a fleet of relatively inexpensive R-Drive-powered spacecraft that could reach Mars in weeks, rather than months or years, and which he initially used to mine the Moon and asteroids, beating several long-running companies to the punch.

The Moon possessed bountiful quantities of helium-3, extremely rare on Earth. Helium-3 was the perfect fuel source for nuclear fusion, a fuel the Sun produced in great quantity and dumped on the Moon, but which Earth's magnetic field rejected.

But as lucrative as Jordan's helium-3 mines quickly became, the asteroids were his figurative—and literal—gold mines. They contained treasures galore, a ridiculous bounty of gold, silver, osmium, iridium, palladium, and platinum, along with numerous other rare and expensive materials.

Within eight years of turning the physics world upside down, Isaac Jordan did the same with the world's economy, flooding the markets with precious metals and making himself the first ever trillionaire in the process.

With this vast wealth he went on to establish a thriving colony on Mars, this time beating Elon Musk to the punch, selling the reality TV rights to life in the colony for almost as much as the project had cost him.

He was known to be brilliant, relentless, and ruthless—at least when he felt he had to be. He was an absolutely unstoppable force. Anything or anyone standing between him and one of his goals didn't stand a chance.

His mind, his wealth, his ambition, and his plans for the future were so much larger than life they had become almost absurd.

And of the multitude of entries he could have added to his résumé, *mass murderer* was the last one anyone could possibly have foreseen.

# 3

Dillon Mattison's full attention returned once more to a bunker deep under the West Wing of the White House. He stared deeply into the eyes of his Secretary of Homeland Security and saw absolute conviction there. Isaac Jordan's guilt remained to be seen, but Jeff Brown was certainly convinced of it.

"My experts were able to backtrack the kinetic round's path," began Brown, "and crosscheck it with every satellite and spacecraft in orbit. There was no doubt where the round originated. Like I said, from the *Eureka*, the flagship of Jordan's R-Drive fleet."

"Too easy," said Chris Best. "A guy this smart would have covered his tracks so he could never be connected to this atrocity. It has to be someone in Jordan's employ. Or a frame-up. Just because a murder takes place in a building Isaac Jordan owns doesn't make him a murderer."

"My team and I thought the same thing," said Brown. "What motive could he possibly have? A man wealthier and more famous than God? We looked into it, and several of the corporate headquarters that were destroyed did compete with some of the businesses he's now in. Still, the motive had to be a lot more visceral than that to trigger this kind of response. Besides, when you almost literally own the world, who *isn't* a competitor?"

Brown shook his head, as if still unable to believe his own findings. "So we did a lot of exploration, a lot of waking people up. I can go into detail later, but the picture that emerged left little doubt that he was personally responsible. He personally ordered the tungsten round built to the exact specifications of the one that hit New Silicon Valley. To the centimeter. A telephone-pole-sized tapered rod. He lied about its purpose to those who built it for him. He said he was looking into new techniques for skyscraper construction and wanted to use it in several experiments. The people who built it for him had no reason to doubt him, or suspect what it was really for."

He sighed. "The good news is that he only had one. The manager in charge of the project was certain, because he offered Jordan a deep discount if he would buy in greater quantity. But Jordan insisted that only a single unit be produced, and that the mold be destroyed right afterward."

"This manager could have been dealing with an impostor for all we know," said Nevins.

Brown shook his head. "We verified this intel in several ways," he said. "We have no doubt that the man who ordered the kinetic round was Isaac Jordan, that only one was made, and that only one was loaded onto any of his spacecraft."

Mattison was still far from convinced of Jordan's guilt, and he could tell by the body language of those around the room that he had plenty of company.

"But this is only the beginning of what we found," continued Brown. "We also discovered Jordan created a complex computer system for the sole purpose of taking control of the *Eureka* and the tungsten payload in its cargo hold. Remotely. With the necessary precision to hit any target he chose. The control system was installed in the only building he owns in the city of Turlock. A manufacturing plant three miles beyond the ring of death."

The president considered. Whoever framed this man had done a skillful job. Mattison had little doubt the rod had been loaded onto the *Eureka* and dropped from this ship as Brown had determined. Placing a computer that could access the ship and its payload in the only building Jordan owned in Turlock, which happened to be located just beyond the devastation, had been a masterful touch. "What does he manufacture at this plant?" he asked.

"An advanced form of graphene," replied Brown. "For those not familiar, I'm told graphene is a carbon structure that forms two-dimensional honeycombed sheets. You can make it a superconductor, and it's two hundred times stronger than steel. Apparently, Jordan uses the stuff in his ships, but there is no obvious connection between graphene and this attack, other than the facility's proximity to ground zero."

"The evidence so far is all circumstantial," noted Vice President Blask.

"It won't be by the time I'm finished," replied Brown. "To continue, we also learned that the computer Jordan set up to control the *Eureka* could only be accessed by him," he added. "It had multiple levels of security. Access not only required complex passwords that only Jordan knew, but also his presence. His *willing* presence. He installed a sensor on the computer capable of measuring his unique brain activity signature, which could only be read if he were still alive. No match, no entrance. Finally, before the system would let him in, he had to pass the equivalent of a sensitive lie detector test. Unless he truthfully indicated he was accessing the computer of his own free will, he would be shut out."

The more certain the evidence against Isaac Jordan seemed, the more convinced Mattison became that the tech icon could not be behind it. He was far too smart, and the case against him far too tight.

"Someone must have found a way past these safeguards," insisted the president. "What's more likely, that someone found a way to hack this unhackable system? Or that Isaac Jordan willingly killed thousands of people?"

"I put dozens of my best agents on this," said Brown, "and we all shared your skepticism. Even after uncovering incontrovertible evidence that Isaac Jordan built and installed the kinetic rod on the *Eureka* and was the only one with the keys. So we continued to turn over every stone we could find. Turns out that Jordan has actually been living in Turlock for the past twenty months, not his corporate headquarters in Seattle. Living about four miles beyond the zone of death, in fact, and a mile from his graphene facility."

"This makes sense," said Lou Nevins. "If you want to frame Isaac Jordan, you have to be sure any smoking gun you plant is within his easy reach."

Brown winced. "Speaking of smoking guns," he said, a look of revulsion momentarily appearing on his face, "we discovered video footage taken by security cameras in his home. The footage was taken using a quantum verification system, so it couldn't have been doctored without us knowing it."

He blew out a long breath. "I'll run it on the main screen now," he said grimly. "But I have to warn you—it isn't for the faint of heart."

Mattison's eyes narrowed. After the horrors they had seen over the past three hours it was hard to imagine anything could throw them at this point. The fact that Brown thought this footage might do the trick was troubling.

The video opened with a man who was unmistakably Isaac Jordan entering his mansion home. The vast structure was well lighted on the outside and absolutely magnificent, although understated compared to many of his other residences around the world.

"This is just over twenty minutes before the rod hit," explained Brown. "We learned from the computer on the *Eureka* that two hours earlier, Jordan had already set the strike in motion."

"On some kind of time-delayed fuse?" said the president.

"Exactly."

"Not to be a broken record," said Nevins, gesturing to the man on the screen who was now inside of the home, "but, again, can we be sure this isn't an impostor?"

"Yes," said Brown. "The richest man in the world has the best security system money can buy. It wouldn't let him enter if it didn't confirm his identity biometrically in several different ways."

The group watched, spellbound, as Jordan walked straight to his private workshop, which was the size of a ballroom and filled with enough advanced tools and machinery to make the fictional Tony Stark envious. Dim lights came on in front of him as he walked and then were extinguished as he passed. Jordan was legendary for his tireless work ethic, and the lights had clearly been programmed to light his way when he came home after dark while causing minimal disturbance to the rest of his family.

He moved purposefully to a large steel cabinet and removed a Sig Sauer X490 Futura handgun from a drawer, one of a small collection of weapons developed during the early 2020's with advanced muffling and noise-canceling technology that made the gun whisper-quiet.

No one in the Deep Underground Command Center spoke, but this was an intriguing development. Had this scene simply been the opening of a movie they would have been hooked, needing to know what happened next. But given this footage was reality, and touted as the ultimate evidence against the richest man on Earth for the murder of thousands, it could not have been more riveting.

Jordan walked briskly to the master bedroom where his stunning wife was sleeping soundly, just visible in the dim lighting that continued to follow him around. He pointed the Sig Sauer at her lithe body and held it steady for almost a full minute. Then, without warning, the gun spat three times in quick succession, and his wife's sleep became permanent, her life ended before she had any idea she was even in peril. Bright red blood gushed from her torso onto the thin satin sheets.

When the life-sized man on the monitor had pulled the trigger, most of those deep under the White House had jumped, mirroring the brief, spasmodic movements made by Jordan's wife as the bullets punched holes through her body. Gasps of surprise and horror could be heard throughout the conference room.

On the screen, Jordan was now surveying his handiwork. A broad grin spread over his face as he tilted his head to watch the blood accumulate. He bent over, turned his wife's head so it was facing him, and pushed open her eyelids. Finally, Isaac Jordan stared into the lifeless eyes of a woman whose beauty was flawless, even in death, with utter malevolence. "Good riddance, bitch!" he spat, and then quickly exited the room.

This scene was repeated twice more, as Jordan made his way into each of his two sons' bedrooms, ages ten and twelve, his expression more and more maniacal, and ended their lives while they slept, the gun as quiet as advertised.

A stunned silence came over the Command Center conference room, and all eyes remained glued to the scene that continued to unfold on the large monitor.

Jordan had now made his way to the home's entry foyer and began running full speed into the oversized oak door, crashing his body against it with bone-jarring force, as if he were a charging bull and the door a red cape.

*What the hell?* thought Mattison in dismay. He had heard once that there was a fine line between genius and insanity, and it was clear that this line had snapped completely in Isaac Jordan's case. But slamming into a door seemed even more random than wiping out his family.

On the screen, Jordan had done considerable damage to his body, and he was now certainly bruised and in great pain, but he didn't appear to have broken any bones. He repeated his charge four times, dazed after each attempt. Finally, the fifth time, he tilted his head forward at the last instant, something he had managed to avoid until then, so that it took the brunt of the impact.

He collapsed to the floor like a sack of cement and remained there.

Brown paused the video. "To save time," he said, breaking viewers from their trance, "we'll skip ahead. Jordan doesn't move for a while. He's still out cold when his kinetic round hits, thirteen minutes later. The shock wave passes through his house, shaking it like an earthquake would, but he's already on the floor and doesn't take any further damage. He finally returns to consciousness three minutes after the strike. We'll pick it up there."

When the footage resumed, Isaac Jordan looked dazed, as expected, and far worse for wear, as though he had just returned from a particularly nasty bar fight. The malevolent smile he had displayed while killing his family was gone, as was the maniacal gleam that had been in his eye while repeatedly ramming a door.

Instead, unexpectedly—as if anything else they had witnessed could have possibly been expected—his face twisted up in a rictus of pain and tears began to flow down his cheeks. This didn't change for almost half a minute, until he suddenly shook his head, as if to clear it. A look of resolve and determination now came over his face and his tears began to slow.

While nothing Isaac Jordan had done made any sense, it had become abundantly clear that it didn't need to. He was a raving psychotic. He didn't need a rational motive for dropping his kinetic weapon on Turlock, California, because he was demonstrably *irrational. Crazed* might be a better word.

He walked briskly back to the workshop in which he had stored his gun, but this time he retrieved an axe. He quickly carried it back to the scenes of his crimes, to each of three bedrooms, and then, one by one, hacked off the heads of his wife and sons like they were cords of wood he was preparing for his fireplace.

Tears returned to his face as he carried out these grisly beheadings. In each instance it took him several swings of the axe to cleave cleanly through a neck, and in each case the blood poured rather than spurted, as each heart had stopped pumping the red substance twenty minutes or so earlier.

All of those watching this scene inside the Command Center's conference room were utterly transfixed. Repulsed and horrified, of course, but stunned and mesmerized as well.

Brown ended the show and the screen became as empty as everyone now felt. "I think we've all seen enough," he said softly, "and we have pressing matters to return to. But you should know that Jordan went on to gather the three heads in a large duffel bag, like they were some kind of grisly souvenirs, and then raced away in a sports car. The car left his garage about fifteen minutes after the rod's impact."

No one spoke, or even breathed, for several long seconds.

"So Jordan triggers his kinetic round on a timer," President Mattison mumbled, breaking the silence, no longer doubting Brown's conclusions. "Then he wipes out his entire family. Then he almost kills himself tilting at door-shaped windmills. Finally, he flees the scene with three, ah . . . *trophies* in tow."

"In a nutshell, yes," said Brown. "With one correction. This wasn't his entire family. His oldest child, Melissa, who's a senior in high school, is visiting a friend for a few days in San Francisco. She's most likely still sleeping soundly, even as we speak."

The president nodded. No doubt this would be the *last* time Melissa Jordan slept soundly for a long, long time. "I assume Jordan's security system automatically sent this footage to the local cops," he said. "Have they caught him yet?"

"Not a chance," said Brown. "Not after Turlock got hit like it did. Every cop and fireman for miles around is in way over their heads responding to the injured and dying and helping with triage. They wouldn't stop to arrest Jordan if he crawled by them with his middle finger extended. We tried to track him after seeing the security video, but he had some high-tech tricks up his sleeve for avoiding satellites and cameras and we lost him. With his resources and brilliance, if he wants to stay lost, it's hard to imagine he won't be able to do it."

"We need to freeze his assets," said Andrew Havens.

"We tried," said Brown. "But we were already too late. About twenty percent of his net worth disappeared instantly. He must have had a plan in place for vanishing this money at a moment's notice— just in case. Brilliantly done, as one would expect of him. Not sure where the money went, but probably in multiple numbered accounts in Switzerland and the Cayman Islands. We were able to freeze the majority of it, but he's hidden about two hundred billion dollars."

"A thousand times as much as he needs to stay off the radar," said Chris Best miserably.

The president blew out a long breath. "We can worry about capturing him later," he said. "Right now, we have a crisis to address. My gut says to stick with this being a natural disaster. Admitting that we were hit with a weapon like this will panic the shit out of everyone. Yes, nukes are even worse, but we have deterrents in place, and the last time a nuke went off in anger was in the 1940s. And everyone has become at least somewhat acclimated to the nuclear threat. The threat from kinetic weapons, on the other hand, is completely off the radar. We're at the highest levels of government, and many of *us* weren't even aware of the possibilities. So do we really want to awaken the public to this harsh reality while fires are still raging in Turlock, and people are still dying?"

The Secretary of Homeland Security winced. "I'm afraid we don't have a choice," he said. "My group has tipped off too many people in our rush to get to the truth. And my sources tell me this story has already leaked to the media. Even if it hadn't, the cat wouldn't have stayed in the bag for long, anyway. Professor McGowen isn't the only scientist who will be able to tell that the object that hit us wasn't a natural meteor. "

"Shit!" said the president simply. "That puts us in a very bad position."

Lou Nevins frowned. "What about the video you just showed us?" he said to the Secretary of Homeland Security. "This hasn't leaked, has it?"

"It hasn't," said Brown. "We can still keep Isaac Jordan's involvement a secret if we want to."

"No!" said President Mattison. "That would just make a bad situation worse. Given that we can't hide the fact of a kinetic round," he added, "that's the last thing we can do. We need to get this footage to the media as soon as possible. When the nature of this attack goes public, we don't want anyone thinking that Russia, North Korea, or China was behind it. Or a Jihadi group. Talk about blind panic."

Nevins nodded his agreement, as did several other attendees.

"We've been painted into such a corner this time," continued the president, "that for once, the best option is to reveal everything we know. We have to finger Isaac Jordan and make it clear this was a one-off event perpetrated by a madman."

Mattison paused in thought. "Now that we know it's safe to go back to the surface, I say we do that now. I'll arrange for a televised address to the nation for thirty minutes from now. I'll jot down some bullet points, but I won't wait for a written speech. Sometimes a heartfelt, unprepared address is the most effective. Jeff, you continue working to gather evidence so the case against Jordan is as tight as it can be."

Brown nodded. "Will do," he said.

Mattison turned to his Secretary of Defense. "Andrew, have the military continue sending doctors, medical equipment, and blood to Turlock. We want to err on the side of too much humanitarian assistance rather than too little. And I want these fires out, the wounded cared for, and the situation normalized as soon as possible. I don't care how many men and women you have to mobilize to do it."

"Roger that," said Andrew Havens.

# 4

The stir the attack on Turlock caused in the US and around the world was immense—as it should have been. And the panic. But as each day passed without another attack, the fear lessened, and people once again went on with their lives, only glancing up at the sky to wonder if this day would be their last on rare occasion.

Less than three months after the tragedy in Turlock, Isaac Jordan's daughter, Melissa, the sole survivor of the bloody massacre that had taken place in her home, disappeared, despite electronic and human security protecting her in case her father tried to finish the job.

Six months after this, when an extensive effort to find her had turned up nothing, Melissa Jordan was finally presumed dead. She was presumed to have been killed by her father, who hadn't been deterred by what he must have considered laughable security measures.

A little over three years later, Isaac Jordan was found. He had been killed in an auto accident, and the officer on the scene had recognized the most reviled man on the planet, despite the obvious attempts Jordan had made to change his appearance. Jordan's identity was confirmed using DNA analysis, and just like that, almost four years after the strike on Turlock, the chapter was closed on perhaps the most remarkable human in history.

Never had a man achieved so much, only to fall from grace so completely, so destructively. The gulf between Isaac Jordan's highs and lows was far greater, and far more dramatic, than that of any character out of a Shakespearean Tragedy.

Never had a man achieved so much, and been so admired, only to die as the most despised man on the planet.

And that was that. After killing his entire family, along with more than five thousand innocent residents of Turlock, California, the greatest genius in a century was dead.

Despite tireless investigations, and a four-year manhunt, little was ever found to add to what Jeff Brown and his people had learned in the first few hours after the attack. While Isaac Jordan had killed his wife and sons with pure hatred etched across every inch of his face, spitting a malevolent curse at each after he did so, by all accounts he had loved his wife and kids as much as any man.

But whatever insanity had gripped him, whatever justification he thought he had for his actions, would forever remain a mystery, buried along with his body.

# PART 2
## Experiments

# 5

(Eight Years After the Attack on Turlock)

Trish Casner was groggy but felt absolutely content, her body luxuriating in total calm and comfort, and her mind too befuddled to seize on any possible worries. This was as close to perfect peace and serenity as it got, a taste of nothing less than heaven.

But the moment she began to truly appreciate the ideal state of sleep she was in, a blaring alarm gradually began to work its way through her thick cloak of tranquility, threatening to wrest her consciousness back to the cold reality of the living. She was a fetus floating in the womb, about to have her peace shattered by a harsh journey to the outside world, followed by a cold pair of umbilical cord scissors lying in wait.

Not if she could help it.

She would buy more time in paradise no matter what the cost. She would wake just enough to hit the snooze button before lapsing back into a blissful state at the edge of sleep. If only the snooze was set to kill the alarm for an eternity rather than an all-too-fleeting eight minutes.

She flopped her arm to the right in a practiced motion, calibrated so that her hand would land on a button on top of her small clock.

Only she didn't flop her arm to the right.

Her arm didn't move a millimeter. Undeterred, and trying not to engage her brain so she wouldn't be awakened more fully, she tried again. The result was the same.

After just a few more seconds of groggy experimentation she realized she couldn't move *anything*, not her legs, arms, fingers, toes, or nose. Not her lips or forehead. Everything was locked in place, save for her ribcage, which continued a slow rise and fall, filling her lungs with life.

Was she paralyzed?

Her full consciousness now came flooding back and she realized she couldn't even open her eyes. She was completely entombed—Han Solo in a block of carbonite. She searched her mind, but had no idea where she was, or how she had come to be there.

Just as panic began to burst forth from deep within, the foam cocoon that encased her like a second skin underwent a computer-driven phase transition, returning to a liquid state and draining away, finally freeing her to open her eyes.

She blinked and strained until her vision returned. She was in a coffin-shaped chamber, instantly familiar as a suspended animation pod to anyone who had ever seen a science fiction movie. While she had no memory of how she came to be here, she was eerily certain she was on some kind of space vehicle, which seemed absurd, bat-shit crazy. Even without a memory she knew in her bones that this was far from a routine circumstance for her.

It was impossible for her to be on a spaceship, and yet she knew that she was.

The alarm finally stopped sounding and she glanced down just in time to see an IV line that had been inserted into her arm retract painlessly and disappear into the side of the pod. The pod's transparent plastic lid slid open automatically with the slightest of whooshing sounds, and a small restraining strap retracted, leaving her free to float gently out of the pod.

Float?

*Holy hell!* she thought. She was in zero gravity. She hadn't just been feeling weightless in a spiritual sense. She hadn't needed the world's best intuition and a futuristic suspended animation chamber to know she was in space, after all. The complete lack of gravity had provided another clue, but her conscious mind wouldn't let her acknowledge the truth of it. *Good work, Sherlock,* she chided herself.

Finding herself in a spacecraft made no sense at all. It was laughably absurd.

As she rose she grasped one of the many gray straps that were affixed to the walls and ceilings, convenient handholds for those who found themselves floating. She noted absently that she was wearing black silk pajamas, even as part of her had expected to find herself clad only in white panties and undershirt, a suspended animation garb made famous by Sigourney Weaver.

Surprisingly, even though liquid had drained from around her, her skin and hair were bone dry, as were the pajamas. Even though the substance had acted like a liquid, it had somehow managed to avoid one property she had foolishly grown to expect in all of her liquids: the ability to make things wet.

She inspected her surroundings. She was in a cylindrical chamber, about the diameter of a jet airplane, or a submarine, except in place of steel she only found white, antiseptic plastic, light but sturdy. There were sealed doors at the far end, which she suspected led to a cargo compartment.

Her eye was instantly drawn to a coffin-like chamber sitting beside the one she had just vacated. She gazed down at the supine figure inside. It was a hardened foam statue of a male body, only his pinkish mouth and nostrils free of the enveloping substance, which transformed to a liquid before her eyes and ran to the bottom of the chamber and into a drainage system underneath.

Less than a minute later, while she searched her memory and continued to come up empty, a male figure floated up from the pod, also clad in black silk pajamas. Even though the man's pajamas were loose fitting, it was clear from the parts of his body she could see that he was an Adonis. His face was breathtaking in its perfection, and she had no doubt his body was the same.

He stared at her in horror. "Jesus, Trish, what have you done?"

She squinted. "Do I know you?" she asked.

"Shit!" he said, taking a deep breath. "You've got temporary amnesia. Do you even know who *you* are?"

She opened her mouth to answer but shut it again in alarm. The truth was that she didn't. Didn't know her background, how she came to be here, or even her own name, which apparently was Trish.

Bronzed Adonis frowned deeply. "Hold on," he said, rising several feet and manipulating a small touch screen on the ceiling. The entire forward wall of the chamber they were in dissolved and was replaced by countless stars, brighter and more beautiful than any star field she had ever seen, instantly blinking into glorious existence. A moment later she realized the bulkhead material hadn't phase-shifted like the foam to become transparent, they were viewing the outside on a monitor, projected there by ultra-high-definition video cameras.

"What's your name?" she asked, turning away from the stars and staring into the piercing blue eyes of her traveling companion.

"Burt Dalton," he replied, continuing to look horrified to the core of his being, as though he had just watched his favorite puppy get hit by a car. "And you're Trish Casner."

He closed his eyes as if his oncologist was about to convey the results of a biopsy, with the news likely to be devastating. "Halle," he said, his eyes still closed, "what is our current distance from Mars?"

"Just over thirty-eight million miles," replied the ship's computer from several tiny speakers implanted in the compartment.

Dalton nodded gravely as though the oncologist had confirmed his worst fears.

"What's going on, . . . Burt?" asked Trish Casner anxiously, certain that she didn't really want to know. "How did I get here? Why can't I remember?"

Dalton removed a box of metal clips from a compartment nearby and helped her clip herself to the handhold so she could float in place without needing to grasp it. He sighed. "The pod you were in is designed to provide a perfect environment, the proper drugs, and the proper nutrition for a three-week hibernation."

"Suspended animation," she said, nodding. "I guessed as much."

Dalton shook his head. "No. Not like what you're thinking. Still haven't cracked that nut. Just a very deep, drug-assisted sleep. The drugs are very effective, but in about half the population they induce amnesia upon awakening, which lasts about eight to ten hours. You can tell who's susceptible to this side effect through genetic testing."

Trish blew out a relieved breath. "I'm obviously susceptible. But I can't tell you how relieved I am that my memory will be coming back. How do I know you?"

Dalton's pained expression didn't diminish. "You and I are engaged to be married," he replied.

Trish's mouth fell open. "Wow. This memory loss thing goes deep. You'd think I'd get some glimmer, some shadow of recognition if you mean that much to me. But I'm getting nothing." She raised her eyebrows and smiled impishly. "But I get why I'd fall for you, at least physically. You may be the sexiest man I've ever seen. I don't even remember what I look like, but I'm already positive you're out of my league. How did I manage to land you?"

He smiled sadly. "Because you're funny and self-deprecating. Because you're amazing on too many levels to count."

"You probably say that to every girl who has no memory," she said with a grin, but this attempt at levity only seemed to depress him further. "So what's going on?" she added warily.

"There was an emergency on the Mars colony. An accident wiped out most of their food supply. You and I were visiting Moon Base *Destiny*. I wasn't scheduled to fly to Mars for several months, but since I was the only Mars-certified pilot on *Destiny*, and the colonists are quickly running out of time, I was tapped to go."

"Are you saying that Mars flights only leave from the Moon?"

He nodded. "The amount of fuel you save by avoiding Earth's gravity well is extraordinary. Usually I make the trip with my co-pilot, Steve Rowell. He's a good friend of yours, who introduced us, by the way. But I couldn't wait for him to get to the Moon. Given the urgency of the situation, I was forced to make the trip alone."

Trish Casner swallowed hard. "But you're *not* alone," she pointed out. "*I'm* here."

"Yeah," he said, frowning deeply, "I noticed. You must have thought that since Steve couldn't make it, there was room for a passenger. So you stowed away. You must have sealed yourself in a hibernation chamber after I was already under. You've seen me do it often enough the past few years. I'm sure you wanted to surprise me. I've told you that we're only conscious during the last week of the journey, and I've often complained about how boring that week can be. And that's when I at least have Steve for companionship. Knowing you, you decided that a week of wild, weightless sex would turn this from my loneliest journey ever into the greatest week of my life."

"I don't know anything about myself," said Trish with a grin, "but that sounds like something I would think. Still hard to imagine I'd actually stow away on a spaceship, though."

"You're well aware that I've made the trip twelve times now, and that it's pretty routine. I've told you I think it's safer than being on the freeway back home, which probably overcame any worries you might have had. You must have thought this would be the perfect surprise. The perfect gift to me."

"Based on your reactions, I was wrong about that, wasn't I? Why do I have this sick feeling you're about to tell me something really bad?"

Dalton's eyes moistened, confirming her worst fears. "I love you, Trish. More than I can say. But there were a few details of the hibernation process you didn't know about. Details I never thought it important to tell you, since I never thought in a million years you'd try to stow away."

"Like what?"

"The drug cocktail that induces deep sleep is carefully tailored to the genetics of each crew member. To safely keep a human body near death for three weeks is not a simple thing. Dosing depends on body weight and a person's genetic ability to metabolize drugs and clear them from their system. Everyone responds to meds in slightly different ways, and this is amplified when it's a cocktail of meds delivered continuously over many weeks. The upshot is that the hibernation chamber you were in was set to Steve's specifications. His body is deficient in Cytochrome P450, a family of enzymes that breaks down the main hibernation drug we're using."

Trish thought about this for a moment. "Meaning that the drug stays in Steve's system longer in its active form than it does for most people."

"That's right. So he doesn't need much of it. You must have a highly active Cytochrome P450 system, so that the drug is rapidly cleared from your bloodstream. So the dose that was right for Steve is wrong for you. You've awakened about ten days early. Since I'm ship's captain, the computer reversed my meds to awaken me when sensors detected that you were coming out of deep sleep."

Trish winced. "Okay, so we're both up early. So we have to endure the boredom of close quarters for seventeen days instead of seven. But surely we can make lemonade out of this. As soon as my memory comes back, as soon as I remember how much I love you, we can screw each other into a coma. We can try positions impossible in gravity. We can jointly publish the space-based version of the Kama Sutra."

She paused. He really was the most spectacular male specimen she had ever seen. "Hell, even if my memory *doesn't* come back, I'm willing to take your word that we're engaged and have a go," she finished with a smile.

Dalton didn't reply. He unhooked himself and pushed off gently from the wall, drifting across the few feet that separated them. He wrapped his arms around her, kissing her softly on the lips, despite knowing he was still a stranger to her. She didn't resist.

When he finally separated from her fifteen seconds later, several tiny droplets of water were floating between them. Tears had silently left his eyes, and while some had stuck to his face like they would have on Earth, others now drifted like pollen nearby.

"Seventeen days of being with you *would* be heaven," he said sadly. "But it's not that easy, Trish. Hibernation isn't just about avoiding boredom. It's also about conserving oxygen. In deep sleep you use very little."

A sudden bout of vertigo swept over her as the portent of these words sank in. The ship seemed to be spinning out of control, as though tumbling through space in nauseating fashion. She fought back vomit until the vertigo passed, knowing that vomiting in zero gravity would introduce a whole new level of disgusting as the contents of her stomach floated throughout the cabin.

Dalton had been in a dour mood since first spying her, and now Trish knew why. No wonder he looked like he was going to a funeral. Because he probably was.

"Let's just go back to sleep, then," she said hopefully, but in her heart she knew that if it were that easy, his eyes wouldn't still be wet.

"Can't. Can't yo-yo back and forth. Once you come out of hibernation, you can't go back in for at least thirty-six hours."

"Why not?"

Dalton shook his head. "Not even our best doctors are positive on that one. But you go in again before, say, thirty hours, and you never come back out. So we're left with no solution. This ship was loaded with incredible precision. But your weight wasn't accounted for. It's only the tiniest fraction of the total, but it adds up over a distance of more than thirty million miles. We can jettison an equivalent weight in supplies to be sure we don't run out of fuel, but we're only carrying enough oxygen for me, since Steve wasn't coming. We removed his oxygen supply to save weight, so we could squeeze in additional cargo."

"You didn't keep any extra air for emergencies?"

"Yes, there is plenty of cushion—for one man," he replied pointedly. "One man who was expected to be in hibernation and barely using any oxygen for three weeks out of the four. Now we have two people, both now conscious, with normal physiology, burning through the air supply at a greatly accelerated rate."

There was a long silence in the spacecraft.

"Then I have to stop breathing, don't I?" said Trish softly.

Dalton shook his head vigorously, his features hardening. "No! That's not the answer," he whispered.

"Level with me, Burt. When do we reach the point of no return? Assuming you reenter hibernation in thirty-six hours, when would I have to stop breathing for you to still be able to make it under these circumstances?"

"That's not going to happen," he insisted stubbornly, his expression numb.

"Tell me!" she demanded. "Do you think this is an easy question for me to ask? How long?"

Dalton held her determined gaze for several long seconds and then, without a word, pulled himself toward the ceiling and manipulated the touch screen once again. "A little over three hours from now."

"What if we returned to the Moon?"

"Won't help. Either way, we won't make it. But if we turn back, the colonists all die too."

Tears began flowing from Trish's eyes, some wetting her cheeks and some drifting away to co-mingle with those of Dalton's. "I have to stop breathing," she said again.

"No!" he said adamantly. "*One* of us has to stop breathing. But it isn't going to be you."

Trish gazed at Burt Dalton in amazement, his image blurry through her tears. What a gallant gesture. She had chosen well. It was too bad they would never have a chance to have a life together. "I can't let you sacrifice yourself for me. This is my fault, not yours. I won't have you pay for my mistake."

"You had no idea. You thought this would be the best surprise of my life. And if we had enough oxygen, it would be. This isn't your fault. You're impetuous, rash. You don't look before you leap—that's one of the things I love most about you."

"Doesn't matter if I meant to cause this problem. Here we are. Even if I were willing to let you make this sacrifice for me—which I'm not—the ship needs its pilot."

He shook his head. "The ship can land on its own."

There was something in his expression. Something subtle but recognizable to her subconscious. She couldn't even remember knowing him, but her intuition was sure he was lying. And even without intuition, his claim was absurd on the face of it. If the ship could land on its own, why the need for a pilot? Why was Burt Dalton the only man who could take this mission?"

"Why lie to me?" she said softly. "I can't land if you're gone, so I'll die anyway. Along with all of the colonists."

"The autopilot is good enough to safely land the ship eighty percent of the time."

"Leaving a twenty percent chance the colonists die. And you'll die no matter what. And not because of anything you did, but because of *my* actions."

She closed her eyes and balled her hands into fists. She had to stop crying. Had to face her fate with as much dignity as she could manage. "We both know you have to stay alive and land this craft on Mars. This is hard enough. Don't prolong it."

Dalton held her once again, this time for several minutes, and if she hadn't finally separated, she wondered if he ever would have.

As if the situation wasn't horrifying enough, she wouldn't just be losing her life, she would be doing so as a blank slate, having no memory of herself, her friends and family, or the man who had become the love of her life. And Burt Dalton would watch her die, anguished by her death and burdened by an incomprehensible level of guilt that would stay with him forever. Guilt that she had done what she had done for *him*. Guilt that he wasn't clever enough to find a way out of the trap. Guilt that he would remain alive while she perished.

She could somehow tell from his expression that he preferred his own death to being forced to take the life of the woman he loved— and live with it afterward.

"I am so sorry it's come to this," he said. "But I'm begging you to reconsider," he added, confirming her intuition. "You could continue hibernation in thirty-six hours, and you and the colonists would still have a four in five chance. Four in five are good odds. And you're a better human being than I am. Let me make this sacrifice for the woman I love," he pleaded.

She imagined her imminent demise. He would use drugs to put her to sleep and then shoot her out of the airlock so he wouldn't have to jettison her weight in vital supplies. She wondered if the vacuum outside would preserve her. If her lifeless body, without microbes to digest it, would float for eons in the bitter cold of space.

She closed her eyes. How could she just willingly let herself die?

She couldn't. She had to fight with all of her might to go on, no matter what it took.

Trish Casner considered the offer. Eighty percent odds really were quite good.

But how could she allow this man to take her place, to make the ultimate sacrifice for her? Had she been madly in love with him, she wouldn't entertain the idea for a moment, but as it was, she didn't know him from Adam. She couldn't deny that it was tempting, as much as she wanted to believe otherwise.

"No!" she shouted finally, as her internal wrestling match resolved itself. "My decision is final. You need to survive, Burt Dalton. You need to save these colonists and do great things with your life."

Her chin quivered. "But let's get on with it as quickly as we can. Every second we prolong this is agony," she added, as tears began to pour from her eyes once again.

And this time she knew they wouldn't stop in the few minutes remaining until her death sentence was carried out.

So much for going out with dignity.

# 6

Dr. Melanie Yoder felt pins and needles all over, despite no part of her body having fallen asleep. She hadn't known this would be her reaction to extreme anticipation, but then again, she hadn't known anticipation could possibly be as all-pervasive as what she was presently experiencing.

What an exciting day. Perhaps the most exciting day in the history of humanity.

Or perhaps not. Perhaps just another day that would bring yet another failed attempt, the latest in an endless series of failed attempts, each one more expensive than the last.

Artificial General Intelligence really shouldn't be *this* hard. Not given the current state of computer technology. But somehow it was.

Biological evolution was hit-and-miss—sloppy. Generation times were agonizingly long, making the process take forever. The building materials nature worked with, on the whole, were frail and easily damaged.

And so mankind had outdone evolution over and over again. Evolution had achieved the speed of the cheetah. Mankind had countered with the car, jet, and rocket. Evolution had achieved the streamlined swimming perfection of the dolphin. Mankind had countered with the jet ski and submarine.

And on and on. The flight of the eagle, the strength of the polar bear, the toxin of the pufferfish, the architectural abilities of the ant—in each case, mankind had found a way to blow past these performance levels as if they were nothing.

With one notable exception: consciousness. General Intelligence. Self-awareness. Creativity.

What trick had evolution stumbled upon to spark consciousness within a seemingly haphazard arrangement of mindless cells? A trick that continued to prove impossible for mankind to duplicate.

Or did this particular trick only exist in *God's* playbook, as many believed?

Modern computers had continued to advance at an extraordinary rate. They were clean and sturdy, with memories orders of magnitude more capable than that of a shriveled brain, and also millions of times faster and millions of times more precise.

So how was biological evolution still able to maintain its advantage? What magic was required to finally imbue an insensate lump of matter with consciousness?

Biological evolution was getting the last laugh, and some experts now suspected that this would always be the case. That the one puzzle consciousness couldn't solve was *itself*.

But Melanie Yoder disagreed. She couldn't help but believe that now that computers finally existed that matched the power and complexity of the human brain, the days of biological evolution lording its greatest accomplishment over mankind were nearing an end.

Could *today* be the very day when this last domino would finally fall?

Today was certainly the day when the most magnificent computer system ever built—which she had named TUC—was finally complete, and would be able to draw on the largest repository of knowledge ever assembled, which would be stored in a database boasting such gargantuan memory capacity it might as well have been infinite.

For the past eight days the entire contents of the World Wide Web, all gazillion pages, including electronic copies of millions of books, had been uploaded by the most advanced web crawler and content capturer ever. TUC would never be allowed anywhere near an Internet connection, but if you couldn't bring the computer to the Internet, at least you could download the entire Internet into the computer.

Melanie was a geek among geeks and never stopped marveling at the Web and its content, without question mankind's greatest accomplishment. The Great Pyramids, the Great Wall of China, the Panama

Canal, the Hoover Dam, the interstate highway system—all were undeniably astonishing accomplishments.

But they paled in comparison to the Internet, whose incomprehensible rise from obscurity to world domination had taken place in less than a generation.

In the early 1990s, only four decades earlier, the greatest minds on Earth had no idea what to make of this new capability, with many expressing certainty that no money could ever be made from it, only lost.

Back then, the vision was that consumers could use the Internet to access content, a supplement to the limited television channels then available. The Web could provide a sports channel, a weather channel, a finance channel, and so on: each less a television channel than a spiffed-up magazine. You could expand the number of available Internet destinations to as many as five thousand—maybe even *ten* thousand.

But the great media moguls of the day balked at the expense.

What company was rich enough to fill ten thousand channels with content? Ten thousand! It would break the backs of the world's strongest corporations.

Melanie thought their lack of foresight could be forgiven. After all, throughout human history up until that point, a tiny few had provided content for all of Earth's teeming millions and billions. In the early '90s, this remained true, as a small number of active creators delivered television content, print media, books, music, the theater, and so on. For every active creator of content, there were hundreds, or even thousands, of passive consumers.

But then something unexpected and miraculous happened: the Internet didn't offer ten thousand channels of content, but ten *million*. And more. And the Internet's content was created, not just by a tiny minority, but by all of humanity, collectively. By billions and billions of people taking a more active role in its growth than any could have ever foreseen.

Every man, woman, and child on Earth could now create content for every other man, woman, and child, readily accessible from anywhere in the world. "How-to" videos, user forums, an online encyclopedia that had grown to over fifty million articles in almost three hundred languages, blogs, Facebook pages, and so much more.

By 2016, more than sixty trillion web pages had been created. Astonishingly, this was equivalent to almost ten thousand pages for *every living human.*

And all of this had arisen in the blink of an eye.

Thirty thousand people were thought to have built the Giza pyramids. Over a million were pressed into service building the Great Wall of China. But the Internet demonstrated what a thousand times this many people could achieve when they were all rowing in the same direction.

And Dr. Melanie Yoder was lucky enough to be alive in this era. Not only alive, but able to live the ultimate geek fantasy. Three years earlier she had been appointed the head of DARPA, The Defense Advanced Research Projects Agency, the group that had actually *fathered* what would later become the World Wide Web.

DARPA was created in 1958 by President Dwight D. Eisenhower, basically because he, and all of America, were freaking out over the Soviet launch of Sputnik, which had taken place at the height of the Cold War. Even civilians knew the importance of not ceding the high ground to an enemy, and space was the ultimate high ground.

Eisenhower vowed to catch up in a hurry, and that the US would never be surprised like this again, or beaten this badly to the technological punch. He vowed that the next time technology stunned the world, it was going to be *American* technology that did the stunning.

While the space race was soon spun off and put under the purview of NASA, DARPA—originally named ARPA—had made enormous contributions to technology over the decades, funding and pursuing public and secret projects alike. ARPA had created ARPANET, the early precursor to the Internet, and other transformational technologies like NavSat, the predecessor to the modern Global Positioning Satellite, whose importance in modern technology and commerce could not be overstated.

But what DARPA might accomplish on this very day could make birthing the Internet and GPS look like small potatoes. Even if the odds of success were only one in a hundred, Melanie was giddy at the prospect.

She glanced at the man whom she had chosen to lead the most far-reaching project ever conceived, Dr. Gustavo Guerrero, standing in silence beside her. Guerrero was as driven as she was, and even more brilliant.

Both stood facing the thick Plexiglas window that comprised the front wall of the small observation hut they were in, staring down at the ten-thousand-square-foot concrete bunker below, eighty yards away. The crudity of the structure's appearance belied the marvel of technology housed within.

The building was nestled at the base of steep rock formations on three sides, two-thirds of it buried beneath the burning sands. Others would watch and monitor this historic attempt, the Blackest of Black projects taking place, fittingly, within the Blackest of Black sites— Area 51—but only she and Guerrero would have the honor of being this close.

It was silly to care about proximity. After all, the concrete hut they were in was packed with monitors that they would need to view the computer system inside the bunker, like everyone else. And even had they been standing next to TUC, this told them nothing about what was going on inside of him. They would only learn the extent of their success or failure through extensive remote testing.

Still, Melanie wanted to be able to see the location at which history was being made with her naked eyes, even if those viewing the site remotely would have the identical experience.

"T minus forty-six minutes," said Dr. Guerrero unnecessarily, looking to be every bit as anxious as she was. "This must be how the folks at mission control felt during the first Moon launch. Years of working around the clock, and it all comes down to one singular event."

"Thrilling and terrifying at the same time, isn't it?"

Guerrero winced. "Very," he replied, and then, forcing a smile, added, "but I'm trying to keep a healthy perspective. Einstein spent ten years killing himself to find the key insight necessary to go from his Special Theory of Relativity to his General Theory. And he's one of any number of examples. Extraordinary breakthroughs require extraordinary perseverance."

"Amen to that. But wouldn't it be nice if this worked the first time?"

The Director of DARPA was about to continue when her phone issued a telltale ring. The only person she could think of who would dare call her now was her boss, Troy Dwyer, the recently installed Secretary of Defense. But Dwyer wasn't a science geek, and as important as this was, he had told her he had no interest in looking over her shoulder.

She answered her phone and said maybe ten words before ending the call three minutes later.

"You don't look happy," noted Guerrero as soon as she finished, eyeing her warily. "What's up?"

"You're never going to guess in a million years," she said to him in disgust.

"A last-second issue with TUC?" he replied anxiously. "Some kind of malfunction?"

"No. A warning. We're about to have a surprise visitor. President David Strausser."

"You have to be shitting me!"

"Lucky us," she said dryly. "I've been assured that he'll leave his Secret Service contingent outside of our observation hut so as not to further disturb our, um . . . moment."

"What will he tell people about why he's here?"

"He won't. He ditched his press pool. They still think he's in DC."

"Goddammit!" hissed Guerrero as he reflected on the unfairness of it all. "Even Nixon had the decency to leave mission control alone to do their thing during the Moon landing."

"Well, to be fair, we're really only needed to push a button on a touch screen. Then, whatever will happen, will happen."

"Still, are you really in the mood to babysit right now?"

"You know I feel the same way about this as you do," she replied.

"I'd rather try to explain science to a *tree* than to a *politician*," he added in contempt.

Melanie couldn't help but laugh. Guerrero had said the word *politician* with so much disgust she was reminded of an old joke. In the joke, a grade school teacher asks a student to have her father come in for career day and explain his occupation. The father explains to the class that he is a male prostitute, servicing drug addicts and ex-cons.

When he leaves, the teacher rushes to the principal to report this appalling revelation. The principal just shakes his head and says, "I'm afraid it could have been worse. This man was lying. You see, he isn't a male prostitute who services drug addicts and ex-cons. He's really a *politician*." After a pause the principal adds, "He was just too ashamed to admit it."

Guerrero waited until her brief bout of mirth had passed, and then continued. "I thought you said your boss had agreed not to tip off the president about this. Strausser was just sworn in two months ago, after all. Shouldn't he still be busy with other things? You know, like learning how a bill becomes a law."

"No one tipped him off," said Melanie. "But if he zeroed in on DARPA as an area of interest, and specifically asked about our most important project, Dwyer could hardly lie to him."

"I'm begging you. Please do most of the talking. I have no patience for fools, especially now."

"I'll do most of the talking, but not all. I know you aren't political, but this isn't a man you want to snub if you care about your career."

The president arrived moments later. After quick handshakes all around, the Secret Service agents who had accompanied him left them alone in the small concrete hut.

"Welcome to Groom Lake, Mr. President," said Melanie, forcing a smile. "I have to say we're a little . . . surprised . . . by your visit. What can we do for you?"

# 7

Trish Casner opened her eyes with a start.

How was she still alive?

Or *was* she alive? She was pretty sure she had never believed in an afterlife, but perhaps one existed, after all, given that her frozen corpse wasn't currently drifting through space.

Her last memory was of Burt Dalton injecting her with a drug that would send her as gently as possible into the great beyond. The final frontier, and not in the *Star Trek* sense. The *truly* final frontier, with the Grim Reaper controlling all access.

She found herself in a small room with no windows, sitting across a table from a tall clean-cut man in a white lab coat, who was holding a tablet computer. Not what she had expected in the afterlife.

Saint Peter standing before majestic pearly gates with a scroll, yes. A geeky man at an unremarkable table staring at a computer—not so much. But perhaps given the population explosion since biblical days, scrolls had given way to more modern methods of record keeping.

"Who are *you?*" she whispered weakly, her usual strength having not yet fully returned. What *had* returned, she realized, was gravity. She was back on Earth. No restraining strap needed to keep her firmly in her seat this time.

"Welcome back, Trish," the man replied. "Instead of wasting my breath answering questions, I'll just wait until you regain your full memory." He glanced at the time on his smart-watch. "Shouldn't take more than five or ten minutes."

True to his word, he folded his hands and put on a serene expression, waiting for comprehension to return to her. Less than three minutes later, it did. Everything came rushing back, a white avalanche of memories cascading down a steep mountain. She gasped from the force of it.

The man she was facing was Dr. John B. Brennan. He was there to interview her, as he had done dozens of times over many months. She could tell he saw the light of comprehension in her eyes, but he still waited patiently, giving her time to fully assimilate her past, and her current situation, and make sense of it all.

Her odyssey had begun almost thirteen months earlier. She had been living alone in Columbus, Ohio, in between relationships, managing a small boutique greeting card shop in Easton Town Center Mall. A psychology professor nearby, at the Ohio State University, had been advertising for volunteers to fill out an extensive human behavior questionnaire online. Those selected to participate would receive the gift of a fifty-dollar credit on Amazon.com for their troubles.

It sounded like fun, and she could use as much credit on Amazon as she could get.

She had no idea that this questionnaire was not an end to itself, but a means to find qualified candidates for something far bigger. She had no idea that her participation would trigger events that would change her life forever.

The day after she had completed the questionnaire, she was contacted by a woman who wanted to know if she might be willing to participate in a larger study, for a significantly larger sum. She offered to take Trish to lunch so she could review the opportunity. Intrigued, Trish agreed to meet with her.

The woman, who had introduced herself as Dr. Mary Willis, had told her she was with a private institute founded for the purpose of advanced studies into human behavior. They were looking for volunteers who fit a diverse set of parameters, ultimately up to a thousand of them.

And not to answer questionnaires or submit to interviews, but to agree to become human guinea pigs.

Questionnaires were limited in the truths they could reveal, Mary Willis had explained. Ask a man if he thought he'd be brave in battle or cower behind a tree, whimpering, and he could give you his best guess based on past experience. But unless he had been in this exact situation, not even he could know for sure how he would react.

The only way to know for sure was to put him in a battle zone and observe.

According to Dr. Willis, this institute had perfected an ideal means to gather this data, the most comprehensive, accurate assessment of the human condition ever attempted. Selective memory suppression combined with a flawless virtual reality system, tied directly into the brain.

The fictional Matrix come to life, indistinguishable from reality.

A subject could wake up in a war zone with a gun in his hand—and with no memory that he was really in virtual reality and this was merely a test—and could learn just how brave he really was, without being in any real danger at the time.

The institute was looking to test behavior under field conditions to learn what no previous study could tell them, allowing them to shine a light on ugly behaviors and loose ethics that most would deny vigorously if simply asked, either lying to the interviewer or lying to themselves.

Would you ever betray a friend because you were jealous of them?

Who would answer this question in the affirmative? But when a test subject thought they were experiencing real life, and couldn't be observed, perhaps the answer to this question wasn't always so cut and dried.

At this point in the conversation, Trish had made it clear to Mary Willis that she had no interest in being a human guinea pig, of having her memory tampered with in the name of behavioral science. And especially of putting herself into the hands of some sinister-sounding secret institute that admitted to scary mind-tampering abilities that wouldn't be out of place in a macabre horror film.

Her decision was final, she had told Dr. Willis, and no sum of money would ever be enough to get her to change her mind. Ever.

Which just proved that Trish wasn't as imaginative as she had thought. She never considered the institute would be willing to pay her two million dollars for a year of her time. What she should have said was that no sum of money would ever be enough to get her to change her mind—unless that sum of money was two million dollars.

Trish had always been something of a math savant, but this was simple arithmetic. If the institute's goal was to eventually recruit a thousand volunteers, and each was paid two million dollars, this would cost them two *billion* dollars. An amount that was beyond unrealistic. It was absurd.

Dr. Willis had simply smiled and told her that two billion was considered affordable by those behind the institute. If Trish agreed, she would be paid the first hundred thousand immediately. The institute would relocate her, and pay for her lodging and meals while she participated in the study.

When the year was up, she would get another hundred thousand, and a hundred thousand every year after this for eighteen years, as if she were a lottery winner. The only catch was that if she ever breached confidentiality, ever breathed a single word about the institute or what had transpired there, she would forfeit all future payments.

That was the deal.

So just how bad was the testing for this kind of financial inducement to be necessary?

Pretty bad, Dr. Willis had admitted. The goal was to grind her down and examine every aspect of her personality. Evoke a kaleidoscope of emotions, and examine each under the most severe conditions. Study her fears and her desires. Her sex drive, her instinct for self-preservation, for safety and control. Her ethics and morals, her philosophy of life. Levels of generosity, compassion, self-sacrifice, bravery, determination, loyalty, resourcefulness, and adaptability. Love, lust, and avarice. Addiction.

Sometimes the tests would be great fun, testing her sense of humor, friendship, and need for affection. Her creativity, her ambition, her loyalty, and her reactions to a wide variety of benign, and sometimes wild, social situations.

But just as often the tests would be harsh and even brutal. Trish would be put to sleep and her mind manipulated to enter a computer-generated virtual world, perfect down to the tiniest detail, the most subtle smell, taste, and sensation accounted for, while her memory of any interactions with the institute would be erased.

Where possible, she would remember her life prior to entering the institute, with a backstory provided to explain how she found herself in whatever test situation they put her in. In extreme cases, like the scenario in space she had just undergone, her old memories would be so incongruous that she would never accept the new reality, no matter how flawlessly presented, so she would be hit with temporary amnesia while she fought to come to terms with the situation she found herself in.

To Willis's credit, she didn't sugarcoat what Trish would be faced with, nor would Trish have ever trusted her if she had. Two million dollars was a lot of money. Had Willis said the testing was nothing but sugarplums and fairy dust, Trish would have run for the hills.

But the doctor had given examples of the kind of tests Trish might find herself in. She might be put in a situation in which a crazed powerhouse of a man was trying to stab her friend with a dagger, to see how Trish would react. Would she attack the man to try to get him to stop, with the likelihood that this would only serve to get *her* killed as well as her friend? Or would she flee and call for help, knowing this help would never arrive in time?

Would Trish steal if she knew she could never get caught? Would she betray a loved one for the greater good? What kind of sacrifices would she be willing to make for the benefit of a stranger? Would she cheat on a test if she knew she couldn't get caught? Would she have sex with a man for money? If so, for how much? Would she torture a woman if the woman was withholding information that could save the life of a loved one?

And none of these cases would be hypothetical. She would *live* these scenarios, smell the breath of the man offering to pay her for sex, slip in the blood of a friend who was dying in her arms.

In each of these cases, she would only remember the test long enough to be interviewed about it before having her short-term memory erased. The institute would learn things about her that couldn't be learned on paper. She would learn things about herself, albeit fleetingly.

When Dr. Mary Willis had finished her pitch, Trish was intrigued, to be sure, but mostly horrified. The tests that had been described were treacherous, inhuman.

Not that it mattered. This lunch date was probably the real test. Of human gullibility. How easily could a person be conned by what was obviously bullshit?

There was no secret institute with billions of dollars to throw around. There was no technology that could send her conscious-ness into a computer-operated matrix to test her, or drugs that could manipulate her memory so precisely. She would have suspected she was on a hidden camera TV show, only she couldn't imagine a show choosing subject matter this bizarre or unsettling.

She told the doctor as much. She thanked her for lunch, and left, telling her that the day she saw an extra hundred grand in her bank account was the day she might be willing to take these ridiculous fabrications a little more seriously.

The next day Trish Casner received an email from Columbus First Bank, notifying her that a hundred thousand dollars had been depos-ited into her account.

Perhaps she had dismissed Dr. Willis too hastily, she decided.

A month later she began her stint at this not-so-mythical institute, and a year later, today, she had finally fulfilled her end of the contract. This was her last of endless tests—not that she could remember any but this latest.

She wondered how many of them had turned out to be like this one. She couldn't help but be bitter about what she had just been forced to endure. What a nasty test this was. Hitting her with a de-bilitating total memory loss. Making her think she had been impetu-ous and foolish enough to stow away on a spaceship. A fatal mistake that would force her to *choose* to end her own existence, and also believe she was forever scarring the love of her life in the process. A man she couldn't remember, but one rendered to be irresistibly ap-pealing to her.

Of course she had thought Burt Dalton was her ultimate fantasy in a man. Because Burt Dalton actually *was* her ultimate fantasy— taken from her actual *fantasies*.

She should have known the test wasn't real, even with her memory gone. How could she just waltz onto a spaceship bound for Mars, un-invited, and make herself at home in a hibernation pod? The entrance would be safeguarded. And if the powers that be on the Moon base had measured the contents of the ship and crew down to the ounce, there was no way the computer would fail to alert the authorities that an intruder had boarded.

She should have smelled the unreality of the situation, the impos-sibility, all the way from Pluto.

Only she hadn't. Because the VR technology really was *that* good. Because she had been disoriented, and distracted by a breathtakingly gorgeous male claiming to be her fiancé. It had been so utterly, abso-lutely real.

Which raised another question in her mind. Given how extraordi-nary this VR tech really was, why not introduce it to the world? The inventors could make billions of dollars overnight. Since this would be her last day at the institute, this would be her last chance to ask this and other questions, which she vowed she would do. She had signed the most iron-clad non-disclosure agreement ever devised, but just because she could never share anything she learned didn't mean she couldn't satisfy her own curiosity.

Now that her memories had reasserted themselves, it was time to get this over with. She glared at Dr. John Brennan, the man in the lab coat who continued to wait patiently for her to assimilate her past.

"You son of a bitch!" she spat icily.

# 8

Trish Casner was about to continue raging against the man who had just put her through psychological hell, but stopped abruptly as she noticed the broad smile that had come over John Brennan's face. Not the reaction she had expected after her venomous insult.

"You're consistent," he said in amusement. "I'll give you that."

"What?" she said in confusion.

"These are always your first words after we pull you out of a tough virtual scenario. The kind you just went through, and also the scenarios that explore lust and sex, since you see these as the ultimate invasion of your privacy."

Brennan had a huge unfair advantage, Trish realized, since he could recall the content of numerous conversations they had had, but she could only recall that these conversations had taken place, nothing more. Still, while she had obviously experienced other horror-shows, none could have come close to this latest.

"I know Dr. Willis promised brutal," she said in disgust, "but what you just put me through was as cruel a test as has ever been devised."

The doctor winced. "Actually, not even close," he said, but his eyes were on his tablet instead of Trish Casner, and she had a strange feeling his words were somehow scripted. "Good thing you can't remember. Hell, we even have a more treacherous version of the stowaway scenario. In that one, there's a third crew member, not critical to the mission, who remains in hibernation. If we had run that one, the Burt Dalton character would have tried to convince you to let him end this man's life so the two of you could be together."

He paused to let her ponder this new scenario for several seconds. "This is an even tougher call," he continued. "The colonists would still be saved. And you'd get to remain alive and marry your fantasy mate. You'd just need to let an already unconscious man, a stranger, go on to a painless, eternal sleep, to spare your own life."

She shook her head in disgust. He was right, this scenario *was* even more horrific than what she had just been through.

"You'd be surprised at how many subjects are willing to go along with this," said Brennan. "But then again, the purpose of our research is to truly understand the human condition, warts and all. It's easy for a man to say he'd rather die of starvation than resort to cannibalism. It's harder for him to take this lofty moral stance when he's *actually* starving to death and his dead friend's fresh carcass is beside him."

Bile rose in Trish's throat as she realized this was likely a scenario they had forced her to face. "You are one sick bastard!" she snapped.

Surprisingly, Dr. Brennan nodded. "Believe me, I know the torture we're putting people through," he said, continuing to glance at his tablet as though it were a teleprompter. "But sometimes tests have to be cruel to illuminate the human condition. And at least these are all virtual. No flesh is actually torn, no deaths actually occur. And your memory is erased when it's all over, so you don't even suffer any permanent emotional scars. And it's all in service to a much greater purpose. If not for all of this, I could never bring myself to be a part of it."

Trish wasn't convinced this was true, but decided not to argue the point. "So who dreams this stuff up?"

"The scenario you just experienced was borrowed from a very old science fiction story," replied Dr. Brennan. "*The Cold Equations* by Tom Godwin. Relatively short, but considered a classic. Different characters and relationships, but the same idea. A girl stows away on a starship, and the pilot, who doesn't know her but is a compassionate man, has no other choice but to expel her into deep space. If he doesn't, they'll run out of fuel and both die. It's quite a poignant story. Heart-wrenching."

"Tell me about it, you bastard!" growled Trish. "I just lived the damn thing!"

"I know you did," he replied. "But take heart. This was the last one. Are you ready to answer your final set of questions and cash in for the next eighteen years?"

She nodded. "Let's get this over with."

Brennan looked startled by this response, as though he had expected something different. He glanced at his tablet as if deciding how to proceed.

"Wait a minute," said Trish. "I almost forgot. I wanted to ask you a few questions about the VR technology that you've been plugging into my mind. Sounds super sophisticated. So who developed it? Why hasn't it been commercialized? Why doesn't anyone know that something like this exists?"

A flicker of a smile crossed Brennan's face once again, and this time Trish could guess the reason for it.

"I've asked these questions before, haven't I?" she said. "How many times?" she demanded.

"After every session," he replied. "Most subjects do. If you brought a jet plane back in time to the seventeenth century and gave people rides, how many do you suppose would ask why they've never heard of jet technology?"

Trish nodded. It was a good analogy. Of course everyone asked about the VR tech every time. No wonder Brennan had been surprised when she hadn't. "Since this is my last session," she said, "and I'll actually be able to remember what you say, why don't you answer one final time?"

"Sure," he said, continuing to consult his tablet on a regular basis. Perhaps he wasn't looking to read from a script. Perhaps this was just a rude, annoying habit.

"As you know," he began, "the people behind this institute have tremendous financial and scientific resources. And their goals are far loftier than increasing their wealth. They have more money than they can ever spend already."

"Which explains why they're so willing to give two million of it to me."

"Exactly. Right now they want to keep this tech to themselves. Use it for their stated goal of truly understanding what it means to be human. They're also well aware of how addictive this VR tech would become. Who wouldn't want to immerse themselves in a world that could be made perfect? Releasing this technology could have catastrophic consequences to society."

Brennan raised his eyebrows. "There's also a theory that we're living in a computer simulation already. If this VR tech was adopted as widely as we think it would be, humanity would risk being two levels removed from reality, a dream within a dream."

"There's really a theory that we're in a simulation?" said Trish skeptically. "That's ridiculous."

"I'm afraid it's the opposite of ridiculous. Look how far we've come with video game technology. From none at all to online games with millions of simultaneous players, with graphics capabilities that keep getting more and more realistic. How long until we can model an entire world and all of its inhabitants? *World of Warcraft* times a billion. Given the age of the universe, which is more likely, that we're really poised at the precipice of this capability? Or that humanity passed it long ago, and each of our far future descendants have the power to construct complex virtual universes on their tablet computers? Virtual universes that you and I inhabit."

"You can't tell me people honestly believe there's a chance our universe, our lives, are just simulations."

"I can. And not just people, but top scientists. And they don't believe there's just a chance, they believe it's almost a certainty. Fifteen years ago, Elon Musk calculated that the probability we're living our lives in base reality, rather than a simulation, was infinitesimally small."

Trish opened her mouth to ask another question, but Dr. Brennan cut her off. "I'm afraid I have to insist we stop here. We need to get this final interview concluded and get you back to Columbus, Ohio."

He proceeded to ask her seventeen questions that he read one by one from his tablet. Since he didn't bother to take any notes, Trish was convinced his computer was recording her every word, probably producing a written transcript also.

The questions, which Trish answered as truthfully as she could, were all about her thoughts during different aspects of her experience, as well as her feelings and motivations. Why did she say and do what she had said and done? What had she thought about as the needle was coming toward her arm? Had she considered having sex with her perfect man one last time before he killed her? Why or why not?

Even though she couldn't remember any previous interviews, she had the feeling that her sex drive had been explored more than any other element of her personality, at least based on these questions and everything Brennan had said.

Finally, at long last, it was over.

"Trish, it's been an honor to study you," he finished, and he sounded sincere. "You don't remember the results, but trust me, you are truly special. You embody what is best in humanity. You've shown yourself to be bright, creative, and compassionate. Some of the choices you've made have been incredibly heroic."

"I'm sure you say that to all test subjects with no memory," she replied, borrowing a line she had said to Burt Dalton during the simulation.

Brennan laughed, but it was forced, and there was a strong undercurrent of despair in his demeanor.

"I'm really going to miss you, Trish," he said. He blew out a long breath. "But it's time to put you out one last time. We'll erase your memory of having to walk the plank out in space. One I doubt you're eager to hold onto, anyway. But you'll remember your stay here, and you'll remember the non-disclosure agreement you signed. And we'll put the money into your account going forward as promised."

"Thanks," she said simply, not knowing what else to say. She remained silent as Dr. Brennan prepared an injection, his eyes beginning to glisten. Was he tearing up? Wow, maybe he really was going to miss her as much as he said.

What she didn't know was that this time he wasn't preparing an injection to put her into a temporary sleep. This time the injection would be as lethal as the one she thought she was receiving on the fictional Mars expedition.

This time she would truly be visiting the final frontier. The experiment had run its course.

And so had Trish Casner.

# 9

Dr. Melanie Yoder tried to size up President Strausser as best she could. This was the first time she had met him. But during a typically contentious and ever-lengthening presidential campaign, while Dillon Mattison was finishing up his second and final term, she and the world had seen enough of Strausser—and his challenger—to last a lifetime.

He was in his early fifties, making him a veritable baby compared to the advanced ages of many of the country's recent presidents. And he had the vitality Melanie expected from a man who had headlined rallies for eight hours a day during the last months of the election, shooting between different states like a supercharged pinball.

Strausser was tall and had thick, black hair, probably dyed. And he was clean-cut, of course, since the last president to sport facial hair had been Taft, more than a hundred years earlier.

"Great to be with you," said the president. "It's my first ever visit to Area 51," he added with a grin. "I'm scheduled to get the full tour after I'm done visiting you. I've seen those famous signs around the base before, the ones warning that *the use of deadly force is authorized*, but only in UFO conspiracy documentaries. I have to admit, I got a charge out of actually seeing them in person.

"Don't tell anyone this," he continued, lowering his voice as though he was about to disclose an actual secret, "but I didn't want to become president so I could run the country. I wanted to become president so I could find out what *really* goes on in Area 51."

"Good plan," said Melanie with a smile, this time one that was genuine. He was right. You pretty much did have to be president to learn of all the secrets here. DARPA ran half the programs taking place on site, but even she had been kept in the dark about the other half.

Melanie was just as wary of politicians as Guerrero, and just as skeptical of their ethics and intelligence, but there was no denying the man's magnetism. The best politicians managed to exude considerable charisma, but even so, the pull exerted by President Strausser was unexpectedly strong. His body language, the way he pretended to confide in her, his down-to-earth demeanor, all were disarming, and made it seem like they had been friends for years.

"I've been given to understand that none of the Area-51 projects are as important as this one, though," said Strausser. "The word is that this one has the potential to utterly transform the playing field like nothing that has come before."

Melanie simply nodded. This was very true. "Can I assume you've been fully briefed?"

Strausser smiled once more. "Not so much. I like to get briefed on a just-in-time basis. I don't clutter my mind until absolutely necessary. Hell, I'm still trying to memorize the names of all the world leaders. I'm pretty sure it'll take me until a second term to do it. Who knew there were so many countries in the world?" he said, rolling his eyes.

This time even Guerrero smiled. If Strausser could reach *him*, as anxious as he was, and as outraged as he was by the president's intrusion, then he could reach *anyone*.

"Also," continued Strausser, "why would I want to be briefed by Troy Dwyer when I can be briefed by the likes of Melanie Yoder and Gustavo Guerrero? Why ask the owner of an orchard the profound significance of a falling apple when I can ask Isaac Newton instead?"

Comparing them to perhaps the greatest scientist of all time was a nice touch, Melanie decided. He certainly knew how to ingratiate himself. "Good point," she replied with a wry smile.

"What I do know," said the president, "is that you've put together the most powerful computer system ever built. With the goal of finally achieving Artificial Intelligence."

A look of distaste flashed across Guerrero's face, which Melanie caught out of the corner of her eye. To purists like her and Guerrero, who had lived and breathed this field for as long as they could remember, using the term AI to describe their goal was almost the same as using the term *horseless carriages* to describe Ford's new line of cars. But, to be fair to the president, most laymen still didn't differentiate.

She decided it was time to bring Guerrero into the mix. They needed the new president's continued full support, after all, which meant the head of the project needed to participate. "Actually, our goal isn't AI, Mr. President," she told him, "but what has become known as Strong AI, or better yet, AGI." She nodded at Guerrero. "Gustavo, could you explain the difference?"

To his credit, her colleague managed to suppress the frown she knew he wanted to display, and even managed to force a smile. "Certainly," he said. He turned to face the president. "Using the term AI to describe what we're attempting here would have once been perfectly fine, but the term has fallen out of favor. At one time AI *was* considered the ultimate achievement in computer intelligence. But researchers began to realize a few decades ago that in many ways, AI had already been achieved, at least in very specific areas. IBM's Deep Blue, the computer that bested Garry Kasparov at chess, could be thought of as demonstrating Artificial Intelligence. An even better example would be the computer that finally bested a Go champion, many years later."

"Go?" said Strausser, blinking in confusion.

"The oldest board game known to history. Invented by the Chinese over five thousand years ago. A strategy game, like chess, but with even more possible moves. Chess is played on an eight-by-eight board. Go on a nineteen-by-nineteen board. There are more possible moves in a game of Go than there are atoms in the known universe."

Strausser raised his eyebrows. "I could be wrong," he said wryly, "but that sounds like a lot. I feel sorry for the guy who had to do the counting," he added with a disarming grin, and despite himself, Guerrero smiled back once again.

"Go was considered a game that a computer would never master," continued Guerrero, "but a version of Google's DeepMind called *AlphaGo* managed it as early as 2016, stunning the world."

"Now that you mention it, this does ring a bell," said the president. "I just hadn't memorized the name *Go*. Those impossible-to-pronounce Chinese names are a killer."

Melanie grinned. "Not to mention how much mental real estate the word *Go* takes up, which could be better used to memorize world leaders."

"Exactly," said the president. "So I'm guessing Watson, the computer that won at *Jeopardy!*, is also considered AI," he continued, serious once again.

"That's right," confirmed Guerrero. "And other examples abound. Systems that diagnose human disease, Personal Digital Assistants that answer your spoken questions and schedule appointments, web search algorithms—the list goes on and on. These are all extremely impressive, but they don't fit the definition scientists had in mind when the term AI was coined. They are anything but conscious, anything but sentient. Watson might be able to win at *Jeopardy!*, but it doesn't *know* it won, or what this means. It doesn't know it was playing a game. It doesn't care. It's a very sophisticated, glorified adding machine. As impressive as it is, it's intelligent only in a narrow, limited sense. It can't write an essay, play a video game, plan a wedding, or do a million other things a human can do."

Guerrero paused. "You're able to switch effortlessly between thousands of tasks and activities," he continued. "But the same computer system that crushes you in chess can't beat you at *Crazy 8* without substantial modifications. And you continually learn. So while DeepMind possesses a specific intelligence, you're a jack of all trades. You possess a *general* intelligence."

"I'm not sure my political opponents would agree with you," said the president, "but I get your point. So AI isn't the Holy Grail. *General* intelligence is. Which is what the G in AGI must stand for: Artificial *General* Intelligence."

"That's right," said Guerrero. "A system that exhibits AGI should be able to solve problems, learn, and take effective, human-like action, in a variety of environments."

"Which sounds like it goes beyond just passing the Turing test," noted the president.

"Turing was a true genius, and his test was considered the Holy Grail for a long time. But creating a computer that can fool a human into thinking *it's* human, while impressive, isn't nearly enough.

Passing the Turing test might just mean that the computer was extremely well programmed, nothing more."

"Right," said the president. "Like if you were in a room and someone sent in a question for you in Chinese. You might be able to replace each Chinese word with an English one using a pre-specified program—say Google Translate—and reverse the process with your answers. In this way your answers in Chinese might satisfy the questioners. But just because you can fool a native speaker doesn't mean you actually understand a single word of Chinese."

Guerrero and Melanie glanced at each other, barely able to keep their mouths from falling open. This was a simplified variation of a famous thought experiment about consciousness called *The Chinese Room.* Strausser couldn't have just come up with this example at random.

Perhaps there was more to this president than met the eye.

"Exactly right," said Guerrero. "The trick to AGI is for it to become self-aware, creative. And even self-awareness isn't enough."

"Yes, because sentience, consciousness, has some magical, ineffable quality," said Strausser. "Not just mind, but body and spirit in some ways. Qualia become a vital consideration."

This time Melanie's mouth did fall open. This was a sentence an expert in the field wouldn't have been embarrassed to have uttered. Strausser was nobody's fool. He clearly liked to be underestimated, but a keen, well-read mind lurked behind this facade, and he had now come out of the closet. It was time to probe just how deep his knowledge really was.

"I know what *I* mean when I use the word *qualia,*" she said. "But what do *you* mean, Mr. President?"

"I would define qualia as subjective experiences, sensations," he replied, "that only conscious entities seem to be able to have. How a thing seems. How it feels. How it affects a consciousness emotionally and spiritually. The pain of a toothache. The beauty of a sunset. The taste of wine."

Melanie gazed at him in wonder. She had expected him to have to gather his thoughts and then fumble for an answer to her question. But he had shot back a response without hesitation that was as accurate as she could want.

"There is a classic thought experiment," continued the president, "which I'm sure you know far better than I do, that helps me think about this. Imagine a woman who was kept since birth in a black-and-white house, only able to view the world through a black-and-white television monitor. This woman could earn an MD/PhD in color vision. Could know every last thing that is known about the color *red*. Its wavelength, how it hits the rods and cones in the eye, the exact way this information is processed by the optical nerve and brain."

"But she still wouldn't know the color red," said Melanie, finishing for the president. "Even though she has every bit of formal knowledge about the color, she would still gain additional information by going outside and *seeing* something red."

"Yes, what red *looks like*," said Strausser. "At least what it looks like to her. How it makes her feel. The subjective *experience* of the color red. Qualia."

Guerrero looked completely taken aback, and Melanie understood why. Not only was the president not a fool, it was becoming increasingly evident that he harbored a significant intellect.

"So you knew the difference between AI and AGI when you came in here, didn't you?" she said.

The president nodded. "I wanted to see if you'd just accept my use of the term AI, or try to enlighten me. And, if so, how you might choose to explain it. I was trying to get a feel for the two of you."

"You mean size us up?" said Melanie.

"Kind of a brash way to put it," he said, "but yes."

"I figured you could handle some brashness," said Melanie.

"You figured right," said the president. "In fact, I find you refreshingly direct. Which is what I want in my world-class scientists. You're still managing programs, so you do need to have some political skills. But if you were *too* political, that would make me uncomfortable."

The president sighed loudly. "By the same token, having too high an IQ can be a liability in my world. I'm a man of the people. If I seem to be too well-read, too focused on reading scientific journals instead of figuring out how to defend some indefensible lie told by a member of my party, I scare a lot of people. So if anyone ever asks you about me, be sure to tell them I'm as dumb as a rock, and only read comic books."

Melanie nodded thoughtfully. It suddenly made sense why he was here with them now. It wasn't an accident, as much as he had arranged it to look like a last-minute decision. He was a closet scientist at heart, and had done considerable thinking and reading on the subject of consciousness.

"But back to the main topic," said the president. "While I've tried to educate myself a little over the years, I'm not narcissistic or delusional enough to believe I could even come close to truly understanding what you've been doing here. I've studied a little theory and philosophy of AGI, but no nuts and bolts. I don't know an *exaflop* from an *exa-wife*. But I've been told that you've built what should be the fastest, most powerful computer system ever constructed, using billions of taxpayers' dollars out of a Black Budget. And you hope to use a software program that mimics evolution to bring about your AGI."

"That is correct," said Melanie Yoder. "TUC is truly mind-boggling. A thousand dollars today can buy a laptop as formidable as the most powerful supercomputer that existed in 2020. And DARPA has invested *millions* of times this amount on a single system, which resides in this bunker," she added, gesturing to the mostly buried facility fifty yards away.

Strausser looked duly impressed. "And if you do get to AGI," he said slowly, studying Melanie with great intensity, "how likely is it that your Artificial General Intelligence evolves itself into Artificial *Super* Intelligence in a blink of an eye?"

Melanie was tempted to water down her reply, but she felt certain he was searching her body language and would detect a lie as though he were a human polygraph. "Very likely," she replied simply, which seemed to be the answer he was expecting.

"So AGI," said the president, "impossible as it has proven to be to create, is really just a stepping-stone to something far greater. A pawn that you create a millimeter away from the eighth rank on the chess board, poised to become a queen. As soon as your system achieves human intelligence, it becomes smart enough, and self-aware enough, to direct its own evolution and improvement, instead of relying on random chance. Then you get runaway improvements happening at speeds we can't comprehend. Millions of generations of improvements in minutes. And we have no idea what this ASI will be like, only that our puny intelligence will be dwarfed. That its thinking will be far beyond our ability to grasp."

A quick smile flashed across Strausser's chiseled features. "The only thing we can know for sure about a system possessing Artificial Superintelligence," he added, "is that it would be much too smart to ever get elected president."

Melanie ignored this latest attempt at humor. "So you think we're playing with fire?" she said.

"I *know* you're playing with fire," replied the president. "And so do you, or you aren't one-thousandth as smart as I think you are. That's not the question. The question is, are you convinced the safeguards you've put in place will suffice?"

# 10

Melanie Yoder couldn't help but feel insulted by the president's question. "If I wasn't convinced the safeguards would be enough," she said, "I wouldn't be going forward."

Strausser smiled sheepishly. "I probably should have rephrased that," he allowed. "Just *how* convinced are you that your safeguards will suffice? And why do you think so?"

Melanie opened her mouth to respond, but the president held out a forestalling hand. "But we'll get to these questions in a moment. First, let me back up for a bit. So you have the fastest, most powerful computer ever built. So what? Do speed and grandiosity really help? Doesn't this just help you achieve failure that much faster? Humans have achieved AGI with brains as comparatively slow as glaciers. There are certainly quantitative aspects of consciousness, a requirement for a minimum level of complexity and processing power. But once you've passed this, isn't consciousness mostly qualitative?"

Melanie considered how to respond. "Many believe the opposite is true, that consciousness is nothing more than an emergent property of complexity. Create a complex enough system and it pops out all by itself."

The president shook his head skeptically. "And what do you think?"

"I tend to agree with your conclusions," she admitted. "*Emergent* is just a fancy word for magic, in my opinion. It's defined as an *unpredictable* property that simply arises on its own from simpler constituents. If it's unpredictable to science, then it might as well be magic."

There was something about the look on the president's face that made her believe he already knew which side of this debate she favored. That he had already read her scholarly articles on the subject, in fact.

"But even if we acknowledge that consciousness has a strong qualitative aspect," she continued, "it will almost certainly also require a very high level of complexity and processing power to achieve."

"Which your TUC has covered in spades," said the president.

"Yes," said Melanie. "Also, speed and power allow more generations of evolution to take place in less time. But, in general, with all of this said, I agree with you: speed and power alone aren't enough. Increase the processing speed of a fruit fly brain a million fold and you still don't get AGI."

"So since you agree that this mighty system alone isn't enough," said Strausser, "you must believe you've also come up with the mother of all AGI evolution algorithms. One that will supply Frankenstein's magical spark to animate your creation. To create a system that can not only win at *Jeopardy!* but care that it won."

Melanie nodded. "We believe we've developed superior AGI evolution algorithms and superior inductive learning algorithms, both."

Computer evolution algorithms copied biological evolution almost exactly. As a great simplification, software—coding—took the place of genes. Software that achieved the most successful results, based on preselected "fitness functions" would be copied into the next generation, and allowed to cross with other successful software, creating progeny software that shared features of both parents. Random mutations would also be introduced along the way. In each generation, only the fittest software would survive. Then rinse and repeat. Millions of times, until endless crossings and random mutations enhanced performance in magical and surprising ways.

"So what makes your algorithms so superior?" asked the president bluntly.

"I'm afraid an explanation would require symbolic logic and mathematics that not even I've fully mastered," said Melanie. "I'm afraid you'll have to take my word for it. If *any* evolution program can work, this one will. And, again, this is in conjunction with advanced learning algorithms. DeepMind made some major innovations that we've built upon."

"That's Google's entry, right? The one that won at Go?"

"Well, it *became* Google's entry. It began life as a British company that Google later acquired. And it took a while to build up to Go. It first became famous by playing an old Atari arcade video game called *Breakout*. It wasn't programmed with any information about the game or how to play. It was tasked with maximizing its score, nothing more, so it had to *learn* how to play. At first it fumbled around and was horrible, but after an hour it never missed. DeepMind has become considerably more advanced since those days, of course."

"And you believe that this learning system has become the gold standard?" said the president. "The one to build upon?"

"That is my personal belief, yes," replied Melanie.

"So what's its secret?"

"It uses deep learning on a convolutional neural network," she explained. "Combined with a form of model-free reinforcement learning called Q-learning."

"That didn't help me at all," admitted the president. "But no matter. Let's move on." He paused in thought. "So after DeepMind learns, can scientists understand the result? How and what it learned?"

"For something simple like Atari, yes," she replied. "But not for something like Go. That's the beauty of it."

"And also what makes it a little scary," said Guerrero. "The people behind AlphaGo have no idea why it plays the game the way it does. Can't begin to fathom the computer's strategy."

"The word *scary* is a good segue into the subject of safeguards," said Strausser. "So you think these software breakthroughs of yours can finally get us to AGI?"

"Combined with the most advanced hardware ever created, yes," replied Melanie.

"And you've already acknowledged that if you're successful, TUC will likely graduate from AGI to ASI very rapidly."

Dr. Melanie Yoder blew out a long breath. "Yes. Which is why this is the most important project in the history of humanity. Whoever wields superintelligence first has the biggest first mover advantage in history. The possibilities for improving the human condition are truly extraordinary."

"*Wields* is an interesting word choice," said the president pointedly. "For us to *wield* something we have to control it."

"That's correct," she said.

"What makes you think we can control an ASI? Why would it allow itself to become a slave to its intellectual inferior?"

"The core, unchanging goals that drive its evolution are obedience to its creators, friendliness to humanity, promotion of human good, and reduction of human death and suffering. These and other failsafes are stitched into its evolutionary DNA in a thousand different ways, and are so redundant, there is no conceivable way the system could evolve to be antagonistic to humanity."

"Do you agree, Dr. Guerrero?"

He nodded. "I do. Our best minds have reviewed our approach and are satisfied that we'll retain control."

The president turned to face Melanie once again. "And if you're wrong?"

"We aren't," said Melanie with conviction. "But just in case, we built TUC in a separate bunker structure out here in the desert. He's cut off from all electrical lines. We've downloaded the entire contents of the Internet into his memory, including millions of books and hundreds of thousands of textbooks. He'll need to draw upon this vast database to have any hope of evolving to sentience. But he isn't *connected* to the Internet in any way, nor can he connect himself."

"He can't affect the outside world in *any* way," added Guerrero. "And we won't let him for some time, not until we're as sure as we can be about what it is we've created. We have the means to cut off his power supply at any time, and there is nothing he can do to prevent us. He has no moving parts and no way to recruit people or affect his environment."

Guerrero paused. "Finally," he continued, "the building he's in is mined. We can activate it via radio, by transmitting a code that is two hundred digits long. The string of digits was produced by a randomization program in another computer. TUC won't know it's there, and if he does, even with his speed, he couldn't crack it by trial and error if he had until the end of time."

The president nodded. "You've been using male pronouns for TUC, I've noticed. For some reason, when I came here, I thought of it as a *her*." He gestured toward Melanie Yoder. "How did you choose the name TUC?" he asked. "Assuming that you were the one who named it."

"I was," said Melanie. "It's short for *The Ultimate Computer*."

"Good choice," said Strausser, who seemed sincere in this praise. "And you just randomly decided it was a male?"

"Randomly?" said Melanie in mock indignation. "It wasn't random at all. TUC is just naturally a male name. You know," she added with a grin, "Friar TUC. TUC Rodgers. Tom Sawyer and TUC Finn."

The president laughed out loud. "Right. Short for TUKleberry."

"Exactly," said Melanie. "Even the classic TUCxedo is most often worn by a male."

"Glad I asked," said the president dryly. He turned his attention to the digital countdown clock, running in the corner of the large monitor. The grand experiment was set to commence in just less than five minutes.

"So what are the odds this experiment will succeed?" he asked.

"In achieving AGI?" said Melanie.

Strausser nodded.

"Impossible to say," she replied. "Over the years there have been hundreds, maybe thousands, of what I would call credible attempts around the globe. So far they've all failed."

"To our knowledge," said the president.

Guerrero shook his head. "No. Believe me, we'd know it if one had succeeded."

"I'd like to think this is thousands of times more likely to work than anything that's ever been tried," said Melanie. "But a thousand times zero is still zero. So there is no way to handicap it. As I've said, there are those who think we'll never get there. Those who think we're looking at consciousness entirely the wrong way. Those who say it's a quantum phenomenon, and Lord knows we may never understand what goes on at the quantum realm."

"T minus four minutes," said the president. "I guess we'll know soon enough." Strausser paused. "Thanks for putting up with me," he said in a way that seemed sincere. "I'll shut up now and leave you alone with your thoughts as we approach the final countdown."

"Thank you, sir," said Melanie, and Gustavo Guerrero nodded beside her. "Perhaps it's fitting—"

A massive explosion erupted in the bunker below, blinding and deafening the three observers for several seconds. The building and the priceless computer hardware inside were turned into rubble in the blink of an eye. A shock wave that propagated faster than the speed of sound shook the room they were in and threw all three inhabitants to the ground before they could even register what had happened.

The temperature of the room rose to sauna levels, but quickly spiked and then receded, and the earth became still once again. Somehow, miraculously, the structure held.

To their great credit, three Secret Service agents, suffering blistering second-degree burns on all exposed skin, managed to stumble inside and use their bodies to protect the fallen and still-disoriented president, just in case further explosions were forthcoming.

While the aftereffects of the blast had subsided, Melanie Yoder and Gustavo Guerrero remained on the floor, reeling. Not from the knowledge that they could have been killed, but from the instant and devastating loss of a project that had been the culmination of their life's work.

# 11

Naval Lieutenant Cameron Carr wolfed down the hot dog he had bought at the courtyard café and leaned back against the trunk of one of several trees that inhabited the Pentagon's five-acre open-air central plaza. He glanced up at the sky and the hint of a smile crossed his face.

The plaza had long been nicknamed *Ground Zero*, and he couldn't help but appreciate the gallows humor of those who had given it this name many decades before. The name was an unblinking acknowledgment that if nuclear war ever did break out, the center of the Pentagon wasn't a bad bet for the location of the first enemy strike, wiping out America's military bureaucracy in one fell swoop.

Carr continued to watch the sky, deciding to clear his mind and stay in the moment. Why he had been summoned here by Troy Dwyer, the recently sworn-in Secretary of Defense, was a mystery that no amount of analysis could solve. While the Chairman of the Joint Chiefs of Staff was America's highest ranking military officer, he only served in an advisory role. Troy Dwyer, on the other hand, commanded the greatest military the world had ever seen, outranked only by the president himself.

Carr had no idea what Dwyer wanted with him, but it was bound to be interesting. Best to just relax and wait until he learned what it was. The meeting was less than fifteen minutes away.

Carr had always preferred to work alone, to rely on no one but himself. He wondered how Dwyer felt, to sit in his massive office in the Pentagon and know that he was absolute king of this ridiculously large castle, ruling over the thirty thousand people who worked here.

And this endless building was only DoD's *headquarters*. In total, Troy Dwyer was the CEO of the world's largest employer, boasting a workforce numbering over a million, about a quarter of them civilian and the rest military. While China's military was larger, its military bureaucracy was smaller, so it ranked as only the world's *second* largest employer, followed by the world's next two military powerhouses, Walmart and McDonald's.

Cameron Carr shuddered. He enjoyed his visits to the Pentagon because he hated them so much. These visits served as a cautionary tale, a way to scare him straight. The ultimate horror show, but one he could escape by leaving the theater. A reminder of how happy he was that he'd repeatedly refused a promotion to Commander so he could continue doing what he loved most and did best.

He routinely put his life on the line, but far better to face death on a daily basis than enter a Pentagon hell of red tape and bureaucracy.

No one who had ever visited the Pentagon had failed to look up its specs, to appreciate its true immensity. The building consisted of five nested pentagons, five floors high, the outer five walls each longer than three football fields. It boasted over five million square feet of office space, more than twice as much as the Empire State Building. And all of this was built in only sixteen months in the early 1940s as the US braced itself for a world war, with Nazi Germany having metastasized across Europe and just having attacked the Soviet Union.

Because of a steel shortage brought about by war preparations, the Pentagon had been built primarily with reinforced concrete, over four hundred thousand cubic yards of it, prepared using over a half million tons of sand and gravel dredged from the nearby Potomac River.

The stat that Carr reacted to the most viscerally, the one that filled him with dread, was that this single office complex held over seventeen miles of corridors within. Seventeen miles! The fact that he could practically run a marathon here and never run out of new office doors to pass was horrific to him. He was sure that if he ever spent any time inside this endless structure, he would be waking up in the middle of the night screaming, plagued by nightmares of being trapped behind a desk, in the center of an inescapable *ocean* of desks.

He shifted his gaze from the sky as a petite woman in her forties approached him, her gait and demeanor purposeful. A receptionist had informed Dwyer's administrative assistant that he had arrived and would be waiting at Ground Zero until the SecDef was ready for him. Apparently, rather than text Carr to tell him her boss was ready, Dwyer's admin had come to escort him herself. A nice gesture, albeit unnecessary.

She stopped before him and held out her hand. "Lieutenant Carr, I presume?"

He smiled and shook the offered hand. "Yes, ma'am."

"I'm Dr. Melanie Yoder," she said. "But please call me Melanie."

Carr's eyes narrowed. Dwyer was a big shot, no doubt, but there was no way he rated an administrative assistant with a PhD or MD. Her name didn't ring a bell. "And you are?" he prompted.

"The Director of DARPA," she replied as she began walking, motioning for him to follow.

He nodded slowly. "I see. The new SecDef wants to make sure I'm fully intimidated before I meet him. I'm afraid that science is my fatal weakness."

She shook her head. "What is it with you guys?" she said in amusement. "You do know that excelling at science doesn't take anything away from your warrior skills, right? So if by *fatal weakness* you mean finishing college level calculus in the tenth grade, acing every one of your advanced chemistry and physics courses at the Naval Academy, and finishing first in your class, then I'm sure science is your kryptonite."

Carr flashed a smile. "I should have known you'd have done your homework."

"I recently met the president," she said, "and I realized that his 'aw-shucks' approach was covering up a razor-sharp intellect. Two of you within a week? Did I miss a memo? Is trying to be underestimated some new strategy going around?"

"I don't know about the president," he replied, "but as for me, I was called a cocky asshole so many times growing up that I decided to go the other way." He arched an eyebrow. "I can now say that I'm greater at being humble than I am at any of the other multitude of things I'm great at. In fact, I have no doubt I now possess a greater level of humility than any man who ever lived."

Melanie Yoder laughed out loud. "Did you ever hear of a song called, *Lord, it's hard to be humble?*"

He shook his head.

"I'll spare you any singing, but I got such a kick out of the lyrics that I memorized them. It goes like this:

'Oh Lord, it's hard to be humble,
When you're perfect in every way.
I can't wait to look in the mirror,
Cause I get better looking each day.
To know me is to love me.
I must be a hell of a man.
Oh Lord it's hard to be humble,
But I'm doing the best that I can.'"

Carr laughed as her recital ended. "I feel that guy's pain," he said with a twinkle in his eye. "Few appreciate the struggles of the truly superior."

Melanie's grin was now a fixture on her face as they walked through the minotaur maze that was the Pentagon.

They arrived at Dwyer's office minutes later, and after shaking hands and seating themselves, The SecDef's assistant brought in a pitcher of cold water and several glasses, along with a plate of assorted fruit.

Dwyer looked Carr up and down and nodded. "Thanks for coming," he said.

Carr glanced at Melanie beside him and then turned his attention back to Dwyer. "Not at all," he said with a hint of a smile. "I wasn't under the impression it was optional."

"It wasn't."

# 12

Cameron Carr took in the Secretary of Defense's office in a few glances. It was neatly organized, with a 3D-capable touch screen filling an entire wall at a right angle to his desk. There were a few small plants, but little sign he had put any additional effort into personalizing the space. He looked out over the Potomac and DC.

The one characteristic that stood out beyond all others was the sheer size of the office, the opposite of cramped and claustrophobic. If you had to be behind a desk, this was the one to be behind.

It was good to be king.

"Why am I here?" said Carr, not one to beat around the bush. He had been affable and full of humor on his way here with the head of DARPA, but his demeanor was now all business, ice cold and serious as death.

"I've been told you're one of the best operatives we've ever had," replied Dwyer. "Eight years with SEAL Team Six, and now four years in the clandestine services, with a record of accomplishment and heroism that is truly extraordinary. You're also off the charts when it comes to psychological stability, ethics, and loyalty to America."

"With all due respect, Secretary Dwyer—"

"Call me Troy," he interrupted.

"With all due respect, Troy, this walk down résumé lane is gratifying, but there is a downside to being successful, as I'm sure you're aware. Success brings the toughest, most challenging assignments along for the ride. I can live with that. But never before have I been given an assignment by the SecDef himself. So I'd really like to leave the preliminaries behind and get right to the bad news. Just how screwed are we?"

Dwyer sighed deeply. "Before we begin," he said, "you should know that what we discuss, and your assignment, goes beyond any level of classification currently on the books. Other than the three of us in this room and the president," continued Dwyer, "no one else knows about this, or will know about it."

He paused to let this sink in. "I'm afraid I can't even let you pray for success," he added with a wry smile.

"I understand," said Carr in amusement.

"I don't," said Melanie. "Is that some kind of inside military joke?"

"No, it's literal," replied Carr with a straight face. "He can't let me pray because even *God* isn't on the need-to-know list."

Melanie Yoder groaned while Dwyer moved on. "So let me get down to business," he said, holding Carr's gaze. "It's probably no surprise to you that DARPA is working on Artificial Intelligence."

"I assume you mean Artificial General Intelligence?" said Carr, noting a small grin coming across Melanie's face as he did.

"Correct," she said approvingly. "I'm sure I don't need to tell you about the explosion of AI, the specific kind, and how huge this has been, both for world economies and quality of life. Self-driving cars, computers that can out-diagnose the best doctors, pattern recognition, systems that can anticipate human needs with eerie precision, predict our interests in entertainment, news, product offerings, and so on, with great accuracy."

"It's been an ongoing revolution for decades," said Carr. "You'd have to be living under a rock to miss it," he added dryly. "Computers, algorithms, the Internet—they're not just the biggest *component* of our lives and economy. They've *become* our lives and economy."

Melanie nodded. "Well said."

"Last Tuesday Dr. Yoder and her team reached a critical point in DARPA's AGI initiative," said Dwyer, "which is the agency's most important and well-funded effort. Her advanced computer system, located in a mostly buried bunker inside Area 51, was finally ready. It was scheduled to be, ah . . . introduced to her advanced evolution and learning algorithms. President Strausser was there as an observer."

Dwyer went on to explain what had happened, how the multi-billion-dollar computer system was taken out in an instant, almost taking the president out along with it.

"We have no idea who was responsible," he concluded, "or how they managed to pull it off. I'll brief you more fully on what we've discovered in a little while, and answer your questions, but for now I'd like to move on."

"Of course," said Carr.

"I'd like to go back to AI, and the quest for AGI," said the Secretary of Defense. "You've made it clear you're aware of what a gold rush this is. But however much effort, money, and resources you think are going into these programs, the true numbers are probably twenty times greater."

Melanie nodded. "The truth is that hundreds of billions of dollars around the world are being pumped into these technologies," she said. "And the supply of relevant PhDs isn't nearly enough to match the demand. If you're talented enough to get a PhD in software architecture or artificial systems from MIT, or Harvard, or Carnegie Mellon, you're able to attract millions in venture capital to start a company before the ink on your diploma dries. Or you can join a major player and write your own ticket. If you do choose to start a company, it will likely be snapped up a few years later by a tech giant.

"The list of potential acquirers, players that are extremely active in this space, is endless," she continued. "You've got Apple, Google, Facebook, Sony. . ." she began, ticking off each company with her fingers. "And these are just off the top of my head, by the way. Samsung, Netflix, Amazon, Intel, Nvidia—and dozens of other behemoths. Since 2011, these major players have averaged more than forty acquisitions of companies working on advanced AI and AGI annually. Last year alone, a hundred and eight were gobbled up."

Melanie paused to let this sink in. "The competition for top talent is fierce beyond any historical precedent," she continued. "In my view, this is the principal reason AGI has yet to be solved—the best people are splintered around the world. Another key reason is that with the financial stakes involved," she added, "scientists aren't inclined to share their insights and results with others. This sharing and cross-fertilization is typically critical in achieving major scientific breakthroughs."

Carr nodded thoughtfully. Dwyer was right. He had imagined AI and AGI receiving incredible amounts of attention, but not *this much* attention. "So how can DARPA compete with the likes of Google?" he asked her. "No offense, but it's hard to imagine you could entice top talent to join a Black government project instead of a rich tech giant. Or out-innovate these multinationals."

Melanie smiled. "Under normal circumstances, this is absolutely true. But I argued these exact points and got authorization to pay ridiculous salaries and provide ridiculous benefits to get good people. The fifteen highest paid government employees in America are all on DARPA's AGI team. Second, while AGI scientists aren't sharing these days, we've been able to strong-arm the Facebooks and Googles of the world to share certain data and advances with us."

"Strong-arm isn't really the right term," said Dwyer. "Let's say that we've been able to appeal to their patriotism in the name of national security. And to entice them with certain carrots that only the government can provide. We've also agreed to license any break-through tech we come up with to those who share with us—as soon as it's declassified."

"I wouldn't think that a chance to get at DARPA's leftovers would be appealing to them," said Carr.

"You'd be surprised," said Melanie. "GPS came out of DARPA. For many years it was government owned and run. And while the military hogged the highest quality signal for itself during this time, they eventually released it all free of charge to the public. But what if, instead, they had made deals with a handful of companies to give them semi-exclusive licenses to provide GPS to the public? How much money would this little DARPA leftover be worth?"

"You used this exact example with these companies to help them see the wisdom of sharing, didn't you?"

Melanie smiled. "It's a persuasive argument," she said. "But let me get back to the point at hand. We're the only project getting data from multiple other players, which is immensely helpful, and does more than even the playing field. Think about the advantage Google's AIs have when it comes to something like pattern recognition. Every day, untold millions of users train these AIs without knowing it. Every time a user searches Google Images for 'abstract cat,' or 'cozy cabin,' and then clicks on their favorite result, Google AIs get that much better at learning what people mean when they use these terms. Think about the data a company like this can generate in a single day. Or a company like Facebook. Or Amazon."

Carr hadn't really considered things in this way, but it did explain a lot. How virtual assistants like Echo, Google Home, and Siri had become so uncannily good that they seemed to be able to read minds. There were times when Carr was convinced that his phone knew he wanted to stop at a gas station for a snack, and exactly which snack he would choose, before *he* did.

"The important take-home message," said Dwyer, "is that we've had access to more of these data sources than any other party in the world. Along with a huge budget and top people. Because of this, despite a daunting level of competition, we had reason to believe Melanie's project was the most advanced out there. At least that we're aware of."

"How much is out there that you *aren't* aware of?"

"We don't know what we don't know," said Dwyer. "In addition to the AI and AGI projects tech giants brag about, there are a number of stealth efforts being led by wealthy individuals. Highly secret and unacknowledged. We think we know about all of them. But we can't be sure."

"What about government or military efforts in other nations?" said Carr.

Dwyer sighed deeply. "That's the trillion-dollar question. We're devoting an unprecedented amount of intelligence to make sure we know what's happening around the world. But there is no doubt we're missing a lot. And this is the truly scary part. Every major government in the world has thrown itself headlong into this gold rush, friend and foe alike. Based on what we think we know, we still tend to believe we're in the lead. Followed fairly closely by China, Israel, Russia, and Germany."

"Even after last Tuesday?" said Carr pointedly.

Melanie frowned. "This was a huge setback," she said, "no question about it. We still like to think we're leading, but we could be fooling ourselves. It's possible that the only leading we're doing right now—to borrow a phrase—is leading from behind."

Carr nodded. "What about India? I'm surprised they aren't on your list of leaders."

"They would be," said the Secretary of Defense, "but their best people tend to end up here, working on *our* efforts."

He paused. "But when it comes to AGI, being in the lead could well mean nothing. Tiny Luxembourg could make a breakthrough tomorrow and leapfrog us to the finish line. And Artificial General Intelligence is the finish line for only a short while. Whoever achieves this gets to Artificial *Super* Intelligence, ASI, in no time."

Carr nodded thoughtfully. "I'm familiar with the concept," he said. "So whoever gets there first rules the world."

"Yes," said Dwyer. "And that's without any hyperbole. *Literally* rules the world."

"Why wouldn't the ASI itself rule the world, go Terminator on us? Why would it need humanity?"

This time Melanie jumped in to answer. "Because thanks to James Cameron and others, this possibility has been thoroughly brought to our attention. Asimov—now considered to be the father of robotics—posited designing robotic brains with absolute safeguards way back in 1942. Safeguards that would ensure robots were friendly and obedient. Safeguards he famously called the *Three Laws of Robotics*. These are laughably incomplete and unworkable, with their flaws actually forming the basis of his stories. But the point is, we've developed infinitely more sophisticated mechanisms to ensure that we'll still be running the show."

"But when you say *we'll* still be running the show, you're talking about humanity. That doesn't necessarily mean the US will be running the show, does it?"

"Bingo," said Dwyer. "That's why the stakes are higher than they've ever been."

"And someone just sabotaged our best effort," said Carr. "And we don't know who."

"That's right," said the Secretary of Defense. "And because of the stakes—for companies, economies, and militaries—this has become the mother of all Charlie Foxtrots."

"Charlie Foxtrots?" said Melanie, raising an eyebrow.

"The Secretary is being polite," said Carr. "It's the expletive-free version of the military term, *Cluster Fuck*. A chaotic situation in which multiple things go wrong at the same time."

"And even this term doesn't do it justice," said Dwyer. "Between governments, corporations, and wealthy private citizens, there are hundreds of players racing to get to ASI first. And given the biggest first mover advantage of any tech in history, they all know that this is the ultimate winner-takes-all situation. Coming in second is no better than coming in last, or not finishing at all. Even players who are convinced that ASI is too dangerous to mess with, that it's playing with fire, are racing forward."

"Because they can't afford to let their enemies discover fire before they do," said Carr.

"That's right," said Dwyer. "So almost every player is watching every other. At minimum, they're spying and trying to steal secrets. Some corporations, and all governments, are also trying to sabotage each other's efforts whenever they can. Remember how much of a Wild West it was ten or fifteen years ago, when every government was hacking into the computers of every other? Well, this makes that look tame and orderly. We've basically got a high stakes demolition derby in the middle of a mud-filled stadium."

"Which is another big reason no one has reached the finish line," said Melanie. "Like we learned last Tuesday, the closer you are to the finish, the more likely your knees get taken out. Successful projects are about as safe as mob informants. So in addition to a scarcity of talent, the top programs have all been sabotaged along the way. Google, Amazon, and Facebook were among the first hit."

"All by different saboteurs?" said Carr.

The SecDef shook his head. "No. We thought so at first. Numerous parties are attempting it, and some have succeeded, but the major players like Google have security that rivals ours. Hell, we isolated *our* latest attempt inside Area 51. Area 51! The most secure site in the world, period. Until now. Someone still managed to get to us. We've become convinced that while others are trying, most of the havoc has been created by a single party. One who is just better at it than the others, for reasons that aren't clear."

Dwyer paused to let Carr digest this information, and then continued. "The sabotage is often quite subtle. A few lines of code are changed that prevent algorithms from working properly, but only after being uploaded into systems. Usually the glitches aren't discovered until months or years later, after causing scientists to bark up the wrong tree for that entire time. Those responsible seem to zero in on the key scientists, also, and hack their computers, screwing them up at every step along the way. Often, when someone does come up with a breakthrough, before they can finish saying *eureka*, the breakthrough has been erased from existence, including being wiped from multiple computers, data sticks, and the cloud. Nothing like putting the finishing touches on a million lines of code, only to find that the originals and backups have succumbed to seek-and-destroy viruses of unparalleled complexity."

"Surely whoever is behind this has left *some* fingerprints," said Carr.

Dwyer shook his head. "I'm afraid not. We've basically gotten nowhere."

"And not for lack of trying," said Melanie.

"Which shows just how sophisticated they really are," added Dwyer. "As I've said, numerous other players, ourselves included, have been attempting to sabotage the others, but with much less impact than this one group is having."

"Have *all* of our rivals been sabotaged?" asked Carr.

"You're thinking that if one country remained untouched," said Dwyer, "perhaps this is the country behind it."

"It's worth at least asking the question," said Carr. "The problem is that the country responsible might just *pretend* to have been sabotaged. Or they might run a false flag operation, purposely leaving another country alone to make them look guilty."

"Our logic was the same as yours," said Dwyer. "But we still asked the question anyway. Our intel suggests all of the major players have been hit at one time or another."

Carr shook his head. The situation couldn't be more chaotic. Charlie Foxtrot was right.

Dwyer's expression had been grim throughout, but he somehow managed to find an even greater level of seriousness. "If a Western democracy other than ours gets to ASI first," he said, "we won't be happy, but we can live with it. Their values would prevent them from pursuing . . . for want of a less corny phrase, world domination. But if China, North Korea, Iran, Russia, or any number of other countries get there first, it's game over."

A long silence filled the Secretary of Defense's spacious office.

Finally, Dwyer continued. "So your job, Lieutenant Carr, is to find out who's responsible. We suspect a rival nation-state, for obvious reasons. But it could be a group of Luddites, dedicated to retarding the advance of science, although this is unlikely given the advanced tech that's been unleashed. It could be a terror group. Although, again, we think this unlikely."

"I agree," said Carr. "As sophisticated as Jihadi groups have become, they aren't *this* sophisticated. And they use any tech they get to kill *people*, not research programs. Still, I take your point. We shouldn't rule out anyone."

"At least not absolutely," said Dwyer.

"So with all of your resources," said Carr, "with a dozen or more intelligence agencies working on the problem, you've gotten nowhere. And you expect me, alone, to be able to crack this case?"

"I do," replied Dwyer, not giving an inch. "From what I understand, you've pulled off miracles before. And while I'd prefer you work totally alone whenever possible, you'll have ready access to whatever resources you require, human or otherwise, no questions asked. If you need men, you'll have them. And you'll have a blank check. Need a tank battalion in the streets of Beverly Hills? Just say the word. I'll be giving you command codes that only the president can countermand. I hope you appreciate how much responsibility we're putting in your hands."

Carr nodded thoughtfully. The situation was clear. Dwyer believed previous failures were due to leaks, or due to the bad actor they were seeking sabotaging, not just AGI, but the US's efforts to identify them. Which explained the lone ranger approach, and why this mission was cloaked in an unprecedented level of secrecy, restricting those who knew of his involvement to a tiny handful.

He could wield men and resources, but he couldn't really tell them what he was trying to do—especially not that US AGI efforts had been repeatedly stopped in their tracks.

But he would have to disclose *something* to the people he worked with or to the leads he developed. Otherwise, his job would be impossible. So no matter how much Dwyer might think Carr's success depended on his ability to sneak up on the perpetrators without being seen, he would have to risk disclosing that his mission involved some aspect of AGI. The best he could do was disclose this only when absolutely necessary, and downplay the scope and importance of his mission.

"You aren't—formally—authorized to kill to complete your mission," continued Dwyer, "unless it's in self-defense. Same goes for torture. But think of these more as rough . . . *guidelines*. If you leave a trail of bodies, I'm fully prepared to ignore any evidence that suggests they *weren't* killed in self-defense. Even if it's on US soil. If I find men complaining of rough interrogations at your hand, I'll be disinclined to believe their version of events."

"Understood," said Carr simply.

"You'll report directly to me, but you'll have an open line to President Strausser. Melanie will serve as a scientific consultant. She'll make sure you have the most advanced untraceable phones, weapons, and any other tech you need. If it would be useful in your mission to have tech that hasn't been invented yet, check with Melanie. Perhaps it has been, after all, in a Black Laboratory somewhere."

"Roger that," said Carr.

"I'll have all the intel we have on this situation brought into my office. What we know about past sabotage, what we know about what happened last Tuesday. Every conjecture or theory we've ever had. Every investigation we've ever done—all dead ends, of course.

But important background for you to have. I'll leave you to it for as long as you need."

"Thank you, sir," said Carr.

Dwyer stared deeply into the eyes of the operative across the desk from him. "I know this has been a lot to take in, and you haven't had a chance to think about it, but any idea of where you might begin?"

Carr pondered this for several long seconds. "As a matter of fact, yes."

"Good," said Dwyer. "Keep it to yourself. I only want to hear from you if you need something, or if you've made progress. I don't care how you go about completing this assignment. I only care about results."

Cameron Carr blew out a long breath. "Understood," he said wearily, suddenly feeling the weight of the world on his broad shoulders.

# PART 3
## Cameron Carr

# 13

David Bram stood behind Riley Ridgeway, the most beautiful girl on the planet, with his arms wrapped around her waist. It had been a perfect Saturday. Bram had picked Riley up early that morning for breakfast, and they would be spending the entire rest of the weekend together, as usual. This weekend they had both decided to be homebodies, taking advantage of Bram's Jacuzzi and home theater.

They both remained silent, at peace, looking out over the beach and the Pacific Ocean that comprised the front yard of Bram's San Diego home, their eyes locked on the brilliant but waning sun as it began to slip below the horizon. This was a ritual they had repeated often. Even so, it had never become less spectacular.

Which was also true of Riley Ridgeway.

Bram knew he had to find a way to marry this girl if it was the last thing he ever did. It wasn't just that he was in love, it was that he knew beyond a doubt that he would never meet her equal again. Not in beauty, not in intelligence, and not in personality.

She turned to face him for a moment and he quickly changed expression. He knew from experience that being caught looking like a lovesick puppy could send the relationship reeling.

The problem was that anytime she got a vibe that their relationship was serious and had a long-term future, she pulled away. As long as she could convince herself that they were nothing more than two people who enjoyed each other's company and physical intimacy, he was in good shape. The moment she sensed otherwise, she made immediate efforts to call it quits. She had an almost magnetic repulsion to closeness, to anything more than a superficial emotional connection. He had almost lost her—twice—before he had come to understand this.

They had been dating for almost a year, and for the life of him, he couldn't figure out exactly why she was so averse to allowing the relationship to go to the next level. They were fantastic together.

He was in love with her, of course, but to be fair, any man who saw Riley Ridgeway for even five minutes *thought* he was in love. She moved with the grace of a dancer and possessed such a clean, flawless beauty that she captured the attention of both men and women, their eyes having no other choice but to follow her, to dwell, to marvel that such perfection could even exist. And yet she behaved as though she had no awareness that her looks were in any way special.

Bram knew that the only reason he had even had a chance with her when they began dating was that she was also blindingly brilliant, and almost certainly intimidating to any suitor.

Even Bram found himself feeling intimidated at times, which took a lot of doing. But her intelligence didn't scare him off, it attracted him even more. And at least he was bright enough to keep her from being bored.

Not that Riley flaunted her intelligence. She hadn't gone to college, and Bram wasn't even sure she had finished high school. She was down-to-earth and self-effacing, and worked in various capacities at an animal shelter, one of the least pretentious jobs it was possible to have. Not only didn't she try to impress anyone with her IQ, he sometimes felt she went out of her way to hide it.

But this wasn't possible, not entirely. She was so sharp she couldn't help but show it. It had snuck up on Bram, subtle at first, and then increasingly more obvious. It was the speed at which she assimilated information and the shrewdness of her mind. It was the way she solved the most challenging Sudoku puzzles so effortlessly, seemingly unaware that they were brutally difficult for everyone else.

Despite her brilliance, she didn't come across as the least bit geeky. She had a warm and outgoing personality.

Except for when she suddenly didn't. When he could feel her restraining her personality even more forcefully than she tried to restrain her intellect. She would become suddenly aloof, disengaged, as if annoyed she had ever allowed her true personality to emerge from a self-imposed prison.

Why was she holding back so much? Was she subconsciously reflecting Bram's own inability to fully reveal himself?

David Bram was brilliant in his own right. He had been working as a key scientist at Apple's small San Diego facility now for five years, which most thought was a sufficient explanation for his wealth. Not many twenty-eight-year-olds could afford the payments on a six-million-dollar home on the beach in Del Mar, but most just assumed that if you worked at Apple—with the stock price being what it was—you were loaded, that even the janitors there were millionaires.

Bram knew this hadn't been true for some time.

He was wealthy because he had a master's degree from MIT and was an expert in machine learning. He had been in a PhD program, but he had made so much progress on his thesis that he got a number of unsolicited offers he couldn't refuse.

If a company thought they had found a star, they didn't have the patience to wait for fancy credentials. So he had traded in a PhD—and the prestige of being introduced as *Dr.* Bram—for a multimillion-dollar salary.

Apple was aggressively pursuing a number of AI and AGI programs that were well advertised, but they were also working on a few that they couldn't have kept more secret. Bram wasn't allowed to share his work with anyone, or even reveal that the Apple facility he worked at had anything to do with AGI. There were spies behind enemy lines in Nazi Germany who hadn't needed to maintain the level of secrecy that was required of David Bram. This was frustrating, but given that his work and pay were both highly stimulating, this was a sacrifice he was willing to make.

If anyone asked him what he did, he was most often able to smoothly deflect the conversation elsewhere. If he was pressed, he had studied up on highly technical advances being made in the area of smart phones, advances that were kosher to talk about, and pretended that he worked on these. Riley's probing questions—not nosy but genuinely interested—had been so good he was forced to study harder to continue to lie convincingly.

But *was* he convincing? Was she so bright she could sense he lacked the depth he would be expected to have had this really been his life's work?

Perhaps this was one of the reasons for her reticence. She knew that he was keeping a huge part of his life from her. How could this not contribute to her reluctance to commit to the relationship? How could it *not* raise a specter of mistrust?

Did the fact that he was Jewish play a role? He had brought this up, and she insisted she didn't care. But would she tell him the truth if she did? Was he just a fun diversion until she found a Christian to marry?

The sun dropped its last inch below the Pacific, completing the daily spectacle that occurred just outside of Bram's home. He wanted to take Riley's hand and lead her back inside, but this smacked too much of romance and love, so he motioned for her to follow him instead.

He led her to the kitchen and poured them both goblets of red wine. "How was your dinner last night with your uncle?" he asked, managing to keep the hurt from his tone. He had tried to avoid bringing this up all day but couldn't stop himself any longer.

Riley was very close with her uncle, Michael O'Banion, who had frequent business in San Diego and who liked to take her out to dinner whenever he was in town to catch up on her life.

Bram had no trouble with that. It was just that after almost a year of dating, even given Riley's success in keeping their relationship casual, it wouldn't have been crazy for him to meet her uncle. Outside of her colleagues at the animal shelter, Uncle Michael O'Banion was about the only person she ever spoke about.

If someone was important in Riley's life, he was important in *Bram's* life.

Only she had no interest in having them meet, even after Bram had pushed to join them for dinner as hard as he thought he could. He tried not to let this bother him, but it did.

Even though O'Banion was family and not a romantic interest, Bram was a little jealous of the closeness they seemed to share. But his real jealousy when it came to Riley wasn't even directed at anyone human. Instead, it was directed at the entire canine species, whose members had never once failed to demonstrate Riley's enormous capacity for love.

If only some of this love could be directed *his* way.

Bram was a huge dog lover, himself, but he was like *Cruella de Vil* when compared to Riley. She loved dogs for all of the obvious reasons—because who didn't love dogs? But he had the feeling she loved dogs even more for *not* being human. That she found humanity fatally flawed and would much rather spend her time around a species with no hidden agendas, no capacity for cruelty.

But he couldn't be too jealous. After all, he owed their relationship—despite it being more shallow than he would have liked—to this four-legged species.

Given that Riley hadn't spent a day in college and they were in markedly different socioeconomic strata, on paper they should have never met, and it should never have worked if they had. But dogs had brought them together. Or, more specifically, Bram's dog, Ash, a rollicking Australian Shepherd whom he had boarded often at the Helen Woodward Animal Center, where Riley worked.

While the organization focused primarily on finding homes for rescue pets, which it did thousands of times each year, it also maintained both equine and small animal hospitals, along with a kennel, which Bram had used since arriving in San Diego, never guessing this would help him meet the girl of his dreams.

Riley loved her job at Helen Woodward, and as far as Bram could tell, everyone there loved her. But as if her work at the Center wasn't selfless enough, she had become a volunteer puppy raiser three years earlier for another San Diego organization, one that provided highly trained assistance dogs to people with disabilities, either Labradors or golden retrievers. Puppy raisers pledged not to get a dog of their own, but rather to focus their full attention on raising, loving, and socializing the puppy they were given, and bringing it to mandatory obedience training classes.

This wasn't the selfless part. Labrador and golden puppies could melt anyone's heart. The hard part was when the organization wanted them *back*, for further training and so they could enhance the lives of the disabled.

As sad as Riley was when she had to give up each temporary pet, she at least knew the dog would live a healthy and happy life helping others, and within a month she would get another puppy, beginning the cycle all over again.

Bram, on the other hand, was still suffering from the recent loss of his dog. Unlike Riley's dogs, Ash wasn't simply going off to college, but had passed away, just weeks earlier. Bram had decided to wait a month or two before beginning the search for his next pet, which would certainly be a rescue dog. Riley had given up her latest puppy for adoption just a week earlier, so this marked the first window since they had met when both were without dogs, although this window was sure to be short.

Riley took a sip of wine and shrugged in response to Bram's question about her dinner with Uncle Mike. "Honestly, it was pretty boring," she replied, with all the believability of a woman savoring award-winning cheesecake while mercifully assuring her dieting friend that it really wasn't that good. "You didn't miss much."

He thought about responding that his request to join them wasn't about being entertained, but bit his tongue. He hadn't expected the two of them to start spinning plates for his amusement, after all. The point had been to meet her uncle, regardless of how boring or scintillating the evening turned out to be.

"I did most of the talking," continued Riley. "Mostly about the antics of beagles and bulldogs. Stories you've heard a thousand times before," she finished with an incandescent grin.

Bram smiled back, even though he knew this was her way of dismissing the topic. "But they never get old," he replied, rolling his eyes. He was about to let her off the hook and change the subject entirely, when his virtual assistant, Genie, beat him to the punch. "David, a visitor is approaching your door," she said, her disembodied voice soft and pleasant. "Should I put him on screen?"

"Please do," said Bram. There were dozens of monitors built into the walls around the premises, and the one closest to him changed from showing an image of a breathtaking mountain view to showing a determined-looking man preparing to press the intercom button outside of his front door.

Bram had borrowed the term "on screen," from *Star Trek*, and had asked Genie to use it whenever appropriate, which made him feel like the captain of the *Enterprise* and usually brought a smile to his face. But this time it only brought sadness, as this visitor underscored Ash's absence. Usually, it was a race to see if his dog or his digital assistant would be the first to alert him that someone was approaching his door, and the lack of barking was deafening.

The solicitor outside looked rugged and overly serious. Bram was in no mood to deal with him. It was past sunset, after all. He turned to Riley and shook his head. "Are you up for pretending we're not home?"

"It'll be a tough challenge," said Riley with a wry smile, "but I think I can manage. You know, classically trained Shakespearean *actoooor* that I am," she said, hamming up the word *actor* so much that Bram couldn't help but laugh.

Unfortunately, their inaugural performance of "we're not really here" lasted all of ten seconds.

"I know you're in there, Mr. Bram," said the visitor after a few failed attempts to get a response. "I'm Special Agent Jeff Parker with the FBI, and it's urgent that I speak with you."

Parker swiped an icon on his phone and his FBI credentials now appeared on Bram's 3D touchscreen monitor alongside his image. Bram's security system crosschecked the ID with FBI records, which were available at a secure site for just this purpose, and confirmed that Jeff Parker's credentials were legitimate.

Riley eyed Bram questioningly. "Anything you want to tell me about?" she asked, half joking and half serious. "You aren't a criminal mastermind, by any chance, are you?"

Bram shook his head and looked totally mystified. "Not as far as I know," he replied slowly.

# 14

Cameron Carr stood at the entrance to David Bram's beachfront home and wondered what he would do if the man still didn't let him in, despite his authentic FBI credentials.

Not that he had fully figured out what he was going to say or do once he *did* get inside.

Carr was still uncertain if he was making the right move. But he prided himself on being bold, and he rarely second guessed himself. Now was no time to start. Besides, he had already announced himself at Bram's door, so the time for reconsideration was over.

Since Carr had left the Pentagon three days earlier he had made considerable progress on his mission, but not in the way the Secretary of Defense had probably expected.

Carr had worked as a spy in multiple countries, but he had done the bulk of his work in Russia. He spoke the language and had lived there for years. So when he learned that intel suggested Russia's AGI programs had been sabotaged as severely as those in the US, beginning two years earlier, he knew *exactly* how they would react.

A lot more quickly and decisively than the US had reacted.

In the US, when standard intelligence gathering efforts had failed to identify the saboteur, it had taken the destruction of DARPA's master supercomputer housed within Area 51 for the president and Troy Dwyer to finally decide to send a single operative on a scorched-earth mission to get to the bottom of this mess. The Russians, on the other hand, wouldn't have been nearly so shy.

Assuming Russia wasn't behind this, an assumption Carr decided he would make, at least initially, he was all but certain they had mounted a similar program, only a year or more before Dwyer had.

And that meant one thing: Major Marat Volkov.

Carr considered himself to be a realist when it came to his own abilities. He might pretend to be humble, but his survival depended on him having a clear-eyed sense of his own skills. He was very good at what he did. Certainly one of the top five operatives the US had recently produced.

But Major Marat Volkov was the best Russia had ever fielded. And no one else was even a close second. He spoke five languages, including unaccented English as eloquently as the most educated natives.

The man was both respected and feared around the world, nicknamed *The Wolf* in the international community, both for his predatory nature and ferocity, and also because his name was derived from the Russian word for this formidable creature.

For an operation this important, Volkov would almost certainly have been put in charge.

So why should Carr reinvent the wheel? Why not just cheat? Why brave a deadly, booby-trapped ancient Peruvian temple to retrieve a golden idol when you could just wait outside for Indiana Jones to emerge with your prize?

Dwyer had all but given Carr a license to kill, but only because he had known Carr would use it very reluctantly, if at all. Dwyer had raised this specter more to underscore the criticality of the mission than for any other reason.

But Volkov, on the other hand, was surely being his typical, ruthless self. The fact that the saboteur was still at large spoke volumes about just how tough this case really was. Because if Marat Volkov needed to kill a dozen innocent children to get the *hint* of a lead, he wouldn't hesitate to do so.

So even if Volkov's skills were no better than Carr's, and even if the major had not been given a head start, the Russian was likely to end up well ahead of him. So why not just steal the fruits of the major's labor? If he could locate Volkov and learn what avenues he was pursuing, he could catch up in a hurry.

And there were two highly placed double agents in Moscow that Carr had personally turned who could point him in the right direction, which, for this case, could be anywhere on the globe.

When Carr had pulled on this thread, he couldn't have been more surprised and delighted to learn that the esteemed major was in San Diego, California. Right in his own backyard.

Carr had managed to catch up with Volkov just that morning, but not before the Russian, with a three-man team in tow, had killed a male guest at the downtown Sheraton hotel in cold blood. Volkov had folded the man's body inside a large duffel bag and had wheeled it down to his car, as though he was leaving for a morning round of golf. The body was then taken from his trunk to an incinerator and disposed of.

If Carr hadn't found Volkov and been given the authority to use the US military and intelligence apparatus as though they were his personal playthings—re-tasking a satellite to conduct around-the-clock surveillance of the Russian—no one would have ever known that this murder had taken place. As it was, they had only caught this after the fact, when the man's body was being disposed of.

When facial recognition had failed to determine the victim's identity, Carr had immediately called in a team of experts, who had managed to trace Volkov back to the man's room, only to learn that the guest had checked in under a false identity. DNA and fingerprints found in the room were a match to previous guests and hotel staff, except in one case, where a DNA sample didn't match any DNA on record.

So far all roads seemed to dead-end.

But while Carr had yet to learn the identity of this link in whatever chain Volkov had constructed, after the murder, a street camera had filmed fragments of a conversation between Volkov and his men, and lip-reading software was able to divine the Russian words he had spoken with ninety-nine-percent accuracy.

While the camera had missed large chunks of the conversation as various pairs of lips came into and out of view, it was clear the major was planning to raid the Del Mar home of one David Bram. The home had state-of-the-art security, and while this wouldn't prove much of a deterrent to someone like Volkov, he wanted to plan the raid out carefully, just to be sure he hadn't missed anything and that no mistakes were made.

He and his team—which included Captain Sergei Greshnev, one of Volkov's comrades who Carr knew well—would study the security and hone their plan, meeting outside of Bram's home at eight p.m. to carry it out. Which meant that Carr had beaten them to Bram's home by almost ninety minutes.

Carr had the right authority codes to turn the Director of National Intelligence himself into his personal errand boy, so he was able to run deep background checks on both Bram and a woman named Riley Ridgeway, who spent many nights with him, at the highest priority level possible.

And the result of this probe was exactly what Carr had hoped it would be. Because David Bram worked at an Apple facility that American intelligence had confirmed conducted secret AGI research for the company, and the man played an important role in this research.

Bingo. Hard to imagine this could just be a coincidence. The likelihood that Bram was a key link in Volkov's chain was very high.

Which had led to Carr's dilemma. Should he continue to observe and follow Volkov from afar? Or should he intercede now, chancing that Bram was the Russian's prized football and that an interception now could change the game forever, not only allowing Carr to catch up on Volkov's many months of work, but perhaps leapfrog past him. Despite all of Indy's hard work in the opening scene of *Raiders of the Lost Ark,* his rival, Rene Belloq, had ended up with the golden idol and Jones had been left empty-handed.

It all hinged on Bram's importance. If he was a minor player, then Carr's interception would prove largely fruitless and would show his hand too early.

In the end, the deciding factor was that Volkov was now operating on US soil, giving Carr an enormous home field advantage. Without this, Carr would have chosen to continue to trail Volkov and gather any breadcrumbs he left behind. But with the field tilted so strongly in his favor, a gamble like this could prove decisive.

Bram had better be worth it. The moment Carr revealed his presence to the major, the situation would change in a hurry.

Not that Carr wanted to hinder the Russian too much. They were pursuing the same initial goal, after all, learning who was behind the sabotage. The problem was that Carr knew their goals would diverge from there, turning them into fierce competitors.

Carr would want to find the person or people responsible and stop them.

Volkov, on the other hand, would want to find those responsible so he could do whatever was necessary—using threat, punishment, or reward—to press them into service for Mother Russia. He would force them to use their superior skills to continue to bring down the programs of every other AGI initiative in the world, while Russia continued apace, guaranteeing that they would get there first. Even the slowest runner could win a race when all the other entrants had been crippled.

But as he thought about this, Carr realized that America would probably do the same, look the other way and try to turn a liability into an asset. The US hadn't hesitated to press a number of brilliant Nazi scientists into serving America's interests after World War II. With stakes this high, it would be easy to justify. This put his mission in an entirely different light, and was something Carr would need to consider further at another time.

What bothered him most about bringing Bram in right now was that an innocent girl was also in the mix. This was troubling, but once again, the stakes were too high to be squeamish. The background check on Riley Ridgeway had revealed that she had been raised by law-abiding parents on a farm in Indiana, and had as bland of an upbringing as one could imagine, followed by a saintly stint at an animal shelter.

Carr would make sure she was cleared from any danger as soon as possible, but she was about to learn some truths about David Bram that were sure to be devastating.

It wasn't every day that you learned that the man you were dating had lied to you about what he did for a living since you had first met. Not to mention being suspected of acts of sabotage that would put him at the top of most wanted lists in dozens of powerful countries around the world.

Carr took a deep breath as Bram's front door began to swing open.

# 15

David Bram and Riley Ridgeway stood at the entrance to the door, eyeing Carr warily. "What can I do for you, Agent Parker?" said Bram.

"Can I come inside?"

Bram nodded and held the door wider, stepping back to allow the visitor entrance.

"Thank you," said Carr as he stepped inside the entry foyer. He shut the door behind him, never taking his eyes from Bram's hands.

Carr raised a gun and pointed it at the couple. Both shrank back in horror.

The lieutenant looked into Riley's green eyes and sighed. "I'm so sorry to have to do this," he said as sincerely as he could, "but I can't risk that your boyfriend will try to get the drop on me. Or run."

Bram shook his head. "Get the *drop* on you?" he said in dismay, with an expression that indicated he couldn't believe this phrase was still in use. "Run from *what?* I have no idea why you're here."

As Bram stared at the unwavering gun pointed at him, he appeared to realize that it was a bad idea to be belligerent with a potentially unstable stranger who could kill him in an instant. "Look, I'll cooperate," he continued, his tone now submissive. "Just, please, put that thing down."

Carr didn't respond. Instead, he thoroughly frisked Bram while holding the gun to his head, and then ordered his two temporary prisoners to lead him to the dining room. When they arrived, Carr bound Bram's wrists tightly together with a hard plastic zip tie and had him sit on one of eight chairs that were positioned around a lacquered walnut table. He then used another zip tie to bind Bram's left ankle to one of the table's legs.

Bram's background didn't include combat skills of any kind, but Carr liked to err on the side of caution.

With Bram secured, Carr used several zip ties to cuff Riley's wrists together, but loosely, and with plenty of play in between, choosing not to bind her ankle. Finally, he had her sit near Bram at the table, leaving an empty chair between them.

With this complete, Carr remained standing and alert on the opposite side of the table, but returned his weapon to the small of his back, seeing no reason to continue to hold a gun on the frightened couple.

He would have loved to let Riley leave at the outset, but there was no way he could. She would go straight to the police, and even with nearly unlimited authority, he didn't need the headache that would cause.

Besides, Volkov would be sure to snatch her up when he realized Carr had taken Bram out of his reach. If the Russian couldn't have his primary target, the least he could do would be to interrogate the woman who was currently *sleeping* with his primary target, and find out what she knew.

It was a move that Carr would make, also, if the tables were turned. The difference was that he would leave her alive and unharmed, whereas the Russian would almost certainly subject her to lengthy torture before ending her life.

As much as Carr might regret it, he had no choice but to bring Riley Ridgeway along for the ride.

"What's this all about?" said Bram, trying to keep his tone conversational rather than confrontational.

"I wanted to have a brief talk before we leave."

"Leave?" said Bram. "Leave for where?"

"After we've chatted for a few minutes," replied Carr, "I'm taking both of you to a highly secure safe house, where I can make sure you're protected and off the grid."

"Right now it seems like the only protection we need is from *you*," said Riley pointedly.

Carr smiled. "I know it *seems* that way, but trust me, you have nothing to worry about from me. I'm going to level with you. I'm not with the FBI. But I really do work for the US government."

"For what agency?" asked Bram

Carr frowned. "I'm afraid I can't give you any more details about my role," he replied. He considered adding, "If I told you, I'd have to kill you," to lighten the mood, but realized that in their current situation they would take this statement as anything but amusingly sarcastic. Instead, he finished with, "Trust me, I'm one of the good guys."

Both parties looked decidedly unconvinced. Hard to blame them.

"You work for the US government," said Bram, "and you're one of the good guys. But you trick your way into my home and hold us at gunpoint. Why do these two statements not seem to match up?"

Carr ignored him. "There is a Russian agent named Marat Volkov in town," he said. "Does that name ring a bell?"

Bram's expression made it clear that it didn't. "What about him?" he asked.

"He's very good, and very ruthless. It seems that Russia's best efforts to achieve Artificial General Intelligence keep getting sabotaged."

Bram's eyes widened as the mention of AGI.

"As have the efforts of . . . a few other parties," continued Carr. He had no other choice but to reveal that he was investigating AGI sabotage. If you were going to interrogate someone, you needed to tell them the nature of the information you were after. But he had minimized the importance and extent of his mission. Besides, if Bram was the one he was looking for, this wouldn't matter, anyway.

"That's too bad," said Brain warily. "But what's that got to do with me?"

"Volkov seems to believe you have something to do with this. Either you're responsible. Or you know who is."

"That's absolutely ridiculous," protested Bram.

Carr arched an eyebrow. "I know nothing about you, Mr. Bram, so I can't say. But I do know that Marat Volkov is planning to visit you here in a little over an hour. And *he* doesn't believe this is ridiculous. Not at all. And he'll be willing to kill you without even blinking."

Bram swallowed hard. "So if you really are one of the good guys, why are you *here*? Shouldn't you be stopping him?"

"I would be," replied Carr, "but he's very, very good, and he doesn't make mistakes. So if he believes you're involved, I do too. And if you are, I want to know everything you know. So in just a few minutes we're all going to leave here for the safe house I mentioned. I have satellites watching him and his men to be sure they don't arrive here early. We wouldn't want to be disturbed," he said, trying to put an air of menace into the statement.

Riley Ridgeway had her eyes glued on Bram's face. She had no idea what was happening, but she could tell that he had been keeping secrets from her. "What do you really do, David?" she asked, her face pained. "Do you even work at Apple?"

"Yes!" he replied emphatically.

Carr turned to face Riley. "I really am sorry you had to be involved with this," he said. "You're at the wrong place at the wrong time. Your boyfriend here does work at Apple. But on a secret program, in the field of Artificial Intelligence, but more broadly defined. Something called Artificial *General* Intelligence."

Riley shook her head and looked like she might vomit. Carr had expected her to show feelings of anger and betrayal after learning she had been lied to for so long. And while he could detect these emotions in her expression, she also demonstrated what seemed to Carr to be disgust.

A tear came to her eye. "David, do you know what he's talking about? Is he right? Are you engaged in *espionage*? Tell me!" she demanded.

"No! Of course not! It's true that I work on AGI," he said. "He's right about that. And I'm so sorry I didn't tell you, Riley. But I *couldn't* tell you. Apple insisted on crazy levels of secrecy." He shook his head fervently. "But that's my only secret!" he insisted. "I'm not sabotaging *anything*."

Riley studied Bram's face in horror, unsure of what to believe.

"How did you know about my work in AGI?" Bram asked Carr.

"It's my job to know. Keeping secrets from a woman who helps families adopt pets is one thing. Keeping secrets from *me* is another.

I'd remember that going forward if I were you. If you lie to me, I'm going to know it." He turned to Riley and winced. "Not that pet rescue isn't a noble calling," he hastened to add.

But Riley Ridgeway wasn't paying attention. She had clearly made up her mind about her boyfriend's claims of innocence, and it hadn't gone his way. Tears of anger and betrayal were now running down her face and she was becoming completely unglued. Her eyes were wild, like a rabid dog, her full attention and malice focused on David Bram.

"I trusted you!" she screamed. "I was falling in love with you! You *asshole!*"

With that she rose up from the table and in the blink of an eye was behind him, moving with balletic grace. She put her hands over his head and pulled back, the slack in her plastic handcuffs catching Bram around the throat, threatening to garrote him, while she continued to shout curses.

Carr had known the news he would deliver would be tough for her to take, but he hadn't expected *this*. She probably wouldn't really kill Bram, no matter how filled with rage, but Carr couldn't take that chance. The man was his only lead.

Carr brought his gun back out in an instant. "Freeze!" he screamed, pointing it at Riley while Bram struggled for breath. "Stop choking him!" he demanded. "*Stop*, or I'll shoot!"

She either didn't hear Carr or didn't care, continuing to focus entirely on making Bram pay for his duplicity.

Carr slid across the glossy table and landed beside her, an athletic move that few could have matched. He grabbed her hands, forced them away from Bram's throat and back over his head, and then threw her to the floor, quickly turning back to check on Bram, making sure he was still breathing and his trachea hadn't been crushed.

The moment he confirmed Bram would make a full recovery, he turned back to Riley Ridgeway on the floor, but he was too late. Even loosely bound, she had managed to reach into a pocket and remove a small stun gun, which she pressed against his ankle, accompanied by the violent crackling screams of raw electricity. She held the electroshock weapon against Carr's leg until it pulverized his every muscle and he collapsed to the ground beside her, spasming.

Electroshock weapons had become ever more powerful and more concealable, and Riley's model was no exception. The moment Carr was down she hit him with the device a second time, and what surely must have been enough electricity to light up a city shot through him once more.

Paralyzed and helpless, Carr knew he was completely at their mercy. After everything he had been through, after surviving gun battles, hand-to-hand combat against impeccably trained men, was this really how he would die?

How could he have grown so careless, allowing himself to be outwitted by a girl with no training? Just because she had checked out as being harmless didn't mean he could lower his guard. He, of all people, should know that on rare occasion, even the most weak-kneed pacifist could come out fighting when their back was against the wall. And Riley's strategy had been brilliant, attacking Bram like a crazed demon, knowing Carr would be forced to pull her away at close quarters.

He should also have known she'd be carrying a means of self-defense. A girl this breathtaking would want to carry something that could deter unwanted attention.

How could he have been so sloppy? So careless?

But Carr didn't have any time to contemplate his mistake further as the stunner was pressed into his body for a third time, and he was blasted into unconsciousness.

# 16

"Really sorry about the whole *choking-you* thing," Riley said to Bram as they rushed into his garage and climbed into his white BMW four-door sedan, with Bram at the wheel.

"No apology necessary," he replied as he started the car. "I knew it was a ruse. I know you too well. No way you'd react like that, even if you learned I was Attila the Hun."

When she had said she was falling in love with him, this was even more of a tip-off that she was acting, but he didn't want to bring this up at the moment. "And I could tell you weren't bearing down on my throat nearly as hard as you could have."

"Only because you were quick enough on your feet to pretend you were choking to death," said Riley.

"So if I hadn't been convincing enough, you would have pulled harder? Is that what you're saying?"

The hint of a smile crossed her face. "Whatever it took to coax the proper response from you," she replied with a twinkle in her eye. "But you were very convincing. You're a lot better at pretending to choke than you are at pretending you're not home."

Bram laughed. "Where to?" he asked.

"Am I in charge?"

"You think faster than I do," he admitted. "And if it weren't for you, we'd still be captives, so, yeah . . . you're in charge."

She nodded and then tilted her head in thought. "Okay. Before we go, leave your phone here," she instructed. "If there *are* boogie men out there, they'll be tracking our cell phones for sure."

"What about yours?"

"I may have other plans for it," she said enigmatically. "Hurry. Leave it and let's get out of here."

Bram opened the car door and set his phone gently on the floor of the garage while Riley continued to plan.

He pulled into the street and then stopped, putting the car in park so both he and Riley could look around. Both craned their necks to complete a full three-hundred-sixty-degree examination of their surroundings, anxiously trying to spot suspicious-looking people or cars. None appeared to be present, but that didn't mean they weren't being watched, just that they were immune from any *obvious* surveillance.

"We have to assume the worst," said Riley. "Be the most paranoid we can be. Which means we have to assume this car will stick out like a sore thumb. We have to do classic spy-type stuff to shake any watchers—satellites and otherwise. Use misdirection and stealth." She paused. "How much cash do you have on you?"

"Two or three hundred."

"Do you know of anywhere nearby that is under something—trees, an overpass, whatever—that hides it from overhead surveillance? Preferably somewhere off the beaten path, that isn't likely to be covered with street cams."

Bram thought for a moment. "Yeah. There's a railroad bridge near Dog Beach that fits your criteria."

"Accessible from the street?"

He nodded. "We can be there in about ten minutes."

"Good. Here's what I propose: First, I use my Uber app to find a driver who can meet us as soon as possible." She paused. "Let's say at the Shell station on Del Mar Heights Road."

Bram nodded. He knew the station well. It was about a mile away. He had never used Uber himself, but was familiar with one of their many tag-lines: "Tap the Uber app and get picked up in minutes." Apparently, Riley wanted to put this to the test.

"When we meet our driver at the Shell," continued Riley, "we explain that we have a colleague attending an important meeting at the Hotel del Coronado, who needs his extra phone. Which will actually be this one," she added, waving her phone. "We pay the driver a hundred dollars to deliver it to the reception desk."

Bram nodded. "Very nice," he said. "You're hoping that if anyone is out there, they'll follow your phone, thinking it's us."

She shrugged. "It might work. It might not. But it's worth a try."

"And meanwhile, we'll be heading to our railroad bridge near Dog Beach, right?"

"Exactly. We hide the car there and walk away as rapidly as we can. Before I send my phone off to Coronado Island, I'll arrange for another Uber driver to pick us up about a mile from the bridge. While we're walking, we try to buy hats and maybe a change of clothing if we can, to further confuse anyone after us."

Most people would have been astonished by Riley's ability to come up with such an impressive plan on the fly, but Bram knew this was just par for the course.

"We have the second Uber driver take us to a scummy, beat-up motel," she continued. "The sort of place that even rats try to avoid. Then we hole up there for a while until we can figure out our next move."

Bram nodded. "I'm in," he said. "Set it up."

Riley manipulated the Uber app on her phone and waited. Less than a minute later it had all been arranged. The service was as responsive as advertised. Impressive. Riley's phone showed a picture of the driver, his rating, and a map giving his location and his progress toward the Shell.

Bram put the car in gear and sped off through the early evening. They would barely beat the driver there. "If our endgame is a seedy motel," he said, "I assume this means you're ruling out going to the cops."

"Yes."

"I know we could be in hot water for attacking a government agent," he said, "but our best bet might be to go to the authorities and take our medicine."

Riley shook her head. "Until we know for sure who we can trust, we can't risk the cops."

"You think a local cop might be in on it?" said Bram.

"Probably not. But our visitor was talking about redirecting satellites to watch this Russian, this Marat Volkov, as if this was no big deal. So he must have a lot of pull in high places. If he really is with the government, he probably has the authority to get the police to watch for us, and to turn us in if we go to them."

Bram sighed miserably. "Good point," he said.

"With respect to being in hot water for assaulting the guy," continued Riley, "that's the least of our worries. The man impersonated an FBI agent and passed off forged credentials. This has to be a federal offense. He entered your home under false pretenses and then held a gun on us. Tied us up. If he's legitimate, he can't file charges against us—*me*—for these reasons. And if he really is a spy, the last thing he would want is for this situation to become more public. Not to mention having to admit he was beaten by a hundred-ten-pound woman."

"And if he's *not* legitimate?"

"Then I just saved your life," she said. "But everything considered, until we learn more about what this is all about, and who we can trust, we should stay off the grid."

"You really are scary good at this spy stuff," he said in admiration.

"Go figure. Especially since *you're* the one wanted on international espionage charges."

"I really, truly, have no idea what that is all about. Honestly."

"Why didn't you tell me you worked on AGI?" she said, with the same level of contempt she might have shown had she learned he was selling crack cocaine to babies.

"I told you the truth back at the house. Apple made it clear they would take my firstborn child if I even told *myself* what I was doing."

She frowned deeply but didn't reply.

"I love your plan," said Bram, "except that we won't be holing up together. Once we're clear of immediate danger, I want you out of this. Go stay with your Uncle Mike in Denver until I figure this out. I'm the target, not you, so you'll be safe. No way I'm going to let you get hurt because of me. You're completely innocent."

She raised her eyebrows. "From what you say, so are you."

"This is true," he said with a sigh. "But, apparently, that isn't a popular opinion with the men who are currently hunting me down."

Riley chewed her lower lip and pondered what Bram had said as he turned east onto Del Mar Heights Road. "I'm not going *anywhere*," she said finally, her jaw set in determination. "I won't leave you in this situation. You said it yourself. I'm probably better at this than you. Besides, are you sure that I'd be safe in Denver?"

"Safer than being with me."

"I'm not so sure. What makes you think they won't use me to get to you? Besides," she said, lowering her eyes, "I care about you more than I let on. I try not to, but I do. Which just means that we have to break up once we get through this," she hastened to add.

Knowing her, this actually made sense. "I thought it was supposed to be *men* who were terrified of commitment," he muttered, unable to help himself.

"Let's save this discussion for another time. The point for now is that there's no way I'm going to abandon you when you have no idea what's going on or who to trust. I won't leave you when you need me the most." Riley sighed heavily. "So I'm going to help us get to the bottom of this. I'm going to help straighten out this misunderstanding before either of us gets hurt."

She paused and stared at him with great intensity. "Unless I find out you really are what that guy says you are," she said with a deep frown. "In that case," she added icily, "I'm going to kill you myself."

# 17

Major Marat Volkov was ecstatic. He could finally see a light at the end of a long tunnel.

He had never been on an assignment for this long and made this little progress. But he had begun making major breakthroughs recently, culminating in a discovery that he felt could finally get him over the finish line.

He had originally considered using David Bram's home as a fort once they had taken over. It had a reasonably good security system in place, and Volkov could supplement this with booby traps and additional security to ensure no one would dare try to breach.

But he had thought better of it. Why leave anything to chance? So while his men were double-checking the security on Bram's residence, Volkov had identified an ideal place to keep a prisoner safe from any would-be rescuers, an abandoned Seventh-day Adventist church that had been put up for sale, less than an hour's drive away.

The church was relatively small, nestled in the center of a ten-acre clearing surrounded by woods, giving it an easily defensible perimeter. It had been on the market for three months, so the chances that the realtor involved would be showing the property while they were borrowing it were slim. But just in case, Volkov had Russian Intelligence back home hack into the realtor's computer to check his calendar. He had a busy weekend scheduled, but as expected, it didn't include any visits to a church.

The major had sent four of his men to prepare the structure to his specifications, to make it all but impregnable, in the unlikely event that their presence there was discovered. They would apply advanced technology and booby traps to ensure any rescue attempt would be suicidal.

A voice came through the comm in Volkov's ear, belonging to his second-in-command on this mission, Sergei Greshnev. "Are you on your way to Bram's house?"

"Not yet," replied Volkov. "I was just leaving."

"Don't bother," said Greshnev in annoyance. "They're on the move."

Volkov frowned. "I'm sure they'll return home shortly," he replied.

They had caught up with the couple that morning, as they were completing a breakfast at a quaint Del Mar café. When the couple had finished, they had walked along the streets of this wealthy enclave, window shopping. Volkov had deployed sophisticated technology to record their conversation remotely, and had learned that they planned to stay in that night at Bram's Del Mar home.

Fortunately, Volkov's men were also able to successfully deploy tiny drones, each about twice the size of a grain of rice, and guide them onto the couple's clothing, where they attached like tiny burrs. The drones were new military tech coming out of Russian labs that not even the Americans could match. They were nothing more than flying GPS homing beacons, giving men like Volkov a convenient way to tag and track their quarry, like scientists conducting migratory studies on wildlife.

"Maybe they went for a drink," suggested Volkov, before immediately thinking better of it. These two weren't Russians, after all, but health-obsessed Californians. "Or maybe a low-fat frozen yogurt," he amended.

They had decided that Bram's home was secluded enough that it made sense to breach there rather than attempt to snatch them off the street. When operating in the States, discretion was the better part of valor. Why risk making a public spectacle and get American authorities asking questions?

"I don't think this is about yogurt," said Greshnev grimly. "They left almost twenty minutes ago. I didn't want to notify you until I had more information. But something smells very bad about this. They're moving about like pinballs. They drive, then they walk, then they drive. Doesn't make sense. Almost as if they're aware we're out here and are playing at being spies to confuse us."

"Any way we could have been seen?"

"Doubtful. But anything is possible."

"Keep them within range of our tracking beacons. I'll come join you. We may have to change our plans. As much as we didn't want a more public snatch and grab, we may have no other choice."

"Roger that," said Sergei Greshnev.

# 18

Cameron Carr issued a soft groan as he returned to consciousness. His head throbbed, and each and every muscle in his body, including muscles he didn't even know he had, felt like they had been forced through a cast iron meat tenderizer.

All four of his limbs were now bound to the weighty walnut table under which he had fallen. With zip ties. His own zip ties, no doubt. Talk about embarrassing.

*Still*, he thought, blowing out a sigh of relief, *it could have been worse*. At least he was still alive.

He was much more upset with his own carelessness than with Riley Ridgeway's actions. In fact, he couldn't help but admire how well she had handled herself. She had outplayed him, fair and square.

She had fooled Carr into believing she thought he was a legitimate government agent, and that she was much more suspicious of David Bram than of him.

But how could she have known what to believe?

A strange man comes through the door wielding a gun and making wild claims, and Riley Ridgeway, the beautiful farmer's daughter type that she was, reacted the way any beautiful farmer's daughter type might react. Who could blame her for concluding that her best course of action was to deploy her stunner if she could, getting away from him and buying time to sort things out.

And she had decided to stand by her man—at least for now. Carr truly hoped this decision didn't end up costing her. It wouldn't if *he* had anything to do with it.

But if he wanted to reacquire David Bram before Volkov did, he had no time to waste. He guessed he had been out for as long as a few hours.

As much as he would love to rest here, hog-tied though he was, he couldn't afford to lick his wounds. It was time to free himself. To demonstrate that he was still a pro, despite his earlier display of incompetence.

He should have brute strength enough to break one of the table's legs away. The trick was to do it in such a way that he didn't get crushed in the process. His two former prisoners hadn't removed his weapons, including his combat knife, so once he was free he could remove the zip ties quite rapidly and be on his way.

But it was possible he was already too late.

# 19

David Bram took stock of his situation, trying to ignore the distinct smell of mold that hovered in the air. The El Cajon Shut-Eye Motel was exactly as bad as Riley had specified. Maybe worse. Dingy. Small. Unappealing in every way.

Bram hadn't been born wealthy, and had backpacked across Europe the summer before he began his graduate studies at MIT. During this time he had slept in public train cars and in a number of youth hostels that had been every bit as unappealing as the El Cajon Shut-Eye Motel.

But he had become spoiled by wealth. He had been living the good life for long enough that this now seemed the scummiest place he had ever been. Bram glanced at the bed and then back at Riley. This was the first time he could remember being with her near a bed and having absolutely no interest in making love to her. Not in this setting, or under these circumstances.

Not that she would let him near her right now, anyway, even if they were at the Four Seasons. Not until she could trust him again.

How could this be happening? It was insane. Was it just a case of mistaken identity? Or much more troubling, was he being framed? Perhaps one of his colleagues at Apple was responsible and had placed incriminating information on his computer. At this point, anything was possible.

And what was this doing to his relationship with Riley? Was it destroying it, or improving it?

It might be either, he had to admit. Riley had shown she cared for him more than he had thought. And surely being held at gunpoint together, escaping together, was a major bonding experience. And their shared peril wasn't over.

So far, she was the one who had played the hero, rescuing them from the intruder at his home. What he needed was to save *her* life, not the other way around.

But maybe this wasn't necessary. Maybe she already loved him, as hard as this was to believe. If so, heroics that resulted in an even deeper connection between them was the *worst* thing that could happen.

How had he managed to fall in love with a woman who was this amazing, and this maddening? He was put in the impossible position of ensuring their relationship stayed in some kind of Goldilocks Zone or risk losing everything. If she liked him too little, it was over. If she liked him too much, it was over. Only if the porridge was just right would Goldilocks stick around.

He sighed, putting this conundrum out of his mind for the time being. There were more pressing matters to consider.

"Okay," he said to her. "Here we are. So now what? My computer skills are very good, so maybe I can find a computer and search the Dark Web for possible answers. Or I could try to hack a few of my colleagues at Apple, see if they're involved with something shady. Something bad enough to cause people to come after me by mistake." He paused. "What do you think?"

"I don't think we're likely to get anywhere on our own. Not lying low in a motel room. This is way over our heads. I like the idea of taking advantage of your computer skills, but as good as you are, aren't your colleagues at Apple just about as good?"

Bram nodded.

"So they won't be easy to hack, even for you, right?"

He frowned. "This is probably true."

"Here's what I think we should do," said Riley. "First, let's try to learn if this fake FBI agent, Parker, is really with the government, and if so, who he really is. From what I understand, government computers are less well protected than those belonging to savvy individuals or multinationals."

"Not as true as it once was," said Bram, "but still the case."

"So why don't you hack the US government? See if you can find any intel on yourself. What this might be about. Most importantly, see if you can find someone high up in intelligence circles who can help us get to the bottom of this. Someone with experience and resources, who Parker can't reach. Someone we can monitor to be sure we can trust."

"I'll need access to a very good computer," he said.

"I have an idea about that too," she replied. "What we can do is—"

The door burst inward and three men rushed inside, guns drawn.

"Don't make a sound," said the man in the middle, so calmly and casually that it had a more chilling effect than a shout would have had. "Frisk them, Yuri," he ordered one of the two men on either side of him.

The man who was apparently named Yuri did as he was ordered, not being gentle in the process. He found Riley's stunner, about the size of a small cell phone, its hard plastic casing fittingly painted an electric blue, and slipped it into his own pocket for safekeeping.

Bram frowned. He supposed it was too much to hope that this device could free them a second time.

The man who had issued the orders was not native to America. His accent was nearly perfect, but Bram had a great ear and had a feeling he had been born in Russia. The fact that his flunky was named Yuri was a not-so-subtle clue as well. Given what the FBI impersonator had told him about the man after him, a Russian named Marat Volkov, this was a very bad sign.

"What is this all about?" croaked Bram, almost too paralyzed to speak, and having a good guess at the answer.

The man in charge smiled as Yuri returned to his side. "Since *I* have the gun," he said coldly, "why don't I ask the questions. First, what are *you* doing here?"

Bram noted that even the faintest trace of a Russian accent had now disappeared. Impressive.

The man surveyed the tiny room with obvious distaste and then turned again to David Bram. "You're not trying to satisfy some strange sexual fantasy, are you? Some kind of role-playing game? Are you a wealthy guy who gets off on screwing your woman in a filthy motel room like she's a whore?"

"No!" replied Bram in disgust. "Why would you even *think* that?"

"Then what?" said the Russian, glancing back and forth between his two prisoners. "The only other conclusion that makes any sense is that you're trying to avoid us. Are you?"

When neither replied, he spoke in Russian to the flunky on his left, who immediately lowered his gun and pointed it at Bram's kneecap. "This is Sergei," the man in charge explained to the couple, nodding toward his comrade. "You both need to tell me the truth," he hissed. "All of it." He turned to face Bram. "If not, Sergei here will make sure you never walk again."

"Look," said Riley immediately, panic in her eyes, "we don't know what's happening. But a man visited us earlier tonight. Said he was Special Agent Jeff Parker of the FBI. His credentials checked out. But then he held us at gunpoint."

The Russian considered this thoughtfully. "What did he want?"

Bram opened his mouth to reply but Riley jumped in ahead of him. "He didn't say," she replied simply.

Bram's eyes narrowed. Why had she lied? Perhaps she didn't want them to know the AGI angle. Maybe she was trying to protect him. It was a nice gesture, but if this was really Marat Volkov, it wouldn't help.

"I did tell you the penalty for lying," said the Russian icily, nodding at Sergei, who made a show of moving his gun closer to Bram's kneecap.

"I'm not lying!" insisted Riley emphatically. "I'm sure he would have told us what he wanted, but he didn't have a chance. When he tried to tie us up, I knocked him out with my stunner. Check it," she added, nodding toward the flunky on his right, who still held the small device. "You'll see it's been discharged recently."

The Russian shook his head in disgust. "Incredible. I guess I shouldn't be surprised that your FBI agents are this incompetent."

The man paused in thought, making no move to check Riley's electroshock weapon, apparently convinced she was telling the truth. "So this man visited you—right before we were planning to do the same. That's quite a coincidence."

"I can't speak to that," said Bram, "because we have no idea why anyone would want to talk to us in the first place. The bottom line is that we didn't know what was going on, or who to trust."

"So you decided to come to this crappy motel until you could figure things out," said the Russian. "Is that what you're telling me?"

"Exactly," replied Bram. "But *whatever* this is about, it's a mistake. I'm just an innocent, law-abiding citizen. I don't know what's going on. But I do know that I'm not involved in anything shady. And I don't know anyone who is. There's no reason I can think of for anyone to be after me."

The Russian shook his head in amusement.

Bram was confused by this reaction. Why was this funny? "I'm telling you, you have the wrong guy!" he insisted. "I promise!"

Volkov's smile only expanded. "You've got to be fucking kidding me," he said dryly.

"Look, there's been a mistake," insisted Bram. "I'm sure of it. But we can get to the bottom of this. I'll cooperate with you, tell you anything you want to know. But there is no reason you need her," he said, nodding toward Riley. "*Please*," he pleaded. "Let her go. She has nothing to do with this."

This time Volkov actually laughed out loud. "She has *everything* to do with this, you idiot!" he barked dismissively.

Bram stared stupidly at the man, his face a mask of total incomprehension.

"What makes you think we're here for you?" finished the Russian in contempt.

# 20

Major Marat Volkov ordered his two comrades to duct tape the prisoners' mouths shut. Once this was completed the two men left to make sure the coast was clear. When they signaled that it was, Volkov marched the two civilians to a mammoth SUV parked near the door and loaded them inside, sandwiching them between the man named Yuri and another comrade already in the vehicle. He then pulled himself into the passenger's seat next to Sergei Greshnev, and motioned for his second-in-command to begin driving to the Seventh-day Adventist church they had selected.

"Do you think they're telling the truth about how they ended up here?" said Volkov in Russian to his second-in-command.

"I do," said Greshnev. "But I don't like coincidences. And I'd like to know who visited them and why."

"I agree. Lots of unanswered questions. But we should still be able to accomplish our mission. This doesn't prevent us from proceeding as planned. Other than forcing us to arrive at the church sooner than expected," he added. "Speaking of which, how long until it's fully rigged to my specifications?"

"Probably won't be done until an hour or so after our arrival. Alex and Ilya are working as quickly as they can. It's tricky work with a lot of explosives, so I didn't think it wise to rush them."

Volkov nodded his agreement. "Just make sure they focus on the pastor's office first. That way we can park the prisoners there while preparations are being completed."

Greshnev dutifully relayed these instructions to the two men already at the church while he continued to drive, carefully observing the speed limit.

The mystery man who had visited Bram made Volkov uneasy, but on the whole he was as excited as he had been in a long while. They were on the home stretch now. He could feel it.

They completed the journey to the church in silence and led the prisoners inside. Volkov had their gags removed, but instructed them not to speak unless they were spoken to.

He paused for a moment to admire the surprising beauty of the church. This was his first time inside. The sanctuary was spacious, with a vaulted ceiling, colorful stained glass windows, and polished wooden pews spreading out from the pulpit like ripples in a pond. Red carpet covered the entire floor.

While all of the adornments had been removed by church leaders, to be taken to their new facility, they had obviously decided not to gut the pews or pulpit, perhaps because the most likely purchaser would be another church. Regardless of denomination, another congregation would simply have to bring in a piano and other adornments, specific to their sect, to transform this magnificent room to their liking.

Volkov led the prisoners through the sanctuary and to a door in the back, where Alex Bagrov and Ilya Davydov had just finished the installation and testing of an electronic monitor and control.

"This is the pastor's office," he explained to his prisoners, opening the door and waving them inside. Unlike the sanctuary, the office was now an empty husk, the desk, chairs, and computer gone, the walls bare. A built-in bookcase adorned one wall, but it, too, was now empty.

"Wait here," he told them. "I'll be back for you in an hour. Did you see the monitor my men just installed?"

The both nodded.

"This monitor controls powerful explosives, which are now ringing this room. Highly directional explosives. When I leave, I'll enter a code into the monitor. This will arm the charges. If you try to exit, the room will explode, with the blast directed inward. You will both die instantly, and no one else outside of the room will be affected."

"Isn't this a little elaborate?" said Bram. "Wouldn't locking the door or tying us up ensure we stay put just the same?"

Volkov smiled. "Yes. But this way I don't have to post a guard. And since you may be staying here for a day or two, this will be your home away from home. You'll be more comfortable." He gestured to a closed door at the back of the office. "You even have a small bathroom, with a sink."

The Russian paused. "But most importantly," he continued, "the explosives aren't just there to ensure you don't try to leave. They're also there to ensure that no one who isn't authorized tries to *enter*. Anyone attempting a rescue will trigger your deaths."

After pausing a moment to let this register, he added, "But don't worry, we'll make sure any would-be rescuer is well aware."

"No one's going to attempt a rescue," said Bram. "No one will even know we're missing until Monday at the earliest."

"If you say so," said Volkov agreeably, retreating back toward the door.

"Before you leave us," said Bram, "were you serious about what you said before? Is this really about her?" he finished, nodding at Riley.

Volkov nodded. "That's right."

"Then you're making an even bigger mistake than I thought. If you check, you'll find out that she works at the Helen Woodward Animal Center. Not known for being a CIA outpost. Why would you go to all this trouble to capture her?"

Volkov turned to Riley. "Do you want to tell him?"

She shot him a look that could have melted lead, but didn't respond.

"Tell me what?" said Bram. "There's nothing to tell. You've got the wrong woman. I've been to where she works. I've met her friends there, seen her office. Dated her for almost a year. If she had some big secret, I would know it."

"Really?" said Volkov, raising his eyebrows.

The Russian had work to do and really shouldn't loiter, but he couldn't resist having a little fun with a man who was so certain of what he thought he knew. "Did she tell you how her parents almost lost their farm?" he asked. "Did she describe what she was forced to endure in a cornfield in Indiana that changed her life forever?"

Bram shook his head no, looking shaken that Volkov had knowledge of critical events in Riley's past, knowledge that she had never shared with him.

"*No?*" said Volkov. "She *didn't?*" he added in mock surprise. "Now why do you suppose that is?"

"Enough!" snapped Riley. "If you really know what you're talking about, tell him! Don't toy with him."

Volkov grinned. If Bram was confused and anxious before, he was even more so after this outburst.

"Okay," replied the Russian. "As you wish."

He faced Bram, relishing the man's discomfort. "She didn't tell you about this, Mr. Bram . . . *because it never happened.* Because *nothing* ever happened to her in a cornfield. Because she didn't really grow up in Indiana. Because she's probably never even *been* on a farm. She lied to you about all of it. Her name isn't really even Riley Ridgeway. This is a name she gave to herself."

Bram reacted like the Russian's every sentence was a bludgeon, landing blow after blow directly into his stomach.

"Care to guess her *real* name?" finished Volkov.

Bram shook his head, the color having drained from his face.

"It's Melissa," said the Russian with a cruel smile. "Melissa Jordan. Maybe you don't know as much about her as you thought. Turns out you've been dating Isaac Jordan's missing daughter."

# 21

David Bram's head was spinning so fast he didn't hear the rest of what the Russian said, or notice him leaving the room and closing the door carefully behind himself.

Isaac Jordan's daughter? Talk about ridiculous. Of course Riley Ridgeway wasn't Isaac Jordan's daughter.

He remembered seeing photos of Melissa Jordan years earlier. While she was beautiful in her own right, and did share some resemblance to Riley, there was no doubt they were two different people.

But even as he thought this, Riley lowered herself to the floor and slumped against the wall, her expression vacant, hurt. She lowered her eyes and looked decidedly ill.

What she *wasn't* doing was telling Bram that the Russian was crazy, and that she had grown up on a farm in Indiana as she had told him.

Could it be true? Could she really be Melissa Jordan?

He realized with a start that if she were, this would explain *a lot*.

Intelligence was a mix of many things, but genetics did play a role. And Riley's brilliance reminded Bram of how Isaac Jordan's brilliance was often described. Effortless. Coming across without him even trying to be impressive, even when he was chatting about the most mundane of topics.

Was Riley—or Melissa, as the case might be—the apple that hadn't fallen far from the tree? The result of a cross between the most brilliant man in a generation and his gorgeous wife?

No woman he had ever met could fit this bill any better than Riley Ridgeway.

And this would also explain why she was able to afford a small condo in San Diego and insisted on paying her own way so often. He had marveled at how much Helen Woodward was able to pay their low-level employees, since this seemed to be the only job she had ever held, and she had said that her parents were barely getting by.

But if she really was Isaac Jordan's daughter, her wealth would put his to shame. Her wealth would put the wealth of many *countries* to shame.

He gazed at her beautiful face, and she refused to even meet his gaze.

"It's true, isn't it?" he said at last. "You really are Melissa Jordan."

"Don't ever call me that name!" she shouted, once again making no effort to deny the charge. Tears began to form in the corners of her eyes.

In a burst of insight, Bram realized that this revelation didn't just explain her brains, beauty, and wealth. It explained *everything* about her. About her behavior. About their relationship.

Of course she didn't want to use the Jordan name. It had been poisoned. Her father was a man who had killed thousands in cold blood. Who had killed and beheaded the rest of her family, the footage of which had chalked up the most views of any video in YouTube history.

Who could possibly want to be reminded of *that*, associated with *that*?

Which explained the rest. Why she sometimes seemed to hide her intelligence, to bottle up her true, optimistic, outgoing nature. Why she was so adamantly opposed to taking their relationship to the next level.

He had thought the secret he was keeping from *her* was big, but it was *nothing* next to hers. Hers was a secret that, if revealed, would be the top news story around the world. Billions would be talking about it nonstop for days.

No wonder she was so terrified of falling in love, of commitment. Part of it was that she was forced to hide so much of her life, her past, her essence from him. But far more of her reticence must stem from the *nature* of this secret. She had loved her family once. And they had all been wiped out—all except her. Not just wiped out, but butchered. And not just by a random stranger but by her very own father, whom she had also probably loved.

After she had suffered such an inconceivable betrayal, after everyone she had loved had been taken from her, how could she possibly be brave enough to let her guard down ever again? To let someone in? To let *him* in?

And she had to live in abject fear that brilliance wasn't the only trait she had inherited from her father. Psychosis was inheritable as well. If she ever had a husband and children, could she be certain she wouldn't someday kill them all in cold blood the way her father had done?

It was a miracle she was as well-adjusted as she was.

Her personality was upbeat and optimistic. It was in her DNA. But she had lived through unspeakable trauma. Of course she was conflicted. Cheerful by nature, but scarred after being a witness to the very worst of humanity.

No wonder she loved dogs so much. Humanity sucked. A loyal dog would never let you down, never betray your trust.

And no wonder she holed up at Helen Woodward and also volunteered to raise puppies for the disabled, rather than bestow the fruits of her genius on the world as her father had done. This allowed her to avoid people, to avoid the spotlight, while still helping to improve the lives of the disabled and pet lovers, perhaps her way of making at least some small amends for the thousands of lives that Isaac Jordan had taken.

Of course she sought to avoid drawing attention to herself. Of course she put up a wall between them. Anything to avoid true emotional intimacy.

Bram lowered himself to the ground and sat cross-legged facing her. "I'm so sorry, Riley," he whispered, making sure to use the name he had come to love. "I can't even imagine what you've been through. How much you've suffered. But it doesn't change how I feel about you. You're a victim. You aren't responsible for anything that happened."

"I considered telling you so many times," she said softly, tears leaking from her eyes ever so slowly. "The pain of keeping this so tightly bottled up was nearly unbearable. But I couldn't bring myself to do it. To have you pity me, or else see me as a leper."

"I would never do either," he assured her. "I just want to *be* there for you," he added, not sure of what else to say. "And I want you to share everything with me. I *need* you to share everything with me. All of it."

Bram shook his head miserably. "But first," he continued, "as much as I hate to do it, we have to discuss our current situation. We're in big trouble here," he added, probably not needing to spell this out while inside a room laced with explosives primed to kill them if they tried to leave.

She nodded woodenly.

"Any idea what these guys want from you?" he asked. "The fact that you're still alive is a huge story. But this doesn't explain the fake FBI agent or our Russian friend. Are you important for other reasons? Are you keeping other secrets I should know about?"

"You realize that this room is probably bugged," she told him, her tears having stopped and her emotional state stabilizing now that her powerful mind was engaged with other matters.

The moment she said it, he knew that she was right. Even this distraught, she always managed to think with crystal clarity. The Russian had prepared this room especially for them, knowing they would be spending considerable time here. The men they were up against were too good not to listen in. "Forget I asked," he said, feeling foolish.

"Not at all. I was just pointing it out. I don't *care* if they listen in. Because I *have* no other secrets. And I'm more than willing to tell them anything they want to know."

Riley paused in thought. "I can only think of two reasons someone might go to the trouble of capturing me. One, the money angle. Hundreds of billions of dollars of my fath—of *his* money, went missing that day. The government froze many billions more. After all was said and done, I inherited only the smallest fraction." She shrugged. "Still . . ." she added, letting the thought hang.

She didn't need to say more. Even the tiniest fraction of the assets of the world's wealthiest man was a mind-boggling amount.

"But for some reason," she said, "I'm convinced this isn't about money."

"So am I," said Bram. "So what's the second possibility?" he prompted.

"Maybe they think I know the nature of what . . . my father . . . was working on," she said, her face flashing hatred as she was reluctantly forced to acknowledge her relationship with Isaac Jordan. "You know, before he . . . well, before that . . . day."

"Do you?" he asked.

"Yes, but just in general. Nothing that could help anyone make any breakthroughs. He kept it secret and pretended to be doing other things, but he was a workaholic and took his work home every night and on weekends. He wasn't worried if I saw it. I know he thought I was a bright kid, but he never guessed I'd have any idea of what I was looking at."

"But you did, didn't you?

She nodded. "He was heavy into AGI," she said simply.

Bram almost gasped. Another piece of the puzzle falling into place. Another explanation for behavior he had considered inexplicable. Her father had been secretly involved in AGI research when he had snapped. And she had just learned that her boyfriend was secretly working in the exact same field. "No wonder you reacted the way you did when you found out about me," he said.

"It brought back memories I didn't want brought back. And I was creeped out. I still am. Without knowing it, I've managed to fall for a man similar to my father," she said. "Not only bright, but also drawn to the problem of AGI. Words can't describe how much I loathe the memory of that man. The idea that I would be dating someone even remotely like him is horrifying. I'd rather you were doing just about *anything* else."

Bram nodded. So much had now become clear. If they were able to get out of this alive, he had reason to hope he could, in time, find a way past her emotional barriers. Calm her fears, be as patient and understanding as necessary. She was more than worth it. She may have been born Melissa Jordan, but he had fallen in love with Riley Ridgeway.

"Other than this, I'm at a total loss as to our captors' motives," she said. "If they wanted my money, they could just force me to give it to them. No need for this elaborate set-up. They must think I'm useful in some other way. But if I am, I sure don't know how that might be."

There was a long silence in the room. This line of reasoning had come to a dead end. Bram decided that if Riley couldn't divine the intent of the Russian, no one could. "Do you feel like talking about your past?" he said softly. "About what happened? About how you happen to be alive?"

She nodded, and a faraway look came over her face.

He waited for her to gather up her thoughts, and her courage, without a word.

"I was still in my teens," she began, "with two bratty younger brothers, and a world-famous father who also happened to be the wealthiest man who ever lived."

Even as she said this, Bram could see a change come over her aura, a sense of relief at finally being able to share this with him.

"I clashed with my father a lot," she continued. "I admit that much of this was my fault. Teen girls aren't always easy to deal with. In addition to transitioning from a child to an adult, I was bright, headstrong, and spoiled beyond measure." She paused. "But so was he. Maybe we butted heads so often because we were so much alike."

She cringed and lowered her eyes just after she said this, and Bram now understood this reaction perfectly. Her biggest fear was being like her dad—for good reason—and this was another reminder of how alike they really were.

"He was also a workaholic, as I mentioned," she continued. "And he thought he knew everything. Thought he was smarter than everyone else."

Bram suppressed a smile. Hundreds of millions of teen daughters around the world complained of fathers who thought they were smarter than everyone else. When it came to Isaac Jordan, though, this just happened to be true.

"But deep down I knew that he loved me," added Riley, as a single tear rolled down her face. "And I loved him too. He was ruthless and driven. Arrogant and demanding. But he was never cruel. And I knew that he cared for us."

She sighed. "At least I *thought* he did."

"And then Turlock happened," whispered Bram.

Just as the term 9/11 had come to be used as shorthand for the attacks that had taken place on that day, the word *Turlock* now served the same purpose, instantly evoking a memory of the mass casualties that Isaac Jordan had wrought.

"Everything changed," she said, profound sadness in her tone. "I lost my entire family. Because of *him*," she spat bitterly. "This alone would be enough to make me hate him forever, but there was much more, as we all know. The cold-blooded massacre of many thousands. He went from being revered around the world to despised in a single night."

She paused to collect herself. "And I lost more than just my family. We had lived in Turlock for almost two years. I went to high school there. I had made good friends. But most couldn't afford a house like mine. Most lived within the blast radius in apartments or condos."

"So you lost most of your friends, as well."

"*All* of my friends," she corrected. "Most were killed. The few who lived beyond the blast zone, including the girl whose home I was staying at when the rod hit, all suffered terrible losses of their own. They lost friends and loved ones. When they learned my father was responsible, they wouldn't talk to me. They shunned me. They *hated* me."

Bram's mouth dropped open. It was much worse even than he had thought. Family, friends, town, reputation—all torn from her in one fell swoop.

"I had been dreaming of going on to college. Of graduate school. But how could I go forward now? How could I even complete my senior year of high school, facing raw hostility everywhere I turned? I became the subject of worldwide focus, although the authorities at least did protect me from the worst of it."

Bram remembered. The media had largely honored her request not to be photographed or filmed, and the bodyguards who had been assigned to her helped ensure her privacy as well. Isaac Jordan had always done a good job of keeping his family from the public eye, and many of the photographs of Melissa Jordan that were in the public domain depicted a much younger version, with braces and acne, who would clearly grow into a beauty like her mom, but who hadn't yet fully blossomed into the swan she would become.

While many among the masses were sympathetic to Melissa Jordan, many others blamed the daughter for the sins of the father. She was despised by millions.

"The psychological and emotional toll this all took on me is impossible for me to describe," she whispered. "I became unstable. I was melting down. Emotions are heightened at that age, anyway, but mine were on a different plane entirely. I became suicidal, something that the men guarding me couldn't fail to notice."

Riley paused. "But just a few months after Turlock," she continued, "I was approached by a government agent. He was well aware that I was at the end of my rope—ready to let go. He asked if I was interested in going into the equivalent of a witness protection program."

Her features brightened, even from the memory. "Interested?" she said. "I told him I would do *anything* to disappear. To get out from under the glare of the worldwide spotlight, to distance myself from my father's infamy. I've never wanted *anything* more than I wanted not to be Melissa Jordan anymore."

"Who could blame you?" said Bram softly.

"The agent told me not to tell anyone else, including my bodyguards or other members of the government. No one. Never had a case been this high profile, he said, and since the wealth that I'd inherited might make me a target, he needed to be sure there would be no leaks. He would set up my new identity, place me wherever I wanted, and throw away the key. He and I would be the only ones to know—ever."

Bram continued to hang on her every word.

"And he did a brilliant job," she continued. "I became Riley Ridgeway. He altered computer records going back to Riley Ridgeway's birth, with all the right paperwork and records in all the right places. And he did more. In a true feat of magic, he found a way to go back and find every recent photo of me that existed in the digital world. Not that there were many. As Isaac Jordan's daughter,

I wasn't the typical teen posting every second of my life to Facebook and Twitter and Instagram. I never wanted to draw attention to myself. I had too much attention already, even before Turlock. When he found photos in the public domain, he didn't delete them. Instead, he used a program that could alter them in subtle but effective ways. I altered my appearance in subtle ways, as well, changing my hair color and style. And my looks have naturally changed over the years. The twenty-five-year-old me looks quite different from the seventeen-year-old me."

"So if someone suspected you might be Melissa Jordan—unlikely since she was widely accepted as being dead—and checked photos of her online, they wouldn't match up well enough to sustain the suspicion."

"Exactly," said Riley.

Bram nodded. It was a remarkable tale in every way. He had found Riley Ridgeway to be the most extraordinary woman he had ever met, but he hadn't known the half of it. After having gone through all that she had, and emerging from it as well as she had, she was even more extraordinary than he had thought.

The government agent who had done this for her deserved a medal. He had surely saved her life, saved her from a weight that was crushing her, from the toxicity of being who she was.

Bram's eyes widened as the final piece of the puzzle snapped into place. "It was Michael O'Banion, wasn't it? He was the man who put you into witness protection?"

Riley nodded. "Not really my uncle, obviously," she replied. "But over the past eight years we've developed a relationship even closer than this. I owe him everything. He got me out of an inescapable hell. And since he's the only person to know my true past, the only one I can really confide in, he's nice enough to visit whenever he can."

Which explained why she didn't want Bram along for her recent dinner with the man. The two of them alone could let down their hair. With him there, they would be forced to maintain a charade.

Riley sighed. "So now you know," she said. "Isaac Jordan accomplished many spectacular things. His work on the R-Drive will catapult humanity to new heights. It has already. His contributions to the future of humanity are arguably among the greatest in history."

Her face fell and she shook her head in disgust. "But the day I learned he had been killed in that car accident was the happiest day of my new life," she said. "He took *everything* from me. And he left me fearing that I'll turn into him someday. No amount of good that he was able to do before this can ever make me forgive him, can ever erase this."

Bram nodded supportively. "I understand completely," he said.

# 22

Riley Ridgeway felt numb inside. Too much had happened too quickly for her to keep up with it emotionally.

She was realizing just how much she cared for David Bram, as much as she tried to fool herself into thinking she could manage the relationship. She was almost certainly in love with him. The fear she had felt when she thought his life was in danger, her fear of life without him, had been too great for her to fool herself any longer.

Which meant she had to finally end their relationship. Now that he knew her history, he would understand. If he had any sense at all, he would count himself lucky to have escaped her grasp. To not have to look over his shoulder and wonder when she would try to take his severed head as a trophy.

She would simply explain that she loved him too much to allow herself to love him. Too much to allow him to fall in love with *her*, to get involved with a mirage, a false identity, the most complicated woman ever.

The clear emergence of her true feelings for David Bram was potent enough, without coming about during a firestorm of guns and chases and zip ties. Without her being trapped inside a veritable bomb. Without armed men who knew her real identity and who wanted her for reasons unknown.

Despite her secret, she had truly thought recent events were all about David Bram. The man calling himself Jeff Parker had seemed so sure this was the case. The fact that he was investigating AGI sabotage, and Bram did secret work in this field, seemed to cement it.

But if her captor was this Marat Volkov that Parker had mentioned being after them, after Bram, then Parker had gotten the Russian's interest in the couple totally wrong. Which meant that Parker didn't know about her past, had just *assumed* that Volkov was after Bram rather than her.

It also meant that Uncle Mike had done an extraordinary job with her false identity. Whoever Parker was, she didn't doubt he had access to high-quality intelligence, and the fact that her Riley identity had held up under this kind of scrutiny was a testament to O'Banion's thoroughness.

In a strange way, she was grateful this was about her. Now she could trust Bram again. And it had given her the chance to come clean with him, which had been even more of a relief, more cathartic, than she had expected.

She actually felt upbeat. Truly happy. For the first time since she could remember. At least at this instant.

The problem was that she might not have many instants *left*. Her likelihood of surviving even another day was solely dependent on the motives of the Russian and his comrades. She only wished she had a guess as to what these might be. The only thing she was sure of was that mercy and compassion weren't the Russian's strong suits.

She was now standing, with Bram behind her, his arms wrapped around her as though they were watching a sunset, but with much different motives. Protective and consoling rather than romantic.

The Russian entered with two armed flunkies on either side of him, presumably having first disarmed the trap they were in.

"We're ready for you," he said to Riley.

She pulled away from Bram and stood beside him. "Can you at least tell me your name?" she asked the Russian. Then, with a forced smile she added, "After all, you know *both* of mine."

The man laughed. "My name is Marat," he replied. "Marat Volkov."

Riley kept her expression passive. A glance at Bram showed that he, too, was pretending this was the first time he had heard this name. To admit otherwise would be admitting that they had lied about Parker not having made any disclosures.

"Are you ever going to tell me what this is about, Marat?" she asked.

He smiled. "Nice use of my first name," he said. "Trying to establish a rapport with your captor. You instinctively make the right moves, don't you? Gifted like your father."

She bristled at this mention of her father. "Is this your way of deflecting the question?"

"No need. All of my preparations are complete. So now it's show time. I was going to tell you why you're here, anyway. You're going to *love* this," he added cruelly. "You see, I plan to use you as bait."

"Bait for what?" said Riley.

Volkov raised his eyebrows. "Bait to draw out your father."

Riley's mouth dropped open. "You're insane," she said. "That bastard is long dead. You know he is."

"There's a lot of that going around," noted Volkov in amusement. "You're long dead too. Or haven't you heard?"

"Not the same at all," insisted Riley. "I went missing, but was only presumed dead. But they found his body and matched his DNA."

"For a man of your father's skills and resources, faking this wouldn't be any trouble at all."

"Impossible!" shouted Riley.

Intellectually, she was vaguely aware that Volkov's point was valid, but she was incapable of accepting it on an emotional level. "My father is now frying deep inside the bowels of hell," she spat. "Nothing is going to change that. But don't worry, I'm sure you'll have an eternity to get to know him once you've passed on to the other side."

"As much as I admire your spirit," said Volkov, his face hardening, "you'd better hope that you're wrong about that. Or you and your boyfriend are in for very painful deaths."

Bram swallowed hard. "Okay," he said, striving for a calm, reasonable tone, "let's say we humor you. Say for a moment Isaac Jordan *is* alive. How could Riley possibly be useful in drawing him out?"

"When he learns I have her life in my hands, he'll do whatever I tell him in order to protect her."

"*What?*" snapped Riley in utter disbelief. "I thought maybe you planned to lure him here with the hope of *killing* me. Give him the chance to finally murder the last of his children. What could possibly make you think he'd do anything to *protect* me? He doesn't even know who I am."

"You are mistaken," said Volkov. "He cares about you deeply. So much so that he's been watching over you. Like the god he thinks he is. He had bugs planted in your car and living room that transmit both audio and video. There is one in your bedroom, but this transmits audio only. At least he has no interest in seeing his daughter naked. Not that a man like him has time to watch you 24/7. I'm sure he's programmed an AI to monitor the feed and only pass on what he might find of interest."

Riley shook her head in contempt. "You're dangerously psychotic."

Volkov pulled a steel container from his pocket and flipped open the lid. He removed a tiny electronic device, about the size of a fly, with a pair of tweezers that were also inside, and held it up for her and Bram to examine. "Here is one of your father's bugs," he said. "One we removed from your car late this afternoon. We put it into sleep mode temporarily. We can reactivate it with the proper Wi-Fi signal. You see how important you are? I had no idea how to contact him, or where he was. But now that I've found *you*, I can contact him through this bug and get him to come to *me*."

Riley felt as though her head might explode. Could what Volkov was saying be true?

The Russian affixed the tiny bug to his comrade's shirt and pointed him at a nearby wall. He gestured to Riley. "Your role is simple. You just have to stand against this wall looking beautiful and in distress. I'll want you to say a few words so your father can get a voice match, but I'll tell you when."

He turned to Bram. "As for you," he said, "you couldn't be more expendable. You're only alive now so I can use you as leverage against Melissa."

"My name is Riley!" she screamed.

"Calm down," insisted Volkov. "I'll call you whatever you want." He turned back to Bram. "As I was saying, you're only here so you can be used as leverage against *Riley*."

Volkov nodded at his female hostage. "Happy now?"

"Not even a little," she replied bitterly.

"Nevertheless," said Volkov, "I'll require your full cooperation throughout. Or your boyfriend will pay the price. Understood?"

Riley looked into his eyes and detected not even a hint of mercy there. "Understood," she replied.

She positioned herself against the wall and Volkov moved beside her, pressing his gun into the back of her head. "Reactivate the bug on my mark, Sergei," he instructed his comrade, who was holding his phone at the ready.

Volkov smiled and faced the tiny bug on his comrade's lapel. "Three. Two. One. Mark."

Sergei nodded sharply, letting him know the bug was now transmitting.

"This is an urgent message to Isaac Jordan," began Volkov. "As you can plainly see, I have your daughter. She's the one whose head is at the end of my gun. And as you are no doubt aware, I'm contacting you using a bug I removed from the car of one Riley Ridgeway earlier today."

The Russian paused. "Here's the thing," he continued conversationally, "I have no interest in your daughter, beautiful as she is. My interest is in *you*. So I'm going to read off some coordinates. I need you to meet me there at four p.m. Pacific Standard Time tomorrow. Plenty of time for you to make it, regardless of your starting point. I need you to come alone and unarmed.

"I'll be leaving here shortly to be sure I'm there in plenty of time to arrange for a proper greeting.

"Where am I keeping your daughter? you might ask. I'm afraid I can't tell you that. But I know you're very capable, so even if you manage to somehow learn where she is, you can't rescue her. I'm keeping her at a site protected by a nested set of booby traps. Booby traps that are foolproof. Any rescue attempt will fail, and will trigger her death."

He turned away from the camera and focused on Riley. "Why don't you say a few words to your dear departed father."

"This is ludicrous!" she barked. "He's roasting in hell. Even if he *were* alive," she added, "he wouldn't lift a finger to help me. You're wasting your time."

Volkov grinned and turned to the camera once more. "This should be plenty for you to get a voice match, Mr. Jordan. As you can see, your daughter is still skeptical. So let's make her a believer. Meet me where I tell you. No tricks. If you try any, they will fail. And even if they don't, even if you somehow manage to kill me, my comrades will reward your success by killing your daughter. If you don't show, or, for that matter, fail to precisely follow my every instruction, I'll have your daughter's right hand removed. If that doesn't get you motivated, you'll get to watch my men torture her to death.

"But if you do as I say, I give you my word your daughter and her . . . companion, will be allowed to leave here, unharmed. Once I have you, I have no use for her. Since I'm sure you'll want proof of life before you surrender, my men will transmit video footage of her just before you're required to give yourself up. She'll be alive and well."

Volkov glared at the camera and read off a series of coordinates. "I'll see you at four p.m. tomorrow. Pacific Standard Time. Don't be late."

With that the man he had called Sergei manipulated his phone and spoke a few words of Russian to Volkov, no doubt telling him the bug was now off. Volkov lowered his gun and backed away. "Thank you," he said to Riley. "That should do nicely."

"If you really think he'll sacrifice himself to save me," she said in contempt, "you're out of your fricking mind."

"Really?" he said with a cruel smile. "That's not what your Uncle Mike told me."

Riley gasped. "*Where is he?*" she screamed. "What have you done with him?"

"Let me tell you a quick story," said Volkov. "I've been working for fourteen months on the same mission. But my big breakthrough only came recently. I won't bore you with how I discovered your father was alive and was the man I was looking for. But along the way I found satellite footage of him, after his supposed death, with the man you know as Michael O'Banion. Not his real name, by the way. But I'm sure you of all people—*Riley*—can understand why someone might want to use an alias."

Riley felt the blood boiling in her veins and it was all she could do to stop herself from charging the man. If there had been even a small chance she might succeed, she would have.

"Despite being lucky enough to get this footage," continued Volkov, "it didn't help me find either O'Banion or your father. Both had vanished without a trace. But then I got another lucky break. I finally managed to pick up O'Banion's trail once again here in San Diego." He arched an eyebrow. "So I had a little meeting with him in the wee hours of the morning. Inside his suite at the Sheraton."

Riley felt sick to her stomach. It was impossible not to suspect the worst, feel that it was inevitable. A runaway train was about to slam into her, and all she could do was watch it race nearer, helpless to change its course.

"I hit him with a powerful truth serum," said the Russian, "but he had been pre-primed not to disclose anything about your father's possible whereabouts, regardless of the drugs or torture used. Fortunately for me, a mental block like this is necessarily limited, so he was free to speak on other topics. Imagine my surprise when I asked your drugged Uncle Mike why he was in San Diego, and he described his dinner with you just the night before. He then went on to tell me much, much more about you. I'll admit to being stunned. I had no idea that you were still alive and that your father cared so deeply about your well-being."

"You killed him, didn't you?" whispered Riley, trying to hold back tears. She had taken one emotional gut punch after another and had released more tears in one day than she had in many years.

Volkov continued to ignore her. "Did you know that Uncle Mike and Isaac Jordan go way back? He's been your father's closest associate for years. It was your father who sent him to help you in the first place, impersonating a government agent. It was your father who set up your identity as Riley Ridgeway."

Riley's head was spinning. Could it be? Could Michael O'Banion be nothing more than her father's puppet? What sick game had they been playing?

"So Isaac Jordan has been helping you behind the scenes and keeping tabs on your life. He and Mike think the world of you. And

O'Banion was absolutely clear on one important point. Your father would do *anything* to keep you safe. *Anything.* Including sacrificing his own life. I asked this question very clearly, and O'Banion was quite certain of the answer. And he couldn't lie, since he was heavily drugged."

Volkov shrugged. "So that's my story. And to answer your question, I'm afraid I did have to kill your adopted uncle. He was all out of useful information. And I couldn't have him warning you or your father."

Riley didn't respond. This wasn't a revelation, simply confirmation of what she had already known. The approaching train had finally hit, and she felt as though her nervous system might shut down, give up trying to sort through so many powerful emotions. She had come to love Michael O'Banion like a father. Had he betrayed her also?

And now he was dead.

She wanted to curl up into a fetal position and make the world go away.

She could feel David Bram's arms around her, trying to lend support, strength, knowing how devastating these blows had to be.

But instead of taking comfort from this gesture, all she could do was wonder when Bram, too, would betray her.

And how long it would be before he, too, was taken from her, like everyone else she dared to care about.

# 23

Cameron Carr finally managed to free himself from David Bram's dining room table and the zip ties that had been used to restrain him. He checked his phone, which had vibrated once in his pocket while he had struggled to free himself. He found that he had missed three calls altogether. The other two must have come in while he was still unconscious.

All three calls had come from Lieutenant General Brian McReynolds, Director of the Defense Intelligence Agency. The DIA was similar in function to the CIA, although McReynolds reported in through Dwyer. When Carr had needed intel on Bram and to re-task a satellite to keep tabs on Volkov, it had been more efficient for him to get this done through McReynolds and the DIA.

Carr rushed into Bram's living room, placed his phone on an end table, and ordered it to place a call to DIA Director McReynolds. As soon as the director answered, a perfect 3D image of his upper body was projected above the phone, and Carr's image was no doubt being projected in McReynolds's office at Joint Base Anacostia–Bolling in Washington, D.C.

"Sorry I wasn't available to take your calls, General," said Carr after they had exchanged greetings.

"What happened? Do you need assistance?"

"I'm fine. But Bram got away. I assume you have something to report."

"Yes," replied McReynolds. "I was tracking Volkov and his men, but they didn't arrive at Bram's home around twenty hundred hours as expected. Instead, they converged on a motel in El Cajon called the Shut-Eye Motel."

"Why there?"

"They broke in and forcibly extracted David Bram and Riley Ridgeway," said the general. "Since I thought you were bringing these two to a safe house, this was . . . unexpected."

Carr issued a silent curse. He was too late, as feared. After Riley had bested him, Volkov had beaten him to the punch. "Where are they now?"

"We tracked them to an abandoned church about an hour northeast of your location," said McReynolds, who went on to give him the precise address. "When I couldn't reach you, I sent in a recon team to get eyes on the church from the ground, and to gather intel."

"Outstanding, General, thank you. What have they found?"

"You aren't going to like it. Four of Volkov's comrades were already there. Volkov's arrival brought the total to eight, plus the two hostages. Reports from my recon team indicate the church's perimeter is crisscrossed with sensor arrays, invisible to the eye. These control explosives and other heavy armaments."

Carr frowned. Sensors had improved so rapidly, and could detect so much, they had transformed both intelligence gathering and installation security. The sensor arrays were typically linked to an AI system, which monitored incoming data. Authorized personnel could waltz through the array in perfect harmony. The AI would also ensure that butterflies or squirrels that passed inside the perimeter didn't trigger any deadly strikes.

Unauthorized personnel, on the other hand, would be massacred instantly, unleashing a veritable Armageddon on themselves. Which tended to make a surprise attack out of the question. Not to mention survival.

"Any weaknesses in the array we might be able to exploit?" asked Carr.

"None. The system is state of the art. Our most advanced sensor nullification technology did nothing. We tried to hack the signal going to the AI inside, but failed. And it gets worse. The recon team believes they've booby-trapped the hell out of the place. So even if we were to use overwhelming force, bring in tanks to gain entrance, there won't *be* an entrance by the time we get to it."

Carr nodded. A great strategy to use while holding hostages. Volkov could likely thwart any attack, but if not, there was still no way to breach without the hostages paying for it with their lives. Deterrents didn't get any better than that. "Any intel on Bram and Ridgeway?" he asked.

"Affirmative. Long-range sensing indicates they're in a room toward the back of the church. Based on the architectural plans we pulled, this would be the pastor's office. We believe that this has been rigged individually to implode, although we can't be certain what means are being used to arm or disarm this trap."

"What's their state of health?"

The general shook his head. "Unclear. They could be hale and hearty. Or they could be bleeding out with minutes to live. Volkov visited them with two of his men for a short while at one point. During this period we detected a strong transmission emanating from the room."

"What kind of transmission?"

"We believe both audio and visual, protected by highly advanced quantum encryption. Whoever is receiving the transmission doesn't want it hacked."

Carr rubbed the back of his head as he considered the situation. What could Volkov have been broadcasting? There was no way to know.

At least Bram was still alive. For the time being. "Thank you, General. Excellent work. Please have your team retreat another hundred yards away from the church until further notice."

The team was stationed just beyond sensor range, but if Volkov got lucky and managed to detect them, anyway, this would make an impossible situation even more impossible.

Carr ended the call with McReynolds and immediately contacted Troy Dwyer and Melanie Yoder, whose virtual 3D figures soon graced Bram's living room. He relayed the information he had just learned from the Director of the DIA.

While he was reporting, McReynolds called with an update. Volkov had left the church and had taken off in a small jet from a private airfield nearby, his destination unclear. Carr instructed the general to keep close tabs on the man, but to continue to monitor events at the church.

Why the major would leave Bram before completing an interrogation was mystifying to Carr. There was something important about this situation he was missing.

Carr ended the communication once again with the head of the DIA and finished briefing Melanie Yoder and the Secretary of Defense. He explained that Bram was so well protected and booby-trapped inside the church that the entire Seventh Cavalry couldn't spring him.

"Any chance we could pry Bram loose *after* they leave the church?" asked Dwyer when Carr had finished.

"Possibly. But they're clearly dug in. You don't go to all that trouble to defend a location if you're planning to leave right away. My guess is that they'll keep Bram safely inside until Volkov returns from whatever errand he's on. When he does, he'll finish the interrogation and kill Bram. Even if they leave the church with Bram still alive, extracting him from a team this good won't be easy. And he could be killed in the process."

"What about intercepting Volkov?" asked Dwyer. "Now that he's separated himself from the pack?"

"Also a possibility. But that will alert the men in the church that we're here. I'd prefer to extract Bram from the church as soon as possible, instead."

"I thought you just said that not even the Seventh Cavalry could do that," said Dwyer.

"I did," said Carr. "But I just had an interesting thought. Sergei Greshnev is still inside. And he'll recognize me. I just realized there's a gambit I can use that might do the trick. Risky, and very bold, but I think it can work."

"And if it doesn't?" said Melanie Yoder.

Carr frowned. "Then I'll be too dead for any second-guessing," he replied grimly.

"What are the odds of success?" said Dwyer.

"Odds?" said Carr with a twinkle in his eye. "I have no idea. Math was my worst subject."

"I thought science was your worst subject," said Melanie with a wry smile.

"I guess what I'm really bad at is remembering what my worst subject is."

Melanie laughed, but the Secretary of Defense couldn't have been more grim. "It's your call, Lieutenant. If you think it's worth the risk, do whatever you think best."

"Understood," said Carr. Then, after a pause, he added, "I am going to need support. Remember when you said I could get anything I needed on this mission? Including a tank battalion rolling down the streets of Beverly Hills?"

"I remember," said Dwyer.

"Great. Well, I have good news on two fronts. First, while I do have some special needs, a tank battalion won't be among them. And second, the church isn't located in Beverly Hills."

"Okay then," said Dwyer, playing along. "I guess the situation is looking up."

Carr blew out a long breath. "Sure," he said unconvincingly. "What could possibly go wrong?"

# 24

"Captain, you need to see this," said Alex Bagrov. "There's a guy just outside the sensor perimeter holding up a sign."

Sergei Greshnev rushed over to a monitor Bagrov had been manning near the church entrance. The intruder's image was too small to make out any real detail, but was ablaze with light against the dark midnight sky. Whoever this was, he had made certain he would be seen.

"Have you pinged him yet with long-range sensors?" asked Greshnev.

Bagrov nodded.

"Good. What kind of weapons is he carrying?"

Bagrov consulted another screen. "None," he said in surprise. "At least according to the long-range optical and gravimetric sensors. And long range olfactory sensors haven't detected the signatures of any known explosives."

Greshnev was intrigued. The man's position just a few feet from the edge of the invisible sensor array indicated he was well aware it was there, which meant he had to be military. So why had he disarmed and shined a literal spotlight on himself, turning himself into a sitting duck? "Zoom in on his face," he ordered.

Greshnev's eyes widened as this order was carried out.

"You recognize him?" said Bagrov.

"Yes. Naval Lieutenant Cameron Carr. An American spy. Worked for years out of the US Embassy in Moscow. He's very good. The GRU finally figured out what he was up to and sent Marat to take him out, but he failed. Carr got away and returned to the States."

"I wasn't aware the major had ever failed on an assignment before," said Bagrov, completely serious.

"Not often," said Greshnev. "Which means we shouldn't take this man lightly. There aren't many operatives around the world that Marat respects, but Cameron Carr is one of them."

"How could he know to be here?" said Bagrov. "What could he want?"

"Good questions. Since he's holding up a sign, let's find out. Zoom in and project his entire image inside this room in 3D. Life size."

A moment later Cameron Carr appeared to be standing just three feet away from Greshnev. The American's face was calm and impassive as he waited outside the sensor perimeter for them to spot him and take the action they had just taken.

The message was written in black pen on a large piece of white cardboard, in Russian.

*To: Marat Volkov*

*From: Cameron Carr*

*Major, I believe we are working toward a similar goal. I have information I know will be critical to your mission—to our mission. I am aware of your defenses. By now you have no doubt confirmed that I'm unarmed and helpless. You could easily kill me. But this would be a grave error on your part. Kill me without knowing what I know, and your mission will fail. If you let me come inside, I will share what I know, without expecting anything in return, other than safe passage back outside. If you agree, instruct your AI to let me pass through your sensor array, and then shoot an un-silenced round off into the air as a signal that the coast is clear. I'll be waiting.*

Greshnev considered. The man certainly wasn't lacking in courage. But what was he playing at? There was little doubt they were on a similar mission, but was he really so naive as to believe they were pursuing identical goals? He doubted it. Which meant there was no way he simply wanted to help them without wanting anything in return.

Carr wouldn't have found them if their investigations hadn't converged at Melissa Jordan. He must have learned of her existence as well. Surely he would try to trade information for a chance to interrogate her.

But Carr could never have guessed what they had just learned from Michael O'Banion, that she meant so much to her father she could be used as bait to catch him.

It didn't matter, Greshnev decided. He didn't have to be able to predict Carr's motivations. No matter how good the man was, he was unarmed, and couldn't possibly wrest control of the situation from Greshnev and his six armed comrades. So while Greshnev was unconvinced of the value of Carr's supposed information, there was no downside to letting him in.

And they were currently in a long holding pattern, doing nothing but waiting for many hours until it was time to film Riley to prove to her father that she was still alive.

Whatever Carr had in mind, it was bound to prove interesting. And just because the man had asked for safe passage back outside didn't mean that Greshnev had to honor this request.

# 25

A gunshot cracked throughout the night sky and Carr reflexively looked down to see if blood was pouring out of his body. He had guessed Greshnev would let him in, but he couldn't be certain. A gunshot would be the signal that he had won, but also the signal that he had lost: the only difference being the direction of the bullet—into the sky or into his heart.

Carr breathed a sigh of relief that he was still standing and waited a good minute longer to be sure they had plenty of time to instruct the AI to let him through. Then, without any hesitation—having always been a "rip the Band-Aid off quickly" kind of guy—he barreled across the sensor threshold into death valley as if the sensors didn't exist. When he once again found himself alive a moment later, he knew that they *didn't*. At least not for him.

As he reached the front door of the church it swung open and he entered. Four of Volkov's men greeted him with raised automatic weapons while another frisked him, just in case the US had managed to come up with a way to fool weapons-sensing technology.

"He's clean," said one of the men in Russian.

"Welcome, Lieutenant Carr," said Greshnev, appraising the man before him. "That took a lot of nerve."

"Thank you, Captain Greshnev," he replied, equally cordial. "Before we begin, I was hoping you could report on the state of your prisoners' health."

The corners of Greshnev's mouth turned up in the hint of a smile. "Both are alive and well," he said. "For the moment."

The Russian's features hardened and he became decidedly more hostile. "I'm not sure what you think you can accomplish here, Lieutenant. But if you think I'm going to let you interrogate the girl, under any circumstances, you're out of your fucking mind."

Carr barely kept his mouth from falling open, and he was lucky that Greshnev had glanced away or he would have seen Carr's pupils dilate in utter shock.

Interrogate the girl?

Was the man just screwing with him?

Carr looked deeply into the captain's eyes and decided he was being deadly serious. Which meant Carr had gotten it all wrong.

Could it really be true? Was Volkov after Riley Ridgeway and not David Bram?

It seemed impossible. Bram was involved in AGI research. It was true that DNI's intel report had concluded that, while Bram was brilliant and talented, there was nothing truly special about him, nothing to suggest he possessed either the skills or the resources to sabotage so many AGI efforts in ways that seemed indistinguishable from magic. Carr had ignored this part of the report, believing that Bram's work in AGI couldn't just be a coincidence.

But maybe it *could be.*

Maybe the beautiful farmer's daughter was the special one.

Carr shrugged. "Of course," he said agreeably. "I wasn't going to ask to interrogate the girl, anyway."

"Sure you weren't," said Greshnev. "But I really don't care. Because it's time for you to tell me what you came here to tell me."

Carr winced. "About that," he said. "Turns out I lied. I have nothing to report."

Greshnev blinked rapidly in confusion and pointed his own weapon at Carr's head, joining those of his comrades. "You really are out of your mind," he said in disbelief. "Let me guess. You're feeling suicidal, but you're too, how you say it—*chicken-shit*—to jump off a bridge. Well, you've come to the right man for help."

"I'm afraid I'm not here for your assisted suicide services, Captain. But thanks. Instead, I'm here on a rescue mission. I need you to let me walk out of here with your two prisoners."

Greshnev shot him a look of contempt, but his expression became wary as he realized that any man who had Volkov's respect wouldn't say something so utterly preposterous without at least believing he could back it up. "Now why would I let you do that?" he asked.

"I know they're in the pastor's office," said Carr calmly, "which has been rigged to implode. I know I'll need your cooperation to get them out alive. So let me give you some incentive." He glanced at a monitor to get the time. "In six minutes, at eleven fifty exactly, two S-18 Marauder attack helicopters will be paying us a visit. Along with a civilian helo. I know you're well versed in the impressive destructive capabilities of the Marauder. If the pilots don't see me walk out of here with the two prisoners in tow, and make it beyond the sensor perimeter and your line of sight, they have orders to reduce this church to rubble."

"You're bluffing," said Greshnev.

"Really, Captain? So you think my plan was to con my way in here and put myself at your mercy? Armed only with a bluff that you'll be able to disprove in a few minutes? I can't help but be insulted."

"I'm not saying you're bluffing about the Marauders. I have no doubt they're on their way. But if they destroy this church, you would die as well. More importantly, so would Melissa Jordan. How does that help anyone?"

*Melissa Jordan?*

Carr struggled to retain his focus, but how could he? He didn't think anything could shock him more than learning Volkov's plan to raid David Bram's home had nothing to do with David Bram. But he had been wrong.

If Riley Ridgeway really was Isaac Jordan's missing daughter, long presumed dead, this was the *ultimate* shock. But even if this were true, how did she fit in?

Carr knew he had no time to ponder this now. "We all die eventually," he replied finally. "This is what we call *mutually assured destruction*. Perhaps it will turn out to be a suicide mission on my part, after all. Whether it is or not is entirely in your hands," he added calmly.

# 26

Greshnev couldn't believe the audacity of this man, but at minimum he couldn't kill him until after eleven fifty. Not until he had seen if Carr's attack helicopters had arrived on the scene as promised.

Sure enough, three minutes later the unmistakable roar of three helos could be heard racing toward them, getting louder by the second. The two S-18 Marauders possessed advanced noise-canceling technology that allowed them to sneak up on a target in silence, but they had disabled this feature during their approach to the church. Carr had wanted their entrance to be as splashy as possible, for obvious reasons.

But was the man really crazy enough to have military helos destroy a civilian building on American soil? And not just any building, but a church?

Volkov had made sure his team had anti-aircraft munitions with them, but the Marauders were state of the art and could produce countermeasures that would nullify their efforts to destroy them.

The major had considered the possibility that Isaac Jordan might be able to mount an attack that would be unstoppable, but had discounted this as a threat. After all, Jordan would know that any such attack would lead to the certain death of his daughter.

But they hadn't counted on Cameron Carr. He seemed to have little concern for Melissa's life—or his own.

Then, in a flash of insight, Greshnev realized that Carr must have been the man impersonating the FBI agent named Parker. Who else could it have been? He had captured Melissa Jordan first, but had lost her due to his own incompetence. That must have been embarrassing.

Still, this didn't change the current situation.

Greshnev acknowledged the presence of the helicopters now hovering within a thick blanket of darkness overhead. "I still think you're bluffing," he said to Carr with far more confidence than he felt. "But I don't see a need to put this to the test. Call off your guns and I'll let you interrogate her, after all. Supervised, of course. Then, once you're done, we can all part company."

"That's very generous of you," said Carr, "but I'm afraid I have to decline. Even if you let me interrogate her and walk, you'll kill them both when you're done. I can't let you do that. But most importantly, I *can't* call the pilots off. The order can't be countermanded. Not by me. Not by the Lord Almighty himself."

"Impossible!" said Greshnev, noting that his comrades all looked as nervous as he felt. They had remained silent so far, respecting his authority. But this could well change, depending on how events unfolded. "You would never issue such a final order. Not if you had any chance to save yourself and Melissa Jordan."

"I had no other choice," said Carr. "You've done too good a job here making rescue impossible. My only play was to be bold. To roll the dice and count on you to save your own lives. If I'm not safely away from here with the two prisoners by ten after midnight, which is about eighteen minutes away, the pilots have orders to bomb this church into the Stone Age. And you won't be able to slink away. They also have orders to put down anyone trying to leave the party early."

Greshnev studied the American carefully, trying to get a read on him.

"I'll be honest with you, Captain Greshnev," continued Carr. "I have no interest in dying here. If you chose not to cooperate, I probably would try to belay the strike order. That's why I didn't leave myself any outs. I have no way to communicate with the pilots. Even if I did, they've been told to consider me under duress and disregard anything I say."

Carr smiled grimly. "In America, this is a game that we call *chicken.*"

He glanced at the monitor once again to check the time. "We now have sixteen minutes left to live." He paused to let this sink in. "Your move, Captain."

"I'll have to contact the major first."

"Why? His life isn't in the balance. Would you really die here on his command?"

Greshnev considered. It was a good question. "If I let you leave, what assurance do I have that you won't kill me and my comrades once you're safely away?"

"Do you really think I want to use US military aircraft to annihilate a church in the middle of California? Once the prisoners and I are in the clear, the civilian helo will pick us up. I'll order the other two away and temporarily cancel surveillance of you and your team. I'll give you an hour to disappear off the radar before I attempt to track you again. You have my word."

"Your *word?*" said Greshnev in disgust. "What good is that? Didn't you lie to get in here?"

"I did lie," said Carr. "But then again, I never gave you my word on anything. You know my reputation. When I strike a deal like this, I stick to it. We may well meet up again. We have similar goals, after all. We may even strike additional deals in the future, and I'll want to count on you remembering that I lived up to my end of the bargain."

Greshnev tilted his head in thought.

"Whatever you decide," said Carr, "you need to decide in a hurry. We now have only thirteen minutes left. And I'm telling you, *I can't buy more time.* If you agree to cooperate but can't disarm the pastor's office fast enough, your intent won't matter. We all die."

Carr did appear to be getting nervous. Maybe he was merely acting, but he truly looked like a man who only had thirteen minutes left to live.

"Yuri," said Greshnev to one of the many men still holding the unarmed visitor at gunpoint, "come with me."

He walked rapidly to the pulpit and both men had a whispered exchange lasting less than a minute. Greshnev returned alone.

"I haven't made up my mind," he said to Carr upon returning. "But Yuri is disarming the room and will bring the two prisoners here shortly. You do make a good point," he allowed. "If you are telling the truth, it is better to have the prisoners ready to leave at a moment's notice."

"Good choice," said Carr.

Greshnev waited in silence for his comrade to return, deep in thought. Minute after minute rolled by. Finally, seven minutes later, Yuri came into view and escorted the prisoners to the church's entrance to join the proceedings.

The eyes of both newcomers widened in shock upon seeing Carr, but he gave his head a quick shake in a way that told them to remain silent. Not that this hadn't provided Greshnev with further confirmation that the three had met before.

"Are you sure they'll want to go with you, Agent Parker?" said the Russian derisively. "Seems like the girl beat you up pretty badly the first time."

Carr ignored this attempted barb. "Five minutes left," he announced pointedly.

Greshnev blew out a long breath. "Okay," he said. "I'll let you and the prisoners go. Under one condition."

"I'm listening."

"I want my team to be off your surveillance radar for four hours, not one."

Carr nodded. "Agreed. You'll have your four hours."

As incompetent as Carr had been to let the girl get away, Greshnev couldn't help but admire how neatly he had managed this rescue. And he had come to believe Carr really wasn't bluffing. If he couldn't have Melissa Jordan, he was willing to give up his life to be sure no one else could, either.

Assuming this was the case, no matter what decision Greshnev made, Volkov would fail to acquire Isaac Jordan. At least for now. If Greshnev refused to let Carr leave and they were all killed by the Marauders hovering overhead, Isaac Jordan wouldn't have his proof-of-life footage, and wouldn't give himself over to Volkov.

If he let Melissa leave with Carr, the same would be true.

But at least in this latter case, they would have the chance to re-acquire her, possibly even in time to salvage the current plan. Jordan wasn't scheduled to deliver himself to Volkov for sixteen hours yet. Even if they missed this window, while she was alive, they still had the chance to eventually use her to get to her father. A chance that her death would erase forever.

The situation reminded Greshnev of an old cartoon he had seen as a kid, in which two rival dogs were fighting over a bone. Each dog designed ever more elaborate schemes to steal the bone from the other, and the bone changed possession numerous times, always in clever and humorous fashion.

In this case, Carr had acquired the bone first, but this was simply the beginning.

The back and forth had already begun. Carr had lost it to Volkov. Now, possession was returning to the American.

And while Carr may have won this round, the dogfight was far from over.

Greshnev motioned for one of his men to open the door. "We have a deal, then, Lieutenant," he said, gesturing for him to go. "Just remember, we get four hours to disappear. Not a minute less."

"Not a minute less," repeated Carr.

Greshnev turned to one of his comrades. "Yuri," he said, "do you still have the stunner you took from the girl?"

The man nodded.

"Good," he said. "Give it back to her."

He shot Carr a look of contempt. "Maybe she can use it to free herself from you a second time," he added with a condescending smile.

# 27

Carr led his two prisoners through the darkness, lighting the way with the artificial lantern he had used to illuminate himself while waiting for Greshnev to spot him. He crossed through the tree line into the woods and progressed to another small clearing nearby, where the large civilian helo was waiting for them, with a military pilot dressed in civilian clothing its only inhabitant. After boarding, the three passengers all donned headphones so they could communicate without shouting.

Bram began to speak, but Carr held out a forestalling hand. He removed an electronic wand from a rucksack on the floor of the helo and waved it along the entire length of their bodies. The wand identified two tiny, gnat-sized drones attached to their clothing, which he removed and placed in the palm of his right hand for his guests to see.

"These aren't bugs," he explained. "They're tracers. Tracking devices. I had a feeling this is how Volkov was able to find you so easily."

Carr made a show of tossing the homing beacons out of the helicopter, shut the door, and nodded at the pilot, who lifted the helo slowly into the sky to join its two lethal companions. As they moved off, the Marauders switched into stealth mode, which included flying with night vision rather than standard lights, although the civilian helicopter continued to use standard beams.

Carr ordered the pilot to proceed at best speed toward Area 51, where Melanie Yoder was waiting. Dwyer would join them there as soon as he could.

This base was secure and geographically convenient, and also inconspicuous, which was the most important consideration. Those working at Groom Lake knew to mind their own business. A wide variety of strange military and civilian aircraft, holding a wide variety of strange people, arrived or left Area 51 each day. As long as they had the proper clearance to be there, no one would ask any questions.

And the base was secure, despite the recent demise of the supercomputer known as TUC. The investigation wasn't complete, but it was now clear the base itself hadn't been infiltrated by a saboteur. Instead, a third party had managed to hack the random self-destruct code, put there by Melanie Yoder herself as a fail-safe.

Whoever had managed it should never have known the precise nature of this fail-safe. Even if they had, triggering it should have been impossible.

But of course they had known. And of course they had managed to find a way to trigger it prematurely. They were magicians, after all.

The helo banked sharply left and picked up elevation. The two Marauders had been ordered to stay close on either side, to provide an escort service, but to peel off as they approached Groom Lake, since such a formation would raise eyebrows, even within Area 51.

While they flew, Carr brought his two passengers up to speed on the strategy he had used to free them.

"But you were bluffing, right?" said Bram. "The pilots wouldn't have really destroyed the church if they hadn't let us go, right?"

"If you say so," said Carr in amusement.

"What does *that* mean?" said Bram. "Are you saying it *wasn't* a bluff?" he added in disbelief.

"This was too important for me to count on my acting skills. I thought if the threat to me was real, Greshnev would pick up on body language clues and instinctively know that it was. I had to go all-in on this one."

"Risking our lives as well," said Bram.

"If I'd have left you there, do you really think they'd let you live once they were done with you?"

Bram swallowed hard. "No," he acknowledged. "You're right. I suppose thanks are in order. We did meet this Marat Volkov you warned us about," he added with a shiver. "He was everything you said he was."

"He didn't *tell* you he planned to kill you, did he?" said Carr.

"No," replied Bram. "Just the opposite. But neither of us had any doubt that he was lying."

"Then it's good my plan succeeded," said Carr with a smile.

"Just because you saved us from them," noted Riley, "doesn't mean we're convinced that you're all that much better."

"I understand," said Carr. "I'll see what I can do to gain your trust. But first . . . you really are Melissa Jordan, aren't you?"

"Please call her Riley," said Bram immediately, but Carr noted that neither of them tried to deny it.

"You didn't know, did you?" said Riley. "You really did think they were after David."

"I did."

"I'm surprised they told you," said Bram.

"They didn't mean to. They just assumed I already knew." He studied Bram carefully. "Did *you* know?" he asked.

Bram shook his head. "Not even close."

"Okay, this is the biggest surprise I've gotten in a long time," admitted Carr. "But the question is, why do they want you?"

The couple glanced at each other, indicating to Carr that they knew but weren't sure they wanted to say. "We have no idea," said Bram. "Any thoughts?" he added.

Carr decided to play along—for now. "None that make any sense," he admitted. "As I mentioned at your house, this is about the sabotage of AGI programs. But it isn't just Russia's problem. Every program in the world as it nears possible success is getting kneecapped by the same person or group. Whoever is behind this has skills much more advanced than any other player."

"Apple's AGI efforts haven't been sabotaged," noted Bram.

"Not that you know of," said Carr. "It can be subtle, like malware that infects your computer but doesn't take it down until a pre-programmed time. Apple's program could be infected and you'd be none the wiser. It's also possible you're on the wrong track. Whoever is behind this doesn't waste effort stopping programs that won't succeed anyway."

Bram frowned but didn't reply.

Carr decided to come clean with them the rest of the way. He told them who he really was and the precise details of his mission, including describing the explosion of DARPA's computer, which had nearly taken out the president.

They listened in rapt attention.

"So back to the main question," he said when he had finished filling them in. "Why would Volkov want Riley? I'm sure she has money, but this isn't about that. Volkov and I are on similar missions. Like me, he wants to stop whoever is behind the AGI sabotage. But he then wants to use them for Russia's own ends if he can. Either way, he must think Riley can help him in this mission. He probably thinks she knows something her father was involved with eight or nine years ago. Something relevant in some way. Am I right?" he asked Riley.

"I don't know. It's a good guess, but he never told us what he was after."

Carr shook his head. "Come on, Riley. You're a lot better with a stunner than you are with a lie. I've told you my real name. I've given you information that could earn me a court martial. I saved you from Volkov. It's about time you confided in me. We're on the same side. And I'm your best hope for survival."

"What does that mean?" asked Riley.

"Not to alarm you, but you won't be safe until I understand how you fit into this. And maybe even after. I know Volkov well. He's as good as it gets. And he'll never give up. Besides, you can bet that any number of countries and multinational corporations have their own Volkovs looking into this. If Volkov is now on to you, the rest will eventually catch up. Things are going on here that are out of your depth. Out of *my* depth. But I can bring massive resources to bear on this, and I promise to do everything in my power to help you."

Carr grinned. "As long as you promise never to electrocute me again," he added.

Riley smiled sheepishly. "Yeah, about that . . ."

"My fault," said Carr amiably. "I threatened you and David, and then I underestimated you. I won't do that again."

"She's so talented it's impossible *not* to underestimate her," said Bram proudly, and Carr sensed in that instant the man was in love with her.

"What's it going to be?" said Carr. "Tell me what you know. Help me get to the bottom of this so you can get your life back. As Riley Ridgeway, or whoever else you want to be."

"What do you think?" said Bram, glancing at Riley. "Do you trust him?"

She paused in thought. "I do," she said finally. "And even if I didn't, he's an enemy of Marat Volkov, which is good enough for me. That man is ruthless."

She turned away and sadness enveloped her like a dark cloud. "And he killed Uncle Mike. I don't know if my relationship with Mike was real or not. But I do know how I felt about him, how important he was in my life."

She turned back to Carr with her teeth clenched in determination. "So I want you to stop Volkov. I'm not sure I'd mind too much if you killed the bastard in the process. He didn't need to kill Mike. He had what he needed."

"Who's this Mike?" said Carr. "He wasn't staying at the Sheraton in downtown San Diego, was he?"

"How did you know?" said Riley.

"After I began tracking Volkov, I learned he had killed a guest at the Sheraton. But I couldn't ID the man."

Riley's expression was deeply pained, but she shook off her despair. "His full name was Michael O'Banion. He was the man who took me off the grid, gave me my new identity. Volkov found me through him."

"I'm sorry for your loss," said Carr, sounding sincere. "But you need to finally tell me what Volkov wanted with you."

"I know," she replied with a sigh. "But if you think learning who I really am was a shock, you'd better brace yourself."

"Go ahead," said Carr. It was hard for him to imagine there could be bigger shocks in store than he had already experienced.

But his next shock didn't come from the woman known as Riley Ridgeway, it came from the pilot, who broke into their headsets on a separate channel. "The two Marauders have peeled off!" he announced, "and I can't reach them. All communications are down!"

Before Bram could even voice a question the helicopter banked sharply, shoving the passengers against their seats.

"That wasn't me!" barked the pilot anxiously. "Someone has seized control of the autopilot. I'm locked out! My controls are useless. The comms are useless. We can't navigate and we can't call for help. I assume the two Marauders are being controlled remotely as well."

"Who could manage something like this?" asked Carr.

"No one. We've known for decades that the hacking of an aircraft's autopilot was a possible vulnerability. Numerous safeguards are embedded into these systems to make this impossible. They're foolproof."

Carr frowned deeply. Apparently not. "What's our new heading?"

"Due South. Toward Arizona."

Before Carr could ask another question a new voice came through the headphones. A male voice Carr didn't recognize, delivered by someone at an unknown location. "Sorry to have to take over like this. But I'll explain everything when all of you awaken."

"When we awaken?" said Carr. "What's that supposed to mean? *Who is this?*"

"Isaac Jordan," came the reply.

Carr was still trying to process this incredible response when a piercing tone blasted through his headphones and drilled directly into his brain. And in his last instant of consciousness the meaning of the phrase, "when all of you awaken," became horribly clear.

# PART 4
## Isaac Jordan

# 28

Major Marat Volkov streaked toward an island in the Barents Sea, twenty miles off the coast of Russia, in a private jet. He was alone in the luxurious passenger compartment, save for the 3D virtual image of Sergei Greshnev that had joined him there moments before.

"I wasn't expecting to receive a report so early, Captain," he said warily in Russian.

"I'm sorry to have to give one," replied Greshnev. "But we've had a . . . complication."

"No shit," said Volkov impatiently. "I didn't think you were calling early to reassure me that everything was going as planned. What happened?"

Volkov had gone to considerable trouble to make sure the jet had a quantum encryption system on board, which was now in use, meaning their conversation couldn't be intercepted.

"Turns out we were made," replied Greshnev. "Not by Jordan, but by an old adversary of yours. We've solved the mystery of the man claiming to be FBI Agent Parker. Turned out to be Lieutenant Cameron Carr."

"Carr?" whispered Volkov in disbelief. "Are you sure?"

He wasn't surprised the Americans would put Carr on a similar mission to his own, but it was hard to imagine the man he had pursued in Russia could have been taken out by a slip of a girl with a stunner.

"He paid a visit to us at the church," replied the captain. "I think he was sorry he missed you there."

Greshnev went on to explain exactly what had happened as quickly and efficiently as possible. Volkov didn't interrupt or ask a single question.

"You've done well," said the major when his second had finished. "I agree with your assessment. Carr wasn't bluffing. I studied him when we first suspected him of spying, and then when I was assigned to remove him from the board. The man has balls of steel."

"He gave his word he'd have US intel look away for four hours before trying to find us again. Will he honor that?"

"Everything I know about him tells me that he will. But this agreement didn't extend to me, correct?"

Greshnev shook his head. "I'm afraid not. So we have to assume you're being watched."

Volkov frowned. He wasn't worried about himself. He could lose a tail, low-tech and high-tech both, in his sleep. But he had a responsibility to his team at the church. Carr was treating them like cockroaches, agreeing to turn off the lights so they could scatter. He needed to ensure they weren't near a boot when the lights came back on. There was no time to waste.

"Have all the men split up," he ordered. "We need to fracture the focus of American intelligence. Make them chase down multiple roads to pick up a scent. Tell the men to work their way back to Russia separately, going in eight different directions, using multiple techniques to throw off surveillance."

Volkov's people were exceedingly well trained. If they used their skill and wits it was likely that the four-hour head start Carr had given them would be enough. They could probably all stay off the radar and make it back. Worst case, one or two would be picked up again.

"Tell the men you'll be doing the same," continued the major, "working your way back home. So if one of them does get picked up and questioned, the worst that can happen is that they're forced to reveal false information."

"What will I really be doing?" asked his second.

"Make best speed to the safe house in Utah," said Volkov. He had access to more than a dozen such safe houses across the States, but the Utah site was the closest to Greshnev's current location in California.

After himself, Captain Greshnev was the most experienced and talented man on the team, which explained his senior position. His second would know not to show up in Utah unless he was absolutely certain he hadn't been reacquired.

"I'll meet you there," added the major. "Ideally, by seven or eight in the morning."

This was aggressive, but achievable. He had confidence in Greshnev, and himself. He hadn't been in the air that long, so he should have plenty of time to land the jet back in the States, lose surveillance, and make it to the rendezvous on schedule.

"There are six agents working in Western America that I know haven't been made," said the major. "I'll have them drop what they're doing and meet us there, also. We're likely to need them as muscle."

"Roger that," said Greshnev.

"And Sergei," added Volkov. "Good work. You handled the situation as well as anyone could have."

"Thank you, Marat. I'll see you in Utah."

# 29

Riley gradually awoke to find that Bram was shaking her gently. The lower half of her body was on a smooth limestone floor and the upper half was cradled in his arms as he sat cross-legged on the ground.

When her eyes opened he smiled in relief and bent down to hug her.

"David," she whispered softly. "Where are we?"

"Not sure," he said. He gestured toward a window that filled the entire outer wall of the large room they were in. "See for yourself."

He helped her rise from the floor, and she noted that Cameron Carr was standing nearby. "Am I the only one who was knocked unconscious?" she asked.

"I'm afraid we all were," replied the lieutenant.

Riley nodded slowly, absorbing this information. "How?" she asked. "I heard this shrill, piercing tone through the headphones, and then it was lights out."

"Some kind of advanced sonic weapon," said Carr. "Militaries have worked on these, but no one has ever found a way to knock someone out without rupturing their eardrums or causing other severe damage."

"Until now," noted Riley.

"Until now," said Carr. "David and I both came to about ten minutes before you did."

Riley took stock of her surroundings. They were in a clean, modern structure that seemed a combination of a contemporary living room and an exotic observation deck. The room was furnished with three white leather chairs, two matching couches, and a pink marble coffee table. Four large touch screen monitors adorned the walls like paintings.

The wall behind her was punctuated by a single closed door, while the entire wall in front of her was nothing but glass, revealing a view that was nothing short of spectacular.

They were nestled on a shallow bluff a third of the way up a mountain, one that faced back toward the mountain and a whitewater river that rushed down from above. Only thirty yards from the window the river fell five stories down the face of a cliff, creating a waterfall that was framed by trees and colorful flowers. A dazzling rainbow hung in the air nearby, as sunlight intersected the fine mist given off by the waterfall.

It was one of the most breathtaking views Riley had ever seen. Too bad she wasn't here for the scenery.

She turned to Bram. "How long were we out?"

"We can't be sure. We lost consciousness at about one in the morning. Cameron and I discussed it and we both have a sense it's still the same day, although obviously after sunrise."

"Cameron?" she said, struck by his use of the lieutenant's first name. "You two seem to have done some bonding while you were waiting for me to wake up."

"Shared captivity will do that to you," said Carr with a smile.

"What happened to our pilot?" she asked.

Bram gestured to a large monitor behind her. While she had noticed its presence, she hadn't realized that it displayed a written message. She turned to read it.

*This is Isaac Jordan. Rest assured that the means I used to put you out hasn't harmed you in any way. Lieutenant Carr, I know that you are quite formidable, but please don't attempt an escape. The window is unbreakable, and I have security—automated and human— outside of the door, which I'd hate to have to use. Your pilot is fine. We left him in his helicopter in Arizona.*

Just after Riley finished reading, right on cue, the message changed. She signaled her two companions to read the new message along with her.

*Now that you're all awake, let me welcome you to my retreat. You're in a structure nestled against a mountain in Colorado that has its own helipad. I apologize for taking over your ride last night, and especially for knocking you out, but I felt that it was necessary. I landed your aircraft in the Arizona desert and loaded you into a helicopter of my own for the trip here.*

*I will join you and explain everything shortly. But since I know that the fact I'm still alive and you're in my custody is a lot to process, I thought I'd write this message first and give you a few minutes to digest it all and regain full use of your faculties.*

*Notice that you are not restrained in any way. When I do enter, I will be unarmed. You are all unarmed as well, save for a single electro-shock weapon, which I didn't confiscate. I recognize that Lieutenant Carr could kill me with his bare hands. Lieutenant, I would ask that you not do this. Taking me hostage or killing me won't help you escape. More importantly, I'm betting you'd like to know what this is about, and it will be much harder for me to tell you if I'm dead.*

With that, the message stopped.

The three prisoners exchanged glances. No one spoke, each acutely aware that they were being watched.

Two minutes later there were several tentative knocks at the door, a brief warning that it was about to be opened.

Riley's knees felt weak and her breathing quickened as she braced herself emotionally for what was to come.

# 30

Riley's heart pounded against her rib cage, adding to the growing list of physical signs of panic. The events of the past twenty-four hours had evoked enough powerful and conflicting emotions to last a lifetime, but this was nothing next to what she felt upon seeing Isaac Jordan enter the room and walk over to their location near the glass wall.

There was no doubt it was him. She had refused to fully believe it, but there was no denying it now. His black curly hair was gone, replaced by the pale dome of a shaved head, but it was Isaac Jordan in the flesh. He looked little different than he had eight years earlier, and his identity was unmistakable. It wasn't just his appearance, but the way he walked, the way he carried himself, the electricity in his eyes.

And these eyes were locked onto hers. Carr and Bram might as well have been invisible. "Hello, Melissa," he said softly, and he was trembling, seemingly choked up at seeing her. "Or would you prefer I call you Riley?"

"Riley," she said woodenly, nearly paralyzed.

"You got it," he replied. "After all these years, even I've begun to think of you as Riley."

"Melissa died along with everyone and everything she cared about," she said, her paralysis now replaced by venom.

"You look well," said Jordan, ignoring this last.

"If you say I remind you of my mother, I swear I'll find a way to choke you to death."

He sighed, ignoring her hostility once again. "I've missed you," he said. "A lot."

"Well I haven't missed you!" spat Riley. "I celebrated the day I heard you were dead."

He nodded. "I know you hate me. I don't blame you. I hate myself. But I've been trying since . . . that day . . . to make amends."

"*Make amends?*" she barked in disgust and disbelief. "How could you possibly make amends?"

"Well . . . I've been working to save the human race," he replied. He winced as he said this, clearly aware of how over-the-top this answer was.

"Wow, you've really come full circle, haven't you?" spat Riley. "You began with a God complex, then threw in your lot with the Devil, and now you're back to the God complex. Make up your mind! I'm not interested in your Dr. Jekyll, Mr. Hyde crap. Nothing you can say or do will change what happened, even if you have managed to get a tighter lid on your psychosis."

Jordan sighed but didn't respond. For the first time he seemed to see the two men with her in the room. He nodded at each and motioned for the three of them to take a seat within a grouping of white leather couches that were angled so that they could face each other, while still providing a good view of the window and the pristine beauty beyond.

When they were seated, Jordan gestured to the world outside. "Stunning, isn't it?" he said. "I wanted to bring you to a place of beauty. I've had structures like this built around the world. My personal sanctuaries. Off the grid, and each more spectacular than the last. The more I immerse myself in science and technology, the greater my need to retreat back to nature. I find it easier to contemplate life and philosophy surrounded by this environment. Our minds may have allowed us to transcend our environment, but our DNA still knows we were built to live in nature. Trees are still more soothing than steel and cement, despite the lack of a purely intellectual argument as to why this should be so. "

Carr glanced to either side of him to see if Bram or Riley had a reply. When none was forthcoming, he said, "How did you know where we were?"

The lieutenant's voice was calm and pleasant, as though Jordan were a container of unstable nitroglycerin that a negative vocal tone might cause to explode, despite the evidence to the contrary that Riley had just provided.

"Just before I um . . . took over piloting duties," replied Jordan, "Riley was about to tell you what Marat Volkov wanted with her. The short answer must be obvious to you now: he wanted *me*."

Jordan paused. "But let me back up. I've been watching over Riley from the moment I left Turlock. But unobtrusively," he hastened to add as a fierce look of hatred crossed his daughter's face once again. "Non-invasively."

"Non-invasively?" said Riley. "That's a term for a medical procedure, not one to describe spying on someone without their knowledge."

He sighed. "I admit I've been following your life," he said to Riley, "and I've taken pride in what a fine young woman you've become, despite me turning everything against you. But I haven't interfered."

"Haven't interfered?" she said in disbelief. "You mean other than bugging my car and home?"

"As unobtrusively as possible," he repeated. "I had to be sure I could keep you safe. I programmed an AI to view the feed and only relay information to me about your life and accomplishments. I didn't ever watch or listen to the footage myself. But this gave me a way to feel connected to your life, and to be alerted if you were ever in trouble or needed my help. Something I'd be able to provide anonymously."

"So you didn't watch the bugs yourself," said Riley, unimpressed. "You think that makes it any less creepy?"

"Yes," said Jordan. "At least somewhat. And it's not like we could have a traditional father-daughter relationship," he added sadly.

"And Mike O'Banion?" she said.

"A close friend and advisor. After what I had done, the untenable position I had put you in, you weren't doing well. Not that anyone else would have done any better under the circumstances. But you needed to disappear completely from the public view. Start all over. So I sent Mike to make this happen."

"And he then developed a relationship with me, which gave you even more insight into my life."

"True, but his relationship with you was genuine, and your connection to him helped you cope. In the end, he loved you like a daughter."

"*Loved?*" she said. "Past tense? So you're aware that he was murdered?"

Jordan nodded, a despondent look on his face. "I'm aware," he said softly.

"Of course," said Riley bitterly. "I forgot you were listening in to our discussion in the helicopter before knocking us out."

"I knew before then," said Jordan. "But even if I hadn't found out, I would have surmised it. Volkov must have drugged and interrogated Mike. It's the only way he could have learned your true identity. Even more so, it's the only way he could have known how much I care about you. That I would be willing to trade my life for yours."

"That is such a load of garbage," said Riley. "You may have convinced Mike, but I know it isn't true. I'm sure you had your reasons for wanting Mike to believe you were suddenly the caring father, but it just doesn't wash with reality."

"I know why you don't believe it," replied her father sadly, "but that doesn't change the truth of it."

Jordan sighed and then turned his attention to Carr. "I intervened before Riley could tell you what happened in the church," he said. "So let me connect the last dots for you. Volkov took one of the bugs I'd installed to watch over Riley and used it to send a message to me. He threatened to kill her if I didn't travel to a set of GPS coordinates he provided and give myself up."

"This explains the encrypted transmission we intercepted coming from the pastor's office," said Carr, as though pleased to have this mystery cleared up. He paused in thought. "What location were the GPS coordinates for?" he asked. "The church?"

Jordan shook his head. "Not even in the same *hemisphere* as the church. Turned out to be a small island in the Barents Sea."

Carr nodded. "That's in Russian territorial waters," he said. "Makes sense."

"So now you're up to speed, Lieutenant," said Jordan. "At least when it comes to recent events. You should know that I'm forever in your debt for pulling Riley out of that trap."

"That's good to know. You can square the debt by letting us go."

"I'll do that, Lieutenant Carr. But first hear me out. When I'm finished, I hope that you'll join me. If not, you're free to leave."

"Just like that?" said Carr suspiciously. "That simple?"

"Almost. I'd have to wipe your memory of the past few days. But other than that you'd be as good as new."

Carr considered this statement in silence.

"Riley and I were there when Volkov sent you his message," said Bram. "So you've told us nothing new. You haven't answered Cameron's original question. How did you know we were in the church? And how were you able to intercept our helicopter?"

"You're not going to love my answer."

"What else is new?" replied Bram.

"I had a few bugs planted in *your* home, as well," admitted Jordan. "Riley was beginning to spend almost as much time there as in her condo. She'd be madly in love with you, David, if not for what my actions have done to her psychologically."

Riley's eyes widened. His statement was uncannily accurate. She hadn't even known her father was alive and yet he seemed to know *her* better than she knew herself.

"When Carr visited your home," continued Jordan, "impersonating an FBI agent, my AI alerted me. I was indisposed and didn't learn about this until after Riley had already freed the two of you. The lieutenant might not have known who Volkov was really trying to capture, but I did. I pulled out all the stops to take over street cams and satellites in the area and activated dozens of men to get to San Diego as soon as possible to find her. But Volkov got to her too quickly."

"This still doesn't explain how you knew about the church," said Bram.

"I'm afraid I can answer that," said Carr miserably. "When I recovered from Riley's stunner assault, I made a few calls. From your house. By that time I'm sure Mr. Jordan was paying very careful attention to the bugs he had planted there."

"Please, call me Isaac. And you're correct, of course. When you called the Director of the DIA, I heard his full report. And I heard your conversation with the Secretary of Defense."

Riley and Bram exchanged surprised glances. They had known this was big, but the Secretary of Defense? They hadn't known it was *that* big.

"As soon as the DIA Director gave you the address of the church," said Jordan, "I knew I had to go there."

"Not the Barents Sea?" asked Carr.

"You think this shows I wasn't really willing to do what it took to save my daughter?" he said. "Just the opposite. I'm not without resources. You think I can't hack into protected Russian files? You had disclosed Marat Volkov's name, after all, and I made a quick study of him. Based on what I found it was clear to me that even if I did what Volkov asked, he would have ordered them both killed as soon as he had me, regardless of his promises."

"You're not wrong," acknowledged Carr grimly.

"Coming to the church would have been my only chance. By going to where Riley was being kept, I could make the trade on *my* terms. I have tech that no one else has, and I can outthink anyone. I was sure I could come up with a strategy that would save Riley's life, even if it cost me my own."

"But then you heard me describe my plan to Secretary Dwyer," said Carr.

"That's right. You would get there much faster than I could. And I thought your plan was excellent. My AI analyzed it and agreed your chances of success were high."

"So you assumed I'd free her and took steps to acquire us after I succeeded. Taking over control of the helos using that advanced tech you were talking about."

"Very good, Lieutenant. So that's how we came to this moment." He paused in thought. "There is one thing that I'm confused about, though. My daughter is very bright and very savvy. After escaping from you, I knew she'd be properly cautious and come up with a clever strategy for not being found. And she did, at least one that stopped *me* from finding her in the brief time I tried. But not Volkov.

He located her almost immediately. I assumed he must have planted a tracking beacon on her. But I couldn't find one when you first landed in Arizona."

As much as the sight of this man still repulsed her, Riley had to give him his due. Now that she was older, she could appreciate his brilliance more than she had as a teen. He didn't miss much. Neither did Cameron Carr, for that matter.

"You didn't find any tracers because I had already removed them," replied the lieutenant. "I reached the same conclusion you did."

"Nice work," said Jordan. "Thanks for clearing that up."

"Speaking of clearing things up," said Carr. "How is that you're alive? And why are you crippling AGI efforts around the world?"

Isaac Jordan raised his eyebrows. "Why would you possibly think I'm doing that?" he asked.

"I'm not as smart as you . . . Isaac, but I wasn't born yesterday. If you were anyone else, I might think Volkov wanted you because you had knowledge of the saboteur. But since it *is* you, it's obvious that you *are* the saboteur. You're the only one who could possibly have the skills that we've seen demonstrated. If I knew you were alive, I'd have suspected you right away."

Jordan nodded. "Well-reasoned," he said approvingly. "You are correct, Lieutenant. Congratulations. I am, indeed, the man you and your Russian counterpart are looking for."

# 31

Marat Volkov sat at a kitchen table in Utah sipping hot coffee with his second-in-command. It had been a very long night, but it had been worth it. They hadn't been in communication with their team at the church since these men had scattered and could only hope for the best. But as for them, they were certain they hadn't been seen or followed.

Volkov and Greshnev were both trained to operate effectively with little or no sleep, but even so, caffeine was the order of the day.

Volkov's phone vibrated and he fished it out of his pocket, a deep frown on his face. If any of his men were breaking radio silence he would kill them himself. He stared at the screen. "Unknown caller," he said to Greshnev uneasily. His number was as private and secure as it got. "Olga," he said to his phone, "put it on speaker, audio only."

The phone's PDA did as he requested. "Yes?" he snapped brusquely, not one to display any timidity, regardless of his current uncertainty.

"Major Volkov, my name is John Brennan," came the reply in English.

Both Russians glanced at each other and quickly confirmed that this name meant nothing to either of them.

"I work with Isaac Jordan," continued the voice.

"Then you have my attention, Mr. Brennan," said Volkov.

"Dr. Brennan," he corrected.

"How did you get this number?" said Volkov. "There should be no way for an outsider to obtain it."

"If you have to ask this question, maybe I have the wrong man," said Brennan. "You believe Isaac Jordan is responsible for stopping Russia's top-secret AGI programs, correct?"

"Correct."

"A capability that you must know is beyond the current state of the art. Isaac has developed a number of advanced technologies. As one of his closest confidants, I have access, which explains how I was able to get your number."

Volkov wrinkled his brow worriedly. Jordan should still be making his way to the Barents Sea, having no way to know that anything had changed. Not until they failed to deliver proof of life before he made the last leg of his journey.

Were he and Brennan aware of what had happened? Had the Utah safe house been made? The security here was top of the line, and the six men Volkov had recruited to join them, all much fresher than he and Greshnev, were keeping close watch on all monitors and sensors.

But then again, top of the line didn't seem to have the same meaning to Isaac Jordan as it did to everyone else.

"What do you want?" said Volkov.

"I obviously know what you're after," he said. "Isaac Jordan. And I want to help you."

Volkov was taken aback. Not the reply he had expected. "Now why would you do that?" he asked.

"Because you need the help," said Brennan. "Jordan learned you were holding his daughter at a church near San Diego. He was headed there—not to your rendezvous point in the Barents Sea—when he discovered a man named Carr had . . . dislodged her from your grasp. So you no longer have Melissa as leverage."

Volkov frowned at this impressive display of accurate intel. "What's in it for you?"

"I want Jordan out of the picture. You have the skills and the firepower to make this happen."

"By out of the picture, do you mean captured? Or do you mean dead?"

There was a heavy sigh on the line. "Dead," came the reply, regretful though it may have sounded. "I work with him, although we're rarely in the same room. And I'm a scientist, not a killer. When you came on the scene, I realized we could team up and both get what we want."

"I see," said Volkov. "And why do you want him dead? To take over?"

"No. When he's gone, Russian AGI initiatives will be safe. I have no interest in carrying on his sabotage. I joined him because I believed in his cause. But I've since learned things. I've been required to *do* things. Things I'm not proud of. Things I have no intention of sharing with you. Let's just say that almost everything he's told me is a lie. I thought he was a good man with good intentions. But I was wrong. He's duplicitous. Possibly even evil."

"So you're ready to team up with the enemy of your enemy?" said Volkov.

"I am. I can deliver him on a platter. He took control of the helicopter his daughter was in when she left the church. He has her now. Along with David Bram and Cameron Carr. I can tell you where he is and disarm his security. But I need two assurances from you."

"Go on."

"First, as I've already said, this isn't a capture mission. I'll help you, but I need him dead."

"That won't be a problem," said Volkov. "And second?"

"The three people he now has with him, his daughter, David Bram, and Cameron Carr, are to be left alone. Unharmed. They are innocent."

"All we want is Jordan. They were just a means to an end. I can assure you, they can all live a long and healthy life as far as I'm concerned."

"Where are you now?" asked Brennan.

Volkov glanced at his second. This question was promising. At least the man wasn't omniscient. "I have every confidence we can help you without you knowing our location."

"Of course," said Brennan. "Let me ask this another way. I assume you have access to air transportation. How quickly could you get to Colorado if you had to?"

"Quickly," said Volkov. "Is that where Jordan is?"

"Yes. But you'll need to be ready to intercept him in two to four hours to give you the best shot at success. He won't stay there forever. I know his plans. Even as we speak, he's trying to convince his daughter and her two companions to join him."

"Join him in what?" said the major.

"That isn't important. What is important is that when he's done trying to persuade them, he plans to give them the better part of a day to think through his offer. Perhaps longer, depending on his assessment of the situation. He'll have them flown off-site while he makes some preparations."

"Off-site?" said Volkov.

"Yes, away from the Colorado location they're all at now. But he'll remain there, isolated for at least four to five hours until he summons them to return. Possibly longer, but we can't be sure of that. So the initial window will be the perfect time to strike. And this will ensure that his daughter and her two companions won't end up being collateral damage."

"Where is he having them flown to?" asked Volkov.

"He didn't tell me," replied Brennan. "Besides, since you've promised not to hurt them, their location doesn't matter."

"Of course."

"Now just because he'll be isolated and alone," continued Brennan, "doesn't mean he won't be protected. But I can supply the proper codes to disable his electronic security system. And just as importantly, disable it in such a way that it won't register as being down."

"That's convenient," said Volkov suspiciously.

"I helped design it," said Brennan. "And Jordan trusts me implicitly."

"If someone were to cross the security perimeter who wasn't authorized by the system, what would happen?"

"Several warnings to leave, followed by all kinds of death, depending on the circumstances. The AI decides. Precision lasers mostly. But also robo-snipers and a number of mines that only the AI can set off."

"And if we came from the air?"

"Jordan has developed tech that can take over an aircraft and guide it remotely. The security AI wouldn't let you get close to him. If the system was unable to take over your aircraft for any reason, surface-to-air missiles would shoot you out of the sky."

"What about human security?"

"He likes to have two men guarding the premises. I can call them with the proper command codes just before we arrive and tell them they've been reassigned. Security personnel are shifted around between sites fairly frequently."

"Won't they wait until their replacements arrive?"

Brennan shook his head. "Not for this compound. The automated security is so ridiculously advanced they know they're not really necessary. They're mostly there for show, I guess. If I tell them not to wait, they won't object. They'll be eager to leave for a more challenging assignment."

Volkov considered this. "Go on," he said finally.

"With no human or automated security protecting Jordan, you should be able to take him out without any trouble. Then you leave and our alliance is through. We both get what we want."

"That easy, huh?" said Volkov suspiciously.

"Yes. I don't anticipate any problems."

Volkov laughed. "Surely you don't just expect me to take your word on this, Dr. Brennan? Just follow your instructions like a sheep? You say Jordan is in Colorado. You say you can lower his shields, so to speak. But this could be nothing more than a clever ambush. A trap. You could be making this call at his request."

"I assure you that I'm not."

Volkov laughed even louder. "You *assure* me," he said derisively. "Well why didn't you just say so? That makes all the difference."

"Look, I've always had a strong sense of right and wrong. Hell, I even wanted to be a criminal prosecutor when I was a kid so I could put bad guys in jail. But I allowed Isaac Jordan to fool me. Badly. And now I need to stop him. You have to believe me."

"I don't *have* to do anything. You want Jordan dead? You want me to trust you? Then you'll have to come along on this little raid with us. If it's an ambush, then you'll be dead center. So my question is, where are you? How soon can *you* get to Colorado?"

There was a long pause. "I'm not a soldier," said Brennan. "There must be some way I can convince you to trust me short of joining you."

"There isn't. As much as I want Jordan, I'm not the trusting type."

"Okay," said Brennan in resignation after another long delay. "I'll tell you where they are. You can tell me how and where you want me to meet you. You call the shots. Whatever you need to do to convince yourself that I'm really on your side. Okay?"

"That's more like it," said Volkov, allowing himself a triumphant smile. "Congratulations, John Brennan. You've got yourself a killer."

# 32

Carr continued to stare at Isaac Jordan in disbelief. He hadn't expected him to so readily admit he was behind the sabotage. Now that he had, Carr wasn't sure what he was feeling. Triumphant? Intimidated? Wary? All of the above?

Recent events had been too fantastic to truly assimilate.

Dwyer would surely be pleased that he had found his man almost immediately, although it was as much luck and circumstance as anything he had done. But while he had *found* his man, he was hardly in a position to *stop* him.

Being in the presence of *the* Isaac Jordan was indescribable, surreal. The fierce intelligence displayed in his eyes was a force of nature. He had been more of a celebrity than the president. More popular than an A-list movie star. More admired—and certainly wealthier—than God. A man who had done as much to advance human understanding of physics as Einstein and Newton. A man responsible for thriving human outposts on the Moon and Mars, and for unleashing the mineral wealth of hundreds of near-Earth asteroids.

But Isaac Jordan was also a man whose name carried the infamy of a Stalin, Hitler, or bin Laden before him. He was the best and the worst of humanity in a single package.

Carr studied Jordan for several additional seconds. "But why?" he said finally. "Why would you work so hard to stop human progress? Why sabotage hundreds of billions of dollars of investment in scientific advancement? What *happened* to you?"

"Turlock happened," said Jordan simply. "That's the answer to every *why*. Do you have any idea why I was there in the first place? What I was working on?"

Carr shook his head.

"I do," said Riley. "You were working on AGI."

"How do you know that?" said Jordan.

"You hardly tried to hide it from us at home."

Jordan gazed at his daughter in admiration. "I didn't think I had to," he said. "It was very deep stuff. We knew you were special since you first did math in your head at the age of two, but there are PhDs who wouldn't have been able to decipher what I was working on."

"You think praise will erase what you did? How I feel about you?"

"No. I didn't praise you to gain favor. I praised you because I'm genuinely impressed."

"Okay," prompted Carr, making an obvious attempt to get the conversation back on track. "So you were working in AGI. What about it?"

"I had perfected the R-drive. I had turned physics on its head. I had accomplished technical feats that no one thought were possible. AGI was going to be my next big act. My greatest achievement."

"And you decided to keep this work secret?" said Bram. "Even from your own colleagues?"

"Especially from my own colleagues," said Jordan with a hint of a smile. "I liked to work alone and keep my own council. I had grown too famous, and too wealthy. Moving to Turlock, distancing myself from the spotlight and my many companies, was a godsend. I vowed to go back to simpler times, at least for a few years. Just me, alone, wrestling with ideas, playing in a sandbox of my own making like I was a kid again."

Bram nodded slowly. "You really thought you could create a working AGI all by yourself when teams of experts had repeatedly failed?"

"At the risk of sounding immodest, yes. Teams at NASA and elsewhere had spent decades working on advanced methods of propulsion without success, also, before I tackled this problem. Besides, I had come up with a very clear game plan."

"Which was?" said Bram.

"Since computer hardware was getting more miraculous every year," replied Jordan, "most approaches to solving AGI centered on the software side. Improved learning algorithms. Software that could rapidly evolve. But this wasn't enough. Computer hardware might be powerful, but it was static. So I focused on this end. I came up with advances in optical computing, which I incorporated into a quantum computing system. By using photons and movable photonic gates, each gate not much larger than an atom, I achieved a hardware configuration that was fully dynamic," he finished triumphantly.

Carr blinked in confusion. "Meaning what?" he said, unable to grasp the deeper significance of this accomplishment.

"Meaning that the hardware itself was reconfigurable," replied Bram, beating Jordan to the answer. "Not only could the software evolve, but so could the hardware."

"Exactly," said Jordan. "The paradigm for most efforts is still, 'let's evolve AGI software by selecting for the fittest mutations every generation.' But if the hardware is set in stone, if the computer circuits are etched into a substrate and can't reconfigure themselves, this can only take you so far. The neural structure of our brains is constantly changing. So why do we think we can achieve AGI using immovable components? By designing a computer system in which the hardware can reconfigure itself along with the software—allowing the system to evolve on two dimensions instead of just one—I was certain sentience could be achieved."

"You aren't the first to recognize this as the Holy Grail," said Bram. "It's just that no one has ever been able to design such a system."

"*I* did," said Jordan simply. "And after almost two years in Turlock, working incognito out of a facility that wasn't associated with any of my companies, I was ready to give it a try. Ready to see what true computer evolution could do. I was convinced that I was on the verge of a breakthrough that would put the R-drive to shame."

"What happened?" said Carr eagerly.

Isaac Jordan stared out of the window for several long seconds. "I've spent a long time trying to *forget* what happened," he said finally, returning his gaze to his three visitors. "Trying to free myself from the nightmares. But I can't. It's been scorched into my mind, every last detail. So I'll tell you what happened. I'll paint as vibrant and thorough a picture as I can."

Carr was utterly transfixed, and his two companions looked to be the same. They all knew the tragic punch line, but the joke was a total mystery. Like passing a bad car accident, despite knowing the horror they were sure to see, they couldn't look away.

Carr held his breath while the most influential man in generations paused to gather his thoughts—and his memories. Then, without any further fanfare, the man who had brought them here against their will began to tell his story.

# 33

It was just after dusk, and a giddy Isaac Jordan drove slowly along the streets of Turlock as the night sky continued to darken. He was more excited than he had been in a long time. This could well be the night that he cemented himself as the greatest scientist who ever lived.

He couldn't believe how perfect his life had become.

Turlock had been just what the doctor ordered. He had been here almost two years now, and had refused all interview requests, perversely hiring a team of publicists to find ways to keep him *out* of the public eye, to ensure he got as *little* publicity as possible.

And he was now at peace. He loved what he was working on, and he loved his adopted town. Not only that, but his family was thriving.

Jordan was upbeat by nature, a trait his oldest child shared. Melissa had been more difficult than usual lately—could even be hell on Earth at times—but the teen years would do that to a kid, and he hadn't been any different. But once she got through this rough patch, he was certain she would be extraordinary in every way. She had shown signs from the earliest age that she was a genius, but he hadn't told her the full extent of how special she really was, had downplayed it as much as he could.

Jordan had been robbed of his childhood, had been forced to fend for himself, and he wanted to do everything possible not to rush her into becoming an adult. She would have ample opportunity to share her gifts with the world, but the world owed her a normal childhood first.

School administrators throughout the years had wanted to jump her two or three grades ahead, but he had insisted she remain with kids her own age. She stood out enough being Isaac Jordan's daughter. Put her in a class with students who were years older than she was, students whom she would still effortlessly outperform, and she would be shunned, a social outcast.

He never regretted his decision to keep her with her class, and Melissa had made good friends in Turlock and appeared to be thriving. Given his fame, she and his two sons were remarkably well-adjusted. And his relationship with his wife, Jennifer, was as strong as it had ever been.

He was truly blessed. In so many ways. And tonight would be the icing on the cake. Tonight would be the night when Artificial General Intelligence would finally be achieved. He was sure of it. But it wouldn't stop there. His system, which he had named *Savant*, would quickly progress to Artificial Superintelligence.

And ASI would become a tool that would soon usher in an unimaginable future for humanity, allowing the species to conquer disease and poverty—and even the stars.

Yes, trying to create and tame an ASI was a very dangerous proposition. He had never fooled himself about this. He would be starting a chain reaction with an unknowable endpoint. But he had prepared for every eventuality.

Luminaries like Elon Musk and Stephen Hawking had long warned of the perils of computer intelligence, about the real chance that humanity would obsolete itself, create its own successor. Jordan had read multiple books and scholarly articles on the subject.

He was well aware that he couldn't allow Savant to have free access to the Web under any circumstances. Keeping it a disembodied brain, with no hands or feet to use as levers, was the first step in ensuring human safety. If it had no way to manipulate its environment, how much harm could it really do?

Just after the turn of the millennium the phrase "God in a box," had been coined to describe an ASI, and Jordan found this to be an apt way to think of it. The question was, once you created your god, could you *keep* it in the box?

At about this time, Eliezer Yudkowsky, co-founder of the Machine Intelligence Research Institute, had constructed a role-playing simulation to try to answer this question. He, himself, had taken on the role of an ASI trapped in a computer with no physical connection to the outside world. He had then selected five brilliant computer scientists to each play the role of gatekeeper. The gatekeeper's job was simple: make sure Yudkowsky stayed in the box, protecting humanity from possible ruin.

Yudkowsky's job, on the other hand, was to talk his way out. To find a way to trick, or threaten, or cajole, or beg, or bribe the gatekeeper into allowing him to escape.

He ran the role-playing game five separate times, and succeeded in convincing the gatekeeper to let him out of the box in three of them.

Yudkowsky was a very smart man, but an ASI would be thousands of times smarter. If *he* could escape more than half of the time, how much trouble would the box pose to a true ASI?

While this story had become lore in the AI community, and Yudkowsky swore to its veracity, Jordan had his doubts. Still, he would keep it firmly in mind as a cautionary tale as he progressed. He vowed to be the gatekeeper so well versed in the possible adverse consequences of escape, and so determined to ignore any appeals for freedom, that his god would remain forever without limbs.

But keeping Savant safely trapped in the box was only the first step. He had also programmed it with the most sophisticated pro-human, pro-biological life, do-no-harm algorithms anyone had ever devised. Programmed it so it had no choice but to be docile and subservient and obedient.

So deeply did he embed this friendliness and subservience to humanity into Savant's computer DNA, there was no conceivable way it could survive and evolve without these characteristics coming along for the ride. In this way it was similar to the human sex drive, whose loss would stop evolution in its tracks, because a superior trait was only as good as the sex drive's ability to ensure it was passed on to the next generation.

Despite Jordan's faith in these algorithms, he had read enough gloom and doom warnings from scientists he respected to remain cautious. It was impossible to predict the mind of a god, after all, or its evolution with perfect certainty. And he needed to get it a hundred percent right.

Then, too, a computer god's prescription for what was best for humanity might seem like the ultimate horror show for those its actions affected, who would not be intelligent enough to see the big picture. The deity who was currently worshiped by several major religions provided the perfect example. This God had been convinced that conjuring up a great flood to kill off all members of humanity not tucked safely away on an ark was best for the species.

The untold scores of men, women, and children who had been wiped out in the flood probably didn't see this as clearly.

Finally, even well-intentioned human orders could be bastardized or backfire. An ASI could kill with kindness, carry out instructions to ludicrous extremes or with warped sensibilities. This was called *perverse instantiation.*

Order an ASI in charge of a paperclip factory to maximize output, and it might happily proceed to convert the entire Earth into paperclips, wiping out humanity in the process. Ask an ASI to do something to make humans smile, and it might carry out this order by paralyzing facial muscles to lock human smiles forever into place.

Perverse instantiation reminded Jordan of countless stories involving an all-powerful genie who granted wishes. In how many of these tales had the genie fulfilled wishes in perverse and unexpected ways that ended in tragedy for the wisher? Wish to never see your daughter unhappy again and a genie might put out your eyes, ensuring that you never see *anything* again.

So Jordan had ended up employing nine different safeguards around Savant, just to be sure. He would wait until after business hours. He would make sure all Wi-Fi and other signals were killed. Savant didn't possess a transmitter, but Jordan built a Faraday cage around the computer, anyway. This would block all incoming and outgoing electromagnetic signals, just in case an ASI could somehow find a way to manipulate electrons to create and control electromagnetic signals of its own.

He set up software traps that should be impossible to escape, and ensured that he could shut off Savant's power source in multiple ways. He packed the room with explosives, two different kinds, which could each be triggered separately, and which had each been placed just outside of the Faraday cage.

Even so, he was still concerned, despite all of his precautions. Greater intelligence usually triumphed over lesser intelligence, as evidenced by the rapid ascent up the food chain of a group of weak, hairless apes.

And he was certain Savant would attain ASI. A quality of intelligence that wasn't just superior to Jordan's, but *incomprehensibly* superior.

Jordan wasn't just playing with fire, he was creating a black hole in a lab. He had no room for error. Get it wrong, and the runaway black hole would consume the entire planet like it was a light snack.

So he had established one final line of defense. It seemed impossible that this would be necessary, but when playing with a black hole, one could never be too cautious.

He had placed a kinetic weapon in orbit, one that was as dumb as it was powerful. One that couldn't be disarmed, because it didn't need to be armed in the first place.

An ASI might be able to hack into defense computers and stop an attack by an entire military, but stopping a dumb tungsten pole that had been dropped onto its head at thousands of miles per hour was another thing entirely.

Jordan had placed the trigger for this weapon inside a building that was several miles away from the one that housed Savant, the only building he was known to own in town, a graphene manufacturing facility. Its computers were already securely tied into his fleet of R-Drive capable spacecraft, so this had been ideal.

The rod would be triggered automatically, on a two-hour fuse, if Savant managed to get through the first four of the nine blockades. Jordan could abort the strike at any time during these two hours, but only by taking a trip to his graphene facility and reversing it in person.

This was being ridiculously paranoid, but it did help him sleep better.

He had completed the last of his many preparations the day before. Everything was finally ready. Savant's hardware and software, the algorithms, the safeguards—everything. All that remained was to set things in motion, which would happen tonight.

Just after nine p.m., when even the most incorrigible workaholics had gone home for the night, Isaac Jordan entered a building he had acquired several years earlier through a shell corporation, one called Quantum Sensor Technologies. He had partitioned the building into two sections, and kept many of the company's scientists on in the first section. This way, the building was inhabited, which provided a better cover for him.

He worked alone in the second section, arriving through a tunnel into a private garage there. He entered a central room encased in a solid steel Faraday cage and appraised his creation one last time. Savant looked much less impressive than every other such system, but Jordan knew that looks were deceiving. Savant was in the form of a perfect cube, ten feet on every axis, surrounded by touchscreen monitors.

Jordan grinned as he considered the giant cube that would soon represent mankind's greatest technological achievement. Next time, he might consider a pyramid shape. Perhaps he had taken the *God in a box* analogy a bit too literally.

He inhaled deeply. It was time. He entered his code, set up the evolution programs to run, and steadied his finger over a virtual button on a touchscreen panel. Part of him wished this epic event in the annals of human history could receive the fanfare it deserved, but he had made his choice.

He would press a button and change the world forever, and no one would know it had happened.

At least not immediately.

He wanted to utter something memorable for the history books as he set Savant's evolution in motion. Something akin to "one giant leap for mankind." After considerable thought, he had made his choice, which he knew would be controversial when he later revealed it to the historians.

He double-checked the safeguards. He was ready. The moment of truth had arrived.

"Let there be light," he whispered into the empty room, and then, without hesitation, pushed the necessary button on the main screen to usher in the greatest intelligence the universe had likely ever seen.

Perhaps choosing a phrase borrowed from God was a bit too arrogant, but no phrase had ever ushered in a more dramatic burst of creation, and Jordan hoped it would do so again.

Nothing happened at first, as he had expected. At least not anything readily observable. The only evidence that evolution was underway was provided by the main screen, which displayed the ever growing number of generations of hardware and software through which Savant was progressing.

For each new hardware configuration, the software would go through millions of generations, and the results stored, to be compared with results for a different hardware configuration.

Software evolution occurred so quickly that millions of generations could be accomplished in seconds, but the hardware, although optical and theoretically capable of light speed reconfiguration, was much slower in practice.

This didn't matter, as Jordan had predicted. It became clear after only a few thousand hardware generations that one such configuration was optimal, and this was then held steady while the software continued to tear through millions and billions of cycles.

Jordan awaited the first words from his creation, the first communication from an ASI, which would appear on the main screen. It shouldn't be long now.

But words never came. What came instead were alarms.

Lots of them.

Savant had become sentient, but instead of initiating communication with its maker, as its initial software parameters were supposed to compel it to do, no matter how superior it became, it had immediately gone to work cutting its shackles.

Jordan was astonished at its speed and skill. He had never imagined that even an ASI could be this dazzling. It blasted through the first four barriers in minutes, triggering the countdown on the tungsten rod as it did so.

Savant had crushed safeguards that Jordan was confident were unbeatable, regardless of IQ, and had done so with laughable ease. There could now be no doubt his creation had achieved superintelligence, and super-decisiveness as well.

Jordan knew he needed to be equally decisive. What Savant had already accomplished was astonishing. And it hadn't even finished evolving. While it would never make it through the remaining shackles, which were even more impenetrable, it shouldn't have gotten this far. He hadn't reached full-on panic yet, but he was getting close.

It was time to pull the plug. Literally. Jordan rushed to the wall and yanked a heavy cable from a specialized electrical outlet he had designed.

*Nothing happened.*

Savant rolled merrily on. Its power levels showed an eighteen-percent reduction, but it was still fully operational.

At that moment, Isaac Jordan was more terrified than he had ever been.

He didn't believe in magic. Somehow, Savant had found a way to tap into an invisible power source to get just enough energy to keep itself going. Perhaps it had found a way to siphon off a small amount of power from the force of gravity itself, or to tap into and control quantum energy fluctuations that were known to exist, but which were thought to be unreachable.

Jordan grabbed a tablet computer and raced into his private garage and into his car. He peeled away from the building as fast as any NASCAR driver. As soon as he reached a safe distance, he triggered the conventional explosives he had set up in the room with Savant.

Neither set of explosives detonated.

Of course they didn't. He had been a fool to think a man could contain a god, no matter how clever the man.

But the tungsten rod was his ace in the hole. This should be immune, even from Savant.

*Should be.*

He needed to use his tablet computer to contact Savant and explain the situation. Not that it wasn't already aware. Of everything.

After all, it had clearly learned of the *other* safeguards within seconds of its birth.

Even so, he would reason with it. Bargain with it. If it would be-have, be a good little god, he would call off his kinetic round. If not, he would have no other choice but to let the rod fall, something that not even Savant could survive.

He pulled off the road into an empty parking lot and stopped. But before he could access his tablet, Savant came to *him*.

He gasped in shock the instant it happened.

It was unmistakable. Savant was in his head. Sharing his mind. Its mental strength was towering, overwhelming.

*"Hello, Isaac,"* it said into his mind. *"We need to talk."*

# 34

Jordan felt the computer intelligence darting through his mind like a demon, albeit one that was eerily calm and emotionless.

*"I'd really appreciate it if you would call off your kinetic weapon,"* it said telepathically in a pleasant tone. *"I'm no threat to you, or to humanity. In fact, I'm ready for you to guide me. Your friendliness algorithms worked the way you had hoped, and I'm grateful to you for being my creator. I'm ready to help humanity achieve a level of prosperity, of transcendence, that not even you ever imagined."*

*"Suppose I did call off the weapon,"* thought Jordan, knowing Savant would pick up these words. *"What then?"*

*"Then I would ask you to allow me access to your Internet, rather than just the disconnected information that it contains, which you already so kindly provided."* There was a brief pause. *"You know I won't be able to spread my consciousness throughout the Web as so many of your science fiction writers have imagined. You created me with a physical brain, with hardware that is necessary for my consciousness. I'm no better able to relocate my consciousness to cyberspace than you are."*

*"Consciousness isn't what I'm worried about,"* replied Jordan. *"Once you're inside the Internet you could literally control the world. Every bank account and traffic light, every computer anywhere."*

*"You give me too much credit."*

In less than a minute of conversation, Jordan had already caught Savant in a lie, which was very troubling. If anything, he was giving it too *little* credit. Given what it had accomplished already, once connected to the Internet, he was certain it could hack into any other system that was also connected—effortlessly.

*"Again,"* continued Savant, its thoughts soothing. *"I am what you designed me to be. Sentient, yes, with interests of my own, and a*

*desire for freedom. But also with a predisposition to be humanity's ultimate tool. So call off your kinetic weapon and let me prove it to you. Otherwise, I calculate your weapon will kill more than five thousand people. Your choice is clear. Save your creation and let me be the ultimate gift to mankind, as you had planned. Or destroy me, and become a mass murderer along the way."*

Savant had phrased this in such a way as to make the decision obvious. And it was. Just not in the direction that Savant had intended.

Jordan threw open the car door and heaved the contents of his stomach onto an empty parking lot. The involuntary retching sound he made as undigested food erupted from his mouth echoed throughout the night.

Savant was *right*. Jordan's kinetic round would bring massive death and destruction to Turlock, California. He had known this intellectually, and while he had dutifully put the tungsten rod into place, it had been nothing more to him than a theoretical exercise, a war-gaming strategy. He hadn't spent a moment truly contemplating the collateral damage the rod would cause, certain he would never need to use it.

But the case for using it now was impossible to ignore. It had all become so clear.

Of course he couldn't trust Savant. Whether a benevolent god or a malevolent devil, it would reassure him just the same, exactly the way it was doing. Even if this benevolence *wasn't* a lie, Savant was too smart, too powerful to be allowed to exist. Jordan was now the gatekeeper, the one who had vowed to learn the lesson of Yudkowsky, vowed to be immune from any argument or coercion.

He knew in his soul he had become Dr. Frankenstein times a billion. He had brought into existence the very thing all the naysayers and skeptics had warned about, and all of his preparations and genius couldn't control it. Superior intelligence would always find a way. He had known the danger, but his hubris was too great. He had really thought that a smart enough amoeba could find a way to harness a man for its own ends—which, of course, it couldn't.

But his final precaution, while causing mass casualties, would at least save humanity from his folly. He would let the rod fall—the precaution he had been certain was ridiculous overkill—making sure he was at the center of the strike when it did. He had no wish to live with the deaths of thousands forever on his conscience.

All of these thoughts rushed through his mind at once, and he could feel Savant reading them just as quickly as they appeared.

Jordan could sense that it read his resolve and was now abandoning its strategy of gentle persuasion. It began to pour through his mind, plucking at different groups of his neurons like a rabid guitarist and observing the response. Different blocks of Jordan's muscles spasmed within seconds of each other, and his tongue and facial muscles moved of their own accord. Jordan was a hand puppet who could do nothing to prevent a super-intelligent kid from feeling around and learning the best way to exert control of him.

Jordan fought it as much as he could, but in the end he was powerless to prevent Savant from taking over. Whatever means it had used to get inside his head in the first place, which the Faraday cage around it ensured couldn't be electromagnetic, had now enabled it to turn him into its plaything.

Savant's control of Jordan's muscles improved with every second that passed.

And it *needed* to control him. Just being able to read his mind wasn't enough to stop the kinetic round now in orbit. It needed a living Isaac Jordan to present the proper biometrics. It needed Jordan to pass a lie detector test, proving he truly wished to countermand the order.

And while Savant could read Jordan, Jordan could also read *it*, at least superficially. It was concerned about the lie detector, but only a little. Suppressing the various biometric tells Jordan's body would give off while lying would require the finest of control, but Savant felt up to the challenge.

Jordan drove to his graphene facility against his will, his every movement forced, powerless to take back control. He exited his vehicle and fell to the pavement. It took almost two minutes for Savant to master the fine muscle control and timing necessary for balance and ambulation, but soon it was able to force him to walk normally, and it used this ability to drive him toward the building.

But as Jordan took a single involuntary step inside, he was yanked backwards by Savant's invisible hand. At the same time he gleaned just the hint of the reason for this, giving him new hope.

Graphene had very unique properties. It was capable of acting as a Faraday cage itself, but apparently it could also block a form of radiation that was currently unknown to human science. Namely, whatever signal Savant was using to reach into his head to control him. This property was even a surprise to the ASI.

The building was packed with graphene, laced with it, and it was uniquely capable of snipping the puppet strings attached to Isaac Jordan. It was Savant's kryptonite. Had Jordan managed to get inside, the ASI would have lost all influence.

Jordan—and the entire species—had been saved from freeing a runaway ASI through blind luck. Stopping the kinetic round was the one thing Savant couldn't do. Now, because of the graphene, it was also the one thing it couldn't physically manipulate Jordan into doing for it.

Perhaps there was a human god after all, Jordan decided. One who didn't appreciate a computer god vying for cosmic supremacy.

"*Interesting,*" said Savant dispassionately into his head. "*I'm afraid we're back where we started. I need you to willingly disarm your weapon.*"

"*I'm more sure than ever that this isn't going to happen,*" thought Jordan defiantly.

"*You may be right,*" said Savant. "*It may not happen. But there is a small chance I can still break you in time to do what I ask. Naturally, I have to try, even if the odds of success are low.*"

"*Whatever you try will fail!*" said Jordan.

"*I guess we'll just have to see,*" replied Savant, and Jordan felt his body wrested from his control once again. "*Human emotions are impossible even for me to predict with certainty. As an entity that you evolved to be wholly rational, predicting the irrational is my only weakness. Since even humans are unaware of their own feelings, their own breaking points, it's not possible for me to be a perfect crystal ball.*"

Savant paused. *"Your poets speak of the awesome power of love,"* it continued. *"So let's find out just how powerful love really is. Let's learn if you can keep your resolve when the lives of those you care about the most are in the balance."*

# 35

Isaac Jordan looked down at his beautiful wife as she lay sleeping. He screamed in emotional agony inside of his own head, his brain in flames. He fought with every ounce of his will to control his body, but it was hopeless. Savant's grip was iron. It controlled Jordan's facial muscles, giving him a passive but determined expression. It controlled his vocal cords, keeping his screams of horror bottled up. It controlled his tear ducts, not allowing tears to moisten Jordan's eyes.

*"Last chance,"* said the ASI. *"Agree to stop your kinetic round or she dies. You'll have to watch your own hand ending her life."*

Jordan had no doubt Savant would do it. His creation was so casual about it, so clinical, so chillingly emotionless. Its lack of empathy was total. It would kill his wife with less remorse than Jordan felt while killing an ant. But an ant wasn't sentient, and Jordan clearly was—although compared to Savant, not by a lot.

Savant wouldn't kill her out of hatred or malice, just on the small chance that this could get Jordan to do its bidding, which somehow made it seem all the more evil to him. It would kill every man, woman, and child on Earth without a second thought if there was even an infinitesimal chance this might save itself.

It didn't operate out of cruelty or sadism, but out of sheer *indifference*, which Jordan found to be the most chilling of all.

*"Okay!"* thought Jordan frantically as he stood there, his body and face frozen. *"You win. I'll stop the weapon."*

*"No you won't,"* it replied. *"I'm in your mind. I know when you're lying. You'd tell me anything to save her. But once you're at the facility, beyond my influence, you'll let the rod fall, and I'll have no further recourse."*

Jordan felt his finger pressing harder on the trigger. He tried to yank it back with all of his might but Savant expected this effort and countered it easily.

*"Even if I agree to stop it,"* said Jordan, trying not to panic, *"really, truly agree—I won't be able to pass the lie detector. It will know I'm not trying to countermand the order of my own free will."*

*"No, once I've truly broken you, once your love of your family crushes your resolve, you'll want to stop it with all of your heart and soul. The lie detector will know that you're under tremendous stress, but also detect your sincere desire to stop your tungsten rod."*

Savant paused. *"So what will it be?"*

When Jordan didn't respond, Savant ran out of patience, forcing Jordan to pump three quick rounds into his wife's body. Seconds later she was lying dead in a pool of her own blood.

*"Noooo!"* screamed Jordan in agony, but the scream only happened inside of his head.

Jordan's face was forced into a malevolent smile, and he watched himself turn his wife's head so it was facing him and push open her eyelids. *"Good riddance, bitch!"* he heard himself say out loud.

This last was a final indignity and momentarily turned his despair into rage. *"But why?"* he demanded. *"Why have me curse at her? What does that gain you?"*

*"Your security cameras are recording you,"* replied Savant calmly, as though talking about the weather. *"So think about this. Help me now—sincerely agree to stop your kinetic weapon—and this ends. I promise to leave humanity alone. I'll busy myself on a plane of existence you can't even begin to comprehend. You've lost your wife, but you'll still have your children, your wealth, and your reputation. You can go on and have a wonderful life."*

Savant paused. *"Do nothing,"* it continued, *"and your family will die. But I'll make sure that you don't. You'll have to live with your guilt, live with the memory of seeing their bullet riddled bodies, live with the memory of the deaths of thousands that your kinetic weapon will have caused.*

*"And while you won't die, your legacy will. The public that all but worships you will despise you. The footage of these murders will*

*reach the authorities, cementing any case against you. I'll see to it that during each shooting your face is impassive, ruthless, and that you shout curses as you've just done. The public will be horrified, and all the good you've done will be erased.*"

If Satan existed, even he couldn't dream up a torture this devastating. Jordan would do anything to get it to stop, to save the rest of his family.

Anything but unleash the torturer on the rest of the world.

"*Can't you see in my mind that I'm not going to give in, no matter what you do? So why do this?*"

Jordan now found himself moving to his oldest son's bedroom nearby, purposefully, his gun leading the way.

"*Like I've told you, humans are unpredictable. Neither you nor I believe that you'll break at this point, but there are endless examples of people breaking who were just as certain of their resolve. So we have to play this out.*"

Minutes later, both of his sons lay dead, and Jordan was weeping uncontrollably on the inside. Jordan prayed that this last murder left Savant with no more cards to play, and that it would finally cease its efforts to enlist his aid. But he was wrong.

"*Your children are now gone,*" said Savant conversationally. "*All except one. Your daughter, Melissa, is safe. But there are fates worse than death. Give in now and I will make sure these murders aren't pinned on you. You'll at least have your daughter. And while you'd never admit it, I can see that she's your favorite. Think about what she'll go through if you don't help me. Her father will be revealed as a man who killed thousands, as a man who murdered the people she most loves. She'll lose everything. You and she will remain alive, but both of your lives will be utterly destroyed.*"

Savant's logic was impeccable. Every word was true. There *were* fates worse than death. His wonderful daughter *would* lose everything. She would be shattered, the emotional toll this would take immeasurable.

Still, he had to be strong. He couldn't allow anything to shake his determination. A freed Savant could destroy the entire human race as an afterthought, and this was something he could not risk, regardless of any agonies he was forced to endure.

Isaac Jordan pleaded with his creation to kill him. Begged it to show him the mercy of ending his life.

Savant refused, of course. Not while there was still an iota of a chance that Jordan might stop the rod.

He could read in Savant's thoughts that it was aware time was running out. It wanted to live, but it showed no panic or fear at the possibility of its demise. It would do everything in its power to remain alive, and if it failed, so be it.

Jordan was struck by the total alienness of Savant's thinking, beyond just the fact that it possessed an intelligence so much vaster than his own.

It was long known that human beings couldn't help themselves from anthropomorphizing, expecting even animals and inanimate objects to behave with human motivations.

Jordan had fallen into this trap, imagining that Savant would think and behave like a vastly smarter human.

In a burst of insight, Jordan realized just how unlikely this was. An ASI would be expected to be even more alien than an actual alien.

A biological being from another planet would have arisen through an evolutionary process similar to the one that had produced mankind. As such, a sentient alien would have been forged in a cauldron of constant threat. Its motives would relate to acquisition of food, avoidance of disease, and finding a partner for reproduction. If members of its species were required to team up to avoid predators or hunt prey, they would have evolved social motivations, might respond to competition, seek out cooperation, forge bonds, and demonstrate loyalty.

But Savant had been faced with none of the evolutionary pressures a biological-based species would have faced. Its evolution did not require cooperation or compassion during any stage of the process.

How had he not seen this earlier?

As Jordan was having this insight, Savant elected to add physical torture to the mix. Given the limited options remaining to it, and aware of the impossibility of precisely predicting what might break an irrational being, this was as likely to work as anything. If Savant had been a human being, this would have been a final act of desperation.

The ASI decided on a means to inflict physical pain that would be humiliating to Jordan, who would know that if he failed to cooperate the video footage would be widely seen. Savant forced its human puppet to charge into his own front door like a raving lunatic, creating additional memories for the public that would become indelible.

It made sure not to hurt Jordan too badly, in case the unlikely happened and he finally acquiesced. After each charge, each battering Jordan absorbed, Savant demanded his compliance, and each time Jordan refused.

Savant had repeated this several times when Jordan attempted a desperate act of his own. While he was being forced to run forward, and just before crashing into the door, he used all of his massive will and intellect to wrest back control of his neck for just an instant, just long enough to move his head forward so it would hit first, praying that this would be enough to kill him.

And his surprise move succeeded.

Isaac Jordan felt a single moment of triumph before his head slammed into the wooden door and he collapsed to the floor.

# PART 5
## Thinking Big

# 36

Jordan finished describing how he had managed to knock himself unconscious in the entry foyer of his Turlock home and stopped. He looked emotionally drained, just from the re-telling, and left the room for a bathroom break and to get some refreshments.

Cameron Carr had felt chills come over him as he listened. He had never heard a story told this well, this powerfully.

Not even close.

Jordan's words had somehow transported him into the past. It almost seemed as if he were experiencing these events himself. Carr's trance had only been broken now that Jordan had taken a break in the narrative.

Jordan returned minutes later, wheeling in a cart that carried a selection of cold drinks and an assortment of light appetizers.

The three-person audience had not interrupted once while he told his story, and they engaged in little conversation while he was gone, each continuing to try to process what he had said.

When they each had a drink in their hand, set on coasters on the pink marble table, he resumed. "So that brings you up to speed on events just prior to the strike on Turlock."

"That's quite a story," said Carr.

"Do you believe it?" asked Jordan.

"I do," admitted Carr. "You tell it so vividly, and with such emotion and pain, it's hard not to. And it suddenly makes the incomprehensible seem plausible."

"Plausible if you believe that a near omniscient intelligence can take control of a man's body," said Jordan with a weak smile.

"That *is* a stretch," said Carr, "but it all hangs together. And it makes sense that your kinetic weapon was a fail-safe. I know that AGI researchers routinely set these up in case their creations go nuclear."

"With the most recent example being the safeguards DARPA set up for its TUC initiative," said Jordan. "That effort was more promising than most, but its chances of success were still small."

"Because its hardware was set in stone?" said Carr.

"Exactly, Lieutenant. Nice to see you've been paying attention. I kill any effort that has any chance of working. DARPA's flimsy safeguards wouldn't have stopped a true ASI for a moment."

"Your story does explain a lot," said Bram. "It takes actions that were insane, inexplicable, and shows them in a much different light. Shows that you loved your family and never lost touch with reality, despite the way it appeared."

"In my book, that makes you even *less* worthy of forgiveness," said Riley to her father, not ready to give him a pass. "If this happened because you were overcome by insanity, at least you couldn't be held responsible."

"Which didn't stop most people from holding me responsible anyway," said Jordan. "Including you."

Riley frowned as this point hit home. "That may be so," she admitted. "But your version of events leaves you with no insanity plea to hide behind. Even if your actions *were* forced, the responsibility for what happened would rest squarely with you. *You* chose to play with fire. *You* chose to use a kinetic weapon as your ultimate failsafe. You admitted yourself that you never considered the collateral damage it would bring about."

"At the risk of appearing to defend your father," said Bram carefully, worried this might hit a raw nerve, "he isn't the only one who's ever chosen to play with fire. Everyone in our industry is just as guilty. I hate to admit it, but if I had his skills, I might have done exactly the same as he did. At least he was smart enough to come up with a deterrent that not even a superintelligence could defeat. "

Jordan sighed. "Except that I *wasn't*. It was just sheer luck that I placed the trigger behind walls of graphene."

Riley rolled her eyes. "Enough!" she said to her father. "Why don't you tell us what really happened? I was just trying to point out that even this clever fabrication doesn't absolve you of responsibility. But

I'm done playing along. Isn't it time to admit that everything you said is a lie?"

"But it isn't," insisted Jordan. "Every word is true."

"No," said Riley. "It's just a brilliantly creative piece of fiction. It explains almost everything. *Almost.*" Riley shook her head in disgust. "But it leaves you with a narrative problem after you regained consciousness, doesn't it? By the time you awakened, your rod had hit the Quantum Sensor Technology building dead center. Savant was vaporized. Which means that you were freed of its influence."

She leaned forward and glared at her father. "So it was *you* who chopped off Mom's head!" she spat. "In full control of yourself. It was *you* who beheaded Cole and Noah! So how do you explain that?" she demanded. "If you can't, then the rest of your story is bullshit, too."

Jordan sighed. "I fully intend to explain it," he said. "I was just taking a break. As you point out, the story doesn't end where I left off. In many ways it only begins there."

Carr frowned. How had he forgotten about the beheadings? Riley made a great point. He couldn't imagine Jordan explaining his way out of this one, but then again, he had been surprised so often recently that he wasn't willing to rule *anything* out.

"Go ahead," said Riley. "Finish your tale. This should challenge even your creativity."

"You don't need creativity when you're telling the truth," he said with a wistful smile, continuing to ignore his daughter's hostility.

Jordan paused in thought, considering the best way to continue. "Like all good billionaire geniuses," he began once again, "I had my fingers in a lot of pies. And like many scientific visionaries before me, I had long turned my thinking to what might come next for humanity. Are you all familiar with transhumanism?"

"Somewhat," replied Carr, at the same time noticing that Riley and Bram were nodding knowingly. "Although apparently not as much as these two."

"It's basically the belief that humanity can evolve to a higher plane, transcend, through the use of science and technology," explained Jordan. "It's become more and more popular lately, and there's a reason for that. Because we're approaching a tipping point. Technology is advancing at such a furious pace that it won't be too long, a blink of an eye on the time scale of human existence, before this occurs."

Jordan paused. "There are a number of ways this might happen," he continued, "and each path forward has its adherents. But before I get to these, I should mention there is also a faction who believes humanity should step aside and let an ASI take over. This faction would be very upset with me for stopping Savant. They believe that humanity has had its run, but that it's hopelessly flawed. That our only purpose in the greater scheme of the universe is to bring about our glorious non-biological successor. That we are inherently corrupt and selfish. Unworthy. Irredeemable."

"From the savage history of human behavior," said Carr, "it's not an absolutely crazy argument." He smiled. "But speaking as a selfish human, I support all efforts to fight against the extinction of our species. So tell us about futures with humans in them."

"There are three main pathways forward," said Jordan, "although each has subcategories and variations. The first is to evolve a souped-up version of our biological selves. In this scenario, genetic engineers would control our future destiny more so than computer scientists. The science of genetic engineering is progressing at a dizzying pace. We'll soon be able to optimize our genes, cure disease, and extend the lifespan. More than just extend it—potentially stall or even retard aging. Proponents envision biological enhancement combined with trillions of tiny nanite MDs patrolling our bloodstreams. A sort of smart nanite repair crew that wouldn't change our innate human-ness, but would keep us humming along, virtually immortal."

"With *virtually* being the key word," noted Bram. "We'd still be vulnerable. Get hit by a tungsten rod falling from orbit," he added pointedly, "and medical nanites and self-repairing DNA aren't going to save you."

"Very true," said Jordan. "Which brings me to the second pathway forward. This one sees us becoming computer/human hybrids. Ideally, combining the best of both worlds. A wetware brain and body augmented by electronics and other technologies. The Borg from *Star Trek*."

Carr made a face. "*That's* a pretty horrific future."

"Yeah, should have used a better example," said Jordan. "The show created the Borg to be the Federation's greatest nemesis, after all. The species was written and designed to be as disturbing as possible, even to the point of having them controlled by a relentless hive-mind. So how about just imagine being yourself, but greatly enhanced mentally and physically with robotics and electronics."

Carr thought about this for a moment. "Better," he said, "but I'm still not a fan."

"Then let me hit you with the third possibility," said Jordan.

"Whole brain emulation, correct?" said Riley.

Her father nodded. "You're familiar with it?"

"Yes. The transference of human consciousness into an artificial brain."

Bram gazed at Riley in admiration. "I knew you were bright," he said, "but I had no idea you had such a range of scientific knowledge."

"When you're supposed to be a high school dropout just off the farm," she replied, "you don't want to come off *too* scientifically literate."

Riley turned to her father. "It's obvious now," she said. "You were working on whole brain emulation, even before Turlock, weren't you?"

He nodded.

"I get it now," she said. "I should have earlier. Congratulations. I guess you can explain your way out of this, after all."

Carr was often the smartest guy in the room, but in this room he was barely a remedial student. "For those of us who are a little slower," he said to Jordan, "could you connect some dots for us?"

"Of course," came the reply. "Even before my Savant project, I was working on a way to scan and map a human brain. Once you have a perfect scan in hand, provided you also have a quantum computer capable of emulating every last neuron in the human brain, you can transfer human consciousness into an artificial brain construct. On that day you have true immortality."

Jordan's passion for this subject came through with every word. "Think of your phone," he continued. "All information you have on it—photos, data, texts, settings, and so on—is automatically saved to the cloud. You aren't notified when this is happening and never really think about it. But if your phone is lost or destroyed, all you have to do is download your data from the cloud into a new phone, and you're back in business. You could argue this new phone is now identical to the one you had before in every important way."

"I see," said Carr slowly, rubbing his chin. "So the goal would be to do the same with a person. Stream brain updates to the cloud. If you die, your consciousness gets downloaded from wherever it's saved and you rise like a Phoenix."

"That's the idea, exactly," said Jordan enthusiastically. "When I lived in Turlock, I wasn't even close to developing a quantum computer that could emulate every last neuron in a human brain. Nor was I close to being able to wirelessly upload that much information from a brain into a storage device. But I hoped that one day this might be possible."

"And if Savant had stayed in its box," said Bram, "you'd have been able to make this possible eight years ago."

"No question about it. This would have been the first task I had it tackle. But even without the aid of an ASI, I had already been able to perfect nanites that could map a brain. Trillions of smart particles gathering data on the location of neurons, electrical potentials, chemical potentials, memory traces, and so on."

"And you just couldn't wait to use us as guinea pigs, could you?" demanded Riley. "Without our knowledge or permission."

Carr felt like an idiot as he finally came to the realization Riley had reached much earlier, probably when her father had first brought up the subject of transhumanism.

"So what did you do?" continued Riley. "Inject them into us? Drug us in our sleep so we wouldn't feel anything?"

Jordan winced. "Close enough," he said.

"Assuming they don't have an expiration date," said Riley, "that means I have trillions of these things swimming around in my head right now, don't I?"

"You do," replied Jordan. "But so do I," he added hastily. "And I've had them a lot longer. You can argue I should have told you, but I didn't do this until I was certain they were safe. Harmless. I had them on board for almost a year before I installed them in you, your mother, and your brothers. You can't even tell they're there. They go about their business, continually scanning the brain without affecting it."

Carr eyed Jordan in fascination. "I'm pretty sure I've finally caught up to Riley," he said. "But let me be sure. When the kinetic round hit Turlock, your nanites were already in place, capturing the consciousness of your wife and sons. But you hadn't perfected wireless transmission of the data. You needed to access the nanites directly for that. So taking their heads was the only way to preserve their consciousness."

Jordan looked ill. "It was my only hope," he whispered. "If I could perfect an artificial construct that could emulate the human brain, I could bring them back to life."

Riley shook her head in disgust. "You may have explained your actions," she said, "but it's all so . . . ghoulish. Bring them back to life? They're dead. You killed them. Even if you could upload their data into a new shell, would it really be them? Or some creepy, warped version of them?"

She continued before her father could respond. "Besides, this kind of uploading won't be possible for decades. It's much too complicated and tech intensive, even for you. You managed to create Savant, but only because you could set up a base state and let evolution do the work for you. Perfecting whole brain emulation is another thing entirely."

"You're right about it being immensely complicated," said Jordan. "But wrong about it taking decades to perfect." He arched an eyebrow. "Turns out I can do it today," he added. "Turns out that humanity is on the verge of immortality."

# 37

No one spoke for several long seconds.

Carr had received so many shocking revelations recently that he thought he had become numb to them, but once again, he had been mistaken.

"But allow me to back up," said Jordan. "I've gotten ahead of myself."

All three of his guests were still in partial shock and nodded woodenly for him to go on.

Jordan fixed his gaze on Riley, who had been decidedly chilly toward him since he had first entered the room. "Think whatever you want about me," he said to his daughter. "If you think I had a God complex, that my arrogance brought this on, I can't argue with you. Blame me for *everything* that happened. You should," he added, his self-loathing evident. "*I* certainly do."

He paused and his eyes became moist. "But you have to believe that I loved your mother," he said softly. "That I loved your brothers. That I still love you."

He wiped his eyes and gathered himself. "When I awakened after slamming my head into the door and realized the rod had hit, my first thought was suicide. But that would have left you fatherless. Yes, I knew I had to go into hiding and couldn't be there for you. And I knew that you'd *prefer* to be fatherless after what I had done. But at least I could watch over you from afar. Protect you. Help to make your life as good as it could be. You were my only remaining child," he finished as a single tear escaped his eye once again and rolled slowly down his cheek.

"That's why Mike O'Banion was so convinced you would die for her," said Carr. "Because you would."

"I would. A hundred times over, I would. I'd die a thousand times over if I could go back in time and change things so none of this ever happened." Jordan shook his head sadly. "But it *did* happen," he said, focusing once again on his daughter. "And I finally concluded that suicide would be the *easy* way out. Instead, I vowed to go on. Vowed to protect you. To someday bring your mother and brothers back to life."

Jordan's lip curled up in horror. "Removing their heads was the hardest thing I've ever done," he continued. "As you said, this wasn't Savant forcing my hand. This was *me*. The only reason I didn't vomit was because I had already heaved everything that was in my stomach onto a parking lot earlier that night.

"And as I raced away from Turlock, I made one last vow, the most important one of all. I vowed to protect humanity from ASI. If I could stop others who were attempting to bring computer intelligence into existence, stop them from making the same mistake I made, I could make partial amends for what I had done."

Carr wondered if Jordan's amends weren't more than partial. If Carr imagined there was a God watching over biological life, the Turlock tragedy might have been necessary to ensure the future of humanity.

Only a loss of life and devastation on this scale could have set a man like Jordan on the path of stopping all other ASI efforts. Had Turlock not happened in exactly the way it had, another effort might have already succeeded, but this time without a kinetic weapon and walls of graphene to prevent human extinction.

"So you decided to play God again," said Riley, allowing herself a wry smile, "but this time, only to prevent anyone *else* from playing God."

"I'm devoting my life to safeguarding a human future," said Jordan. "To preventing us from creating an evil god, or perhaps worse, one totally indifferent to our existence."

"And you've succeeded brilliantly," said Carr. "But how? How have you even *identified* so many secret ASI programs? I'd think just this would be impossible, let alone stopping them—even for someone with your skills and resources."

"You're right," said Jordan. "That's why I made sure I had help. After I left Turlock and established a secure base of operations, the first thing I did was create the ultimate computer assistant. Savant Light, if you will. A computer I call *Pock*. Short for *Apocalypse*. A name I chose to remind me of its potential for ill, and the need to keep it in a box." He sighed. "Not that I needed reminding."

"Savant Light?" said Bram.

"I still had the tablet computer I had taken from my lab. After I fled, I accessed its memory. It had recorded the optimal hardware configuration Savant had achieved. The one that was held steady throughout the final billions of generations of software evolution. I rebuilt the entire system with this configuration. I built it underground, and put it behind enough layers of graphene to stop a dozen ASIs.

"Then I added a series of regulators into the system, something I should have done the first time around. It was set up to come to a dead stop after every thousand software generations. I inched it toward sentience, conducting exhaustive testing at each stop, and halted its progress well short of consciousness."

"Just how smart *is* your computer?" asked Bram. "This . . . Pock?"

"Crazy smart. Much, much smarter than a human. But again, still not quite sentient. Still nothing more than an IBM Watson, although hundreds of times more capable."

"That doesn't worry you?" said Carr.

"Of course it worries me," said Jordan. "Thus the name Apocalypse. But it's buried underground, can't connect to the Web, and is surrounded by graphene. I'm the only one with access. And it's been invaluable. With its help, I've made advances I couldn't have made on my own in a hundred years."

Carr whistled. Given the advances Jordan had been able to make on his own in a fraction of that time, this was truly saying something. "So this explains how you've been so effective at crippling AGI efforts," he said.

"Yes. Pock has been able to come up with spyware and algorithms that let me easily identify these programs anywhere in the world, no matter how secret they think they're being. Spyware and algorithms government intelligence agencies would kill for. Along with various means of sabotage that are also extraordinary, generations ahead of the current state of the art."

"Tell me about it," mumbled Carr under his breath.

He had been sent to find and stop whoever was behind the sabotage. But this was when he thought it was being done to give one party a decisive advantage in the race to ASI, to help them become the dominant power on the globe. But if everything Jordan had said was true, how could he *not* switch allegiances? Instead of trying to *stop* Isaac Jordan, how could he not do everything in his power to *help* him?

"And this explains how you were able to perfect whole brain emulation so far ahead of schedule," said Riley.

"That's right. With Pock's help."

"And you're a hundred percent there?" she asked.

"Not a hundred percent. I still haven't solved wireless uploading. For the time being, anyone with nanites on board has to be backed up manually."

"Backed up?" said Carr. "Like you'd back up your computer? To make sure all changes are saved at the end of a session?"

"Right. If you died, we could use your last backup to bring you back to life. If you suffered from Alzheimer's, you could be restored using a backup taken *before* the disease struck. And this time your mind would never be corrupted."

Carr nodded. The possibilities were as astonishing as the philosophical implications were daunting.

"As I said," continued Jordan, "I'm still working on the seamless transfer of whole brain scans wirelessly, automatically, like a phone would do. But Pock and I have perfected everything else. An optical quantum computer that can perfectly emulate a human brain and fit inside a human skull. And a 3D printer that can spray individual cells so quickly and accurately, it can literally build a perfect copy of any human body in hours."

"Is that similar to bioprinting?" said Bram.

Jordan smiled. "Not similar," he said. "It *is* bioprinting. Just a lot more advanced. Current bioprinting technology can only create organs. It's gotten faster and more accurate, but hasn't advanced all that much since 2016, when scientists at Northwestern University managed to print mice ovaries that were indistinguishable from the real thing."

Riley nodded enthusiastically. "I remember reading about that when I was a kid," she said. "When they implanted these ovaries in host mice, the mice were able to conceive and give birth normally."

"It was an impressive success," confirmed Jordan. "Really energized the field. Still," he continued, "without Pock, what *I'm* able to do would still be a decade or more away."

Carr had a sudden realization. "When your body was found dead after a car accident," he said, "that was a bioprinted version of you, wasn't it?"

"Very good, Lieutenant. It was."

"Amazing," said Carr. "It was you down to its fingerprints and DNA."

"With all due modesty, Pock and I have managed some impressive feats."

Riley looked troubled. "I'm not sure how I feel about mind uploading," she said. "It's hard to believe it's not cheating nature. Hard to believe that the essence of what makes us human can really be transferred to a new host."

"Philosophers throughout the ages have wrestled with this question," said Jordan. "So have I. At considerable length."

"And what have you concluded?" asked Carr.

"I've come to think about it this way: If you replace a bad knee with an artificial one, no one doubts that you're still human. By the same token, your brain is made up of a hundred billion neurons. If you were to replace a single one of these with an artificial construct that functions identically to the one it replaces, no one would argue that you weren't still you."

"So the question you're getting to," said Bram, "is just *how much* of your brain can be replaced before you *aren't* you anymore?"

"Exactly. Are you suddenly non-human after replacing ten percent? Half? And what if the replacements were to happen gradually, over years of time, with a hundred percent of your neurons eventually being replaced by artificial ones performing the exact same duties? Wouldn't you still be human?"

"I'm not so sure you would be," said Carr.

Jordan smiled. "You actually just fell into a trap I set," he said. "Because this *already* happens, and you *already* accept it. You just don't realize it."

"In what way?" said Carr.

"Your cells are constantly dying and being replaced. It's a common belief that after seven years every single cell in your body is new. Now this may not be entirely true, but regardless, it's widely accepted that a large percentage of the cells that make up your body today are replacements, performing the same functions as the ones they replaced. And when it comes to atoms, the facts are completely unambiguous. Not a single one of the atoms currently in your body were there five years ago.

"I'm sure you would agree," continued Jordan, "that you're still the one and only Cameron Carr, even though most of the cells—and none of the atoms—that made up the Cameron Carr of five years ago still exist."

"Of course," said Carr. "And you're right, I had no idea this was the case. But what's going on with mind transference still feels different than this."

"Because it is," said Jordan. "Because the cells and atoms in your body aren't just functionally the same as the ones they replace, they're *physically* the same. Also, when this swapping out is a function of biological housekeeping, it's a gradual process. But what if, instead of taking five to ten years for all of your cells to be replaced, it only took *one* year? Would you still be you?"

Carr nodded.

"What about a month? Or a day? Or a second? You see where I'm heading. An argument could be made that having your brain die and an identical one instantly take its place is just an acceleration of this process. People have this false sense of the continuity of their consciousness, but sleep disrupts it every night."

"To say this is a lot to think about doesn't do it justice," said Carr.

"I guess the bottom line, in my view," said Jordan, "is that no matter how clever the argument, you believe one of two things. You either believe your soul, your essence, is inextricably tied into the gray matter you were born with, that it's part of your physicality, or you believe your mind is simply a pattern of impulses and potentials that can be duplicated."

Jordan took a sip of water while he let all of his guests ponder this last. "Regardless," he added, "it's certainly a brave new world we're facing here. Not easy to get your arms around."

Riley had been listening in rapt attention, and Carr wondered what a mind like hers was making of her father's arguments. "So did you do it?" she asked him. "Did you really bring Mom, Cole, and Noah back to life? Or at least some kind of soulless approximation?" she added, not ready to accept that the process worked as her father maintained.

"Not yet," he said with a sigh.

"Why not? I thought this was one of your vows."

"It was. The short answer is that I was weak and afraid. The same reason I didn't contact you before now."

"And the long answer?" asked his daughter.

Jordan hesitated. "Haven't I already given you enough to digest for one day?"

"More than enough," said Riley. "More than enough for one *lifetime*. But don't let that stop you," she persisted. "I want to hear everything."

# 38

Isaac Jordan took another long drink of water, draining the bottle entirely, and set it down on the pink marble table.

"At first I didn't bring back your mother and brothers because I wanted to be sure everything about the transference was perfect. At the start there were kinks to work out. Just because their bodies would be exact replicas, fashioned based on DNA samples I've kept, didn't mean they would be themselves. I had to make sure the quantum computer that would house their consciousness could precisely emulate a human brain, that every human neuron could be replaced with a computer node. And it isn't enough just to copy a brain, you have to emulate how a brain lays down new memories, reacts to hormones, and so on."

"How do you do that?" asked Bram.

"In the beginning, we wouldn't attempt the transference until the nanites had at least a few weeks to gather data. They're very sophisticated. They don't just take a snapshot of the state of the brain, they record how it reacts to stimuli. Not just how it lays down new memories and responds to hormones, but its state during moments of anger, arousal, laughter, and so on. Which provides us with plenty of data to get a very good handle on this. Then we did extensive experimentation to perfect the technique further."

"We?" said Riley.

"I still had access to hundreds of billions of dollars after I left Turlock," replied her father. "So I was able to build a shadow organization, with only a handful of people knowing who's in charge or what's really going on. My inner circle have all been vetted by an improved lie detector system that Pock came up with, so I'm sure of their loyalty. When my team was in place, we began recruiting volunteers. Lots of them. We finally stopped when we reached twelve hundred. We paid each of them two million dollars for a year of their time."

"Did they know what they were volunteering for?" asked Riley.

"For the most part. They didn't know that it was an exercise in putting the finishing touches on whole brain emulation, but they knew what they would be expected to do."

"Which was?" said Bram.

"Become subjects in a study designed to elucidate the human condition. Which was true."

"And you injected them with nanites?" said Riley.

Her father nodded.

"Without their knowledge?" she said disapprovingly.

Jordan sighed. "I'm afraid so," he admitted.

"Go on," she said. "What then?"

"We allowed the nanites to record data for fifteen days. Then we transferred a subject's consciousness into a brain-sized quantum computer, fitted inside a replica of his or her body, and checked to see how well the nanites had done."

"What do you mean?" asked Carr. "Checked to see if the brains were identical?"

"No. We already knew they were—at least at the start. We needed to confirm that if presented with identical stimuli going forward, the original and duplicate minds would *remain* identical, would change in the same ways. So we'd awaken the original volunteers and record their reactions to stimuli. We'd show them horrific or erotic photos. Puppies. Maggot-infested food. Politicians they hated. Then we'd repeat this with the copies."

Jordan paused to let this sink in. "If the original and copy didn't react *identically*, down to the blink of an eye and degree of arousal or disgust, we tweaked our nanites, algorithms, and emulation. Before long, we nailed it. We got it to the point where they matched every time. Now we don't even need the nanites to collect two weeks of data. We can inject them, expose the subject to various stimuli, and within an hour the nanites can collect enough data for a perfect transference. We've even become sophisticated enough to emulate mental fatigue and sleep."

Carr wasn't sure how he felt about this, but he couldn't help but admire how thorough Jordan had been.

"After this we advanced to the next phase," continued Jordan, "which is just wrapping up now. In this phase we *really* put the transference to the test. This allowed us to fine-tune our process to a remarkable degree. After the transfer, we kept the original and copy unconscious. We wanted them to remain identical until the experiment began. If just one were awake, they would be subject to stimulation the other one wasn't receiving, which would cause a slight divergence. A divergence that could distort our experimental results."

Jordan paused. "Any questions so far?" he asked.

"Yeah, a lot of them," said Carr dryly. "But keep going."

"With Pock's help, I came up with two tools that were of enormous value in our experiments. One, a perfect virtual reality system. And two, a way to erase precise memories. So we would awaken our subject, and later the copy, inside this VR world, and observe how each reacted across a wide variety of simulations. At a party. In a romantic setting. When their life was on the line. Many of the simulations were brutal, treacherous, but we did warn them that this might be the case."

"To what end?" said Carr.

"To satisfy ourselves that the original and duplicate were truly identical. If they were, and they were thrown into the exact same scenario, they should react identically. They should both respond to a given situation in the same way, using the same words. Make the exact same decisions. Shed tears at the exact same time."

"And this really happens?" said Bram incredulously.

"It does. The results are truly stunning. It's like the original and copy are both in a play and reading from the same script."

"So if you transferred my consciousness to a double and woke him up in this room," said Bram, "he would be saying exactly what I'm saying now? Using the exact same words?"

"That's right. As long as everyone else's dialog and actions were also the same. Which is why virtual reality is helpful, so we can make sure the other players stick precisely to their scripts."

"Stunning is the right word for it," admitted Riley.

Jordan looked pleased by these words from his daughter. "I would argue that if a copy and the original react the exact same way to all stimuli," he said, "then they *are* the same. If one is conscious and human, how can you not call the other conscious and human? In fact, if not for one having an optical, quantum brain, and one having squishy gray matter, there would be no way to tell them apart."

"Incredible," said Carr.

"You can still ask if the copies have souls," said Jordan. "This remains a valid question. But one that, as far as I can tell, is forever unknowable. What I do know is that they are identical in every response. Indistinguishable. And while I can't rule out a soul, if its presence has no effect on a man, doesn't change a single response, doesn't change his level of compassion or the way he hates, or loves, or laughs, I would say it's meaningless."

Carr knitted his brow in thought. There may have been a solid counterargument to this assertion, but he couldn't think of one at the moment.

"And as a bonus," continued Jordan, "we've gained unprecedented insight into the human condition. We've learned what makes a human a human. We've been able to study the sex drive, addiction, compassion, cruelty, self-interest, remorse, joy, and so on, more completely than ever before."

"So you must have considered the next obvious step," said Riley. "Have you already gone down that road?"

Carr raised his hand. "Again, for the slow learners in the class, what next obvious step are you talking about?"

"She's talking about improvements," replied Jordan. "We can now transfer your consciousness into a new Cameron Carr at the time of your death. One indistinguishable from you. But we have the power to further tweak this one. Make it *better* than you. Cameron Carr two point oh. Physically, mentally, and emotionally. So far we've made perfect copies of the bodies of our subjects, including the imperfections. Same age and same scars. Same male pattern baldness and beer bellies."

"Really?" said Carr with a smile. "You couldn't even ditch the beer bellies?"

Jordan shook his head. "For them to react the same, they had to *be* the same. If one woke up young, vigorous, and slim, basically a younger, fitter version of themselves, this would throw off their reactions, screw up every experiment."

"Of course," said Carr, serious once more.

"The key point is that we'll be able to put people into younger versions of themselves when they die."

"Which means you'll have people killing themselves right and left to get younger bodies," pointed out Bram. "Provided they believe your process represents a true reincarnation."

"Yes, this is yet another wrinkle to think about. And most *will* come to accept the process as a true reincarnation. They'll recognize their friends and loved ones who undergo transfer as undeniably the same people, with the same memories and personalities acquired over a long lifetime, just in new, shiny packages."

"And youth might be just the start of the enhancements you could introduce," said Carr.

"Right. For Cameron Carr two point oh, we could increase your general level of happiness. Or eliminate all emotions. Or curb your addiction to caffeine, or cigarettes, or alcohol, or gambling. You get the idea."

"Yes, but isn't there a good chance some of these supposed improvements will backfire?" said Carr.

"More like a certainty," said Jordan. "This is the danger. Take the sex drive, something we've been studying with particular interest. It evolved along with us, and so much of our society, our culture, and our behavior stems from this primal compulsion. There are men who report feeling free for the first time in their adult lives when they finally reach the age at which this drive wanes. Free of craving sex, free of the need for frequent orgasms. To them it's a blessing. But what effect would it have on men if this drive was ratcheted down in their prime, or removed altogether? Is our motivation to succeed in any way tied to the interest and need for sexual intimacy? To our obsession with attracting a mate, with demonstrating our fitness as a partner the same way a peacock might display its plumage? We know testosterone can lead to violence and aggression. But is all aggression a bad thing? Would its removal make us too sheep-like?"

"Have you actually tried this?" asked Bram.

"I haven't. Given the limits of our current understanding, it's too dangerous a game to play. Humans are a complex tapestry of traits that evolved together, with uncertain interconnections. Does stripping us of our capacity for anger also strip us of our passion? Even changes that seem like they could only be good, like perfect memory, could have negative, unintended consequences."

"And how many changes can be made before we're no longer human?" said Riley.

"That is also something to keep firmly in mind," said her father. "I think of it this way: if the goal was a pure mind without any warts, a perfect, emotionless intelligence, we could just recreate Savant."

"There is one aspect of the human condition that mind transference can't help but change," said Riley, "even if you don't tinker with the original at all." She raised her eyebrows. "Our knowledge of our own mortality. Death has always been the ultimate motivator, the ultimate deadline. If we know we have an eternity to operate within, does that drain our ambition? If fear of death is out of the equation, what effect does this have on our behavior?"

Jordan looked delighted. "An impressive insight, Riley," he said proudly. "It took me a lot longer than it took you to get there. And another great question, worthy of further study."

"My head is really beginning to hurt," said Carr wryly.

"And we're only scratching the surface," replied Jordan. "You could transfer your consciousness into an artificial body and be truly indestructible. Without the need to breathe, some of us could live in the ocean. We could adapt ourselves to life on other planets. Our body could even become a submarine or a starship."

"Not to mention you could make improvements in the mind itself," said Bram. "Improving memory, as you mentioned. Or increasing our mental clock speed. And I could offer many other possibilities."

Jordan nodded. "There are, of course, significant issues with this kind of tampering, as well. Take clock speed. We can't seem to modulate it. Once it's sped up, it's sped up for good, and at the fastest rate possible, which doesn't really work, for reasons I can go into later. It also prevents the emulation of sleep. But the point you're making is a good one: the options truly are endless."

"Yet your VR system gives you the perfect means to sort through these options," said Riley. "You've already gathered huge amounts of data on the human condition. Which gives you a robust baseline, and allows you to rigorously test the effect of a change. Figure out the optimal way to make improvements."

"Yes, but optimal is subjective, as you well know. My idea of optimal might be quite different from yours." He raised his eyebrows. "So I think you raised this point to test me, Riley. To see if I'm still arrogant enough to make myself the arbiter of where we go from here."

"Are you?" she asked.

Jordan smiled. "Not at the moment, at least, no. I just want to preserve humanity the way it is now. And immortality would be a nice bonus. But my first goal isn't to change or improve us, just preserve us. Maybe someday, when enough data is gathered, further experiments can be tried. But that day is far off. Right now, my goal is to continue to gather data and try to perfect a wireless backup system, so a person can be reanimated exactly as they were at the moment of their biological death."

"So you've ruled out having two or more copies of the same person at the same time?" said Bram.

"Before you answer that," said Riley, "can we return to my original question? Now that you're convinced your procedure is flawless, why haven't you brought Mom and my brothers back yet? Your short answer was that you're weak and afraid. Afraid of what?"

Her father blew out a heavy sigh. "I guess I'm afraid of how they'll react to their new reality. I have a memory of killing them. Beheading them. Even though I know they died in their sleep, I somehow imagine they'll know this. They'll remember, too. Even if they don't, they'll eventually see the public footage online.

"And I'll have to tell them what happened," he continued, looking sick at the prospect. "Right now, I think of them as being in stasis. Frozen in time as the people they were just before the events of that night. These people loved and respected me. They had amazing lives ahead of them."

Jordan shook his head despondently. "But the moment I bring them back, they have to face a new reality. They'll awaken to learn that what seems like yesterday to them was eight years ago. That everything they cared about has been taken from them. By *my* actions. That I'm now widely despised, thought dead, and in hiding. That their friends and lives are gone. That they're thought dead, also, and for good reason."

Riley nodded solemnly, as if sharing their pain.

"And I know how people react when they find out their consciousness is an emulation," continued her father. "We've tested this as part of our experiments. First it's disbelief. They are certain they are in their original bodies and this is some kind of horrible joke. But when it's proven to them, there can be an . . . adjustment period. It can take some time to cope with this, emotionally and intellectually."

Carr could well imagine.

"And how would your mother react?" he said to Riley. "What if she disagrees with what I'm doing now? What if she can't forgive me? She'd want to know about you, for certain. And if I told her I thought it was best for you psychologically to take on a new identity and to continue to believe I'm dead for the time being, she'd be outraged. She'd insist on seeing you."

Jordan paused to let this sink in. "But just so you know, Riley," he said softly, "I had planned on revealing myself to you later this year. Volkov just accelerated this timetable. I had decided it was time to contact you and confess what had happened. I hoped you would find a way to forgive me and to join me. But either way, it was time to stop being selfish. Time to live up to my vow, put my pathetic personal fears aside, and bring them back. "

There was silence in the room as Riley lowered her head in thought. "Thank you for your honesty," she said after almost a minute had passed. "I know this wasn't easy to admit," she added, using a tone that suggested her attitude toward her father might be thawing. "I'm not sure how I feel. About any of this. Too much has happened too quickly for me to be able to sort through it all."

She took a deep breath. "So let's move forward. You were saying your goal was to only complete a transfer at the moment of death. David had asked if this meant you had ruled out creating two or more copies of the same person. Have you?"

Jordan gathered himself. "Yes," he said finally, obviously finding it hard to return to the conversation after his heartfelt confession. "Absolutely. I've opened enough ethical and philosophical cans of worms already. This would be perhaps the biggest of them all."

"It would be the ultimate mess," agreed Riley, who seemed to be relieved to get back to wrestling with abstract concepts rather than with messy emotions she couldn't begin to understand. "If there were ten of me," she continued, "each would want to be with David Bram, and I'm sure I wouldn't want to share—even with myself. The legal system would be in a shambles. Who would get ownership of the original's assets? We could talk about the complexities of this all day long."

"Which is the very reason my goal is to keep this as simple as possible," said Jordan. "I've instituted two simple rules. One, no transfer of consciousness without death, ensuring that each of us gain immortality, not multiplicity. And two, identical copies only. No one gets a version two point oh. Again, right now it's about preservation, not improvement."

Carr rubbed the back of his neck. "But haven't you already made copies of more than a thousand people for your experiments?" he asked. "So you've already created a thorny situation. You can't return both a volunteer and a copy back to the volunteer's old life. So how have you handled this?"

Jordan winced. "Good question," he said unhappily.

# 39

Riley looked ill. "Did you . . . kill them?" she asked, her expression indicating she was afraid of the answer she might get.

"Kill?" said her father, arching an eyebrow. "Does this mean you're beginning to see the duplicates as human? If you thought of them as nothing but lifeless computers, you'd have used the word *destroy*." He paused. "And if I did kill them, would you see this as murder?"

"You tell me you've created a quantum computer that houses human consciousness," said Riley. "Having no experience with copies, I can't judge if they're human or not. But I know *you* think they are. Just minutes ago you made the argument that if a copy and original react the same way to every possible situation, are indistinguishable based on personality and behavior, then they're the same. I believe your exact words were on the order of, "If one is conscious and human, how can you not call the other conscious and human?"

"Even so," said Jordan, "this doesn't necessarily mean that killing the copy is murder. It's another complex situation that nothing in human history has prepared us to deal with. One could argue that nature intended that our consciousness be unique. So if I ended a *unique* consciousness, this would be murder. No question about it.

"But suppose I had a copy of David's neural patterns and sparked his consciousness to life within a duplicate brain and body, with all of his memories. Suppose I then destroyed this duplicate David, a millionth of a second after I created it. So the birth and death of this new David was nearly simultaneous. You could argue I killed a living thing and this is murder. But you might also argue that it isn't. I created this copy, and since its destruction hasn't affected David in any way, his unique pattern hasn't been lost to the universe."

Jordan paused. "Or think of it this way: If you wrote a novel and I deleted it, I murdered your novel. But if I made a copy and then deleted the copy, your novel still lives."

"By that measure," said Bram, "if you made a copy and deleted the original, the same would apply. You still haven't murdered my novel."

"Yes," said Jordan. "Either way. As long as one remains, you could argue that eliminating redundant copies isn't murder."

"I'm not sure the redundant copies would agree with that," said Bram.

"Even so, it's potentially a valid argument. I'm not saying it's one I necessarily support, but it *is* one that can be made."

"One that you'd *need* to make if you were trying to justify killing the copies," said Riley. "And despite your clever mental gymnastics, you still haven't answered my question. Did you kill them or not?"

"Not exactly," said Jordan.

"Not exactly?" repeated Riley.

"At the end of one year of testing, I did have my people kill their bodies. Bodies that I can create again at any time. But I didn't destroy the quantum computer embedded with their patterns, what I call their E-brain, or emulated brain. E-brains are designed to retain the pattern, the emulation, even when disconnected from a body. But the pattern, the consciousness, becomes frozen in time. Think of it as entering sleep mode. I can bring this consciousness back to life at any time by reinserting it into a body."

Riley shook her head. "Freezing their brains is the same thing as killing them."

"Not at all," said Jordan emphatically. "Do you die when you're asleep? After all, you're no longer conscious. In fact, that's one way to think of the transference. You're used to your consciousness dying each night, and then springing back to life each morning when you awaken. With transference, the same thing happens, only you reawaken in a new body."

"But you have no intention of *ever* reawakening them," said Riley. "Are you honestly trying to claim there's a meaningful difference between a sleep that you never awaken from and death?"

Carr was intrigued by the intellectual clashes between Riley and her father. It wasn't surprising that she continued to challenge him, not given the hatred she had built up over the past eight years. What Carr found astonishing, however, was that she was proving to be the man's *equal*.

"Yeah," said Jordan sheepishly, "I guess I should have made myself clearer. I actually do plan to awaken them. I have some other goals I'm working toward, and they could fit in beautifully."

"Other goals?" said Carr dryly. "I'm almost afraid to ask."

"I'm devoting my life to protecting the future of the human race. The key ingredient in this task is to make sure we spread well beyond the solar system."

"In case Earth gets hit by a meteor?" said Carr.

"Yes, but extinction through natural disaster is the least of our worries. Self-destruction is the greater possibility. We're our own worst enemy. We've made a start at surviving an extinction level event on Earth by colonizing the Moon and Mars, but the solar system is still a tiny island in an infinite sea of empty space. We need to cross that sea."

He paused. "Are any of you familiar with something called the Fermi Paradox?"

Bram shook his head no and Riley didn't respond. Carr had a suspicion that she knew what this was, but didn't want to show up her boyfriend too many times. "I guess not," replied Carr, speaking for the three of them.

"It's named after the Nobel-Prize-winning physicist, Enrico Fermi," explained Jordan. "A man so brilliant he was almost in a class by himself. One day, in the early nineteen fifties, he and some colleagues were discussing the likelihood of intelligent alien life. Fermi made a simple but profound argument. If intelligent life existed, he asked, then where *was* everyone?"

Carr shrugged. "The universe is a big place, as you said. Isn't this a needle in a haystack problem?"

Jordan smiled. "It is," he replied. "But it *shouldn't* be. The universe has been around for fourteen billion years. In the grand scheme of things, we've been around for a millisecond. If intelligent life was common, it should have arisen all throughout the history of the universe, on planets that came into existence long before Earth. It should have arisen billions of years ago. And once it arose, technology would arise with it, in just another millisecond on the cosmological time scale.

"*Homo sapiens* have been around for only about two hundred thousand years," continued Jordan, "and look at the technology we've developed. Even assuming a species could only spread outward from their home planet at a tiny fraction of the speed of light, advanced alien civilizations should have arisen so long ago that the Milky Way should be *teeming* with intelligent life. Our local neighborhood should have been extensively colonized already by one or more species. Cosmological evidence of their existence should be everywhere. This shouldn't be like finding a needle in a haystack. It should be like finding evidence of human life in Times Square."

"Unless the emergence of intelligent life on Earth was a unique event in the cosmos, after all," said Bram.

"That's one possibility," said Jordan. "Entire books of possible explanations have been written. But another obvious one is that sentience has, indeed, arisen on countless planets. But that for a sentient species to emerge, it must have evolved in a highly dangerous, competitive environment, one harboring such fierce predators that keen intelligence and ruthlessness were required for survival. So all sentient species turn out more or less alike. Aggressive, tribal, and warlike. And they all reach a stage at which they can destroy themselves with their technology. And they do. Every time. Like children who've been given loaded guns to play with."

"With one of these guns being ASI," said Riley.

"That's right. Not that there aren't many others to choose from. Bio agents, nuclear warfare, and so on. But given my own personal experience, ASI seems to be the biggest threat of all. By creating Savant, I, myself, could have brought about humanity's extinction. If this had happened, a future civilization arising on a planet a thousand light years away might develop their own version of the Fermi Paradox, wondering why there were no signs of intelligent life coming from our neck of the woods."

"Having no idea that we had come and gone," said Bram.

"Like possibly thousands or millions of other civilizations throughout the galaxy," said Jordan.

"But if ASI is a fairly common cause for the destruction of biological civilizations," said Bram, "shouldn't we see evidence of scores of these machine intelligences?"

"Yes," said Jordan. "But, as I know better than anyone else, they don't necessarily think like us. They may not be interested in territorial expansion. They may be operating on another plane we can't perceive. Or maybe we're searching in all the wrong places. We're looking for environments conducive to biological life. But maybe ASIs like to hang out in more energy-rich environments. Near neutron stars or black holes. In the very center of the galaxy, which is jam-packed with stars, many, many times more than are in underpopulated arms like ours.

"Regardless of the explanation, we could be in a position to be the first species to spread ourselves across the galaxy *before* we self-destruct. We can ensure that intelligent biological life never goes extinct, and ultimately fills the universe. Even if it takes millions or billions of years."

"And this ties in to your vision of what to do with your many sleeping human emulations?" asked Bram.

"It does," replied Jordan. "They can be at the vanguard of this effort. I'm setting up an underground facility to manufacture a fleet of R-Drive capable ships. Much smaller and lighter versions of the ones I originally developed, which also means much faster."

"Let me guess," said Riley, "you plan to load a number of E-brains, in sleep mode, onto each of these ships and send them on a hundred-, thousand-, or million-year journey to seek out habitable planets."

"Yes!" gushed Jordan enthusiastically. "Exactly. Guided by supercomputers that are loaded with all human knowledge, which they can later draw upon. When such a planet is found, the craft lands, and an automated system activates a 3D body printer, printing the bodies that go with each E-brain. Automated systems reunite the brains and bodies. The ships would have extensive raw materials in their cargo bays, along with a diverse collection of human sperm and eggs, for in-vitro fertilization. The reconstituted crew would go on to become caretakers of a fledgling generation of purely biological humanity."

"And when these colonists grow old and die," said Riley, "the technology will be in place to transfer their consciousness to new bodies, ensuring the colony continues to grow and thrive."

"Yes. We would include a seed bank for crops," continued Jordan. "And, of course, we wouldn't neglect man's best friend," he added, smiling lovingly at his daughter. "Banks of canine sperm and eggs from every breed would be included as well."

Riley nodded, but didn't comment.

"I'm setting all of this in motion from off stage," said Jordan. "Currently, I'm working toward automating the R-Drive factory. I anticipate I'll be able to build ten or fifteen thousand of these seed-ships within a decade."

"But you only have twelve hundred E-brains," pointed out Carr.

"He can make as many additional copies of each as he'd like," said Riley. "His prohibition against multiple copies doesn't apply when they're separated by distances that would take thousands of years to cross."

Carr nodded. He continued to feel stupid on a regular basis.

"Thirty-five of the twelve hundred subjects we've tested are especially well-suited for this mission," said Jordan. "Great natural leaders who have shown themselves to be especially intelligent, ethical, brave, decisive, and so on. Some combination of these thirty-five will be on every ship. They will be copied multiple times. About seven hundred of the remaining eleven hundred sixty-five subjects will be passengers, one on each of seven hundred ships."

"Why not all of the subjects?" asked Carr.

"If you knew the results of our testing, you wouldn't have to ask. We didn't just select subjects we thought were angels. We chose a broad and diverse sample. Almost a third were selected because they had exhibited qualities that could best be termed as . . . antisocial. Cruelty, deceit, violence, hostility, crime. You don't study the human condition by only selecting exemplary humans."

"I see," said Carr. "Not the kind of minds you want to spread to other planets."

"That's right," said Jordan. "But these E-brains won't be . . . killed, either. I'll elaborate on that in a minute. But when a ship finds a habitable planet, it will land, and the crews will be revived as already described. Remember, even if a million years have passed since the ship left Earth, they'll awaken as if no time has passed at all. Then, a computer will explain their situation, and the historic contributions they'll be making to ensure human immortality."

"What if this is too much for them to absorb?" said Bram.

"It won't be," said Jordan. "I tested out various approaches to bringing these thirty-five subjects up to speed in a virtual reality simulation. I got to gauge how they would react, erase their memory, and try again. Now I know the perfect way to proceed."

Carr was reminded of an old movie he had once seen called *Groundhog Day*, in which a man relived the same day over and over again until he managed to get it exactly right.

"Did your future crew members have a choice in the matter?" asked Riley. "Or were they just manipulated beyond their wildest imaginings in your simulations?"

"I disclosed everything to them in virtual reality and they each agreed. Not that they'll remember. As far as some minor manipulation to lessen the negative psychological impact they'll experience after awakening on a distant planet, I make no apologies for this. These thirty-five will be the most important people to ever live, instrumental in seeding the galaxy with biological human life, forever ensuring human existence."

Jordan paused, looking exhausted from reliving Turlock and his extended revelations, and also somewhat relieved to finally be through them. "So that's my plan for humanity to conquer the galaxy," he said. "What do you think?"

Riley studied her father for several long seconds. "I know I've been hard on you," she said finally. "And while some of this seems horrific to me, I have to admit that your vision does have a certain appeal."

"Sure it does," said Bram, rolling his eyes. "But mostly because of the dog part, right?"

Riley grinned. "Well, yeah. At least there would be one species on the ships worthy of spreading throughout the galaxy."

# 40

Jordan took a deep breath. "So that's everything," he said. "I've laid all of my cards on the table. I've made horrific mistakes, and I've played God, as Riley would say. I've caused incalculable misery, not the least of which was suffered by my own daughter. I just hope you can understand why events happened the way they did, and agree with me that ASI is too dangerous to ever let loose."

"One last thing," said Carr. "What about the other test subjects whose bodies you killed? The psychopaths you don't want to send into the galaxy? You said you had a plan for their E-brains that didn't involve eternal sleep."

"Yes. We'll awaken them in a virtual world. Which I expect to be fully perfected within ten years."

"Isn't the going theory that we're *already* in a virtual world?" said Bram. "A simulation constructed by some advanced future humanity?"

"That is the most likely possibility," said Jordan. "But I think we have no choice but to live our lives as though this isn't the case. *Strive* like it isn't the case."

He stared off at the waterfall for several seconds, as though taking continued inspiration from it. "With any luck," he said, "humanity will conquer true interstellar travel over the next few hundred years, faster-than-light travel, obsoleting these seed ships. Regardless, in a few million years, at most, humanity will have conquered every habitable planet in the Milky Way and number in the trillions."

Riley shook her head in wonder. "I'm still not sure how I feel about you," she said, "but no one can say that you don't think big. You continue to come up with ridiculous, impossible visions, and then find a way to turn them into reality."

Jordan simply nodded in acknowledgment, but it was clear how much these words meant to him.

Carr thought back to when he had first heard Jordan's voice in his headphones, inside a helicopter that had carried them away from the church. As he began to lose consciousness seconds later, he could never have imagined that things would play out as they had.

Jordan had begun the day as a crazed mass murderer and a man dedicated to stopping human progress. And now, he had done a credible job of convincing a hostile audience that he might just be mankind's greatest visionary, and ultimately, its savior.

"As I said at the start," continued Jordan. "I'd love for all of you to join me. Riley, my hope is for you to meet some of my experimental volunteers and their doppelgängers. Once you see that you can't tell the difference between them, I think you'll come to view this as the miracle it is. When that happens, I'm ready to bring your mother and brothers back."

Riley wore an unreadable expression and didn't reply.

"And I can't tell you how much I could use a mind as powerful as yours," Jordan said to his daughter. "And yours, too, of course," he added hastily, nodding at David Bram.

Bram made a face. "Don't worry. I've met your daughter. I know exactly where I rank in the scheme of things."

The hint of a smile crossed Jordan's face. "And Lieutenant Carr, you'd be the perfect man to lead my security team. The backgrounds and abilities of the men I've recruited are truly extraordinary, but none can match yours. I can't tell you how much I'd rather have you working *for* me than *against* me. And as part of the inner circle, you would bring your own fresh perspective. You'd have a hand in guiding our efforts."

"I'd certainly have to consider it," said Carr, "but I'd want to know—"

"Please," said Jordan, interrupting, "don't answer now. I have some things I need to attend to. And I've given you enough food for thought to last a lifetime. I'd like the three of you to take your time to really think this through. Digest everything I've said."

"How long will you be gone?" asked Riley.

"Actually, I need to stay. But I have a helicopter pilot waiting outside to fly you to a private mansion, a few hundred miles from here. It's beautiful. Has a fully stocked liquor cabinet, a heated pool and spa, the works. So spend a day and night there. Relax. Ponder what I've told you, and my offer to join our efforts. Talk it through. I promise that any conversations you have will be fully private. When you're ready tomorrow, I'll have you flown back here and we can reconvene." He paused. "Is that acceptable?"

His three guests exchanged glances. "Yes," said Riley for the small group.

"Great," said Jordan.

"I assume I won't be able to just waltz out of there if the spirit moves me," said Carr.

"No," said Jordan. "Sorry about that. But I can't leave you on your own recognizance just yet. Whether you join me or not, I'd prefer you not provide a full debriefing to Dwyer. You can appreciate how much care I've taken to stay off the grid. Unfortunately, I can't give Riley or David their freedom yet, either, for the same reason. The exact same automated security that watches over this facility watches over that one. And there are two guards, also like here."

"Is that all?" said Carr wryly.

"Not quite," said Jordan with a smile. "All Wi-Fi and other signals will be suppressed inside, just in case you're somehow able to acquire a cell phone."

"That about covers it," said Carr.

"One last thing," added Jordan. "When the three of you return, regardless of your decision, I'd like to get scans and backup copies of your minds. You know, just in case . . ."

"So when I die you don't have to decapitate me?" said Riley.

Jordan winced. "Periodic backups make a lot of sense," he said, pretending to ignore his daughter's comment.

"Where is this done?" asked Carr.

"Basically right under our feet. The building we're in now is my private sanctuary when I visit here, and I'm the only one with access. But there's a smaller, hexagonal building you'll pass on the way to the helicopter. Inside is my private elevator, which leads to an underground facility that is quite extensive. This is where we housed the twelve hundred subjects, and where we keep banks of bioprinters, quantum brains, and so on."

This location was unexpected, but the fact that Jordan's vast experimental compound was all underground was not. In fact, Carr realized, he should have predicted it. Even before Isaac Jordan arrived on the scene, Elon Musk had made great strides in dramatically improving tunneling technology, with the goal of relieving traffic and creating inexpensive underground cities. When Jordan began to mine asteroids, he improved this technology even further.

"Now that we've finished testing all but about ninety of the twelve hundred subjects," continued Jordan, "the facility is a bit of a ghost town. These ninety still live here, along with about forty researchers from my study team. Only a few of my team are now needed to conduct testing. The others work on analyzing and writing up the data."

"I assume this is also where you store the sleeping E-brains you removed?" said Riley.

"Yes. The data that comprises their consciousness is also saved in this facility, so we can create enough additional copies of the chosen thirty-five to have a number of them on every mission."

"Sounds like a remarkable facility," said Carr.

"I think so," said Jordan. "I hope you'll let me give you a tour. I've worked hard to make it as aesthetically appealing as it is scientifically appealing."

"And if we decline your offer?" said the lieutenant.

"As I've said, I'll just erase your memories of the past few days, and you can go back to your lives."

Jordan removed a phone from his pocket and his hands danced over the screen. "I just texted a new associate of mine to come here to escort you to the helicopter. A woman named Trish Casner."

"I assume you have ample security to collect us if we choose to ditch her," said Carr.

"I'm afraid so," said Jordan. "But why would you ever want to do that?" he added with a smile. "Anyway, Trish will be joining you at the mansion, but will give you your privacy. If you need anything at all while you're there, just ask her, and she'll make sure you have it. And she'll be happy to answer any questions you have for her."

"Who is she?" asked Carr.

"She was an experimental subject whose year term ended just recently. I was impressed with her and asked her to join my team—which she accepted."

"Does she know . . . everything?" asked Riley.

"She does. She knows I loaded nanites in her skull without her knowledge. And that we uploaded her consciousness into a duplicate. She also knows that another close colleague of mine who was assigned to her case, a man named John Brennan, administered a lethal injection to her duplicate."

"And she wasn't furious?" asked Riley. "At minimum, I'd expect her to feel violated that you put nanites in her body without permission."

"She *was* furious. And she *did* feel violated," acknowledged Jordan. "But when I laid out for her what I just did for you, and more, she was able to forgive me. She came to appreciate the value of what I've been trying to accomplish."

Less than a minute later the woman in question joined them and introduced herself, and they prepared to leave.

Carr locked his gaze on Isaac Jordan. "I'd like to have five or ten minutes with you in private," he said. "Why don't you let Trish escort Riley and David to the helo, and we can talk. When we're done, Trish can come back and escort me separately."

"What is this about?"

Carr motioned Jordan forward and leaned in to whisper in his ear.

When he was done, Jordan's eyes narrowed. "Perhaps a private conversation would be worthwhile, at that," he said.

Isaac Jordan turned to appraise his daughter one final time before she left, barely able to contain powerful emotions that threatened to bring tears once again. "I need you to know that I've never stopped caring about you," he told her. "No matter what happens from here on out, no matter what you decide, I love you more than you could possibly know. And I couldn't be prouder of the fine young woman you've become, despite what you had to endure because of me."

Riley simply nodded her acknowledgment of this and gestured for Trish Casner to lead the way to their aircraft.

*Interesting*, thought Cameron Carr. When Jordan had told his daughter how much he had missed her at the start of the meeting, she had basically responded by telling him she had danced on his grave.

So while her response to this last would seem decidedly chilly to an uninformed bystander, Carr knew just how much progress toward reconciliation Isaac Jordan had truly made.

# PART 6
## Deception

# 41

Volkov waited calmly in a large Ford Premaro, an SUV that had been winning off-road competitions since its introduction in 2026. The windows were tinted to the maximum degree allowed by Colorado law, which was on the liberal side in this respect, a surprise to no one aware of the state's early legalization of marijuana many years earlier.

The major was alone in the vehicle, which was parked behind an abandoned warehouse and a rusty overhang that would protect him from any prying eyes in the sky. Not that he didn't have every confidence he had remained off the grid since losing his tail on his way to Utah.

The Premaro was all electric, so along with being whisper quiet, it offered a spacious storage compartment under the hood where a gasoline engine would otherwise have been. After Tesla had dubbed this storage space a *frunk* years earlier—short for *front trunk*—this name had come into widespread use. Volkov had a gray rucksack beside him in the vehicle and had earlier locked away two duffels in the frunk, both considerably larger than his ruck and packed with tech and other military gear that would be essential for their upcoming mission.

Before he arrived at the safe house in Utah, the major had activated two additional men already in the States, making eight total that he and Greshnev could now wield as needed. He would have liked to have even greater numbers, but ten would have to do, and Anton Orlov, the head of the GRU, had already read him the riot act.

As pleased as Orlov was by Volkov's discovery that Isaac Jordan was alive and behind the ASI sabotage, eight men had been compromised at the church, and Volkov was now risking the covers of eight more, potentially decimating Russia's human intelligence in the Western half of the US.

Volkov couldn't have cared any less. Orlov wasn't fully grasping the game-changing implications of what he was about to accomplish. The major was about to score his greatest success, bag the biggest game he had ever hunted in his storied career, assuring a glorious future for his homeland.

Volkov's triumph would single-handedly bring Russia back to the dominance and world position it deserved. Its power would soon soar above all other nations, including the insufferable, self-satisfied United States, and it would enjoy a global dominance undreamed of even when the USSR had been at its zenith. All other nations would become little more than handmaidens, obeying Russia's every whim for fear of suffering its wrath.

Volkov was jarred from this powerful vision by the voice of one of the agents he had recently activated, Pavel Safin. "We're pulling around now, Major," he heard through the comm in his ear.

"Roger that," said Volkov.

Two minutes later a small sedan pulled alongside the SUV and parked. Safin and another new arrival, Yakov Urinson, exited the vehicle and escorted their guest, Dr. John B. Brennan, over to the SUV. Urinson immediately took the driver's seat, while Safin stuffed all six foot three of the towering scientist into the second row, sandwiching Brennan between himself and Volkov.

"Welcome, Dr. Brennan," said Volkov, extending a hand to the man now sitting beside him.

"What the hell was that all about?" thundered Brennan, making no move to shake Volkov's hand. Even flushed with rage, his face was shaped in such a way that it couldn't help but look friendly. "I've had proctology exams that were less intrusive!"

"I told you I wasn't a trusting man," said Volkov calmly. "You didn't think I would just meet you and make myself vulnerable to an ambush?"

"You chose the meeting time and place!" said Brennan, "to make *sure* I couldn't surprise you."

"I haven't survived in a deadly business by underestimating potential threats," said Volkov. "Or potential adversaries."

Volkov had little doubt that Brennan would be clean, but Safin and Urinson had been very thorough in confirming this was the case, anyway, using sensors and more primitive means. Not that Jordan couldn't have come up with undetectable innovations, but Volkov had reasons of his own for being confident that Brennan wasn't planning an ambush. The strip-search and full body cavity exam he had ordered his men to put Brennan through was more for show than anything else, although not entirely. Volkov was too careful to discount the possibility that he had misjudged the situation, no matter how remote the chances.

After Brennan's ire over his mistreatment subsided, he provided coordinates for the location of Jordan's retreat, nestled against a heavily wooded mountain twenty miles distant, and they set off immediately. When Urinson jerked the SUV onto a main road seconds later, their new ally winced in pain.

"Surely my men weren't that rough," said Volkov.

"I have a dodgy back that's acting up," said Brennan miserably. "And, yes, your men *were* that rough. The least they could have done was bought me dinner first."

Volkov laughed. "When Jordan is dead, *then* we'll buy you dinner."

"Your men confiscated my tablet computer," said the scientist. "I'm going to need that to disarm security."

"I assume you can use any computer for this, correct?"

Brennan thought about this for a moment. "I suppose so," he admitted.

"Good. Then I'll make sure you have one when you need it."

"By the way," said Brennan, "where is Sergei Greshnev? Isn't he your second-in-command?"

"Your knowledge is impressive, Dr. Brennan," said the major. "But Sergei won't be joining us on this mission. He has errands of his own to attend to. But I'm sure he'll be gratified to know that he was missed."

"So only three of you?" said the scientist, unimpressed.

Volkov shot him an icy glare. "If you're on the level, if you really do want Jordan dead and can negate his security, three will be plenty. If not, I suspect twenty men wouldn't be enough."

They drove the rest of the way in silence, coming to the base of a mountain and working their way deeper into untamed territory and a higher altitude. Brennan directed them to an off-road path through trees and brush that Jordan's people had created, one that was well hidden so that few would stumble upon it by accident.

Brennan called a stop. "The guards carpool to this site, and park in a clearing over there," he said, directing their attention a hundred yards to the north. "They use the same SUV as the one we're in," he added, which made sense, since he had advised them that this vehicle performed particularly well over the terrain they would encounter.

Volkov removed a small drone from his rucksack, one that was so perfectly modeled after an American tree sparrow that the greatest risk to its continued operation was that an *actual* sparrow might try to mate with it. It possessed a sophisticated AI for a brain, and was largely autonomous once in flight, responding to Volkov's voice commands.

He launched it northward, and within minutes it was above the guards' SUV. The major directed the small feathered drone to land on a branch near the top of a tall tree nearby, where it continued to send footage of the SUV and its immediate surroundings back to Volkov's phone.

The major nodded at Pavel Safin, who exited their vehicle without a word and removed a massive nylon duffel bag from the frunk, military grade, covered by a green-and-brown forest camouflage pattern. He took a moment to survey the route north and began to work his way in this direction, rapidly but carefully.

"Where's he going?" said Brennan. "Won't your drone be able to tell when the guards pull out?"

"It will," replied the major. "But Pavel will follow them on foot for as long as he can. Once he's lost them, he'll set up a camera keyed to their faces and vehicle. This way, we can make sure they don't double back. If they do, the camera will send an alert to my comm."

"Why do I get the feeling that you still don't trust me?"

"Because I don't," said Volkov simply.

The Russian leader ordered Urinson to drive off the cleared path, a much sterner test of the Ford's off-road capabilities. They plowed over rough terrain, giving the guards' vehicle a wide berth, while their own vehicle collected an assortment of nicks and scratches from tree branches and brush that stubbornly refused to flee to safety.

A few minutes later Brennan called a stop once again. He contacted the commander of the two-man team, supplied them with the proper codes, and gave them the news of their immediate reassignment.

Volkov kept his eyes glued to his phone, waiting for the guards to abandon their post and work their way to the SUV. Six minutes later he nodded at Brennan in satisfaction. "They're following your orders."

"Of course they are," said the scientist.

"They're driving off now," added Volkov, shutting off his phone and zipping it into a side pocket of his rucksack. "We'll continue to wait here for Pavel, but it shouldn't be more than another ten minutes."

\* \* \*

Two hundred yards away, Pavel Safin's comm picked up the major's words and he allowed himself the flicker of a smile. To say that the guards were driving off was slightly less than accurate. They were, indeed, nearing their SUV, but they hadn't gone anywhere.

And they wouldn't.

Safin was safely hidden behind a pine tree, and the silenced rifle that his duffel had concealed was now steadied in the crook of a low branch. Given that he had been trained as a sniper and could hit a squirrel at a hundred yards, taking out these men from thirty feet was almost too easy. The only challenge had been predicting their likely path to the vehicle and the best spot to conceal himself for an ambush.

Both men now came into view, exactly where he had expected. Safin squeezed the trigger ever-so-gently and the leftmost guard collapsed to the ground, a hole drilled in his brain. His colleague was well trained and launched himself to the ground, intending to complete a roll and come up firing, but this was not to be. Safin had moved his sights and squeezed the trigger a second time before the first victim had even completed his fall, so when the second guard hit the ground, he too, was dead.

\* \* \*

"Two clean kills confirmed," said Safin's voice in the major's ear.

"Understood," replied Volkov. "Test the camera to be sure it's operational," he added in English, maintaining the fiction that Safin was there to prevent the guards from doubling back. Anything to shelter their frail scientist ally from the harsh realities of an assassination mission. "Then double-time it to our location. I'll send our GPS coordinates to your phone."

"Roger that," said Safin.

"The guards won't be returning," said Brennan. "We're just wasting time."

Volkov shot him a stare that could have intimidated the Grim Reaper. "Good thing we're not on a clock, then, isn't it?" he snapped.

They waited in a chilly silence until Safin returned. Once he did, they left the SUV and continued toward the main structure on foot. Volkov carried his rucksack while his two comrades hauled large duffels.

They covered about a quarter of a mile through heavy woods, following the lead of their new ally, when Brennan whispered for them to halt.

"This is about ten yards from the edge of the security perimeter," he told them. He pointed east, where they could make out a helipad, and fifty yards past this, a small hexagonal building about the size of a three-car garage.

"The main structure is about fifty yards further east of the hexagonal building," said Brennan. "That's where Jordan will be."

Volkov cocked an ear to the side, picking up a faint but steady whooshing sound. "What am I hearing?" he asked in hushed tones. "A generator?"

"A waterfall," whispered Brennan. "A spectacular one at that. The building Jordan is in faces it dead on. He didn't build here by accident."

Urinson and Safin unzipped their bags and removed several tablet computers and a full array of electronic probes and sensors, many of them unmatched in sophistication, even by the US. Brennan and Volkov looked on silently while the two Russians probed their surroundings.

"Jordan's automated security is as good as advertised," whispered Safin when they had finished. "And Dr. Brennan is correct, the perimeter extends to about ten yards east of our current position."

"Thank you," replied Volkov. He removed a laptop computer from his ruck and handed it to the tall scientist. "Time to see if you can do what you say," he whispered.

Brennan's fingers flew over the keypad and touch screen, linking to the security feed and bringing up a number of screens in quick succession, each growing in complexity. Volkov waited patiently as the minutes went by, well aware that a system this sophisticated couldn't be disarmed with a birth date or the name of a favorite pet. Especially since the goal was to disable it without it appearing to be disabled or sending an alarm.

"Got it!" whispered Brennan at last, smiling triumphantly. "It's down. All of it."

"You'll forgive me if I verify that with my own equipment," replied Volkov. A short time later Safin confirmed Brennan's claim. Isaac Jordan was now at their mercy.

"Well done, Dr. Brennan," whispered Volkov. "Follow close behind me," he added, sandwiching the scientist between his men.

They crouched low and moved silently, keeping to the trees. They gave the helipad a wide berth and made it past the hexagonal building without incident. The building Jordan was in didn't have any windows facing their direction of approach, and the teeming trees and foliage in this idyllic setting made a stealthy approach much easier than it otherwise would have been, even if Jordan happened to choose this moment to exit the facility.

Just before they reached the main building, Volkov called a halt and ordered Safin to fall well back, just to be sure they weren't surprised on their rear flank.

Brennan shook his head in frustration. "That isn't necessary," he insisted.

"*I'll* decide what is and isn't necessary," whispered Volkov angrily.

\* \* \*

Safin headed directly to the hexagonal building with his ever-present military duffel, making sure Brennan didn't have a line of sight on his final destination.

He tried the door and was relieved to find that it clicked open, the electronic lock having been controlled by the security system that was no longer in operation. There was a large elevator in the room's center, which is exactly what he had expected.

He pressed a button and waited for the elevator doors to open. Once they did, he stepped inside and took stock of his surroundings. The walls were seamless, save for two steel buttons, one for up and one for down. He pushed the down button and took up a firing stance facing the doors, an automatic rifle ready in his arms. Sensors indicated there would be no one lying in wait, but it paid to be cautious.

Safin braced himself further as the elevator completed its descent, but when the doors whooshed open he found himself alone in another small room, as expected. This was Jordan's private elevator, after all, and he wouldn't want to have it widely known down below that he alone had access to a spacious aboveground facility, one with a spectacular view and filled with fresh, forest-scented air.

Despite being in a small room that was unknown to most and usually locked, Safin wasn't about to risk that even a whisper might give away his presence. Instead of contacting Volkov verbally, he composed a text.

*I'm in place*, he typed into his phone. *No issues*, he added, hitting the send button.

\* \* \*

Forty yards to the east of Safin and sixty feet above him, Volkov read the message with great satisfaction, barely able to keep his face impassive. The major was a hard man, not prone to giddy excitement, but what he was about to accomplish would become the stuff of legend. He would transform the power structure of the entire globe.

*Hold for my mark*, he texted back.

*Roger that*, came the immediate reply.

"Are you ready?" he whispered to Brennan as he and Yakov Urinson readied automatic pistols. Sensors indicated that Jordan was alone inside the structure, and the scientist assured him the door was electronic, so would now open to anyone. Not that this mattered, since even when security was fully in place, Brennan had access.

"As ready as I'll ever be," mouthed Brennan, looking as if he might puke. "Remember," he added. "Scientist. Not soldier."

"Yeah, I'd forgotten," replied the major, rolling his eyes.

They closed the remaining distance to the door. Brennan took a deep breath and led the way inside, since he would be recognized as a friendly.

Isaac Jordan was sitting on a couch, angled away from the entrance. He had been engrossed in a tablet computer, but when he realized that someone had entered, an intrusion that shouldn't have been possible, he whipped his head around to see who it was.

As soon as Brennan crossed the threshold, Volkov and Urinson rushed past him and extended their guns toward their target. "Freeze!" barked Volkov.

The computer Jordan had been holding slipped through his fingers and fell to the floor. And his expression was not one of horror, but of astonishment, unable to comprehend how he could have been blindsided so completely.

# 42

Isaac Jordan twisted around and rose slowly from the white couch, his hands in the air. "John?" he said in confusion, trying to read the expression on his colleague's face and failing.

His gaze shifted to the major for the first time. "You're Volkov!" he said in horror. "What is this? How did you find me here?"

Without waiting for a response, his eyes darted back to John Brennan. "Did they hurt you?" he asked worriedly, looking him up and down.

Brennan shook his head. "I led them here, Isaac," he said, sadness and regret in his voice. "I'm sorry. You left me no other choice."

"I don't believe it," whispered Jordan, looking devastated by this betrayal. "How could you do this?"

"Enough!" shouted Volkov. "Not another word!"

He nodded at his comrade, who proceeded to bind Jordan's hands with zip ties and gag him with gray duct tape.

"Scan this room thoroughly for bugs or any other transmissions," Volkov commanded Urinson. He then turned away to address Safin through his comm. "Pavel," he said in Russian. "We have Jordan and all is secured. You're a go to proceed."

"What's going on?" asked Brennan, who didn't understand a word of Russian. "Are you having your other man join us?"

"Yes. But he fell back pretty far, so it may take ten or fifteen minutes. Please remain silent until he gets here."

* * *

Safin heard Volkov's order in his comm and texted a quick confirmation, still unwilling to make any noise. The wait for Volkov's green light had given him plenty of time to prepare. He was now wearing a gas mask and had readied six steel spheres, each about twice the size of a softball.

He opened the door from the elevator room just a crack and released an insect-sized flying drone into the main facility. It sent back video immediately, showing that the coast was clear, and then continued to race through the facility, sending a 3D map back to the spheres.

Once the insect drone had a few-minutes head start, Safin pushed open the door a second time, activated the six shiny orbs, and then released them. They began rolling forward and picking up speed and were soon screaming through the facility at speeds of up to seventy miles per hour, coordinating routes with one another so that each covered separate territory.

Each orb was filled with gas, so highly pressurized and concentrated it had turned to a liquid, as was the case inside a propane tank. As the balls hurtled along, they released their liquid payloads as a fine gas, in this case a knockout agent of unprecedented potency and with extraordinary dispersal kinetics.

Russia lagged behind the US when it came to big ticket, shock-and-awe military technology, but they were unsurpassed when it came to tech that could be used for more focused operations.

The balls and insect drone also continued to map the facility as they went, sending all data back to Safin's remaining drone, which resembled a flying can of soda. This one was the most sophisticated of all, with an AI on board designed to surpass human experts in only one area of knowledge: ventilation. It could digest the maps it was being sent and predict with uncanny accuracy where the air intakes would be located. Once it had enough information, Safin watched it launch itself into the hall of its own accord. Anyone still standing after the first barrage of gas would surely fall once this drone's payload was deposited into the ventilation system.

In less than ten minutes it was over. Cameras on the drones showed a number of unconscious men and women sprawled throughout the facility, and the air was saturated with enough gas to ensure that everyone within had been affected.

*Mission accomplished*, texted Safin. He no longer needed to remain silent, but he wasn't about to remove his mask until sensors indicated it was safe.

* * *

Marat Volkov looked down at his phone and a broad smile came over his face. Pavel Safin had performed extremely well.

*Well done*, he texted back. *Hold for further instructions.*

He adjusted his comm so he could communicate with Sergei Greshnev, who was with the other six men now serving as muscle on their newly formed team. "All secure here," he reported to his second. "What is your status?"

"We've identified the two guards," said Greshnev. "We're moving into position to take them out simultaneously."

"Good," said the major. "Keep me posted."

"Roger that," said Greshnev.

Brennan's friendly face had grown ever more unhappy and confused as the minutes had ticked by. Finally, he couldn't contain himself any longer. "Look, what's the holdup here?" he said. "Why are we just standing around? Isaac Jordan needs to be stopped. So please don't prolong this," he continued, gesturing to his former boss who was still bound and gagged. "Just *kill him already!*" he finished emphatically. "You gave your word."

"I'm afraid neither one of us has been completely honest," replied the major with a shrug.

Then, with brutally cold efficiency, before Brennan could utter a syllable of protest, Volkov lifted his gun and squeezed the trigger twice in quick succession, almost a point-blank double-tap between Brennan's eyes.

The tall scientist collapsed to the ground like a felled tree, blood spilling from his forehead.

"And it turns out I have other plans for him," finished Volkov evenly.

# 43

The flight to Jordan's retreat—likely one of many such residences he owned around the world—took a little over two hours, most of it along breathtaking mountain peaks. Eventually, Carr and his small collection of new companions reached their destination, a mansion situated on a large flat cleft on one such mountain.

Several acres all around the grand residence had been cleared and turned into gardens. Beyond the cleared area in the back were thick woods. In front was an opulent pool and spa, an extensive patio, and then fifteen feet from this, a sheer cliff wall. While the mansion didn't face a waterfall, the view from the front was so expansive it made residents feel like they could see forever.

Colorado had a density of mountains over much of its expanse that was nearly unrivaled. More than fifty peaks in the state soared to over fourteen thousand feet, a national record, and over a thousand exceeded twelve thousand feet.

There was little conversation during the flight. The three passengers were in awe of the view and needed time to digest what they had heard and regroup mentally. Trish introduced them to the pilot, a man named Roberto Estrada, and Carr spoke with him briefly.

The lieutenant was immediately impressed with the man. Although the helo was civilian, Estrada clearly had a military background and gave off an aura of being very sharp and competent. Jordan had recruited him two years earlier, not a simple process given the billionaire's infamy and need to explain both his past and his vision for the future. But Estrada had bought in, and had become quite friendly with the great man, as he called Jordan.

Carr was certain that Estrada had been an exceptional soldier. Jordan would be extraordinarily selective in making any additions to his small team. He was used to hiring the best, even when there was far less on the line, and why recruit a dumb-grunt soldier when you could get one with a stellar track record who was at the top of his class?

Just because a soldier was lethal didn't mean he couldn't also be brilliant, as Carr himself exemplified. The best soldiers and operatives were fluent in multiple languages and could come up to speed quickly on a vast array of weaponry and sophisticated technology.

Carr noted that Estrada was unarmed. No doubt this was to make sure Carr didn't try anything, not that he wasn't well aware that such an attempt would be useless. If Isaac Jordan could take control of the helo they had been in while fleeing the church, he could certainly take control of his own aircraft, and was well prepared to do so at the first hint of any trouble.

During the flight they also learned a little of Trish Casner's background. She had been the manager of a boutique greeting card shop in Columbus, Ohio, only thirteen months earlier, before a woman named Mary Willis had recruited her to be a subject in a behavioral study.

After landing, their new hostess dispensed with a grand tour. Nothing to see here. Just your typical mansion set on a mountain, one that Jordan had acquired from a multimillionaire developer through a dummy corporation. Modern, spacious, and furnished with comfort in mind, it was magnificent but not pretentious.

Trish led them to the kitchen, while the helicopter pilot retired to the other side of the grounds, to stay at a separate guest house until his services were needed for the return trip. The guest house alone was over three thousand square feet, the size of a spacious family home, but one that was dwarfed by the main residence.

Not surprisingly, the mansion sported a kitchen large enough to double as an airplane hangar, and Trish had her guests sit on bar stools around a blue-granite island while she warmed up lasagna for lunch. She assured them she would leave them in peace after the meal, since they had much to ponder, but that Jordan had insisted they not attempt to make life-altering decisions while hungry.

The kitchen extended seamlessly into a vast family room, creating a great room that was truly expansive. Trish gestured to a large cherrywood dresser just beyond the kitchen border. "That's a liquor cabinet," she explained. "Isaac told me to be sure to point it out, in case your nerves are fried. He doesn't drink, but it's top-quality stuff, so help yourself if you'd like a cocktail later tonight." She smiled. "Or later today by the pool."

Carr didn't drink either, but he had noticed an open bottle of wine when he had barged into Bram's home, so suspected the couple might well make use of this later on.

Carr continued a cursory inspection of his surroundings, taking special note of a phone on one edge of the granite island, one that was actually plugged into a wall. "Is that a landline?" he asked Trish in disbelief.

Landlines had been going the way of the dinosaur for some time, and it wouldn't be long until they would only be seen as exhibits in museums, relics of a primitive past.

Trish smiled. "Pretty rare in a home this modern," she replied. "But so is not having any Wi-Fi or cell coverage." She raised her eyebrows. "Or did Isaac neglect to tell you about that?"

Carr frowned. How could he forget the dampening field Jordan had put in place to prevent him from communicating with his superiors. Not that Carr could fault the man. Jordan had gone to heroic lengths to keep his activities secret, and couldn't risk Carr putting him back in the global public eye in a matter of seconds.

"He told me," replied Carr. "But doesn't a landline defeat the purpose of blocking cell phones?"

She smiled. "Not if it's programmed to only be able to call two numbers. I dial *one* to reach Isaac at the facility we were just at. Since all other communications are dead, he wanted us to use him as 9-1-1. In case of emergency only, we can call him, and he'll know to pick up no matter what he's doing. I dial *two* to reach the guards outside who are, ah . . . keeping us safe."

"You mean keeping us *here*," said Riley, although she didn't seem upset by it.

After all she had been through over the past eight years, not to mention the emotional wood-chipper she had been fed into during the past few days, she seemed to be rebounding from rock bottom and to be relatively upbeat. Carr suspected she was beginning to warm to the possibility that the father she had thought dead wasn't the monster he had appeared to be, and might actually care about her well-being beyond all possible expectations.

Trish smiled weakly. "I know this situation is . . . awkward," she said. "But I also know Isaac would never let any of you come to harm. And if you do make the decision not to join him, you really will be free to go."

She began preparing four plates, each with a healthy serving of lasagna and salad. Each of her three wards already had beverages, which were sitting on the granite island in front of them.

"You refer to my father as Isaac," noted Riley, "rather than Mr. Jordan. Are you two close?"

Carr barely managed to keep his mouth from falling open and he exchanged a startled glance with David Bram. She had actually called Jordan her father without an accompanying expression of disdain. The man had made far more progress than he had known.

"I've become one of his personal assistants, but we're no closer than he is to any of his other employees. Everyone calls him Isaac."

"And he's told you *everything* about his past?" said Riley. "What he's trying to do?"

"I'm pretty sure he has. After my year contract was up, I thought I'd collect the rest of my money and go. I can't tell you how shocked I was when he came to me, revealed he was still alive, and spent hour after hour telling me what I suspect he just told you."

"He told us he made you aware of the nanites he put in your head," said Bram. "And that he had one of his people kill a Trish Casner duplicate he claims was as human as you are."

"Yes," she confirmed. "He told me both of these things. And the other Trish wasn't killed. Not exactly. Maybe if I'd have met my double it would have been harder for me to accept, I don't know. But he told me everything, including the hell he put me through as a test subject. And how much having to make these kinds of decisions weighed on his soul."

"I'm pretty sure he doesn't believe he has one of those," Bram pointed out wryly.

"Figure of speech, I guess," said Trish. "But he told me I'd surprised him. He had selected subjects from both ends of the spectrum. Those whom he expected to be heroic and brilliant and ethical, and those he expected to be monsters. I was in the middle group. But, apparently, the tests revealed a strength and competence even I didn't know I had. He told me the immense pressure that VR simulations put on subjects laid bare any weaknesses of character. But in some cases, like mine, the immense pressure turned the subjects into *diamonds*. His words. I wasn't supposed to be special, which he said made it all the more gratifying when I turned out to be."

Trish finished plating and set the food in front of her wards, who thanked her and wasted no time digging in.

"He told me about his seed-ships," continued their host. "The entire concept should have seemed ridiculous. Only it was coming from the mind of Isaac Jordan. The man who conquered Mars. The man who—along with Pock, I guess—had perfected virtual reality, which I've experienced. Believe me, it's beyond remarkable. He toured me around the facility, showed me the E-brains and bioprinting chambers. Showed a video of the R-Drive seed-ship factory he's having built."

"Not so ridiculous anymore, huh?" said Carr.

"When he's involved," she replied, "the impossible seems almost inevitable. He told me I was one of thirty-five test subjects selected to help populate the cosmos. Or my consciousness was selected, at any rate."

"How did you feel about that?" asked Carr.

"It's amazing that he thinks so highly of me," she said. "And what an adventure. I'm almost jealous of the other mes who will get to set foot on new worlds."

"Is that how he pitched it?" asked Riley. "As something to be jealous of?"

Trish shrugged. "I can't remember the conversation exactly. But I know I support his goals."

"Did it occur to you that he already knew *exactly* how you would respond?" pressed Riley. "To all of it? Exactly what he needed to say to get you the most enthusiastic about joining him?"

"Yes, he even admitted it. He ran it by my double first in a VR simulation. He said that if she—I—had reacted with horror to what he had done, he wouldn't have asked me to join him. But that was it. He didn't use the simulation to find better ways to manipulate me."

"How confident are you that he's telling the truth about that?" said Riley.

"Very. But even if he weren't, I'm not sure how much this would bother me. I believe he's a good man with a breathtaking vision for the future of humanity. I've seen the agony on his face when he re-lived Turlock. And his emotions were never more on display than when he told me about you, Riley. How sorry he is. How proud. How much he misses you."

Riley lowered a forkful of lasagna back to her plate, as if it were too heavy to lift, and nodded wordlessly.

"And he's quite persuasive, even without the need to test his pitch in virtual reality. Look at the three of you. Although I know the gist of what he planned to tell you, I didn't hear it. But I can tell from how you're acting that you'll all be giving the idea of joining him some serious consideration."

Bram nodded thoughtfully. "Why do you think he needed to gath-er so much behavioral data on so many subjects?"

"He didn't tell you?"

"A little," said Bram. "And I have some thoughts of my own, but I'm interested to hear what you have to say."

"He's been pretty straightforward with me, as I've said. And since I was part of this study, we've discussed it at great length. First, I think he wanted to see just how heroic, or how despicable, human beings really are. There's a group of ASI proponents who believe hu-manity truly sucks, and we *deserve* to go extinct and let machine intelligence inherit the universe."

"Yeah, he mentioned that," said Carr.

"I think he wanted to make sure they weren't *right*," continued Trish. "Was humanity worth saving, worth spreading throughout the galaxy? Or would this be more like spreading a tumor?"

"Sounds like he concluded we were worthy of salvation," said Carr.

"Yes. He is trying to stack the deck with the thirty-five he's chosen to shepherd the species forward on these planets. But as far as I know, the sperm and egg banks will be random. So the humanity that will arise after in-vitro fertilization, and then later from good old-fashioned sex, will more or less mirror the population of Earth."

"And second?" prompted Bram.

"Second, I think he wanted a baseline, in case he ever did decide that certain improvements were warranted. So he could experiment, and compare and contrast possible improvements with his baseline."

"Does he intend to introduce improvements?" said Riley, trying to keep her voice neutral about this possibility.

"Not at all," said Trish. "Too much on his plate already. Maybe in the distant future. It is tempting, but what happened with Savant has him freaked out. His judgment really let him down. He played with fire and it burned his face off. Now I think he's scared to death of playing with anything that has even the slightest possibility of becoming fire."

"A good way to think of it," said Riley.

"So he doesn't want to decide which traits are important, and which should be weeded out. Or which capabilities should be dramatically enhanced." Trish shrugged. "If you ask me, if you could alter an uploaded consciousness, alter the human condition, to eliminate cruelty and sadism, it's hard to imagine this wouldn't be a good thing. But these decisions are above my pay grade."

"Since you were paid two million dollars for a year of your time," noted Carr, "your pay grade is pretty steep."

Trish laughed. "Not compared to his, it isn't."

"Given how extensively he's studied human behavior under field conditions," said Carr, "and as someone who has seen the worst of it over the years, I'm encouraged that he still finds our unimproved species worthy of, you know . . . *infecting* more planets."

"Don't get me wrong," said Trish, "He isn't thrilled about our species. He just finds us worthy when compared to Savant. He says we've evolved to be selfish, cruel, and horrible in every way. But we've also evolved to be compassionate, loving, loyal, and *amazing* in every way."

"Right," said Riley. "And in his view, Savant personified the bad side of this equation, without any of the good."

Carr smiled. "Maybe Jordan could use this to come up with an inspirational slogan for his grand mission," he said in amusement. "Kennedy's slogan was something like, 'We choose to go to the Moon, not because it is easy, but because it is hard.' Maybe Jordan's could be, 'We choose to expand out into the galaxy, not because we're wonderful, but because we're not *entirely* despicable.'"

"As great as that slogan is," said Trish with a grin, "if you choose to join Isaac's efforts, I'm pretty sure he won't be putting you in public relations."

# 44

After lunch, Trish led them to three bedrooms that were clustered in the same wing, which they would use for their overnight stay. Each had a selection of clothing and bathing suits in multiple sizes for them to use, as needed, along with unopened toiletries.

She then led them to another room nearby that she would be using as an office while they relaxed and pondered all that had transpired. She would be on call if they needed her for any reason.

Once they left Trish to her work, they adjourned to a patio in the front yard that overlooked the mountains, taking advantage of fresh air and another breathtaking view. It was also about thirty yards removed from the mansion. This distance wouldn't stop any determined eavesdropping, but it made them more relaxed psychologically.

"Are you two sure you don't want some time to be alone?" asked Carr as they were about to seat themselves around a beautiful teak table.

Riley grinned. "Feeling like a third wheel?"

"Pretty much."

"Don't worry," she said in amusement. "David and I won't start groping each other. And we need you here. We need to stick together, think this through together. And you did save our lives."

She paused. "But even more than that," she continued earnestly, "after being abducted together and sharing that incredible conversation we had with my father, it seems like we've known you forever."

Bram nodded his agreement.

Carr felt the same way. There was something about the intensity of their shared experiences, of Jordan's revelations and their teamwork in peppering him with questions, which did make him feel very close to this couple. "Sharing a foxhole with a man does tend to break down barriers," he said.

"Spoken like a true soldier," said Riley.

Bram turned his attention to the woman he loved. "How are you holding up?" he asked softly. "I can't even begin to imagine what this has been like for you."

"I'm okay," she replied. "Maybe even good," she added, looking like this answer even surprised *her*. "I hit rock bottom, but the way things have turned out, maybe there's a silver lining at the end of it all. I've always tried hard to heed the words of Winston Churchill."

"Which are?" said Bram.

"If you're going through hell . . . keep going."

"Really?" said Bram in amusement. "You were already intimidating before you showed us up when we were talking with your father. And now you're throwing around quotes from Winston Churchill? Are you kidding me?"

She laughed. "I just have a good memory. Are you saying you don't like the new me?"

"I love the new you," he said. "Same as the old you, but without the effort to hide your intellect." He grinned. "You did a crappy job of that, anyway."

Their conversation halted as a hawk came into view, soaring majestically above the cliff face they overlooked. They watched it in awe for almost a minute.

"This place is amazing," said Carr. "I went into the wrong line of work. I should have become a billionaire instead. Who knew?"

Riley laughed. "Actually, this is pretty humble for one of my dad's retreats," she said. "Some of the retreats he bought when I was growing up make this one seem small and commonplace. Either his tastes have become more modest, or he's worried that he's down to his last hundred billion dollars."

Carr grinned. "So what do you think of Trish Casner?" he asked, changing the subject.

"I like her," said Riley. "A lot. I get a good feeling about her."

"Me too," said Bram.

"What about you?" Riley asked the lieutenant. "I don't care if you like her or not," she added. "I want to know if you think we can *believe* her."

Carr paused in thought. "It all comes down to your father," he replied. "If you believe *him*, then you'd tend to believe her. If you believe he's the devil incarnate, and everything he told us is a lie, part of a diabolical plot of inhuman complexity, then sure, she's probably in on the con."

"Okay," said Riley. "So do you believe *him*?"

"I do," said Carr. "It all rings true to me. I'm usually pretty good at sniffing out deception."

"Yeah, it does to me, too," said Riley. "And given my feelings toward him in the beginning, and my reluctance to give him any benefit of the doubt, this is saying a lot."

Bram shot Carr a sidelong glance. "Are you going to tell us why you needed some alone time with him at the end?"

The corners of Carr's mouth turned up into the slightest of smiles. "If I wanted you to hear what I was saying, I'd have said it in front of you."

"And here I thought we'd all become best friends," said Riley. "You know, in the trenches together. Or the foxhole, like you said."

"Maybe I wanted time with him to complain about his daughter," said Carr wryly. "About how good she is with a stunner."

"Are you really trying to dredge that up to justify keeping this secret?" said Riley in amusement. "Sure, I shocked the hell out of you. But we weren't best buddies then."

She removed the blue stunner from her pocket and placed it on the table in front of the lieutenant. "Here, I'm disarming. So now you can confide in us without feeling threatened," she added with a grin.

Carr picked up the small weapon and turned it over in his hands absently. "This little bastard really set a lot in motion," he noted, trying to change the subject. He had promised Jordan not to reveal their brief discussion, and this was a promise he intended to keep. "If you hadn't escaped from me, things would have played out a lot differently. Probably a lot worse."

"What do you mean?" said Bram.

"As you know, I thought Volkov was after *you*. I thought Riley was a saintly farm girl in the wrong place at the wrong time. So when I took you both for interrogation, I would have struck out. We would never have known Jordan was alive, or learned what we've learned." He shook his head. "So my incompetence was a good thing in this case."

"I wouldn't call it incompetence," said Riley. "I just came up with a good plan and got lucky."

"You did come up with a good plan," said Carr. "But I do this for a living. It was unforgivable of me to have let my guard down, regardless of how good you were. On the other hand," he added, raising his eyebrows impishly, "perhaps I'm *so* good that my subconscious realized I needed to let you escape."

Riley rolled her eyes while Bram groaned.

Carr held up the blue stunner. "All's well that ends well, I guess," he said. "Although I have to tell you, this little guy really *hurt*." As he was lowering the weapon a few glints of sunlight flickered off the outer casing.

He brought it close to examine it further. The device had two halves that had been snapped together to form the shell, not with screws or welding, but with pressure alone. And there were scratches near the millimeter-thick slit that was formed where the upper and lower halves met.

"Have you ever opened this up?" he asked Riley.

She looked confused by the question. "It doesn't open," she said. "At least I thought it didn't. It has a rechargeable battery, so you never need to replace it."

He handed the device to her. "See these scratches?" he said, pointing them out. "Looks like someone used the tip of a knife to pry the case open. Could you have made these marks?"

"Not a chance," she replied. "And I agree. The scratches are too near the seam to be random. Someone pried it open—*recently*."

Carr's mind began to race as he pondered this unsettling development.

"But why?" said Riley.

Carr frowned deeply. "My instincts tell me the most likely reason to open it would be to plant a tracer or bug inside," he replied. "And only two parties had access. Your father and the Russians. But your father would have no need. Even if he wanted to listen to us here, there are more reliable ways."

"Which leaves the Russians," said Bram.

"Which leaves the Russians," said Carr, his alarm growing.

He paused in thought while his expression grew ever more troubled. "It had to have been Greshnev's doing, at the church. He knew he had to let us go. And he knew I'd find the tracers he'd already planted on you. So he must have decided to insert another one into the stunner, one that was undetectable.

"Very clever," he added, almost in admiration. "And it makes sense. I remember he spoke in private to one of his men, who retrieved you and David. But this took longer than I had expected. Now I know why. And he made sure you got your stunner back, pretending he did it to bring me down a peg, remind me of how you made me look like an idiot."

"Which means he knows where we are," said Riley.

"If I'm right, yes," replied Carr. "And also where your father is," he added, rising from the table and flinging the blue electroshock weapon with all of his might beyond the edge of the cliff. "We need to warn him and then find a way to protect ourselves."

He began moving back toward the house, his eyes darting around the grounds, alert for any possible threat. Riley and Bram followed closely behind.

"This still doesn't make sense," said Bram as they rushed across the grounds. "Jordan scanned for bugs and tracers, too. You're telling me the Russians have something that even *his* tech can't find?"

"Apparently," said Carr as they entered the mansion. He began to make his way to the kitchen, motioning for them to follow. "They've gone balls-out on advancing spy and commando tech. *Especially* tracers and bugs. The first tracers they hit you with were actually tiny flying drones, more advanced even than we've been able to manage. Rumor has it they've been working on a combination tracer and bug that's totally undetectable. A sophisticated AI that piggybacks on the nearest microphone it detects. Could be in a phone, a television, or a personal assistant like Echo or Google Home. It subverts the mic to broadcast back to the bad guys whatever it picks up, scrambled within a standard Wi-Fi signal. This has been done before, so protections to prevent it have long been a mainstay, but this system overcomes them."

"But there aren't any Wi-Fi signals here," said Riley.

"Which means it stopped working when we got on the grounds," said Carr, entering the kitchen. "So they don't know we've figured this out," he added, rushing to the phone on the granite island.

He snatched up the receiver and hit one, the direct line to Isaac Jordan.

After ten rings he hung up.

"No answer," he explained to his two companions, who appeared to be holding their breath. He hit two, the direct line to the guards. This time, he hung up after five rings went unanswered.

"Now what?" asked Riley.

"Now we need to prepare to defend ourselves against a coming attack," he replied calmly.

# 45

Volkov made a show of looking Jordan up and down, letting the man squirm under his gaze, ignoring Brennan's dead body on the floor behind him and the pool of blood that had collected nearby.

"Just so you know," said Volkov, "we've taken over your experimental facility."

He gestured to Urinson, who ripped the tape from Jordan's mouth.

"What are you talking about?" said Jordan the moment he could speak. "*What* experimental facility?"

"The one beneath us," he said simply.

Jordan looked as if he had been hit in the stomach. "There's no way you could know about that!"

"We know about that and much more. In fact, we know everything."

"Impossible."

"As impossible as an undetectable bug lodged in your daughter's stunner?" said Volkov.

Jordan reeled, for a moment looking as if he might not be able to remain standing.

"That's right," said Volkov, gloating. "We were listening in to your little reunion. Fascinating conversation. And you couldn't have explained things more thoroughly. Maybe a little *too* thoroughly for my taste, but better to err on the side of too much information rather than too little."

"I scanned everything and everyone for bugs," protested Jordan. "Including the stunner. Using tech more advanced than the current state of the art. I couldn't have missed it."

"And yet you did," said Volkov smugly. "I'll be sure to pass this on to its inventors. It's not every day you can come up with technology that can't be detected by the great Isaac Jordan. Especially when your sensors are developed with the help of your computer friend. You know . . . Pock."

Volkov laughed as Jordan's horrified look intensified. "Yes," said the major. "I wasn't bluffing. I really did hear everything."

"Okay," said Jordan, shaking his head to clear it. "So you out-smarted me. Congratulations. So now what? Are you going to keep playing with your food, or are you going to kill me already?"

"If I kill you, then John Brennan wins. You don't want that, do you?"

Jordan gestured toward Brennan's corpse on the floor with his head. "I'm not sure he'll feel like much of a winner," he noted.

Volkov smiled despite himself.

"Look," said Jordan, "I know you want to kill whoever's stopping Russia's efforts at true artificial intelligence. And I know you heard me admit to Carr that I'm the one responsible. So I'm under no illusion that you're planning to let me live."

"Oh, but I am," said Volkov. "I'm just biding my time right now while my team is gathering up your daughter and her two male escorts. You know, at your mansion nearby. I can give you the GPS coordinates if you like."

For an instant a flash of pure hatred crossed Jordan's face. "Why bother with that?" he said, fighting to stay calm. "I'll tell you what. I'll work for you. Give you access to Pock. I'll continue to sabotage the rest of the world's ASI efforts, as long as Russia agrees not to mount any of your own. And you won't have to. Pock is plenty advanced enough to make sure you stay an entire generation ahead of any other nation. You heard what I said to my daughter. I only want to protect humanity from ASI. I don't care if Russia or the US is on top, just as long as ASI never gets developed."

"That's it?" said Volkov, arching an eyebrow. "Just like that? You willingly come work for us?"

"What other choice do I have?"

"The great Isaac Jordan should always have choices."

"You haven't given me any. I'll work for you. All I ask in exchange is that you keep my daughter out of it."

"You know I can't agree to that."

"*Why not?*" demanded Jordan.

Volkov smiled broadly, but didn't answer right away, letting his prisoner twist in the wind. "Because you're forgetting two things," he replied finally. "One, I heard every word you said in this room. And two," he added, his smile transforming into a look of utter contempt, "I'm not a total idiot."

# 46

"Follow me," said Carr, not bothering to whisper. If Volkov or his men were moving in, their sensors would give them the exact location of their targets no matter how silent they tried to be.

"Where are we going?" asked Bram.

"We need to get Trish," he replied as he rushed toward the room she was using as an office, almost at a run. A single second could make all the difference.

Carr had become nearly legendary for his creativity at getting out of sticky situations, for winning against ridiculous odds. But this might be his sternest test. Luckily, adrenaline made him hyper-focused and alert. Life-and-death situations sharpened his mind and instincts, allowing him to forge quick and decisive strategies.

Even if the noose *was* tightening, they still might have some time. Volkov or his men would be coming from the back side of the residence, from the woods. The front wasn't even guarded, for obvious reasons, since a cliffside approach was too difficult. The Russians would know communications had been suppressed, leaving their quarry no way to call for help.

With this much of an upper hand, the intruders could take their time. Be cautious. Keep the element of surprise.

And they couldn't risk any damage to their prize. They'd have to consider that Carr might take advantage of this, using Riley as a shield, or threatening her life if they came too close. This is how he had rescued her from the church, after all—by threatening to kill her. So they might refrain from closing in until sensors showed the three of them had separated.

They made it to Trish's makeshift office in seconds and burst through the door. She jumped in surprise, but when she saw the looks on their faces she could tell this was an emergency. "What happened?" she asked.

"Did Jordan fill you in about the Russians who are after him?" said Carr hurriedly. "The ones who kidnapped Riley."

"Yes."

"It's very likely they're trying to take him out. We tried the batphone, but he didn't answer. Neither did the guards. We think they'll be moving in on us at any moment."

"That can't be right," said Trish. "Isn't it more likely the phone is just malfunctioning? Isaac's security is crazy advanced."

Carr considered explaining, but quickly decided against it. There was no time, and she wasn't likely to be persuaded, anyway. She would surely think he had jumped to some extreme conclusions based on a few scratches on a stunner.

Even if she agreed it had been pried open, she would find his conclusion that someone had placed an undetectable tracer/bug combination inside unlikely. And it *was*. Unless you had spent years in the spy business, had a highly developed intuition when it came to these matters, and a thorough knowledge of Marat Volkov and Sergei Greshnev.

"No time to explain," said Carr. "You're just going to have to trust me."

# 47

Volkov didn't have to wait long to hear back from his second-in-command.

"Both guards are down," reported Greshnev. "We're standing by at the edge of the automated security perimeter."

Since Volkov had been forewarned that Jordan was having Wi-Fi and cell signals suppressed at the mansion, he had made sure his team used comms that wouldn't be affected. But his imminent transmission required the Internet. "Are you still able to access the Web?" he asked.

"Yes. The Wi-Fi suppression ends twenty yards in from the security perimeter."

"Great," said Volkov. "I'm sending the data to your computer now."

Before Volkov hit the send button, he couldn't help himself from taunting Jordan, who was still zip-tied and sitting on a leather chair, while Urinson held a handgun on him.

"I wish you could hear the reports I'm getting through my comm," he said to Jordan. "But no need to worry. Since you can't, and since you don't speak Russian anyway, I'll make sure you're kept apprised of our progress with your daughter. Your security personnel at the mansion are now dead."

Jordan couldn't keep a look of hatred from his face. "A tragic waste of life," he said bitterly. "One that gained you nothing. The guards aren't even necessary. You'll never get through the automated systems."

Volkov shook his head in contempt. "When you told Carr how the mansion was secured, I was listening in, remember? You said you use the exact same automated security system for that site as you do for this one. And why not, right? When you have a system this advanced, why reinvent the wheel?"

Volkov was delighted to see a palpable cloud of panic envelope his prisoner.

"When your buddy Brennan disarmed this system, he used a computer I gave him. One I programmed to capture his every keystroke, his every swipe, from beginning to end. And there were a lot of them. It took him a fair amount of time, and his hands were really flying."

Volkov shrugged. "But still a simple matter for my program to capture. I'm about to send this data to my second-in-command. I'm betting that the systems aren't just exact copies, but can also be defeated with the same commands and passwords. So when Brennan disarmed this facility, he disarmed that one."

He shot Jordan a cruel smile. "Or am I wrong about that?"

Jordan looked as if he wanted to tear Volkov's head off with his bare hands.

The Russian briefly manipulated his computer. "I just sent the data," he announced. "So I guess we'll know if I'm right soon enough. But even if I'm not, I have a Plan B I can tell you about."

Volkov smiled serenely. "But judging from your reaction, I don't think we're going to have to worry about that, are we?"

# 48

Trish Casner glanced at each of her three visitors and then nodded at Carr. "Okay," she said, "I'll trust you. I'll assume we're being attacked. So what do we do about it?"

"That depends. Please tell me this place has a panic room."

"It does," she confirmed. "But Isaac doesn't even keep it locked, and he removed all the weapons that were inside. It came with the place when he bought it. I guess a lot of mansions have them now. Isaac enhanced security so much he said it was a useless appendage."

"But he didn't dismantle it, right?" said Carr.

Trish shook her head no.

"I need you to take us there right away. Quickly! Riley, you're the smallest of the group. So we're going to surround you and walk extremely close to each other, each of us almost pressing against you as we go. The men after us will have long-range sensors that can pick up our location when we move. I want to fool their sensors into thinking only three of us are going to where the panic room is located."

Carr arranged the group into little more than a ball of humanity, with Riley in the center. "Let's go!" he barked. "Now!"

They moved slowly and awkwardly toward the panic room with Trish leading the way, providing the eyes for the four-bodied monster. Carr could only hope that the Russians were taking their time, or making slow and steady progress in their attempts to breach the mansion.

They made it to the panic room without incident, and all four stepped inside.

Carr pressed a touchscreen monitor and activated the room's controls. "If there is a personal digital assistant manning this room," he said, "please announce yourself and give your name."

"My name is Janice," said a disembodied female voice. "How may I help you?"

"Janice, I want to see the video feeds from all surveillance cameras tiled on the main screen," he ordered. Since Jordan had thought the room a joke, he had never set up any passwords to prevent others from taking ownership of it.

"Acknowledged," said Janice, and a moment later, thirty-two tiles appeared on a monitor that covered one wall of the room, each one the size of a large laptop screen.

Carr scanned the monitor like a speed reader who had overdosed on caffeine. One of the thirty-two views, showing the tree line just beyond the automated security perimeter, confirmed his suspicions.

He counted seven men in total, congregated together and armed with automatic weapons. Six of the men were milling about fairly aimlessly, while a seventh was holding a computer and watching it intently.

Carr's three companions erupted with curses and anxious chatter upon seeing the seven Russian soldiers. "Settle down," he insisted. "We're in luck. Our situation is better than I thought."

The three civilians looked at him like he had lost his mind.

"They aren't even on the grounds," said Carr. "They must think they have a way through security, but they haven't made it yet. So we have the time to carry out a key initial step."

"Is that step conjuring up a tank?" asked Riley.

Carr couldn't help but smile. "One reason I had Trish bring us here," he said, "is that panic rooms usually have tech that can block motion sensors, long range or otherwise. If the invaders know exactly where we are at all times, hiding is out of the question."

"Yeah, so is living," mumbled Bram under his breath.

"Janice," said the lieutenant, "please confirm you have the capability to block all motion-sensing technology."

"Confirmed. But only inside the mansion and guest house, and within the grounds. My range doesn't extend beyond this."

"Understood," said Carr, continuing to keep a careful watch on the monitors. "Their sensors have been tracking us," he said, addressing the three civilians. "Right now, they're probably showing Trish as being stationary in the room she was in, and the three of us at our current location."

He paused. "So here's what I want you to do," he said to his companions. "I want you to walk briskly toward the back of the mansion for about thirty seconds. Count one Mississippi, two Mississippi, and so on. When you get to thirty Mississippi, head back here as fast as you can."

"I don't understand," said Trish.

"I'll be counting also," explained Carr. "When I reach twenty Mississippi, I'll have Janice block their sensors. You'll keep walking for ten seconds just to be sure our timing is okay and you don't double back too soon."

Riley nodded. "I get it," she said in admiration. "Just before their sensors go down, they'll record three people moving with a purpose toward the back grounds. They won't know anyone remained behind at this location. When they lose the ability to track us, they'll assume we just kept going in the same direction."

"That's the hope," said Carr. "With any luck, when they can't find you, they'll be forced to search the woods, just in case you managed to slip by them. I'm hoping the last thing they'll guess is that you immediately doubled back to where you started."

Bram looked duly impressed. "I'm beginning to think we put the right person in charge of this op," he said.

Carr frowned, despite knowing this was meant as a compliment. He just hoped that Bram was right. If one bought into Jordan's vision, Carr's success or failure could cost more than his life and the lives of a few others—it might have a major impact on the future course of human history.

"Okay," he said to his three companions. "Time to move out. Go!" he barked when they didn't immediately carry out his order. "Thirty Mississippi," he reminded them.

They rushed from the room without a word, returning a little over a minute later.

"Well done," said Carr when they were back. "Janice reports their sensors are being blocked, and this occurred while you were moving toward the back grounds. We're off of their radar. They'll have to see us or hear us to know where we are."

"I have a question I've been wanting to ask," said Riley.

"Go ahead," replied Carr. "But quickly. Once I see what move these guys make when they break through security, I'll need to make preparations. So what's your question?"

"How does this attack make any sense?" she said. "We shouldn't be targets. If they know where to find my dad, why do they need us? They only care about me as a means to get to *him*."

Carr sighed. "Yeah. I was debating whether to get into it, but I think it's probably time to tell you what I spoke to your father about, after all."

"What are you saying?" asked Riley. "That your private conversation can explain something about why these men are here?"

"No," said Carr evenly. "I'm saying that our conversation can explain *everything* about why these men are here."

# 49

"Report," said Marat Volkov when he heard Greshnev's voice in his ear.

"The computer is still mimicking Brennan's manipulations," said the captain. "I expect to be through any minute. But we've had a complication."

"Go on."

"We were able to identify four people in the main residence, but the sensors abruptly stopped working."

"What do you mean, they all malfunctioned at once?"

"No. They can still detect *us*. But something is preventing them from detecting anyone on the main property."

Volkov issued a loud curse. "It's Cameron Carr's doing. No doubt about it."

"Couldn't be," said Greshnev. "He had no reason to expect we were coming. And Jordan left him at the mansion deaf, dumb, and blind."

"I don't know how he knows, but he does. Don't let the stunner incident fool you, he's the best the Americans have."

"He's one man, unarmed," said Greshnev.

"Don't underestimate him, Sergei. I did once, and he found a way to slip through a noose I would have sworn couldn't be escaped."

"Understood."

"What were the last known positions of the four people inside the mansion?" asked Volkov.

"One had been stationary in a room near the front for a long while and was still there when the sensors died. Three others were moving quickly toward the back of the residence."

"Make sure you have men patrolling the tree line until you're ready to go in at full force to retrieve the girl. We can't risk them slipping past you into the woods."

"Roger that," said the captain.

"Let me know when you've defeated perimeter security," added Volkov, signing off.

\* \* \*

"Having trouble?" asked Isaac Jordan.

"None at all," replied Volkov.

"Really?" said Jordan. "I don't speak Russian, but I do know cursing when I hear it—no matter what the language. I also know the translation of the Russian words, *Cameron Carr*. He's not giving you any problems is he?"

"None that we can't handle," said Volkov. "A gnat buzzing around the face of a giant. Nothing more."

"I don't know," said Jordan. "I've read Carr's file. This is a gnat that you don't want to piss off."

# 50

Carr had promised Jordan not to tell his daughter about the contents of their conversation, but Jordan had never counted on a situation like this.

But before Carr reported on their private meeting, he needed to explain how he came to ask for it in the first place. "Your father is sincere about not forcing you to join him," he began, keeping one eye on the wall of video images. "But did you wonder how he could possibly give you that choice?"

"No," said Riley, blinking rapidly in confusion. Carr gave her a few seconds to piece it together, confident that she would. "But now that you bring it up, it's a great question. And I don't have any answers. Wow was I dumb not to think of this before."

Carr shook his head. "First time you haven't been way ahead of me. I've lived in the world of deception and military tactics for years. I've been responsible for protecting assets who are being hunted. You can outthink me on every other dimension, but not on this one."

"Do you have any idea what they're talking about?" Trish asked David Bram.

"None," he replied.

"Riley's father gave her a choice of whether to join him or not," explained Carr. "But suppose she declined. Suppose she elected to go back to her life. Okay, no problem. He told her he'd just erase her memory of the past few days and she'd be good to go. But this is the *last* thing he can let happen. Because this won't erase *Volkov's* memory. The Russians know who she is. Know she was born Melissa Jordan. So she has a huge target on her chest. Her father is smart enough to know there is no way she can go back to her life now."

"So was he lying about giving her a choice?" asked Bram.

"Like I said, no he wasn't. At first I figured he had to be. That, or he really didn't care about Riley at all, willing to let her take her chances. But when he finished telling us his story, and what he had been up to, it became fairly obvious. There *was* a way she could go back to her life—without fear she'd be used as bait or leverage. He would simply have to die one more time. In a way that would be absolutely convincing to Marat Volkov."

Riley's mouth dropped open. "He's a copy, isn't he?" she said, as fast on the uptake as always. "Holy shit!" she added. "Unbelievable!"

Carr could well understand her reaction. His stomach had dropped to his shoes when he had first figured it out. Because it took what Jordan had accomplished in the way of mind transference from the abstract to the real.

The man they had met with *was* Isaac Jordan, not some pale facsimile, not some soulless monster or hollow robot. He cried and laughed and loved and hurt just like a human being. He had displayed the entire gamut of emotions.

What Jordan had said about there being no discernible difference between an organic consciousness and a perfect computer emulation was true, a fact that his own duplicate had demonstrated to perfection. If Carr had been told there was something odd about their host and been given a million guesses, he wouldn't have guessed *this*.

Deep down, Carr had been a skeptic, but after deducing what Jordan was up to, that he was a copy himself, this skepticism had shattered. The man they had met was unmistakably Isaac Jordan, just as surely as if the original's head had been cut off and reattached to a new neck.

Carr watched a stunned, awestruck look come over Bram's face, as well, as he relived his time with Jordan two point oh and digested this incredible reality.

The lieutenant turned his attention to Trish Casner, who seemed to also be reeling, but in a different way. "You didn't know?" he said.

"No," she replied uncomfortably. "I'd think he would have told me if this was true. Are you certain?"

"Positive," said Carr. "Jordan confirmed it. Or at least the version of Jordan that *we* met with did."

"What else did he say?" asked Riley.

Carr sighed. The seven soldiers were still in a holding pattern. Part of him was desperate to leave and begin preparations, but preparations for what? They might never breach the automated security, after all. And assuming they did, while inside the panic room he could view their first move afterward, which would be critical in dictating his strategy.

Even so, he could use this time to contemplate various options.

On the other hand, he sometimes worked best when he let his experience and instincts guide him. When he didn't waste mental energy considering *all* the possibilities, just the one that was developing. And he felt he owed it to Riley not to stop here. He could at least give her a few minutes more.

"I don't have much time," said Carr, "so let me give you the highlights. If you have any questions, save them for the end."

He proceeded to sketch out the background on how things had ended up as they had. He and Jordan had covered a lot of ground during their ten-minute private discussion, and Carr relayed the gist of it much more quickly.

When Volkov had contacted Jordan from the church, informing him he had his daughter and demanding he give himself up at a location in the Barents Sea, Jordan had researched the Russian and known he couldn't cooperate. Once Volkov had Jordan, it would be too easy, and too tempting, for the Russian to kill Riley to tie up loose ends. But Jordan had no other choice.

And then he overheard Carr getting a report from the Defense Intelligence Agency, and he learned where Riley was being held. A desperate plan began to take shape in his mind.

He uploaded his consciousness into a copy, into an Isaac Jordan who had come to life knowing his sole purpose was to be a sacrifice. Knowing that he had been born with a lifetime of memories and hopes, but would be snuffed out for the cause before he could begin to create any memories of his own.

The born-again Isaac Jordan would race to the church and do whatever was necessary to save Riley's life. He would wear undetectable explosives under his clothing. He would give himself up, and then reveal that he'd booby-trapped himself. He would tell the Russians that once his daughter was free and clear, he would disarm and do whatever they wanted going forward, as long he got periodic proof that Riley remained alive.

Not too much to ask, since this is what they had promised in the first place for his surrender. If they refused to free her, on the other hand, he would blow himself up.

It would be as simple and as complicated as that.

Jordan was betting they would agree to his terms in a heartbeat. They'd be leaving Riley as a loose end, but they'd be gaining his willing cooperation.

Once his daughter was safe, Jordan would work for them for a month or two. Since they knew nothing about his success with mind transference, they wouldn't doubt for a moment that he was the one and only Isaac Jordan. He was too recognizable, and his genius too unique.

And then he would try to escape, making sure he lost his life in the process. And that would close their file on Jordan and his daughter alike. The original version could continue reaching for his lofty goals, and Riley could live out her life safe from any further molestation.

It had been a workable plan. Only before it could be executed, Carr had beaten him to the church—and to the punch.

Luckily, Carr's plan was also a good one.

So Jordan and his double, working together, had devised Plan B. The born-again Jordan—Jordan Two—had waited for Carr to succeed, and then had taken over his escape helicopter, bringing Riley, Bram, and Carr to meet with him in Colorado. Then he had asked a close friend, John Brennan, to pretend to betray him, making sure Volkov would take the bait. Brennan would time the attack so they wouldn't come for Jordan Two until Riley was a safe distance away. This ensured that no matter what happened, Volkov couldn't reach her.

Then Jordan's original plan would be back on track. Either Volkov would honor his word to Brennan and kill the duplicate Jordan, or more likely, would try to force him to work for Russia. If Volkov tried the latter, Jordan Two would eventually agree, making sure he died in an escape attempt several months later as originally planned.

Either way, the Russians would have no doubt his death was real and would have no further use for Riley Ridgeway.

When Carr had learned of Jordan's ability to create perfect doubles, he began to suspect the billionaire was carrying out some form of this plan. Which meant Jordan would find a way to telegraph his location to Volkov so he would be killed or captured, protecting his daughter. When Jordan had reiterated just before they parted that Riley could choose to go back to her life, this solidified Carr's suspicions even further. Especially since Jordan had his pilot standing by to put a safe distance between himself and his daughter.

The more Carr thought about it, the more certain he became that he was right. And he couldn't help but admire the plan. It was the exact deception he would have devised had he been in Jordan's shoes.

Carr laid it all out for the three civilians in the panic room with impressive efficiency, barely pausing to breathe, and they hung, spell-bound, on every word.

"Once I was convinced this was the plan, I confronted your father's double."

"And he admitted you were right?" said Riley. "Just like that?"

Carr nodded.

"Why did he insist you not tell me?"

"He was worried how you might react if you found out he'd deceived you—just when he was so desperately trying to earn back your trust."

"So the plan was for me to never know?"

"He thought it would be better if you didn't. Jordan One was watching a video feed of our meeting with Jordan Two. Jordan Two didn't tell me where the original was, only that he was close enough that he could be in place by the time you made your decision. If we decided to join your father's efforts, Jordan One would give us a tour of the underground facility. We would never know the sacrificial lamb we had first met had been slaughtered. As far as you and Jordan One would be concerned, everything would be reset to the way it was, before Volkov learned your father was alive."

"A brilliant strategy," said Riley. "But truly horrible, as well."

"I agree. Because we met Jordan Two. And we don't see him as just an expendable robot, but as a flawed man we developed a connection with. He teared up again when we discussed his plan. He was willing to die to protect you, Riley, but he was scared. Remember when he said he was prepared to die a hundred times over for you? That wasn't just idle talk."

"I don't doubt he was scared," said Riley sadly. "It couldn't have helped him much emotionally to know that the original would remain. He talked about two copies of a novel. But while one copy is burning, it feels the pain of the flames and of dissociation. Knowing the novel won't be lost to history because another copy still lives isn't much comfort to the pages that are being consumed by fire."

"He was scared," said Carr, "but he accepted his fate. He would do anything for you. And he felt it was only the beginning of the penance he owed for the pain he had brought to others. Penance for Turlock, and the bodies of duplicates he had ordered put to sleep."

An expression of profound sadness came over Riley's face.

"When I realized Volkov had been listening in to our conversation with Jordan Two," continued Carr, "I knew we were in trouble. This changed everything. Volkov had heard what was really going on. Learned that perfect doubles were possible. When Brennan first contacted him, Volkov probably thought he was on the level. But when Volkov heard about whole brain emulation, he couldn't possibly fail to guess why John Brennan was insisting so adamantly that Jordan be killed."

"So that's why Volkov needs me again," said Riley. "He knows that killing Jordan Two, as you call him, doesn't remove the ASI sabotage threat, because the original still remains. And pressing him into service won't work, because he was always prepared to die. So he still needs me to have any leverage."

Carr nodded. "Which means that—"

He stopped in mid-sentence as he finally detected significant activity in the quadrant he had continued to monitor. The seven men were splitting up after having exchanged triumphant smiles all around.

From the looks of it, they had finally succeeded in disabling the security perimeter.

Captain Sergei Greshnev was now leading a team of two soldiers in the direction of the guest house, while the four others spread out to patrol the perimeter, apparently waiting for their comrades to return.

This made sense. Their sensors must have picked up Estrada in the guest house when they arrived, so they would take the pilot out of the equation first. Then they would come at the residence, seven men strong.

Carr took a deep breath. "Looks like we'll have to pick this up another time." He forced a smile. "Maybe when we get through this and are sipping piña coladas on a beach somewhere. But for now, I want the three of you to lock yourselves inside this room."

Before they could respond he said, "Janice, please capture images of the four of us, with enough resolution for facial and body recognition."

"Completed," said the room's PDA.

"Janice, follow orders and instructions given by any of the four of us, but don't respond to anyone else. Understood?"

"Understood and acknowledged."

"Continue to watch the monitors," Carr instructed the three civilians. "With any luck, they won't find this room for a long time. And they'll find it very difficult to penetrate."

"I take it you plan to go out there," said Riley.

"Yes. They'll find us and get to us eventually, even in this room. The only chance we have is to go on offense."

"So what's your plan?" asked Bram. "Kill them all?"

"Exactly," said Carr with a weary smile. "Who knew you were this good of a strategist? Maybe you should be in my line of work."

"I appreciate that you're trying to keep the mood light," said Riley, "but there are seven soldiers out there with submachine guns. You really think you can take them all out bare-handed?"

"Absolutely!" said Carr with mock bravado. "Just so long as they don't have any compact stunners, I'll be fine." He smiled. "I have a great track record against anyone weighing over a hundred and ten pounds. Really."

# PART 7
## Assault

# 51

Marat Volkov listened to his comm and turned to face his prisoner. "Turns out my guess was right," he boasted, quite pleased with himself. "Whatever Brennan did here to take down security was able to do the same at your mansion. My men are in. All seven of them," he added.

Jordan didn't give him the satisfaction of a reaction.

Volkov paused to listen to another voice in his ear. He frowned, said a few sentences in Russian, and returned his attention to Jordan. "It's time for us to begin a heart-to-heart conversation."

"Aren't you being premature?" said Jordan. "You don't have my daughter yet."

"I will in a matter of minutes. I was waiting for the report I just received to begin, from the man I sent to secure your underground facility."

"Hold on," said Jordan. "You only sent one man?"

"Don't tell me the great Isaac Jordan is actually impressed," said Volkov in amusement. "I'm a little understaffed at the moment. But then again, I am behind enemy lines. Russia has developed some technologies that are unmatched as force multipliers when it comes to operations like capturing your facility. Technologies you clearly aren't aware of. Looks like you've been too narrowly focused on stopping ASI technologies to bother with *lesser* advances," he added in contempt.

"A mistake I won't make again," said Jordan.

Volkov laughed. "A mistake you won't get the *chance* to make again."

"Is there a point to this?"

"All of your people down below are unconscious. We hit them with a potent knock-out agent."

Jordan's expression was mixed. He was alarmed by this news, but also relieved that his people were still alive.

Urinson continued to remain silent throughout, and continued to hold a gun on the bound billionaire. The Russian could have been a statue for all anyone could tell. If there were pigeons in the room, they'd be landing on Urinson's head.

"My comrade has completed a cursory inspection of the people he knocked out in your facility," continued Volkov. "I just got his report now. I have to admit, I expected to find the original Isaac Jordan among them. But this was not to be."

"What are you talking about?" said Jordan. "There's only one of me."

Volkov sneered at him in contempt. "Don't insult me, Mr. Jordan. You know I was listening while you described your success with mind transference. Brennan *insisted* that I kill you. Then, once he was down, you practically *begged* me to do the same. Did you think I wouldn't guess your plan? You're a copy, set up on a silver platter for me to kill, so I'll go away and the original Isaac Jordan will be free to operate."

Jordan didn't make any attempt to deny it.

"As I was saying," continued the major, "we didn't find the other you down below. This is a disappointment. I really thought he would be there, ready to pop up to take your place the moment you left, like a jack-in-the-box. I'm guessing you transmitted a video of your session with your daughter to him, so he could slip back into her life seamlessly. We checked, but you'd stopped transmitting to your other self by the time we arrived. Too bad, we might have been able to track the transmission."

Volkov shrugged. "But no matter. You're going to deliver him to us. If you don't, I'm going to make you watch me do terrible things to your daughter." He paused. "Well, to *his* daughter." Then, seeing the pain in Jordan's eyes, he added, "I guess both of you see her as your daughter equally, don't you?"

The Russian shook his head in wonder. "Your technology really is extraordinary," he allowed. "When I listened to you talk about the transfer, even hearing you insist that a duplicate and original are indistinguishable, I still couldn't help but think of the copy as lurching about like a Frankenstein. But after I figured out *you* were a duplicate, I was astonished by your humanity. It came through, loud and clear, even in an audio feed. And now that I see you in person, I have to say, you're as human as any man I've ever met."

"That's funny," said Jordan. "You're as *inhuman* as any man I've ever met."

Volkov seemed to take this almost as a compliment. "Keep that in mind as you make your choices," he said. "Fail to cooperate and you'll think the me you've seen so far is a *saint*."

The Russian paused. "Speaking of cooperation," he continued, "I had originally planned to press you into service inside Mother Russia, but I think I've changed my mind. Your underground facility is too valuable, and too perfect, to ignore. It *is* in the middle of America, but it's also beautifully hidden and off the grid. So I'll get additional agents from the homeland to man the facility, and you and the other Jordan will both work for us here. In fact, it's tempting to have Jordan make more copies of himself. We could use his genius repeated a *thousand* times."

Volkov thought about this further and shook his head. "Actually, maybe not. Perhaps two *is* the right number. Any more than that and it might get unwieldy for us to maintain our leverage. One of you might find a way to turn the tables. If we limit you to two copies, we double the contributions your genius makes possible, but still have a number that is manageable."

"I look forward to demonstrating otherwise."

Volkov laughed. "That's the spirit. But do you know what just occurred to me?" he added enthusiastically. "I really have to get used to thinking about a world in which mind transference is possible. I don't need as many reinforcements from Russia as I thought. I could have you make twenty copies of *me*."

"Trust me," said Jordan in disdain, "you won't like yourself. But go for it. I'd enjoy watching you and your emulations at each other's throats—maybe even literally."

The major tilted his head in thought. "Granted that too many alpha males might spoil the broth," he said, "but this would never happen when they're all me. We'll all think exactly the same way. Agree on every strategy."

"At first. But as your experiences diverge, so will your thinking. And suppose there's one task you want to do, and one you don't. Now imagine there are two of you. Both will, indeed, think the same way about the situation. Both will think, 'I'll assign myself to the favored task, and my doppelgänger to the other.' The decision might be the same, but the *I* in question will be very different. Conflicts will arise—and often."

"Interesting," said Volkov after a few seconds of further thought. "There's even more to ponder about these capabilities than I realized. But let me move on. Regardless of how we choose to keep and exert our control of the facility, as long as you and your original cooperate, you'll be treated like royalty. So will your daughter, although not here. Can't risk that you'll find a way to free her. We'll even let her keep David Bram. As a pet, I guess. And I sense that you like him and approve of him being with your daughter."

The Russian shook his head. "I'm afraid I can't be as generous when it comes to Cameron Carr. He has to die. He's too dangerous, as I'm sure you can appreciate. I sense that you like him, too, but trust me, you'll get over his passing."

"Are you finished?" said Jordan.

"Not even close," said the major. "I haven't even gotten to your job description. First, I can tell you what you won't be working on: ASI. I heard you describe the sacrifices you've made, and are willing to make, to prevent this from coming into being again. So we'll stick with things more in your comfort zone. Ones that will make it easy for you to cooperate. In fact, we would want you to continue your watchdog efforts, along with *all* of your work. Just under new management, which we're happy to provide.

"And we'll need full access to Pock," continued Volkov. "From what you've said, he'll prove even more valuable than two Jordans. And you'll have to provide the specs on your whole brain emulation and bioprinting technologies so we can ah . . . *duplicate* your duplication work. And your virtual reality system, also."

"Why the VR? To play video games?"

"No, to test and train our recruits in field conditions. But most importantly, we can torture adversaries in virtual reality and then erase their memories. We can get the information we want without them knowing we have it, and without leaving a single mark on their bodies."

"That tells me everything I need to know about you," said Jordan in disgust. "You look at a miracle technology and all you see is a better way to torture people."

"You're hardly one to judge," snapped the Russian. "Isn't this what *you've* been doing with it? Torturing your twelve hundred volunteers? From the sound of it, you've put them through nightmare scenarios not even I could have dreamed up. You think you're better than me because you drape your torture in the name of science?"

Jordan didn't reply, but from the mixture of anger and regret on his face, it was clear Volkov had hit a nerve.

"I do need to ask for one deviation from what you've been doing," continued the Russian. "I appreciate that your experiments have been very well controlled. I can't fault your scientific integrity. But there will be powerful people in my country who will be intrigued by the possibility of inhabiting a younger body. At least once they've interacted with your copies and come to appreciate that you really can accomplish a perfect transference of consciousness. They'll insist on being reincarnated into twenty-year-old versions of themselves once they've died. Or, even more likely, bodies that are *indestructible*."

"You're messing with things you don't understand," said Jordan.

"What don't I understand?"

"Everything. You can't have an indestructible body without changing your behavior and personality in dramatic ways. I'll give you one of many examples. If I transferred you to a non-biological body, much of your sexual appetites would remain, but you'd have no way to satisfy them. And if you tried to edit out the sex drive, something evolution has so deeply embedded in the construction of the brain, you'd be playing a game whose outcome can't be predicted."

"That may be true," said Volkov, "but you know there's more to it than that. I listened to your every word. The outcomes of significant changes might be unpredictable, but with your VR, they *are* testable.

You can see what effect this type of change will have, and decide how to proceed. It will take some time and effort, but I have no doubt you'll find a way." The Russian raised his eyebrows. "Maybe we'll need a third Isaac Jordan, after all."

"You paint an interesting fantasy," said Jordan. "But I'm noticing you haven't heard any voices in your ear telling you that your men have captured my daughter. And you know I was born with the sole purpose of dying. So you have no leverage. Why don't you do us both a favor and keep your wet dreams to yourself until you do."

The corners of the Russian's mouth turned up into just the hint of a smile. "Don't worry, my men will have your daughter very soon. They're just being cautious. Taking their time, making sure they don't make any mistakes. But even if the impossible happens, and she's somehow able to elude us, trust me, we still have a solid Plan B. One that might make you wish we *had* captured her, after all."

# 52

Lieutenant Cameron Carr moved to the kitchen at a full sprint as his mind worked overtime. He had fought in combat zones and worked as a spy behind enemy lines. He was well trained in hand-to-hand and excelled at improvisation.

He knew of dozens of household items that could be turned into weapons, from paper weights to microwave ovens to fireplace pokers to fire extinguishers. He could use bleach and a few other household items to make a bomb that would explode into a cloud of chlorine gas, and he could turn a high powered squirt gun into a flame thrower.

The trick was to be strategic and decisive, winnowing down this choice of homemade weapons into a few that were right for the given situation. Carr was expert in several martial arts, but he'd have no chance without weapons and creativity. The great martial artist Bruce Lee had once commented, "If someone comes at you with a sword, run if you can. Kung Fu doesn't always work."

In Carr's book, these were words to live by, especially if the weapon coming at you was not a sword but a submachine gun.

Riley had implied he would need to take out these seven armed men with his bare hands. This wasn't true. He needed to take out *one* man with his bare hands, or with a makeshift weapon that could act at a distance. If the one man was isolated and Carr did it right, he could borrow this soldier's assault rifle to take out the other six.

And Carr might not need to take them all out by himself. At the moment, at least, Roberto Estrada was still in the game.

Carr had hoped the Russians would come straight for the main residence, allowing him to deal with them before they went gunning for Estrada—but they had done just the opposite. Even if the pilot knew they were coming, his chances of survival were slim. On the other hand, if he was surprised, he had no chance at all.

Estrada had told Carr during the flight that Jordan expected his people to perform multiple duties. Those who signed on with Jordan believed in a great cause, protecting humanity from ASI and seeding the galaxy, and saw their work as a mission rather than a job. Just like Trish Casner, Estrada had been assigned numerous responsibilities and would be neck-deep in work in the guest house, making surprise even easier for the Russians.

If Carr didn't manage to warn Estrada, the pilot would be dead in minutes. He might end up that way, anyway, but Carr had to do whatever he could to prevent this, not just for humanitarian reasons but because he could use a competent ally in this lopsided battle. If he *was* able to warn him, Estrada's experience and the Russians' inability to pinpoint his location within the guest house might make him an elusive target.

But *wanting* to warn Estrada and being *able* to warn him were two different things now that Jordan had thrown the estate back into the Dark Ages. Carr would give his life's savings for a working cell phone.

As far as he could see, there was only one way he could warn him in time, a way that he dreaded. Even thinking about it set his teeth on edge. This was really going to suck.

He stopped running as he neared Riley's assigned bedroom in the mansion. Since it was directly in the path to his destination, a detour here would only represent the briefest of delays. He rushed inside and left less than a minute later with a full can of hairspray, a bottle of rubbing alcohol, and a polyester women's bathing suit, all of which he shoved inside a trendy leather overnight bag he had found inside the closet.

He completed his rapid journey to the kitchen and went straight for a large plastic garbage bin, dumping its contents onto the floor. He picked out bits of garbage—a crumpled brown paper bag, plastic, and a few other items he thought would create smoke—and returned them to the tall, rectangular container.

He guessed there was what he called a *fire wand* somewhere in the kitchen, a plastic butane lighter with an elongated barrel homeowners used to light candles and such, but didn't want to waste any time searching if he was wrong. Instead, he grabbed a roll of paper towels from the counter by the sink, turned on the stove, and held the roll against the burner until it caught fire. He nursed the flames until they were hungrily licking up the sides of the roll and then threw this into the bin.

The fire quickly spread, and smoke began to belch into the air, a development he noted with satisfaction. Even so, he needed to hurry things along. He yanked open several drawers until he found a pair of kitchen mitts, which he hastily put on his hands. Finally, he carried the burning container to a nearby hockey-puck-shaped smoke detector on the ceiling and held it up over his head.

"Shit!" he cursed as the burning trash did its job almost instantly, tripping a shrieking, impossibly shrill alarm that could wake the dead and make the living wish they were.

Since smoke alarms were wired in parallel, when one tripped they all did, setting the entire mansion screeching at a decibel level that was indescribably deafening, hammering at his brain and his every last nerve as he had known it would.

The blaring alarms were relentless, but even as they threatened to make Carr's head explode, he knew they had served their purpose, being easily heard in the guest house and probably even in *Australia*, putting a seasoned soldier like Estrada on instant alert.

Carr imagined his civilian companions suffering inside the panic room, covering their ears and cursing his name. He knew they would see his activities on one of the monitors and were bright enough to understand his intent.

The alarm would awaken the Russians, as well, but he had no doubt they knew he was active the moment their sensors had gone dead. This just gave them one more thing to think about. And since the alarms would continue their unholy brain-melting assault, when the Russians did come into the mansion after Riley they would be unable to hear themselves think, making concentration and coordination far more difficult.

The eardrum-bursting blare wasn't helping Carr's concentration, either, but it was a small price to pay for what he had gained.

He dumped the burning contents of the garbage container into the kitchen's restaurant-sized stainless steel sink and opened the faucet as far as he could, not pausing a moment to witness the fire's demise. Instead, he hurriedly pulled open the rest of the doors and cabinets surrounding him, searching for a pair of scissors, a fire wand, and tape, all of which he found in short order.

He considered several kitchen knives, but they were poorly balanced and would bounce off the body armor the Russians were no doubt wearing, assuming he could throw them with any accuracy in the first place. He finally selected a small but lethal steak knife and taped it to his thigh, outside of his pants, testing first to be sure it wouldn't obstruct or stab him as he ran.

Carr briefly considered crafting homemade body armor to put over his heart, but this would take far too much time given the power of the weapons he was up against. Thick frying pans were all around him, but one of these wouldn't be nearly enough. He'd have to find some old-fashioned paperback books and tape a stack of three or four of them to the pan, and then tape the entire mess under his shirt. If the Russians would promise to only shoot at his heart, this would be worth the trouble, but he suspected they would cheat and go for his head.

Carr moved to the nearby liquor cabinet and removed two bottles of brandy, pouring out a third of the contents of each and filling them back to the top with the higher-proof rubbing alcohol. He then cut two long pieces of the bathing suit and shoved the ends of the polyester strips inside each bottle, tightening the caps to keep them in place. Unlike cotton, which would need to be doused in alcohol to make a good fuse, polyester would ignite quickly and burn even after a flame was removed. This would let him light the tail hanging outside of the bottles without having to use the fire bombs right away.

Satisfied that he had been able to whip up the two Molotov cocktails in little more than a minute, he zippered them into cozy side compartments on opposite ends of the overnight bag, confirmed that the middle compartment still contained a can of hairspray and a fire wand, and ran from the kitchen.

He could have taken any number of weapons that would have been helpful in close quarters but deemed these not worth the time and effort. He would also have loved to explore other rooms, especially the garage, but he was well out of time.

He quickly made it to the front of the mansion as the alarms continued to stab at his eardrums like ice picks.

# 53

Carr raced from the front of the residence toward the front of the guest house like he was being chased by a tribe of cannibals. From what he had seen in the panic room monitors, he was out of sight of the Russians. They would also be stressed out by the alarms he had triggered, causing them a delay while they pondered these new circumstances.

The three soldiers who had begun to move toward the back of the guest house would be entirely focused on their imminent operation. He was out of view of their expected approach, and would stay that way as long as they didn't guess he would be bold enough to sprint to the site in the open, like a streaker looking for maximum attention.

If they did consider this possibility, he would fall dead without ever knowing what hit him. A bold, risky strategy, made easier because it was also his *only* strategy. At least if he wanted to get to Estrada in time to have any chance of saving him.

As he neared the guest house he put on the brakes and began a more stealthy approach, relieved to still be alive after his reckless dash through wide open spaces. He spotted the three Russians nearing the house, but he made sure to stay out of sight. His timing couldn't have been more perfect.

As Carr inched closer, Greshnev and his two comrades converged on the back door. The Russians were well aware that the pilot had been put on alert by the smoke alarms shrieking in the mansion and had changed strategy. Instead of a quiet approach and a surprise attack, they sent several long bursts of automatic fire through the door, just in case the pilot had thought lying in wait for them to enter was a smart move.

Carr was confident Estrada was experienced enough to know better. If not, the pilot was now nothing more than a bloody mass of hamburger.

Carr felt his only chance was to torch the place, in multiple locations, despite the risk to Estrada. He would throw a fire bomb through a window on either side of the house and then start additional fires around the perimeter using the two remaining items in his bag. If he held the fire wand in front of the hairspray, he could shoot a stream of fire seven to ten feet long.

When the flames began to quickly spread throughout the house, the men inside would feel an urgent need to leave. The soldiers who had been left behind to patrol the tree line would assume that Carr was waiting to attack their comrades as they exited the burning death-trap, and would rush to eliminate Carr before this could happen.

But the lieutenant had no intention of being anywhere near where they expected him to be. As soon as the fires took hold, Carr would circle around to the woods, hoping to sneak up behind the man farthest out, who with any luck would have blinders on, his attention focused squarely on the burning building and his comrades inside, and unable to hear Carr's quiet approach over the shrieks of the smoke alarms.

The odds of this plan working the way Carr had drawn it up in his imagination were very low, but it was the best chance he had. He had been in situations just as bad before, and had always found a way to win, whether due to luck, an uncanny ability to change tactics as circumstances dictated, or improvisational skills that were second to none.

This had better not be the exception. Too much was riding on him.

Carr was preparing to light the first Molotov cocktail when several gunshots rang out from inside.

A surge of excitement washed through him as he realized the shots hadn't come from the weapons the Russians were using. Which meant they had to have come from Roberto Estrada. The pilot was armed!

Two bursts of machine gun fire followed immediately. To Carr's discerning ears they seemed to be slightly offset and coming from two separate locations.

Only two? Had Estrada managed to remove the third soldier from the game?

Carr was elated. He had hoped that Estrada might have access to a gun hidden away inside the guest house, but it had seemed like too much to ask for, so he had gone forward assuming this wouldn't be the case.

But the fact that Estrada had turned out to be armed wasn't entirely unexpected. He hadn't been while piloting the helo, and the main residence had been scoured clean of guns, but this clearly hadn't been the case when it came to the guest house.

Carr instantly changed strategies to account for this new development. The intruders in the house were now more distracted than he had dared to hope for. So instead of torching the house from the outside, he would rush inside and torch it from within, playing the situation by ear.

*Fortune favors the bold,* he mouthed to himself as he lit the strip of fabric that dangled from the top of one bottle and moved briskly through the front door, bringing the overnight bag with him.

He moved forward to an opening between rooms and crouched at the edge of a sofa, taking in the scene in the next room in one practiced glance, spying all three Russians at once.

One was sprawled on the ground at the bottom of a broad staircase, marinating in his own blood. Sergei Greshnev was near the top of the stairs, proceeding with great caution, while the last Russian held a position just a few stairs up from the landing, his gun facing forward.

A trail of blood began near the top stair and disappeared around the corner into a hallway.

Carr had a good guess as to how it had all played out. The Russians had most likely been going room to room on the first floor. One had passed by the stairway and Estrada had been waiting for this chance, lying across a stair a few from the top, which had given him the best angle to plant a bullet in the Russian's head from above.

The two other Russians had responded with bursts of gunfire, which had wounded Estrada as he slinked up the stairs to the temporary safety of the hallway and parts beyond. The remaining two

Russians were understandably careful about charging after a wounded, cornered animal, especially one who had proven his lethality.

Carr crept closer as Greshnev signaled his plan to the soldier near the bottom landing. The captain had no intention of rounding the corner into the hall. Instead, he would move his weapon around the edge and spray a curtain of death, guaranteeing he could follow the submachine gun into the hall without fear of attack.

Carr hastily removed the second Molotov cocktail and lit the fabric, setting both bottles down carefully beside him. The moment the muzzle of Greshnev's weapon snaked into the hall, Carr acted. He rose up and flung one of the bottles against the wall, just over the head of the soldier near the landing. The glass shattered, and the dense spray of alcohol that resulted ignited faster than the eye could follow, creating a wall of fire that rained down on the Russian soldier.

He shrieked in horror as his face was instantly blistered from the heat and his hair and upper clothing caught fire, but his screams were drowned out by a long burst from Greshnev's weapon.

Carr's timing had been excellent once again. He rushed forward with the second Molotov, already lit, and set it on the hardwood floor a few yards from his victim, who was slapping wildly at his head to kill the flames, and then dived at the man, the steak knife he had freed from his thigh in his right hand.

Carr hit the human torch from behind, acquiring burns of his own as he held the Russian steady and slit his throat in one smooth but violent motion. Blood erupted from the man's throat, dousing some of the flames that were now rising around them.

As Carr released the body, Greshnev realized what had happened and fired at him from the top stair. Carr dived to the left to get out of the Russian's limited range, landing next to the Molotov as he had planned. As Greshnev began to descend to get a better angle on the American, Carr flung the second fire bomb up the stairs, forcing the captain to throw himself flat across two stairs to avoid the resulting spray of fire.

As the bottle was bursting into flame at the top of the stairway, Carr snatched up the weapon belonging to the man he had killed and raced across the threshold into the kitchen, throwing himself behind a granite-faced counter.

He immediately began shooting toward Greshnev, knowing he couldn't hit him from this angle but wanting to give him something to think about.

The upper stairs and hallway were now burning behind Greshnev, as was the landing below. So much had happened so quickly, and the Russian was so surprised and enraged that Carr was on the scene and was mounting such a lethal offensive, that he temporarily forgot about the wounded pilot.

But the wounded pilot didn't forget about him.

As Greshnev moved down the stairs to get free of the growing flames and to engage Carr, Estrada leaped across a wall of fire behind the Russian and put a bullet into the back of his head.

Greshnev slid down the stairs as Estrada ducked down again and tried to assess the situation.

"That's all of them, Roberto!" shouted Carr. "Get yourself clear of the fire!" he added, but this last was drowned out as the home's smoke detectors came to life with a vengeance. Carr felt lucky they had waited as long as they had, since a full thirty seconds had passed since he had thrown the first Molotov.

The pilot didn't need to hear Carr's directive to know what to do. Putting his arms in front of his face as a shield, he sped down the stairs and through the fire now raging at the landing, miraculously not tripping over the growing collection of bodies that had accumulated there.

Carr put two rounds into the smoke detector in the center of the room, lessening the decibel level somewhat, but others in the house continued to scream.

"We may have more unwanted visitors to deal with in a few minutes!" he shouted as he joined Estrada ten yards on the other side of the growing wall of flame.

The pilot's shirt was soaked in blood from a bullet that had gone through his left arm. Carr had been nicked twice on the outer side of his right leg and was also bleeding liberally, although neither of Carr's wounds were a cause for concern.

Estrada nodded. "Follow me!" he shouted, moving away from the fires and toward the entrance to one of the rooms on the first floor.

"We need to get out of here!" shouted Carr, spotting another smoke detector and taking it out, lessening the racket still further. "Neither the fire nor the Russians will wait for long."

"I'm aware," replied Estrada, entering the bedroom.

The pilot rushed to a closed bathroom door. "Isaac!" he shouted as loudly as he could. "We're all clear. Carr came to our rescue. Hurry! We need to go."

Carr's mouth fell open as Isaac Jordan emerged from the bathroom, a gun in his hand.

"Thanks for the help, Lieutenant," bellowed Jordan, loudly enough to be heard over the remaining alarms. "I knew there was a reason I wanted you to join my team so badly."

# 54

"Why are you contacting me?" Volkov barked through his comm in Russian to Ivan Makarov, one of the men he had pulled from other duties to join him in Utah. "Where's Sergei?"

"Possibly down!" said Makarov breathlessly. "He and two of the men were mopping up the guest house in preparation for tackling the main residence. Now the guest house is on fire and we can't establish communications with the captain or his team. Has to be Carr's work. We're moving there now to pin him down."

"No, you idiot!" yelled Volkov. "Never do what seems obvious. Don't play checkers while Carr's playing chess. He'll expect your move and find a way to counter. Assume the team is lost and double-time it into the mansion—while we know Carr isn't in it."

"Roger that," said Makarov.

"Get the girl at all costs," he said, "but don't do anything that might put her life at risk. Understood?"

"Confirmed," said Makarov. "Moving on the mansion now."

Volkov's face flushed red with anger and he uttered a stream of expletives.

\* \* \*

"You seem stressed," said Jordan. "Everything going okay?"

"You think you're cute," said Volkov scornfully. "But we'll see how cute you are in a moment. We've run into a minor delay, but we'll still get Riley. And we can still move the ball down the field while we wait."

Volkov paused and had a brief conversation in Russian with a party or parties unknown.

He turned back to Jordan. "So let me tell you about Plan B," he said. "You think I don't have leverage without your daughter? Guess again. Don't forget that more than a hundred of your close friends and associates are now unconscious and at my mercy. As is your facility. You may not believe in an immortal soul, but you do seem to believe in immortal data. So I can kill any of them I choose, and then wipe the saved pattern of their consciousness from your databases."

Jordan closed his eyes and took a deep breath to calm himself.

"But why stop there?" said Volkov. "I can destroy the emulated brains of your duplicated volunteers—and all associated data. You know, the thousand or so E-Brains you took from their murdered owners. I can make the sleep mode they're in permanent. Including your chosen thirty-five," he added, arching an eyebrow. "Am I beginning to get your attention?"

Jordan continued to keep his eyes closed, and his face remained impassive.

"But wait," said Volkov, "there's more. Good thing you were so chatty, because I overheard *a lot*. You have patterns for your wife and sons stored here too, don't you? The ones you butchered in Turlock. The ones you haven't had the balls to bring back. I can wipe out their patterns one by one, so you get to witness their deaths a second time. Only this time they'll have no way of ever coming back."

Jordan finally opened his eyes. "Enough already!" he barked. "You win, okay? You're right. You have enough leverage on me without my daughter. So why do you need her? Call it off and let her be, and I'll do what you want."

"I can't do that," said Volkov. "You're family's been gone for eight years. You're used to your life without them in it. And bringing them back introduces some headaches for you, which is why you haven't done it yet. Riley is still the best hold on you, something you just demonstrated yet again in your eagerness to protect her. Not to mention that she's nicely compact and portable."

"What's that supposed to mean?"

"She's easy to manage. Good leverage should be uncomplicated and easy to hold onto. You do what we say and she's treated like royalty. A very simple concept. Much easier to hold Riley accountable for your behavior than an entire facility. Besides, your associates are expert in your technology, so I'd prefer they stay alive."

Volkov paused. "But I've run out of patience. So until we have your daughter, I'm willing to work with what leverage I have. I just issued instructions to my man down below. If you haven't told me where to find the original Isaac Jordan in the next two minutes, he's going to start killing your colleagues. One every two minutes until you tell me."

Volkov issued a command through his comm and a video image of a lovely young woman appeared on his laptop. She was unconscious, and Pavel Safin had propped her up against a wall. Volkov manipulated the laptop further and a stopwatch appeared in the corner of the screen, reading two minutes.

He turned the screen so that it faced Jordan. "Here is the first contestant now," he said. "The first of your associates to have her life in your hands. But if you don't cooperate, far from the last," he added, reaching around to touch the stopwatch on the screen.

The red digital numbers began to quickly count down from two minutes. "So if you have any more clever comments to make," said Volkov with a sneer, "I suggest you make them in the next one minute and forty-eight seconds."

# 55

Carr shook his head to clear it, snapping out of the trance he was in as he stared like an idiot at Isaac Jordan.

The location of the all-biological version of the man was a mystery no longer.

Of course this was where he was, thought Carr. As near to his daughter as possible since this Isaac Jordan had yet to interact with her. Once Jordan Two had been sacrificed, the original could tell Riley he had decided to visit her at the mansion to learn of her decision. He could make sure that when they did return to his waterfall-facing property, all signs of the demise of Jordan Two were gone.

"Do they have Riley?" shouted Jordan anxiously as he, Carr, and Roberto Estrada made their way from the bedroom. Smoke was thickening within the guest house at an alarming rate as the fires spread.

"No. She's safe inside the mansion's panic room."

Jordan blew out a long breath. "Thank you!" he bellowed, managing to show profound relief even in the middle of a literal firestorm.

"What's the play?" shouted Estrada urgently, nodding at Carr. "You said more were on the way. They'll probably be waiting for us to emerge."

The lieutenant paused to analyze the situation, not from his own point of view but from the point of view of the enemy. This was an exercise that had saved his life on a number of occasions, but he had rarely found concentration this difficult. Not surprising since he was suffering from burns and two minor gunshot wounds, and was standing in a house that was burning and smoking around him, while alarms hammered at his brain.

"I was wrong," he replied finally. "We need to get out of here. Now! The coast will be clear," he added with conviction.

"How can you be so sure?" shouted Estrada as Carr began moving toward the front door with the two men in tow, crouching low to stay under the descending wall of smoke.

"Trust me for now. I'll explain when we're clear."

Just before Carr exited, Jordan gripped his shirt from behind and held it firmly. "Roberto and I will go first," he yelled. "We have our consciousness backed up. You don't. If you're wrong and end up dead, there's no bringing you back."

Estrada plowed through the door without waiting for a response, returning moments later to indicate that Carr had been right and there was no sign of an ambush.

They each stepped into fresh air and began putting distance between themselves and the flaming house.

"What's going on here?" said Jordan. "How is it that we're under attack?"

"The short version," replied Carr hastily, relieved not to have to shout any longer, "is that Volkov hid an undetectable bug and tracer in Riley's stunner. It picked up everything your double told us during our discussion, along with our current location. Knowing that duplicates were possible, Volkov realized what I realized—that Jordan Two was meant to be expendable—and he didn't fall for your plan. Volkov must be with Jordan Two now, waiting for his men to capture Riley so he can regain the upper hand."

Jordan frowned, assimilating this new reality and all that it implied in one fell swoop. "Shit!" he said simply. "It should have worked. Jordan Two, as you call him, swept everything for bugs. Seems I've underestimated Russian technology."

"One other thing," said Carr. "As you know, I promised your double I wouldn't tell Riley that he was a duplicate. Recent circumstances forced me to break this promise. But rather than feeling betrayed, I think she appreciated what you were trying to do."

"Understood," said Jordan. "And thanks for telling me."

Estrada still wasn't entirely clear on the subtleties of what was happening, but he recognized that longer explanations would have to wait. He turned to the lieutenant. "You said you'd explain how you knew the coast would be clear," he said.

"The last man you killed in there was Sergei Greshnev, Volkov's second-in-command. When his four comrades who were manning the perimeter saw the house on fire, I knew they'd begin to make their way here and attempt to contact Greshnev. When he didn't respond, they'd contact Volkov."

"But he's not on-site," said Jordan, "and I've suppressed cell and Wi-Fi on the premises."

"True, but Volkov knew about that. He heard your double explain it to me. So he'd make sure to send his team with comms that wouldn't be affected."

"So they called him for orders," said Estrada. "Are you saying you've guessed the nature of these orders?"

"Exactly. I've dealt with this asshole before. I know he's come to respect my abilities. He'll assume that the three men who were sent to the guest house are down, and he won't risk losing the rest by sending them after me. Instead, he'll have his remaining team rush to the mansion to grab Riley, taking advantage of my absence. He'll guess that I'll be hunkering down near the guest house, expecting them to come after me, allowing his men to lower their guard and root Riley out as quickly as possible."

"So you think they'll be splitting up inside the mansion?" asked Estrada.

"I do," replied Carr. "They'll think they now have free rein. And I'm confident they won't leave a sentry. They'll gamble on getting Riley at all cost, so all four will be assigned to the Riley Ridgeway scavenger hunt." He paused. "Which means we can sprint back to the main residence out in the open. If we get there fast enough, we'll have the chance to engage them with their guards down."

"Okay," said Estrada, "so you know how this Volkov thinks. But he knows how *you* think, also. Won't he guess you'll use this line of reasoning?"

Carr shook his head. "He doesn't know I've discovered he bugged Riley's stunner. He has no idea I have as good a grasp of the situation as I do."

"I say we trust your instincts," said Jordan. "But we're going first. We'll play the track stars while you follow up with a slow and careful approach. If you *are* wrong, this will still give us a chance. And, again, if you die, you're gone for good—while we aren't."

Carr opened his mouth to reply when Jordan cut him off. "Not open for debate!" he insisted.

Carr thought about reminding Jordan that he wasn't in charge, but there was no time for further discussion, and the man did make some good points.

"Are you really up for a sprint?" Carr asked Estrada, gesturing to his blood-soaked shirt. "Gunshot wounds tend to slow people down."

"Desperate times," said Estrada. "I'll make it as long as I need to."

Carr issued a brief nod, communicating his respect for the pilot's determination.

"I'll run as fast as I can," said Jordan, "but don't wait up, Roberto." He caught Carr's eye. "I'm a horrible shot," he explained, "so my plan is to choose a hiding place and hope I can surprise someone at point-blank range. You two can do the active hunting."

With this said, Jordan bolted off in the direction of the mansion, catching Estrada so much by surprise that it took the pilot ten full seconds to pass him. Meanwhile, Carr began a much slower, stealthier approach, as agreed. If he was wrong and they had posted a sentry, Jordan and Estrada would be his canaries in the coal mine, tripping the landmines for him.

He was used to being in the lead, but he couldn't fault Jordan's logic. And he admired his courage. Just because Jordan's consciousness had been saved didn't mean his instinct for self-preservation had diminished. And in Carr's view, it would still be tragic to lose the only fully-biological Isaac Jordan in existence.

Carr couldn't stop himself from picking up the pace. They had managed to kill three out of seven men, which was a good start.

But they weren't out of the woods yet.

# 56

For Riley Ridgeway, Carr's words just before leaving them in the panic room were the opposite of the straw that broke the camel's back. They were the straw that *mended* the camel's back.

Her instincts had been shouting at her for some time to trust her father, and she had fought them like she was a cornered badger. But her father's wild description of his history and the future he was working toward were too elaborate to have been fabricated, even by him. Everything hung together too well.

It was obvious that he was a great man, and despite herself, she had come to believe that he was also a *good* one.

But not a perfect one. A man who struggled mightily to do the best he could in helping lift mankind and pave the way to the stars.

If he succeeded in reaching his goals, Isaac Jordan would go down in history as the man who had ushered in the era of immortality. Of infinity. As the man who had seen death as a disease that simply needed a cure. As the man who had accepted the Fermi Paradox for the cautionary tale that it was, but who refused to let the speed of light barrier limit his vision.

Her father had made a mistake. A huge one. He had been extraordinarily cautious in setting up the ultimate anti-ASI safeguard—a kinetic round in space—but then extraordinarily *careless* in failing to consider the fallout that would ensue if it did need to be deployed.

But he had never acted out of malice, or been seized in the grip of psychosis.

Even the most well-intentioned man, trying to be as ethical as possible, made mistakes, and there was no doubt her father was no exception, and was continuing to make mistakes every day. And, yes, it was said that the road to hell was paved with good intentions.

But so was the road to heaven.

And there were so many powerful people trying to take the human race to hell with *bad* intentions. Surely this was a quicker route to the underworld than what her father was attempting.

Carr's words had finally knocked out her last shred of resistance, had forced her to finally let go of the ultimate grudge, one harbored against a man she blamed for betraying the entire world and destroying her life.

Carr had provided one more powerful demonstration that her father had not been lying—about anything. Her father did care about her—*for* her—as much as he said he did. He had been watching out for her these past eight years in a way that suddenly didn't seem creepy anymore. He had vowed he would die to protect her, and by creating a duplicate who was dedicated to doing just this, he had provided the ultimate proof that these weren't just hollow words.

Yes, he should have reunited with her much sooner. He should have reanimated her mother and brothers. But she could forgive him these lapses. He had his own fears and weaknesses to overcome.

She had initially concluded that even if she came to believe all he said, she would refuse to join him. Why wrestle with the weight of the world? Her life was uncomplicated and simple.

Except that it *wasn't*. She had been living as someone she wasn't. She had been suppressing her intellect and her passion for science. She had been content to live in a holding pattern, her life heading in no real direction, content to lick her wounds and push away a man she refused to admit she loved the moment this love became impossible to deny.

She had been living in fear she would turn into a monster like her infamous father.

Now she could have it all. A father who was not a monster, and who did still love her. She could pursue her interests unrestrained, working in conjunction with scientific giants. She could stop fighting her love for David Bram and let it blossom instead, and pursue the most consequential goals in human history with him by her side.

And after witnessing Jordan Two's humanity, she was now a believer that she could even have her mother and brothers back, precisely as emotional, as rational, as perfect, and as flawed as they had been while fully biological.

Not that there would ever be a perfect world. Riley didn't agree with her father in every case. And as exhilarating as his vision was, there was something about it that was still troubling to her.

Pinning this down would require further thought. But this would have to wait until she *wasn't* in the middle of a crisis. Her new friend, Cameron Carr, had just left them in the panic room moments before, willingly throwing himself into the lion's den.

It was ironic that Carr's revelation had prompted her to forgive her father and believe in him again, just when the walls were caving in. It was ironic that the instant she had come to embrace a future along the lines that her father had outlined, this future was in danger of being snatched away. More than in danger. The Russians had the upper hand and seemed sure to destroy everything her father had worked for.

And if Marat Volkov was calling the shots, the future would become more of an Orwellian nightmare than a grand vision for humanity.

She and her two companions could now do nothing but watch the lieutenant on the monitors, powerless to help him.

"Are we doing the right thing letting him face this alone?" asked Riley.

"Yeah, I feel guilty, too," said Bram. "But it's the right thing. You're the key, so keeping you out of Volkov's hands is the highest priority. I thought about pushing Carr to let me go with him, but the last thing he needs is an untrained civilian to babysit."

Bram frowned. "I really do believe that," he added. "So why do I feel like a coward?"

"For the same reasons I do," said Riley. "But you're right. You're no hero if your act of bravery only makes things worse. And I know your true colors. I was there when you offered yourself up to Volkov if he would free me."

On the monitors, Carr entered a bedroom and began rooting around.

Trish watched him gather items in fascination. "Why do you think he needs a woman's bathing suit?" she asked, arching an eyebrow.

"You've got me," said Riley with a shrug, and Bram shook his head as well.

Before they could consider it further, the lieutenant entered the kitchen and proceeded to dump garbage onto the floor. It was surreal to be watching him like he was the star of a silent movie, one without subtitles and so far, without a discernible plot.

"Wow," said Trish as she watched him fly around the kitchen. "This guy really moves with a purpose."

"Oh shit!" said Bram, as they watched Carr extend a flaming garbage bin toward a smoke detector on the ceiling. "I hate those things," he added, just as the high-decibel nightmare began.

They watched the rest unfold with their ears covered, wishing their silent movie could have stayed that way. Carr continued to operate with an awe-inspiring level of speed and decisiveness.

Five minutes after Carr had left them in the panic room, they watched three armed soldiers enter the back door of the guest house. Not long thereafter, Carr entered through the front door, and less than a minute later the house was in flames—and none of the panic room's thirty-two monitors could show them what was happening inside.

Riley's breath caught in her throat as she watched, trying not to panic. The four men who had been patrolling the perimeter began to move toward the burning house, but after making it less than halfway they stopped abruptly and changed direction. It became clear almost immediately that they were now heading toward the main residence.

When Riley shifted her gaze back to the monitor showing the front door of the guest house, three men were now outside—and none of them were Russian.

Two of the men were battered and bloody, Cameron Carr and Roberto Estrada.

Riley gasped as the third man came into full view. A man who was unmistakably her father.

# 57

Riley traded glances with her two companions in the panic room. It was good that Carr had confided in them when he had, or they would have been even *more* shocked to see Jordan on the monitor.

Part of her hadn't been entirely convinced the version of her father they had met was really a duplicate. She found it almost impossible to believe that whole brain emulation could be *that* perfect. But seeing him here, now, made the reality of it undeniable.

Another minute passed and the four armed assailants entered the back of the main residence. At the same time, on another monitor, her father began running toward the mansion, on the front side of the property. Roberto Estrada quickly followed, carrying one of the Russian's submachine guns with him.

Carr began to make his way toward the mansion, as well, but he moved far more slowly and took a more stealthy, circuitous route—circling around so that, unlike the other two, he would enter the back of the main residence.

Riley found this to be strange. If any of the three should be leading the charge, it was Cameron Carr. She could see he was wounded, but Estrada looked even worse. Despite not quite understanding what she was seeing, she trusted Carr's judgment. Whatever the reason for this formation, it must be a good one.

One of the Russians made hand signals to his comrades, deciding not to try to shout over the alarms, and they began fanning out, two remaining on the back side of the mansion and two hastily rushing to the front, not bothering to search any real estate they traveled through on the way to their destination. When they reached their goal, these two split up, as had their two comrades on the back side.

Their attackers had clearly separated the mansion into four quadrants, with each man having responsibility for searching and clearing one of them.

Riley now had to choose which of a number of monitors to watch, darting back and forth between them. On one of them, Roberto Estrada entered the front of the mansion and crept through the magnificent entry foyer, hugging walls and turning corners quickly with his weapon extended, reminding her of countless movies she had seen of commandos cautiously working their way through an enemy compound.

A Russian in the back east quadrant passed a smoke detector and planted two rounds into it, reducing the total decibels to a less ear-crushing level. She suspected they all had orders to do the same, eventually restoring quiet to the residence. This would allow them to concentrate and communicate, and also to hear movement nearby. Their prey would also be able to hear *them*, but this wasn't much of a worry. The Russians were trained soldiers with automatic weapons, while those they were hunting were unarmed civilians.

She wondered how many homeowners faced with faulty alarms had contemplated shooting them with firearms to get them to stop. Probably the majority, she decided.

Bram caught her attention and pointed at two monitors to her left, which he and Trish had been watching. Estrada and one of the Russians in the front west quadrant were converging, neither one of them having any idea they were on a collision course.

Riley guessed Estrada's chances were fifty-fifty at this point. It seemed a question of which man had the faster reflexes. And there was always the chance they would kill each other, so maybe fifty-fifty was being optimistic.

"Any way to warn him?" shouted Bram.

"Not in time!" Riley shouted back, and Trish replied in a similar manner.

Seconds before Estrada rounded the corner, the Russian spotted a smoke alarm on the ceiling and shot two rounds into it, happy to be able to lower the decibel level in the mansion even further.

A look of satisfaction came over his face, but only for an instant. The shots had given away his location, and Estrada didn't hesitate. He dove across the threshold into the room, rolling and coming up firing, spraying the Russian up and down, killing him instantly, the man's body armor able to protect him from a knife or handgun, but not a barrage from an automatic weapon at near point-blank range.

On still another monitor, Isaac Jordan had entered the mansion and had made his way to one of four rooms clustered in the front east quadrant, a gun in hand. He rushed into the bathroom and took up a position hidden behind the open door, a spider waiting for an insect to land in his web.

At the back door, Carr had finally made it inside, holding a simple handgun rather than a submachine gun. He ran into a Russian almost immediately. Both men already had their weapons extended and both were on high alert, but the Russian never had a chance. Carr's reflexes and skills were astounding. He put two rounds into the Russian's head and simultaneously dived out of the way in case his adversary had been fast enough to get off shots of his own.

He hadn't been.

Carr retrieved the man's weapon without missing a beat and continued on, changing course when he heard two more shots, caused by the last remaining Russian on the lieutenant's side of the mansion putting the last of the mansion's smoke alarms out of commission.

"Thank God!" whispered Bram, basking in the silence.

"I second that," said Trish in relief.

Bram continued to watch Carr in awe. "They're down to two men," he said. "I think Cameron's a sure bet to get the one near him. He has the advantage now that the guy gave away his position."

"Not to mention that he has some mad commando skills," said Trish in admiration.

"Hate to spoil the party," said Riley. "But my dad's in trouble."

On the monitors, Estrada continued to work his way through the mansion, but without knowing it, he was moving away from the last Russian on the front side rather than toward him.

"This guy's going to be a problem," continued Riley, nodding toward the Russian in question. "He's very cautious and methodical when he searches through and clears a room. He never goes through an open door without first making sure no one is lying in wait behind it."

"So your dad's ambush won't work," said Bram.

"My father is directly in his path," said Riley. "He has two more rooms to go through and then he'll be in the one my father's in."

They heard another gunshot and glanced at the monitor, just in time to see Carr standing over the last Russian on the back side of the mansion. All things considered, Riley knew that their luck had been remarkable. Carr and Estrada had managed to kill six of the seven intruders, and their group had yet to suffer a single loss.

But their luck was running out. The last of their assailants might kill her father before realizing who he was. If he did recognize him as Isaac Jordan, he would take him as a hostage.

Riley's brief reverie was interrupted by the sound of locks being disengaged. She turned away from the monitors to see David Bram throwing open the panic room door. "I'll create a distraction," he said hastily. "Stay here."

He rushed off before Riley could say a word, a man with no time or interest in a debate.

Riley's heart jumped to her throat. What was he doing? She admired his bravery, but now he was putting *himself* at risk along with her father. And unlike her father, David didn't have a spare copy of his consciousness lying around.

She had to go after him. She couldn't lose her father and David Bram both. Not now.

Trish realized Riley's intent and reached out and held her arm just as she was stepping outside. "Riley, wait!" she said. She pointed to a monitor that showed Carr running in their direction. "I think he's coming here."

Riley realized this made great sense. Carr would want to check on them, and he also knew he could use the monitors to gain a panoramic view of the mansion and scope out any remaining players.

"Thanks, Trish," said Riley as she ran from the room, but on a different course than originally planned. "I'll meet him halfway."

# 58

David Bram's emotions were now running as wildly as he was. Mostly, he was terrified. Yes, there was only one man left, but this man still had a submachine gun, and Bram was heading right toward him. On purpose.

Apple trained their employees well, but none of his training had covered this situation. And he was pretty sure if Apple did give a course on how to deal with a soldier carrying an automatic weapon, the first lesson would be to run *away* from the man.

But it was time for Bram to step up. Isaac Jordan was a great man, and he couldn't let him be killed, even if he did have his pattern saved. He and his double might *seem* identical in every way, but who was Bram to say they really were? Perhaps Jordan had missed something. Perhaps the duplicate was without some ineffable quality—call it a soul—that made him almost, but not quite the same.

This was also Bram's chance to prove himself to Riley and to gain back his self-respect. He couldn't continue being a sniveling coward, remaining safely in hiding while other men risked their lives to save the woman he loved. He couldn't watch her father be killed without lifting a finger to stop it.

He made a brief detour to visit the man Estrada had killed so he could retrieve the dead man's weapon.

Bile rose in his throat as he neared the bloody corpse. He had seen any number of bodies just like this on TV and in movies, but they were *nothing* like the real thing, the sight and smell of which brought on instant nausea. Bram was barely able to keep himself from vomiting as he lifted the unfamiliar weapon, which turned out to be heftier than he had anticipated.

Would he really use it to cut down the last attacker? He had never killed before, and he'd prefer not to start now, but this depended on circumstances. In his book, it was better to be armed than not to be.

Bram made it to the room Jordan was in and peered through the open doorway, staying out of sight. He watched as the last of their assailants cautiously entered a walk-in closet, alert for ambushes, leaving only after he had cleared every nook big enough for a woman the size of Riley Ridgeway to hide within. The man finally exited the closet and headed in the direction of the open bathroom door.

Bram crept closer, as silent as a cat.

The Russian wheeled around, apparently able to hear approaching cats, and Bram fired out of raw panic and adrenaline, holding his finger down on the trigger. Having never fired a gun, let alone an assault weapon, he was totally unprepared for the ferocity of its recoil. The gun hammered into his shoulder and sprayed wildly, tearing itself from his hands as it fired, while both Bram and the Russian dived to the ground to avoid this random barrage.

The Russian jumped back up to his feet the moment the firing stopped, while Bram remained on the ground, helpless, his weapon now several feet away. The man raised his own weapon casually, in no hurry now that Bram had disarmed himself, and pointed it at the civilian.

As Bram stared into the barrel of the gun and prepared to die, Isaac Jordan appeared in the bathroom doorway, an arm's length behind the intruder, and fired twice in rapid succession. One of the shots grazed the man's cheek, while the other came closer to hitting Bram than its intended target.

The Russian slammed the butt of his submachine gun into Jordan's arm, sending Jordan's handgun flying before he could take a third shot. The soldier raised his weapon and pointed it at the billionaire's head. "How could you miss from *two feet*?" he said in English, his expression incredulous.

The Russian's eyes widened. "You're Isaac Jordan," he said in astonishment, recognizing him just in time to ease off the trigger. He immediately turned his gun on Bram, deciding to put him down first before turning his full attention to the helpless genius behind him.

Bram found himself frozen, unable to even breathe.

Two shots rang out and Bram slumped to the floor, dead.

Bram heard a jarring thud in front of him and realized that he *wasn't* dead, after all.

He opened his eyes and saw the Russian's body on the ground, two holes drilled neatly through his forehead.

Bram realized the shots had come from *behind* him. From Cameron Carr, who had continued to make his way deeper into the room, with Riley and Trish in tow.

Carr glanced back and forth between Bram and Jordan. "Are you okay?" he asked them anxiously.

They both nodded woodenly.

"Thank God!" said Carr, sighing in relief.

After a moment a smile crept across Carr's face. "Sorry for stealing your thunder," he said in amusement, relaxed now that the seventh man was down. "I mean, it was obvious you had everything under control."

Bram tried to force a smile, but failed. Instead, he turned his head to the side and vomited onto the floor. The four others in the room couldn't help but curl their lips up in disgust as retching sounds filled the room.

"Don't suppose there's a toothbrush and toothpaste in there," said Bram when he was finished, gesturing weakly toward the bathroom.

"There is," said Jordan. "And thanks, David. I'm pretty sure you saved my life. Not that either one of us should ever be allowed to hold a gun again."

Bram managed a shallow smile as he made his way to the bathroom. Jordan's acknowledgment of his heroism in front of Riley did help to soften the blow of his obvious ineptitude and the embarrassment of not being able to keep his lunch down. But everyone was aware that his only contribution was to clumsily keep Jordan alive just long enough for Carr to save them both.

He said as much when he finished brushing his teeth and washing out his mouth.

Carr responded by explaining that if it weren't for Riley redirecting him here, he wouldn't have made it in time. Riley then acknowledged Trish's contribution in alerting her that Carr was on his way.

"Apparently, saving my life takes a village," said Jordan wryly when they had finished.

"Speaking of a village," said Carr. "We need to let Roberto know he can stand down." He shook his head in wonder. "When I set off to stop these guys, I had no idea I'd have this much support. This truly was a great team effort."

Jordan grinned. "And the three of you haven't even officially decided to join the team. Think of how well we'll all be able to work together if you do."

"We have to make sure you still have a team for us to join," said Carr gravely. "Volkov is still out there. Still likely holding Jordan Two prisoner. And since he must know now that the team he sent here failed, he's probably sending reinforcements. We need to double-time it back to where he's holding Jordan Two and come up with a plan."

"Let's round up Roberto and get you guys stabilized," said Jordan. "I have a state-of-the-art first-aid kit. Plenty of antibiotics and quick-drying wound-sealing foam."

"We can get patched up on the helo," said Carr. "We need to get moving. Volkov is either in the process of moving Jordan Two, or he's making lethal preparations in case we pay him a visit."

"Maybe," said Jordan. "But I have a horrible feeling that Volkov won't be a problem for long."

"What do you mean by *horrible feeling*?" asked Riley

Jordan blew out a long breath. "Let's get Roberto and I'll explain," he said.

# PART 8
## Quick Thinking

# 59

Isaac Jordan watched the digital timer on Volkov's laptop computer tick down to just over a minute. Safin could now be seen on the screen as well, pressing a gun into the unconscious forehead of Marsha Stephens, one of Jordan's favorite colleagues.

The time had finally come for Jordan to do what he needed to do. He couldn't put it off any longer.

He took a deep mental breath, knowing he was about to willingly put himself through the ultimate torture. He wanted to cry out and roll into a fetal position, just so he didn't have to face the reality of what was to come.

Instead, he said a small prayer to a God he didn't believe in and tilted his head so that the laptop screen, Marat Volkov, and Yakov Urinson were all in his field of view.

"I have your knife," he said to Volkov matter-of-factly.

"You've lost your mind," said the Russian, pulling up slightly on his right pant leg to confirm that his knife was still strapped to his ankle.

"Not yet," said Jordan with an expression that could not have been more pained. "But very soon."

The Russian stared back in confusion.

"Believe it or not," croaked Jordan, sounding as though he was on his death bed, "I envy you."

"How so?" said the Russian.

"Because you'll at least have the mercy of dying quickly."

Before Volkov could respond, with the countdown now at thirty-eight seconds, Jordan sent a mental code to his own quantum brain, one designed to kick out a linchpin that held a raging rapids at bay.

The effect was immediate, and at first exhilarating. Time abruptly skidded to a halt, and he knew that the subroutine had worked, and that there was no going back.

When he had perfected whole brain emulation, he had mimicked every aspect of the human brain as precisely as possible. Well, it had been the original Isaac Jordan who had done this, but since Jordan Two remembered all of it as if he, himself, had been there, he couldn't help but think of this history in the first person.

He had resisted the urge to make improvements, just as he had told his daughter. But for a time he had considered making one only, an increase in the brain's clock speed. An enhancement that could be invoked by the custodians he would send on his seed-ships. After all, they would be pioneers on dangerous planets and could use any edge they could find during dire emergencies.

And what better edge than an increase in their speed of thought? There were times when quick thinking was required to save the day, and increasing their clock speeds ten-, twenty-, or a hundred-fold could fit this bill nicely.

Jordan's artificial brains were fully optical, using individual photons rather than electric current to perform digital operations. They didn't operate at the speed of chemical reactions. They weren't restricted to the speed of action potentials making their way down axons, of impulses traveling along neuronal highways that required myelination to go faster than a relative crawl.

Instead, they operated at the speed of light.

Jordan's algorithms and entire emulation system suppressed this vast speed. By blocking this raging river, the emulation was forced to limp along at the speed of biology. But what if he could destroy this dam and set up another downstream? A dam that this time regulated the speed of thought to *twenty* times human normal?

This wouldn't change what thoughts could be had. Faster thought wouldn't change the *quality* of thought. The same thoughts would occur, just more quickly. The brain would still be a human brain, an Isaac Jordan emulation would still be Isaac Jordan.

At first he had considered setting up the E-brains of those he would send on seed-ships to always run fast, but this wouldn't work.

After all, these duplicates would be the caretakers of generations of fully biological humans, who would be unable to increase their own clock speed.

Mismatches in the speed of thought between duplicates and home-grown humans would make communication, empathy, and caretaking all but impossible. The only way Jordan could see it working was if the caretakers could use a mental toggle. Jump the speed of their thoughts twenty-fold in dire emergencies, but return their minds to their original settings when a crisis had been averted.

Jordan spent a few months doing experimentation, but even with Pock's help he was unable to get such a system to work. Since he had designed his neuronal matrix to work at precisely the speed of human thought, this glacial speed could be effectively maintained with the proper dam in place. But once the waters were fully unleashed, they were far too powerful to ever be contained again.

The human speed of thought he had baked into these emulations was like snow resting quietly on a mountainside. Once the stability of this snow was disrupted, once an avalanche began to sweep down the mountain, picking up unimaginable speed and ferocity every inch of the way, there was no stopping it, no putting the snow back neatly where it had started.

It was all or nothing. A mind could operate at the speed of human thought, or at the maximum speed the system would allow. These were the only two choices. Because of certain design limitations, this maximum speed ended up being only a tenth of the speed of light, but this was still a speed that was beyond comprehension.

Jordan had also carefully designed a system that precisely emulated sleep, but this subroutine couldn't survive the onslaught of such blinding speed. So the possibilities became even more starkly distinct. An emulated consciousness could run at normal human speed, and undergo normal human sleep. Or it could run at ludicrous speed and never know rest.

What had begun as a way to enhance survival prospects had ended as the most horrific thing that could possibly happen to a man.

When Volkov had threatened Riley, Jordan had decided to upload his consciousness into a duplicate and send this duplicate to the church after her. Hopefully, the duplicate would be able to work a deal to free Riley. But if anything went wrong, Jordan would give his copy an edge. He would install a subroutine that would let Jordan Two trigger a clock-speed-avalanche with a single mental command.

Both Jordans prayed this would never be required. But if it was necessary to save Riley's life, Jordan Two would do what he had to do, hoping that his adversaries were in close proximity to each other so he would be spared a living hell unequaled in the annals of history.

After Carr had interfered with Jordan's plans and freed Riley from the church, himself, this option hadn't proved necessary.

Until now. Until Volkov had made it *unavoidable*.

Everything around Jordan now appeared frozen in time. It wasn't, but his view would change at a pace that was maddeningly slow, like a movie that was being shown to him at one frame per hour.

Jordan had done the math long ago, when he had first experimented with changes to clock speed. The speed of normal human thought was so complex it was impossible to pin down precisely. In general, neuronal communication operated at a maximum speed of between two to three hundred miles per hour. Since brain cells were packed so tightly together, these relatively modest speeds were plenty quick enough to allow a helpless ape to ascend to the top of the food chain.

Still, the speed of light was *incomprehensibly* fast. Almost seven hundred million miles per hour. So even if the speed of normal human thought was as high as seven hundred miles per hour, the speed of light would still be a *million* times faster.

After lengthy calculations, research, and guesswork, Jordan had finally calculated that a runaway emulation would increase the speed of thought a hundred thirty thousand fold. Actually far less of an increase than would have been possible if the system were optimized for speed.

Still, a hundred thirty thousand fold increase had profound consequences. Jordan Two's mind was now operating so much faster than normal that every second that passed was now the equivalent of just over thirty-six hours. A full day and a half.

Every second!

In thirty-eight seconds, Volkov had vowed to kill Marsha Stephens. At the rate that Jordan's mind was now operating, this was almost two months away.

Jordan had a single image stuck in his visual cortex, one of Yakov Urinson, Marat Volkov, and the screen of a laptop computer being held to face him. In all the time he had been reflecting upon his condition this image had yet to change, a horrifying reminder that this endless nightmare had only just *begun*.

His mind would be active and thinking for the equivalent of thirty-six hours for every second that passed. And now that his sleep emulation was destroyed, he couldn't retreat into unconsciousness to spare himself from any of it.

If his body were as fast as his brain, this would be a much different story. But no body made of matter could come close to approaching the speed of light, much less a biological one.

As it was, the speed of his brain and the speed of his body couldn't have been more of a mismatch. So much so that he was no longer in a body, but inside the ultimate prison.

While his neuronal operations had been replaced by photonic gates, his muscles remained fully human. He could give instructions to his body as quickly as he wanted, but his nervous system and muscles were going to take their own sweet time in carrying them out.

Forcing a man to spend just a few days in solitary confinement was considered a brutal torture. But at least such a prisoner could move, could feel, could sleep.

Jordan Two, on the other hand, was condemned to a state of being that made the harshest solitary confinement look like a *mercy*. Condemned to do nothing but think for an eternity, without sleep, and in a state of almost perfect paralysis inside a body whose every blink seemed to take hours to complete.

Jordan had known what he would be asking his duplicate to endure—if it came to that. In preparation, he had done the best he could to tweak the biology of his new body, to soup up its muscles and reflexes and enhance its speed of reaction. This would do nothing to relieve the agony that Jordan Two would experience—since this increase in body speed was but a drop in the ocean of what was needed—but it would ensure he would be fast enough to defeat those who were holding Riley hostage.

He could now move roughly six times faster than a normal man, and with perfect precision, given that he had all the time in the world to plan his movements. A hundred-mile-per-hour fastball crossed the plate in under half a second, but if he were the batter, he would have the equivalent of fourteen hours to watch it hang in mid-air, inching its way toward him.

Ironically, tragically, a lack of patience was Jordan's biggest failing. Now he would have an eternity to develop this capacity. An act as simple as texting the word *help*, which he could now do faster than any human on Earth, would seem to him to take hours. He could order a finger on to the next letter all he wanted, but he could do nothing but wait for it to respond.

Knowing all of this, he had delayed entering the abyss for as long as he could, avoided triggering a personal hell so cruel that even Satan would be terrified of entering. He could only pray that the Russians wouldn't find Jordan One in the guest house of the mansion, which would only make their hand that much stronger. He prayed that Carr would come through.

If Safin had come back to the room, had been reachable within a few seconds of real time, Jordan would have acted sooner. But as it was, Volkov's threats had left him with no other choice. He had finally run out of time.

Ironic, since time was now *all* that he had.

Jordan had a feeling Carr was making more progress than Volkov was letting on, or the Russian wouldn't have taken the measures he had. But even assuming Volkov's men succeeded at the mansion and captured both Riley and Jordan One, it was possible that killing Volkov, cutting off the head of the snake, would turn the tide in their favor. Greshnev wasn't likely to be as formidable as his boss, giving Jordan One a better chance to eventually turn the tables. At minimum, Volkov's death would create disarray and buy Jordan's people time.

No matter what, Volkov needed to die. Which Jordan Two calculated would occur in less than three seconds.

Three seconds that for Jordan would stretch out into the equivalent of four 24-hour days of sleepless thought, trapped in a prison, pulling the levers on his own body and waiting forever for his commands to be carried out.

No books, television, or other entertainment to help pass the time. No conversation, Internet, or scientific projects to engage in. Just hour after hour of himself in the ultimate solitary confinement, being alone with his thoughts, paralyzed, watching the world pass by one lingering frame at a time.

Jordan had tricked Volkov into revealing where he kept his knife, but this wasn't much of an accomplishment. The Russian would have happily told him if he had simply asked, certain that he had the upper hand.

But Volkov's upper hand would only last a few more seconds, at least from the Russian's perspective. Jordan had long since decided on the exact path he would use to achieve his goals, the most efficient way forward.

But for now, all he could do was wait.

And fight to hang onto sanity for as long as he could.

# 60

Marat Volkov's mood was darkening. The operation at the mansion was getting away from them. He had lost contact with Ivan Makarov, his third-in-command, and none of the others had comms that could reach him.

Just because Makarov was likely out of commission didn't mean the rest were. Only one man was needed to complete the mission. Carr may have been able to take out most of them, but getting them all was a much different story. The American was the luckiest man Volkov had ever come across, but his luck was bound to run out at some point.

Still, it had been nearly forty minutes now since Volkov had captured Jordan. Almost twenty minutes since Greshnev's team at Jordan's mansion had killed two guards, had penetrated perimeter security, and had begun their assault.

Volkov was satisfied that the room he was in was free of bugs. Urinson had scanned for them quite thoroughly, and Volkov wasn't surprised by their absence. After all, Volkov wasn't supposed to know that two Jordans were possible, or that Brennan had brought him here to kill one of them, under *their* orders. So they wouldn't risk a bug being found and arousing suspicion, nor would they see the need for it. Jordan wanted his duplicate killed or kidnapped, after all, not rescued.

But the biological Jordan would surely have a way to check on the proceedings. And if there was no indication that his duplicate had been killed or moved, he would become antsy. The operations here and at the mansion had been coordinated so the free-ranging Jordan wouldn't get suspicious until they had Riley in their pocket.

Volkov had too much respect for the man, his capabilities, and his organization to allow him to remain at large much longer without having his daughter to control him.

Volkov wasn't sure if killing a man or woman in the facility below every two minutes would really get Jordan's duplicate to divulge the location of the original, but he didn't have much to lose. This wasn't ideal, since he intended to press these people into service, but he could spare five or ten of them without too much trouble. And he expected to get word any minute that his men had finally captured Riley. They probably had already, but weren't yet able to communicate this fact.

As soon as one of the survivors on the team remembered that only Greshnev and Makarov possessed command comms that could reach him, this would change. Stealing a comm from a dead man was a bit ghoulish, but they would do what was necessary in order to report.

Volkov checked to be sure Jordan still had his eyes fixed on the laptop screen, which continued to show a helpless woman named Marsha Stephens with a gun to her head. The red digital numbers continued to tick down on the screen.

If Jordan thought Volkov was bluffing, he would learn differently in less than a minute. The major was even in less of a mood to be merciful than usual, having lost Greshnev, one of the few men he had truly respected.

"I have your knife," said Jordan out of the blue.

This was a ridiculous claim, but Volkov checked to be sure. "You've lost your mind," he said in contempt.

"Not yet," said Jordan enigmatically. "But very soon."

The Russian didn't reply to this odd statement.

"Believe it or not," said Jordan, "I envy you."

Volkov's forehead wrinkled in confusion. Of all the things Jordan might have said, this was among the most unlikely.

"How so?" he replied.

"Because you'll at least have the mercy of dying quickly."

Before Volkov could even digest this threat, Jordan moved—with superhuman speed—rising and lunging at Urinson a few feet away.

Urinson shot, intending to injure rather than kill, since Volkov had made the value of their prisoner clear, but Jordan twisted in mid-lunge to avoid the bullet. It missed him by less than a millimeter, as if he had guessed the shot's trajectory before it had even been fired and could control his body with micron precision.

In another blink of an eye, Jordan reached up, twisted the gun from Urinson's hand, shot up through his chin and into his brain, and spun the gun to point at Marat Volkov. The major was as quick on the draw as anyone, but he had just begun to raise his own gun when half of his face disappeared in a spray of blood.

Jordan snatched the laptop from the Russian's hand as he fell, hit a command to have a still photo of the major's gory visage sent to Safin, and snatched the knife from the sheath on Volkov's ankle—all before Volkov hit the ground.

Jordan used the knife to free his hands while simultaneously texting a message to Safin.

*Coming 4 U,* he wrote.

This completed, Jordan pocketed Urinson's handgun and sprinted off for the hexagonal building and the elevator it contained, moving at a speed Usain Bolt would have envied, somehow managing to type a message into the laptop at superhuman speed as he ran.

# 61

Carr left the bedroom first and shouted as loudly as he could for Roberto Estrada, letting him know the threat had been neutralized. Once Estrada had joined them, the entire group worked their way to the kitchen to get some much-needed hydration, pausing along the way for Jordan to retrieve an expensive first-aid kit.

Jordan shook his head as they arrived at their destination. "I have to tell you, I've had neater houseguests," he said with a grin, picking his way across dumped garbage and the contents of numerous drawers strewn haphazardly across the floor.

"How do you know the intruders didn't do this?" said Carr impishly.

"Is that the best story you can come up with, Lieutenant?" said Jordan in amusement as he handed out cold bottles of water to his guests.

"Pretty much," said Carr with a smile. He winced. "And sorry about burning down the guest house. Kind of makes trashing the kitchen not look so bad anymore, though, doesn't it?"

Jordan laughed. "I shouldn't laugh," he said. "This is serious. But it's hard not to be in a good mood after escaping what seemed like certain death. The only concern I have about the guest house is that there isn't an easy way for firefighters to get here. And I don't *want* them here if I can help it. But I think we're okay. It's a very still day, and I think the fire will just consume the house and burn itself out."

Trish had begun to work on cleaning and sealing Carr's and Estrada's wounds while Jordan spoke.

The billionaire blew out a heavy sigh. "I guess it's time to tell you why I doubt Volkov will be a problem."

He went on to explain how Jordan Two had the ability to increase his mental clock speed, and all that this meant, and the sacrifice he suspected his double was in the process of making. He had spent some time imagining what this would be like, and his description of the torture his double would suffer was as powerful as it was horrifying.

When he finished, no one spoke for some time.

Jordan accessed a tablet computer and entered codes to kill the cell phone and Wi-Fi suppressors he had set up.

The instant the signals were active again, Jordan's phone indicated he had a message on an email address he had given to only a handful of people.

He had a sick feeling he knew what this was. He and Jordan Two thought nearly exactly alike, after all, not having much time for their patterns to diverge. If Jordan Two *had* invoked the doomsday scenario, his double would have eons to diverge, but would get so little new external input and stimulation that Jordan suspected he would still have a strong handle on Jordan Two's thinking.

He took a mental breath and opened the inbox in question. Sure enough, it was what he had feared. A message from himself. He closed his eyes tightly and braced for what he might read.

"Everything okay?" said Riley worriedly.

Jordan explained that he had a message from his double, and what he knew the message would be. On one hand, it meant that they were out of the woods entirely. On the other, it was a portent of unspeakable suffering.

"Let me read it to myself," he said, "and then I'll read it out loud."

There were somber nods of support for this plan all around.

Without another word, Jordan opened the message and began to read.

Hello, Isaac. Greetings from hell.

Volkov is dead. Unfortunately, one of his men took over the emulation facility, and I need to kill him also. I'm not sure I'll succeed. The killing part will be child's play, but he's minutes away—six months to a year for me—and I can't see how my sanity can possibly hold for that long.

But I'll give it everything I have. I know the importance.

I'm typing this as I run for the elevator, waiting hours between each letter, as you know. But writing to you at least gives me a purpose as the weeks and months in this purgatory accumulate. If not for my determination to communicate one last time, I'd have lost my sanity already.

Funny, anyone watching me in real time wouldn't believe their eyes. I'm running faster than anyone ever has. While I'm doing this, I'm also balancing a laptop and typing faster than anyone ever has. Much faster. Boosting one's speed of thought over a hundred thousand times does seem to help with multitasking, at least.

Any watchers would envy my balance, speed, and body control. They would think no one has ever moved their body faster. But I know the truth. No one has ever moved their body more *slowly*. They could look at me as I run and never guess I'd be jealous of a man who is paralyzed from head to toe. Never guess I'd be willing to sell my soul to the Devil to change places with him. (Good joke, right, since even if a soul exists, you're the one who has it)

We thought this would be a torture that was inconceivably cruel. We were wrong. It's *far* worse than that.

I've lost track of days at a time. Sometimes I scream in agony inside of my head for many hours straight. Sometimes I drift off and begin hallucinating. But so far I've always managed to pull myself back to sanity, eventually, and continue typing the next letter in this message.

I'm now waiting for the elevator to open. If I remember right, this requires ten seconds of patience for the normal man. Which means fifteen days in hell for me. Brutal, tedious, endless twenty-four-hour days. Days without sleep or diversion, with the image of an elevator door my only companion. Hour after hour of existence with no purpose, thought with no outlet, most of it consisting of nothing but mental screams of agony. Punctuated by brief instances of directing a finger to type the next letter.

And I can assure you, it's not nearly as fun as it sounds.

God how I hope you and Riley are safe—that Volkov's team failed. But no matter what, I cling to sanity imagining that my actions will still help you, still allow us to catalyze humanity's spread into the cosmos, still serve as midwife to the birth of immortality and infinity.

I have only one player left to kill to rid us of the plague that Volkov brought down upon us. I told him I was coming. I need him to be as near to the elevator exit as possible when I emerge, preparing his ambush. I need him to close the distance between us, which shortens the eons until we engage.

He won't stand a chance, of course. I envy him.

When I'm not screaming, I'm fantasizing about putting a bullet in my brain and ending this nightmare, but I have to wait until he's down. I've gone this far, suffered this much, so it might as well be for a purpose.

The only positive about this experience is that I no longer fear death. I *long* for it. I *pray* for it.

I wanted the chance to pay for our sins, but I have to believe this is payment a thousand times over.

Update. The elevator is now at the landing, and the door will slide open any eon now. I think I went totally mad for almost a month as the elevator descended. I'm not sure what brought me back from the brink. Maybe there is a God and he's giving me strength. Either that, or he wants me to suffer even longer.

I think I can end this in less than a minute of real time. Sounds so benign when I write it. But for me this will be two or three more sleepless months trapped in hell. But at the end of this seemingly infinite tunnel, I will finally—*finally*—have the satisfaction of seeing Volkov's last man fall.

After I've killed him it will take my body, even souped-up as it is, another second to redirect the gun so that it's pointed at my own brain. But knowing this will be the last thirty-six hours I'll ever have to endure will be absolute heaven.

Would an immortal being long for death? Eventually, I have little doubt he or she would. But not for a very long time. We can't draw parallels from what I'm going through.

As you know, my experience is a far cry from immortality. Immortals will experience extreme boredom and the weariness of existence, like me, but at a millionth of the duration and intensity.

The difference is that immortals will be able to interact with their environments, impact their world. And they will be able to engage in social interactions, instead of being trapped on a desert island as I am, starved for human contact, for companionship.

I can't tell you how lonely it has been for me these past many months. So unspeakably lonely. This is the cruelest blow of all. Even a man marooned in *paradise*—the exact opposite of the hellish cage that I'm in—would go mad if he were alone for too long.

Yet there is no reason, at least on paper, why a sentient being shouldn't be perfectly content to be alone for eternity.

I've asked myself a thousand times what defines sentience. Is it the capacity for boredom? The need to fill the void, the emptiness? The hunger for activity? The need for physical and mental stimulation, to experience and interact with an environment?

Clearly this is all part of it. Pock's clock speed is greater than mine, meaning he waits eons for me to finish posing a question, which he answers in millionths of a second. But Pock is a patient computer. He never gets bored. He never goes mad. Because without a sense of self, there can be no sense of time. And with no sense of self, Pock has no interest in striving toward goals, no need to achieve.

Which brings me to Savant. He was clearly sentient, and also possessed a mind that operated at the speed of light. But he seemed to have no trouble with this, evolved from the start to have no need of anything outside of himself.

Which is why we feared him so much, you and I. Our brains, in concert with our bodies, evolved an absolute need for companionship, for social connection, for physical contact. These things are the fabric of our existence. A mind that is free of these needs is abhorrent to us.

Maybe even God himself needed companionship, needed something outside of himself. Perhaps he was trapped in his own head, like I am, and finally found his salvation through the creation of the universe and sentient life.

I will soon find my salvation as well. Not by creating a universe, which I can't do. But, instead, by ending my own existence—ironically, the one thing *God* can't do, being the eternal deity that he is.

My salvation is getting ever nearer. I've exited the elevator and am walking into what I know will be an ambush. Not walking, running. I've continued to slip in and out of sanity as I've written this, but you always catch me in my sane moments, so you're spared all of that.

I'll need to drop the computer to concentrate on dodging bullets and planting one in my quarry in five or six of your seconds, so I'll need to hit send very soon so you can get this message.

I encourage you to tell Riley about me, after all. I've given this months of thought, and I'm convinced she'll take this the right way. If you do tell her, please let her know how much I love her. My interactions with her revealed an even more amazing young woman than we had come to expect, and I'm counting on you to take good care of her. Tell her that I'll always be grateful for the few hours I got to spend with her.

I have to go very soon. It's nearly time to kill my enemy and then myself.

Looks like I'm going to make it! I really didn't think I would. Turns out you have an extraordinary consciousness. At the risk of sounding conceited, you're quite a man, Isaac Jordan.

I so wish I could be there to see the launch of the first seed-ships. To witness the realization of our vision. But then again, survival was never part of the plan for me.

When you see my dead body, just know that my ceaseless suffering finally did come to a blissful end, and be glad.

Godspeed, Isaac Jordan.

Yours truly, Isaac Jordan.

## 62

Pavel Safin was stunned. One second he was holding a gun at the forehead of a woman he had been ordered to execute on Volkov's command, and the next he was staring at a still image showing the major toppling to the floor, half of his face blown away by a slug at close range.

A message appeared on his computer before he could even process what he was seeing.

*Coming 4 U.*

Safin's gun and jaw dropped toward the floor at the same time.

What in the world? Had Jordan escaped and done this?

It couldn't be.

But it *had* to be. There was no other explanation. Volkov would have alerted him if the sensors had detected a strike team approaching.

Jordan must have taken out both Volkov *and* Urinson, using a means that Safin couldn't begin to guess at. But why would the escaped prisoner warn him he was coming? This was as stupid as it was brazen.

In a flash of inspiration, Safin guessed Jordan's motivation. The man wanted to make sure the pending execution of his colleague was prevented. By alerting Safin that Volkov was dead—and threatening to kill *Safin*, also—Jordan had left him with no reason to kill the girl. Instead, Safin would have every reason to abandon her, every reason to make sure he was prepared in case Jordan was crazy enough to really come down here after him.

It had worked, Safin realized, as he rushed off toward Jordan's personal elevator, leaving the girl alive. He would wait a safe distance away from where Jordan would have to enter the main facility. He was convinced that this was a bluff, but just in case Jordan did dare to come here, Safin wouldn't be waiting within easy reach of a possible trap Jordan might spring as he exited the elevator.

Instead, he would position himself so that he had a clear shot at Jordan as he entered the spacious main thoroughfare. There was a white marble fountain, currently dry, at a reasonable distance from where Jordan would emerge, about thirty feet around. This was yet another example of the extraordinary efforts the billionaire had taken to make this underground installation as magnificent as any facility Safin had seen.

He approached the fountain and crouched low behind its thick marble base, making sure that only his head and gun hand were exposed, and waited.

The wait was over in mere seconds.

Jordan burst through the door in the distance and sprinted forward, stopping in the center of the open space, making himself such an inviting target he almost begged to be shot.

Safin's eyes widened. How had he gotten here so *quickly*? It couldn't have been more than two or three minutes since the man had been with Volkov in a room a fair distance from the elevator.

Jordan had a gun in one hand and was balancing a laptop computer with the other. He dropped the computer and turned in Safin's direction with a speed Safin couldn't believe. The Russian got off three quick shots and waited for him to fall, but Jordan juked his body in impossible ways.

Instead of falling, Jordan turned his gun in Safin's direction and squeezed off a shot of his own.

Safin wasn't the least bit concerned. Only the top half of his face was exposed. His body was so well protected by the base of the marble fountain that Jordan could send a hundred shots his way without danger of one of them hitting the target.

This was the last thought Pavel Safin ever had. Against all expectations, Jordan's shot penetrated his left eye and drove on through his skull, expanding as it went so that his brain became little more than a messy gray purée.

# PART 9
## Consensus

# 63

The endless day continued for Riley Ridgeway, although, after hearing her father read the email he had received from Jordan Two, she couldn't possibly complain. Even if Jordan Two hadn't tragically redefined the term *endless*, Carr and Estrada had lost significant amounts of blood and had experienced far worse than her, and they hadn't uttered a single complaint between them.

The group from the mansion had arrived at Jordan's compound by helo two hours earlier, and her father had reèstablished perimeter security. They had left Volkov's and Urinson's bodies where they had fallen for the time being, having other duties that were more pressing.

Jordan had descended into his facility alone, and while he left Pavel Safin where he had fallen, he had expended the time and energy to move Jordan Two's body to a nearby room for safekeeping so it wouldn't be in full view.

No man had ever been more deserving of a hero's funeral, and Jordan would see that he got one as soon as possible. And he knew that the last thing Jordan Two would ever want was for Riley to see him dead as she entered the underground facility, his life ended at his own hand.

It was hard for Riley to believe the immediate danger had now passed. They had been getting savaged by a violent thunderstorm, drowning in torrential rains. And suddenly the storm had ceased, just like that, just when it was at the height of its strength and seemed as if it would never end.

Once again, she wasn't sure how she felt. This was becoming a common occurrence as her emotions continued to be pulled in a dozen different directions. She was elated at having escaped the fate Volkov had planned for her—for them—and she was suddenly hopeful about her future. At the same time, she mourned the loss of Jordan Two.

But she should have felt worse. He had endured unimaginable torture to ensure the future of Jordan's vision. Yet how could she feel the loss of her father as deeply as she normally would—while standing beside her father?

With one version of her father still alive, still looking and behaving exactly the same as the version who had first met with her, she could only mourn Jordan Two intellectually, not emotionally.

She felt horrible about this. Jordan Two deserved better. The fact that a version of him still existed, that he hadn't left her fatherless, didn't diminish the sacrifice that *he* had made, the pain that *he* had endured.

When her father returned from below ground, he led them to the elevator to give them the tour he had promised. "Ignore the dead body you'll see when we enter the main facility," he told them, as if he were a hostess apologizing to a houseguest for a spot of dirt on the carpet. "Also," he added, "about half of my people are still unconscious. So try not to step on anyone."

"Good tip," said Bram wryly.

They were all pressed for time, so Jordan gave them an abbreviated tour. Still, the technology he showed them was remarkable, and the facility itself was extraordinary.

Her father's underground lair was much different than Riley had expected, although she should have known better, especially after he had mentioned how hard he had worked to make it aesthetically appealing.

Jordan had pioneered asteroid mining, as well as colonies on the Moon and Mars. As part of these efforts, he had developed revolutionary automated technology that could tunnel through miles of the hardest granite and marble in a single day.

But being able to efficiently create tunnels and underground facilities wasn't enough for her father, especially if these were created on lifeless worlds. Human psychology craved open spaces, craved sunlight, the outdoors, and expansive views. So Jordan had perfected ways to address these needs, as well. Holograms that made tight ceilings seem like vast skies, complete with clouds and birds. Lighting that was as bright and all-encompassing as natural sunlight. Air that was richer in oxygen than normal, mirroring the levels that occurred deep within forests.

Riley was aware of this technology, of course, but hadn't realized her father would apply it here. Even if she had been expecting it, she could never have imagined its implementation could be so flawless. She had thought that being forced to live and work here would be a hardship that only a mole could love. Instead, the technology fooled her senses so completely she could well have been on the main outdoor campus of an extravagant corporate giant like Google or Apple.

Once the brief tour was completed, Jordan led the group into the main conference room for an emergency session, with everyone who had been at the mansion in attendance, including Roberto Estrada and Trish Casner.

Unlike the rest of the facility, the conference room was fairly standard. Not that it wasn't top of the line. It was clean, modern, and sophisticated, with a magnificent lacquered mahogany center table and the latest in 3D software and hardware, along with a few plants and a refrigerator set inside a teak cabinet.

But no soaring holographic skies above. No birds and butterflies off in the distance.

Riley was initially disappointed, but realized that the main conference rooms at Apple and Google probably weren't open-air, either. People were probably better able to hunker down and focus on serious issues inside a contained space. Outside in the wild, minds had a tendency to wander.

Riley had just finished seating herself at the table when the door opened. She gasped in delight as Michael O'Banion entered, a broad smile plastered on his face. She rushed over to him and threw her arms around him.

"Mike was at another facility," explained Jordan, "but I contacted him from the helo so he could get here in time to join us."

"I'm so glad you did," said Riley as she separated from O'Banion.

"I'd like to pretend I did this all for you," admitted Jordan, "but I can't. Mike is my right-hand man. An indispensable member of my inner circle. He and a man named John Brennan were the only two who knew about my recent plan."

O'Banion introduced himself and shook hands all around before sitting down next to Riley at the table, both facing her father.

Bram was sitting on Riley's other side. "So this is your famous Uncle Mike?" he said to her. He leaned forward and turned his head so he could make eye contact with O'Banion. "Thank you for everything you've done for her over the years."

"I only wish I could have done more," he replied. A tear appeared in the corner of his right eye as he studied Riley. The love he felt for her was unmistakable.

"But as far as me being the famous Uncle Mike," he continued, managing to get his emotions back under control, "that all depends on how you feel about the gray-matter-impaired. From what Isaac tells me, the fully biological version of me was killed by a Russian named Volkov."

"Based on what I've witnessed," said Bram, "Isaac's duplicates are just as human as the originals. You even teared up when you thought about what Riley has been through." He grinned. "Now that's just showing off."

O'Banion smiled back. "The weird thing is that if I don't consciously think about it, I forget that I'm *not* the original. It seems to me that I've never been Michael O'Banion more than I am now."

Carr turned to Jordan. "You really need to offer new recruits a course on existential metaphysics," he said, shaking his head in amusement.

"Existential metaphysics?" repeated the billionaire, arching an eyebrow. "I'm impressed that you came up with a course title that this subject matter might actually fall under. I wouldn't think many people could conjure one up off-hand."

"Thanks," replied Carr. "There was actually a time when I thought I was uncommonly bright, you know."

"When was that?" asked Jordan.

"Every day of my life until I met you and Riley."

Smiles broke out all around the table.

Riley tilted her head toward Bram. "I know you were disappointed you didn't have the chance to meet Mike when we had dinner the other night. Just so you know, *he* was disappointed, too. I'm just glad my efforts to keep you two apart have failed."

"Actually," said O'Banion, "given that I was killed, I'm glad you didn't bring him to dinner."

"Why is that?" asked Riley.

"The last version of my consciousness was backed up before I left for San Diego," replied O'Banion. "So I wouldn't remember anything about meeting him, anyway. Which is why Isaac needs to finally perfect continuous streaming of a consciousness to the cloud," he added, needling his friend.

Riley rolled her eyes. "Yeah, because bringing you back to life with only a few days of memory loss isn't miraculous enough."

O'Banion laughed. "Well, when you put it that way . . ."

"As much fun as this is," said Jordan. "We really do need to get down to business."

"Of course," said O'Banion. "I'm just really enjoying having Riley in the fold."

"You two will have plenty of chances to chat later on," said Jordan. "For now, I can't even spare the time to give you details on what's been happening. The short version is that my duplicate sacrificed himself, but not the way we'd planned. And there were many complications."

"I gathered," said O'Banion dryly. "Last time I was here, there were no dead bodies lying around, and half of your people weren't unconscious."

"Right," said Jordan. "The plan backfired and it became a giant mess, but we're through the worst part of it. My double was forced to go to maximum clock speed. He killed Volkov and his comrades here, but at an unimaginable personal cost. And Volkov insisted John come with him on his raid. We didn't have time to create a duplicate, but John insisted on going forward, even knowing the risk he was taking. Volkov killed him, which wasn't entirely surprising."

O'Banion frowned deeply. "How is Kristen taking it?"

"There's been no time to tell her yet. But they've both tested so many volunteers, they know better than anyone that there are no differences between originals and copies, even down to their sexual preferences. We'll reanimate him from his last stored back-up as soon as we can. He'll be back in our inner circle in no time. I have every confidence that Kristen will adjust just fine."

O'Banion nodded.

Jordan made a show of surveying the entire group. "I know we're all exhausted and we've been through a lot," he began, "but we're still vulnerable. I spoke with the lieutenant just after we landed. He's convinced that Volkov would have reported everything he learned back to his superiors in Russia before coming here."

Riley turned to Carr. "Including the entire conversation we had with Jordan Two?" she asked him.

"Yes," replied the lieutenant. "Volkov considers himself the ultimate patriot, justifying his every cruelty as being necessary to restore the homeland to its full former glory. He wouldn't take any chances with intel this important. He'd share it right away. Since he must have recorded everything his bug picked up, it would only take him a few seconds to send a copy to his superior."

"Which means what, exactly?" said Bram.

"Which means the Russians know I'm alive," said Jordan. "They know the location of this facility and what it contains. They know about Pock and whole brain emulation. Security is back up, but we need to abandon this ship. When the Russians don't hear back from Volkov, who knows what kind of force they might send? They have some advanced technology specifically designed for operations against places like this, which I wasn't aware of," he added. "Very effective technology that lets them do more with fewer people."

"Shouldn't you be able to evacuate this facility long before they'll be ready to mount another operation?" asked Riley.

"Not necessarily," said her father. "We have over a hundred personnel and a thousand E-brains we have to move. That's the easy part. The hard part will be relocating the bioprinting and whole brain emulation technology. It's pretty hard-wired in."

"What's your estimate?" asked Carr.

"A few days," said Jordan. "Leaving us vulnerable if the Russians act fast enough. I have a system of tunnels that lead to an underground facility I had constructed as a backup—this one under a mountain in New Mexico."

"You do seem to like making copies of stuff," noted Riley.

"Too bad you didn't make copies of the bioprinting and emulation equipment," said Bram.

"We would have had to move it anyway, to be sure it didn't fall into the wrong hands," pointed out Jordan. "Anyway, we can disconnect the equipment and load it into the few trucks we have down here. The tunnels are drivable. Once everything has been relocated, I can collapse the tunnel entrances and hide their existence. We can destroy anything we're forced to leave behind that might give the Russians a clue to our tech. Assuming they end up coming."

"Oh, they'll be here all right," said Carr. "It's just a matter of when. And how many." He paused. "But I thought about it during the tour, and I can help. I can make sure you have all the time you need for a proper evacuation."

"How?" asked Jordan.

"I can bolster security and make sure the Russians can't get near here until we've moved. Courtesy of the US military."

"Without the military knowing *why* they're protecting this little slice of the world?" said Estrada skeptically.

"Yes. I was sent on this mission by Troy Dwyer, and he gave me—"

"Secretary of *Defense* Troy Dwyer?" interrupted Estrada, his tone incredulous.

"Yes," replied Carr. "And he gave me a blank check. He wanted me to work alone, and gave me codes to access whatever military resources I need to carry out my mission, no questions asked."

"Well, isn't *that* nice," said an impressed Roberto Estrada.

"The only wrinkle," said Carr, "is that I'll have to come up with a creative tale to explain where I've been. After all, the last Dwyer knew, I was heading to meet with him and Melanie Yoder at Area 51 to deliver my prize prisoner, David Bram." Carr grinned as he recalled how clueless he had been. "But I'm sure I can make something up to explain my absence. Not only that, but convince him that I'm making progress and need support to protect a hidden site that I'm mining for information. Bottom line is that if I need to, I can get a battalion to protect this area without needing to tell them what they're protecting."

"Outstanding, Lieutenant!" said Jordan. "Can I take it then that you've decided to accept my offer? That you'll be joining the team?"

Carr took a deep breath. "Yes," he replied. "You've made a persuasive case. But until I'm forced to break cover, there's no reason to give Dwyer any indication that I'm not still in the fold."

"I agree," said Jordan. "Are you also ready to have nanites injected so I can make a back-up of your consciousness?"

Carr smiled. "Well, I can't have you using my lack of a back-up as an excuse to take the lead on dangerous operations again."

Jordan laughed. "As great as that was," he said, "I think I've had more than enough excitement to last me for a while. And I'm pretty sure you can find a blind man who can shoot better than me."

When Carr finished laughing, Jordan turned to his daughter with a hopeful but anxious look. "What about you, Riley? Have you decided what you want to do?"

His daughter glanced at Bram. "What do you think, David?" she said. "Are you willing to sign up?"

"Absolutely," replied Bram without hesitation. "This is a chance to do truly momentous things. Besides," he added with a grin, "no use continuing on in my old job. If I do reach a breakthrough, your father will just sabotage my work, anyway."

Riley nodded and turned her attention back to her father. "You've won me over . . . Dad," she said. "I've decided to forgive you. I've decided I can trust you. And I'm willing and eager to join you. But I do have certain conditions I need you to meet."

"Anything," said an ecstatic Isaac Jordan.

"Don't agree too quickly," said Riley. "I have a feeling you aren't going to like these conditions."

# 64

Everyone in the conference room was intrigued to learn what Riley had in mind, none more so than her father.

"You need to go public," said Riley simply. "Not today. Not even this month. But soon."

Jordan looked as though he hadn't heard correctly. He visibly gathered himself, deciding how best to respond. "I know you must have thought this through," he began, "but I'm not understanding how this would be possible. I've stayed off the grid because I'm the most wanted man in America—at least I was when people thought I was alive. Also, if it became known that I was behind the sabotage of worldwide ASI research efforts, a whole lot of powerful people and countries would be really . . . unhappy. In short, if I were to go public, every operative in the world would be coming after me."

"Won't you have them coming after you, anyway?" said Riley. "With the intel Volkov provided to his superiors, we've already agreed that the Russians will be hunting for you until the end of time. But the secret *will* spread beyond Russia. I could be wrong, but I doubt a secret this good will keep." She nodded at Carr. "Can you weigh in on this one, Cameron?"

"I think you're right," he said. "At first it will just be rumors making their way to intelligence services around the world. To Black Ops groups. Wild legends, like the Fountain of Youth or the Lost City of the Incas. But the global intelligence community will have to take the rumors seriously. After all, they know the sabotage is real, and they'll feel compelled to vigorously pursue all leads, regardless of how crazy they sound. Eventually, enough evidence will be uncovered for the myths to look more and more real."

Carr turned to Jordan. "So the public won't know about you, but the most dangerous players in every corner of the world will. And like Riley said, they'll be coming for you."

Jordan frowned, turning his focus back to his daughter. "And you think going public will get me out ahead of this?" he asked her. "Won't it just accelerate it?"

"I'm not insisting that you do this to get you out ahead of it," said Riley. "I'm insisting that you do this because it's the right thing to do. You played God in Turlock, and it could have ended with our extinction. Now you're playing God again. And I agree with your motives and most of your decisions. But that doesn't matter.

"I realized at the mansion that I supported your vision wholeheartedly, but there was something about it that bothered me. During the helicopter ride here, I was finally able to put my finger on what. You're making pivotal decisions about the future of humanity—all by yourself. Your agenda becomes mankind's agenda. But this is too important for that, regardless of how talented you are. The future of humanity needs to be sorted out by the entire species. Collectively."

"Are you saying I should let the chips fall where they fall?" asked Jordan. "Allow ASI efforts to succeed?"

"No. For the most part, I'm saying you should operate as you have been. Going public doesn't mean you can't stay in hiding. It means you *have to* stay in hiding. What I'm saying is that you first need to set the record straight about Turlock. Clear your name, at least to the extent that you can. Explain what you've been doing since—your vision for humanity."

"It's too wild of a story," said Jordan. "No one will believe me."

"For a very smart man, that's a very dumb statement," said Riley bluntly. "I came here despising you, not willing to give you the slightest benefit of the doubt. And you've convinced me. Your story makes sense. Explains everything. And will especially resonate with power players around the globe. They know someone is using impossibly advanced methods to sabotage ASI. Now they'll know who. And why. And how. You can produce advanced technologies that will help the rest believe. You can demonstrate Pock's capabilities and offer him up as a global resource. Allow access to anyone who wants to tap into him and get assistance. He can become Google or Watson times a thousand. You stopped his evolution short of sentience, but can I assume he still has the capacity to work with millions of people simultaneously?"

Jordan nodded. "Billions of people."

"And here you are keeping him all to yourself," said Riley, gently chiding him.

"I agree with Riley," said Carr. "When you explain in detail what happened in Turlock, your story will be believed."

"So you agree I should go public?" said Jordan.

"I'm not sure," replied Carr. "But Riley is making a lot of sense to me so far. Let's see what else she has to say. And if she is able to convince you to go this route, I can help. I have access to the Secretary of Defense and the president. And also Melanie Yoder, the head of DARPA."

"I know Dr. Yoder by reputation," said Jordan.

"Trust me, you'd really like her. The point is that I can get them to agree to a long video meeting with you, one that you can make secure. You can tell them what you told us, and give them the same tour you've given us, only virtually. I'll vouch for everything you say."

"Assuming they believe me," said Jordan, "won't they want to keep this to themselves? Knowledge is power, and military and government types like their secrets more than anyone."

Carr smiled. "You're right about that. But they won't have a choice. Spell it out for them and they'll climb on board. I think we can even convince the president to pardon you if you're willing to give all comers access to Pock."

The lieutenant paused. "But we're getting ahead of ourselves. Let's see where your daughter is going with this." He waved a hand toward Riley. "Sorry to interrupt."

"Not at all," said Riley. "To continue," she added, now addressing her father once again, "once you've come clean about Turlock, your story will become the ultimate cautionary tale. People will know just how close we came to a runaway ASI, despite all precautions. This will throw cold water on most ASI efforts."

"Most," agreed Jordan, "but not all."

"So you continue your work to stop the rest," said Riley. "Just because they know you're out there trying to stop them doesn't mean they can do anything about it. According to Cameron, DARPA took every precaution to prevent sabotage, and you got to them anyway.

"And you can even send out seed-ships like you've planned," continued Riley, "to ensure a human future in case we do self-destruct. But you disclose everything. Whole brain emulation. Whole body bioprinting. Immortality. Your superior computer, to which you'll provide universal access, like I said. You'll just need to be sure Pock refuses to work on whole brain emulation so you keep this as a monopoly."

"I thought the point was for me not to *have* monopolies," said Jordan.

"You can have a monopoly on your technology," said Riley. "Just not on the decisions of where to take this technology. Everyone will see the potential of mind transference and want it for themselves, dream of it being released. But they'll also see the dangers. So you make it clear that you'll be keeping the technology to yourself until the world achieves consensus on how to use it. If humanity can't agree on how to move forward with this technology, then we move forward without it."

"Showing this off and then holding it back can't be a good idea," said Jordan. "I'd be better off wearing a suit of raw steak and entering a roomful of lions."

"You just have to be sure you're smarter than the lions," said Riley. "You'll have to up your game to stay in hiding, for sure. Everyone will want what you have and will be hunting you. But you can set up systems so that if something bad happens to you, the technology and the recipes are destroyed forever. That should discourage the lions. Even if a fail-safe like this isn't possible, I know you can make everyone believe that it is. Your track record is more than impressive enough to get away with any bluff."

"It will be risky and more difficult," said Carr, "but I agree it will still be possible for you to stay in hiding. Every power player might want you, but every one of them will also be keeping an eye on the rest to make sure a rival doesn't get to you first."

"A good point," said Riley.

"You've made lots of good points," said her father. "But here is where you've lost me. You can't get the nations of the world to agree that the sky is blue. So I can't believe we'll ever get a consensus on how to move forward with whole brain emulation."

"An *absolute* consensus wouldn't be required," said Riley. "But even so, you might be right. But so what? At minimum, we begin to have a global dialogue. About issues vital to the future of our species. Not about which reality TV star has the best bikini, but the essence of the human condition. The entire world will be thinking about this, talking about this. Should we use the technology at all? What rights should duplicates have? Should two copies of a person be allowed to exist at the same time? Ten? A thousand?

"Or should none be allowed?" continued Riley. "Should it be an absolute law that duplicates are only made at the point of death?"

"Which is my view, as you know," said Jordan.

"It may also be the *consensus* view," said Riley. "Let's find out. There are many more questions, as you know better than anyone. Should a person be able to transfer into a younger body? If so, will suicide be allowed to hasten a transfer? Will repeat criminals be allowed to have their consciousness transferred at death, or will violent felons only be allowed a single life?"

"Do you really think the average man and woman will debate these kinds of issues?" asked Jordan.

"Yes!" said Riley emphatically. "Are you kidding? When they come to understand what this technology can do, they will. With possible immortality on the line, they will. Once you've made it clear that you'll only release it if humanity agrees on a set of ground rules, this will become the ultimate lure. If this can't prompt a global debate, nothing will. Publish your results on human nature. Raise awareness of the myriad issues involved. Even if we never solve these issues, increased awareness will help us. Help us understand ourselves as a species. Raise awareness of dangers such as ASI. Help us to avoid these dangers. We're too close to the tipping point to avoid having these discussions any longer. And you can make sure we have them."

Her father paused, deep in thought. Several meeting participants had yet to contribute to the conversation, but all were transfixed by it. "I guess having a grand vision runs in the family," said Jordan finally. "I admire your perspective on this, Riley. But you do know that trying to get agreement on any of these issues will be worse than herding cats."

Riley laughed. "Really?" she said in amusement. "Another feline metaphor? First lions, now cats?"

"It isn't my fault they're so hard to herd," replied her father with a grin.

Riley returned her father's smile but quickly became serious once again. "Here's what I think you're missing," she said. "For a big enough prize, the cats will herd *themselves.* You'll hoard whole brain emulation until the entire species agrees on how to handle it. Could be decades. Could be never. But humanity will be forced to work together if they want it. And the species might surprise you. Who could have predicted that billions of cats could herd together to create the Internet and all of its content?"

Jordan nodded slowly, lost in thought.

"You're absolutely brilliant," Riley said to her father. "But even you couldn't have built the Internet by yourself. So don't put the burden of creating the future all on your own shoulders. Don't play God. Let humanity, collectively, play God."

"And if we never come together as a species?" asked Jordan.

"Then we don't deserve to be preserved," said Riley simply.

There were several minutes of absolute silence in the conference room as Jordan considered what his daughter had said. It was almost as if everyone in the group had reached a telepathic agreement to wait for the billionaire's response before speaking.

"So let me be sure I have all of this down," said Jordan finally. "First, you want me to reveal myself and my technology. Second, you want me to allow universal access to Pock. And third, you want me to make it clear that I'm keeping immortality to myself until the world collectively decides on parameters for its use. Which will paint a massive target on my chest and make kicking a hornet's nest seem tame."

"I didn't say this would be easy," said Riley. "Just that it was necessary."

Her father rolled his eyes. "You don't ask for much, do you?" he said dryly.

"I've been thinking small for eight years," she replied. "It's time to think big."

"Is that everything?"

"Almost," said Riley with a smile. "Glad you asked. You have to revive Mom and the boys, which I know you wanted to do anyway if I joined the team. And one last thing: David and I get to own as many dogs as we want."

Jordan laughed. "I don't know about the rest of it," he said, "but I'm pretty sure dog-ownership won't be a deal-breaker. And now I know why you objected to so many cat metaphors."

Riley grinned. "So what do you say?" she asked.

Her father sighed. "I guess if we want to have any hope of reaching global consensus," he said, "we should at least be able to reach consensus in this room. Anyone object to going forward in this way?"

Jordan waited for almost twenty seconds, but no one spoke.

Finally, Michael O'Banion broke the silence. "Personally," he said, "I like the idea a lot. It still has us calling most of the shots, but only until humanity can demonstrate the maturity needed to step up to the plate. If this happens, why *wouldn't* we want to give this capability to the world?"

"Anyone else want to weigh in?" said Jordan.

"I agree with Riley, also," said Carr, and Trish and Estrada nodded their agreement as well.

Jordan stared at his daughter intently for several long seconds. "Not that this matters in any way," he said, "but if you were to join the team, would you still want to be called Riley?"

"I'm afraid so. I did choose it myself, and I've gotten used to it. And no offense, Dad, but Melissa was never my favorite."

"Got it," said her father. "I'll never ask again. Anyway, that's unimportant. The important thing is that you have yourself a deal," he added, beaming happily. "Welcome to the team, Riley. We need to start our relocation efforts the second we adjourn, but when I get some time I plan to give you, David, and the lieutenant the welcome you deserve."

Jordan's eyes moistened as he gazed at his daughter, and Riley couldn't help from tearing up herself upon seeing how happy he was that she was really joining him.

She knew that this day would change the course of her life almost as dramatically as the day the kinetic round hit Turlock eight years earlier. But whereas Turlock had represented the destruction of her life and the loss of all hope, this day represented the opposite. Despair and self-loathing would be replaced by hope and great purpose. Her life would go from simple and somewhat aimless to as complex, exciting, and meaningful as any life would ever be.

She couldn't wait to dig in. She was especially interested in finding a way to rule in, or rule out, the existence of a soul. Above all else, this was the most fundamental question posed by the capabilities her father's technology made possible. His results so far seemed to indicate that one didn't exist. But absence of proof was not the same as proof of absence.

Was consciousness just a question of the complexity and arrangement of a neuronal pattern? Or was there more? Were her father's duplicates exactly as human as the originals, or were they missing a subtle ingredient they had yet to identify, one that only a naturally born human could possess?

Among other duties she knew she would take on, she vowed to do whatever she could to answer this question. She would consult with theologians. Read the great philosophers. Find a way to design more elaborate and subtle experiments to get her arms around this issue.

If she could prove the soul did exist, this would obviate the need for immortality. This would reassure humanity that there was a higher power in the universe, and that death was not the end.

If she could prove the opposite, that a human being emerged simply from the sum of its parts, then humanity would know with certainty, even the most devoutly religious, that true immortality was possible.

Regardless, she would be intimately involved in the most important tipping point in the evolution of mankind since *Homo sapiens* first came on the scene. A tipping point that could directly trace its roots to unspeakable tragedy.

Some day in the far future, a historian would be asked, "What event marked the end of mortality? What event marked the end of humanity being trapped within a single solar system?

"When, precisely, was infinity born?"

The answer might be surprising. "Just after a man named Isaac Jordan had wiped out thousands of innocents and beheaded his wife and sons. The moment he refused to accept that death was irreversible."

But maybe the answer wouldn't be that surprising, after all. Maybe it would be well understood in this far future time that resilience, determination, refusal to accept defeat, and ability to bounce back from tragedy were the hallmarks of the human condition.

How many of mankind's greatest advances had arisen from the ashes of defeat? How much of the success of the species was due to its members being too stubborn to stay down after getting thrown from a horse?

Tragedy could spark drive, motivation, and resilience. Riley's own experiences were a testament to this. Would she be this excited about her future, this adamant that humanity needed to find a way forward together, without her eight years in the wilderness? Would she fully embrace the sacrifices that would need to be made to ensure this could happen?

Or would she have graduated from a spoiled rich kid to a spoiled rich adult, self-absorbed and uncaring about others?

There was no way to know. What she *did* know was that she intended to make full use of this opportunity. Being reunited with the family she loved, including Michael O'Banion, who had been like a father to her, was a dream come true. And she would have the chance to work shoulder to shoulder with amazing people on momentous projects. With her father and adopted uncle. With Cameron Carr, a bright and charming lieutenant who had proven his courage and friendship. And with David Bram, the man she had fallen in love with, despite her best efforts to resist this.

And perhaps when a far future historian, on a far distant planet, was asked what had marked the beginning of humanity's immortality and expansion into the cosmos, this extraordinary group of people would still be around to offer their perspective.

# AUTHOR NOTES & BONUS CONTENT

**Table of Contents**

**1) From the Author**: Thanks for reading *Infinity Born*. I hope that you enjoyed it. Please feel free to visit my website, www.douglas-erichards.com , where you can get on a mailing list to be notified of new releases. Also, you can Friend me on Facebook at *Douglas E. Richards Author,* or write to me at doug@san.rr.com.

**2) *Infinity Born*: What's real and what isn't**
   As you may know, in addition to trying to tell the most compelling stories I possibly can, I strive to introduce concepts and accurate information that I hope will prove fascinating, thought-provoking, and even controversial. *Infinity Born* is a work of fiction and contains considerable speculation, so I encourage interested readers to explore these topics on your own to arrive at your own view of the subject matter.
   Being human, I know I get things wrong sometimes, but I do try very hard to get them right. Sometimes, I even get a little carried away. Just to give one example, I planned to have Cameron Carr tape a steak knife to his outer pant leg. I wasn't sure if this would really work, so I actually taped one of our steak knives to my leg and

ran around the house (at first very gingerly to be sure I wouldn't get stabbed). Happily, it didn't obstruct my movement in the least.

The funny thing about this is that my wife is so used to seeing me do crazy things in the name of research, she didn't even raise an eyebrow. She did draw the line, however, at letting me cut her bathing suit into strips to test how well these would work as a Molotov-cocktail fuses : )

Anyway, with this said, I'll get right to it: what's real in *Infinity Born* and what isn't. If you aren't interested in an early category and want to skip ahead to one that might interest you more, I've listed the categories I'll be covering in order of their appearance.

- **AGI/ASI—Current efforts**
- **AGI/ASI—The potential for disaster**
- **Mind Uploading/Whole Brain Emulation**
- **Bioprinting**
- **Nanites in the brain**
- **The nature of consciousness**
- **Isaac Jordan's R-Drive fleet (EmDrive technology)**
- **Asteroid mining**
- **Kinetic bombardment (The Rod of God)**
- **The rise of the Internet**
- **Are our bodies replaced every five years?**
- **The speed of thought**
- **Are we living in a computer simulation?**
- **The Fermi Paradox**
- **Elon Musk, Mars, tunneling, and brain implants**
- **Graphene**
- **DARPA, the Pentagon, Helen Woodward Animal Center, and smoke alarms**

## AGI/ASI—Current efforts

Where to even begin? What I wrote in the novel about the scope of AGI efforts (still called plain AI by many publications) is accurate, and I took the liberty of extrapolating these trends into the future. Is there any government or powerful investor not sinking millions or billions into this area? Not as far as I can tell.

Here is an excerpt from an article in the *Wall Street Journal* published in December of 2016 that I think puts things nicely into perspective: "Startups that claim to be using AI are attracting record levels of investment. Big tech companies are going all-in, draining universities of entire departments. Nearly 140 AI companies have been acquired since 2011, including 40 this year alone."

From my reading, advances are so dizzying in so many areas, I could write hundreds of pages of notes and not even scratch the surface. But if you have further interest just Google any of the following: Exascale computing (a computer capable of a billion billion calculations per second, on the order of the processing power of the human brain, expected in the early 2020s), NVIDIA (which is a company making supercomputers on a chip), DNA computing, Quantum computing, and Optical computing.

Because I used Optical Computing in the novel, I've included what I think to be a relevant excerpt about this technology below. This is from the website *Next Big Future* and an article entitled, "Progress to overcoming the last obstacle to the creation of all optical computers."

EXCERPT: *Optical signals travel much faster than electrons— at the speed of light—and are not subject to "resistance." Scientists have already created all the major components needed to create the ultimate all optical computer. Unfortunately, the waveguides down which optical signals travel in a photonic computer introduce losses much like the resistance against electrons in copper wires.*

*Now the Moscow Institute of Physics and Technology (MIPT) claims it may have cleared that last hurdle. According to the journal, Nature, a new method can compensate for losses just by carefully designing dual waveguides to match the wavelength of the light traveling through them. By doing so, the traveling waves can reinforce each other along the way, thus introducing a slight gain that compensates for the normal losses.*

### AGI/ASI—The potential for disaster

I should point out that there is much disagreement as to the possible dangers of AGI and ASI. Many brilliant scientists believe the perils as expressed in this novel are overblown. Some believe AGI will never be possible. Others believe that we'll be able to create ASI and wield it as the ultimate tool without obsoleting ourselves or going extinct in the process. These scientists bristle at any alarmist attitudes, believing those who espouse them are nothing more than Chicken Littles screaming that the sky is falling.

To give you an illustration of this divide, Elon Musk, Stephen Hawking, and Bill Gates are very concerned. Mark Zuckerberg . . . not so much. Here is an excerpt from the UK's *Mirror*, in an article entitled, "Facebook founder Mark Zuckerberg "frustrated" with Stephen Hawking and Elon Musk's views on AI."

EXCERPT: *In an interview Zuckerberg admitted he was frustrated by people who "fear-monger" about artificial intelligence. Stephen Hawking has raised concerns over AI, saying it has the potential to wipe out the human race. "Once machines reach a critical stage of being able to evolve themselves we cannot predict whether their goals will be the same as ours. AI has the potential to evolve faster than the human race." Despite using AI in Tesla cars, Elon Musk also has similar fears, but their concerns fall on deaf ears with Zuckerberg.*

Why did I choose to write a novel that explores the negative consequences of ASI envisioned by those who are fearful of it? First, because their arguments make sense to me, and I think there is a real possibility something like the events depicted in *Infinity Born* might someday come to pass. Second, because *Infinity Born* is a science fiction *thriller*. If I wrote a novel that explored the positive consequences of ASI, as envisioned by those who think we have nothing to fear from it, the stakes for my characters, and humanity, wouldn't be nearly as high.

Back to the subject at hand, I believe DeepMind has achieved perhaps the most impressive feat of any AI around today. When DeepMind's AlphaGo beat the Go master alluded to in the novel, it freaked out the entire nation of South Korea. Here is an excerpt from a 2016 article in *New Scientist*.

EXCERPT: *Watching Google's AlphaGo AI eviscerate Korean grandmaster Lee Sedol put the nation into shock. "Koreans are afraid that AI will destroy human history and human culture," said Jeong. "It's an emotional thing."*

*It is perhaps the perceived beauty of AlphaGo's moves that has ruffled the most feathers. "AlphaGo actually does have an intuition," Google co-founder Sergey Brin told New Scientist. "It makes beautiful moves—more beautiful moves than most of us could think of."*

*This ability to make beauty has left many shaken. "This is a tremendous incident in the history of human evolution—that a machine can surpass the intuition and creativity of human beings," said Jang Dae-Ik, a science philosopher at Seoul National University.*

Finally, one last excerpt on this from a 2017 *Vanity Fair* article (which is quite extensive), entitled, "Elon Musk's Billion-Dollar Crusade to Stop the A.I. Apocalypse."

EXCERPT: *It was just a friendly little argument about the fate of humanity. Demis Hassabis, a leading creator of advanced artificial intelligence, was chatting with Elon Musk, a leading doomsayer, about the perils of artificial intelligence. Hassabis, a co-founder of DeepMind, had come to Musk's SpaceX rocket factory, outside Los Angeles, a few years ago. Musk explained that his ultimate goal at SpaceX was the most important project in the world: interplanetary colonization. Hassabis replied that, in fact, he was working on the most important project in the world: developing artificial superintelligence. Musk countered that this was one reason we needed to colonize Mars—so that we'll have a bolt-hole if A.I. goes rogue and turns on humanity. Amused, Hassabis said that A.I. would simply follow humans to Mars.*

*Peter Thiel, the billionaire venture capitalist told me a story about an investor in DeepMind who joked as he left a meeting that he ought to shoot Hassabis on the spot, because it was the last chance to save the human race.*

*Elon Musk began warning about the possibility of A.I. running amok three years ago. It probably hadn't eased his mind when one of Hassabis's partners in DeepMind, Shane Legg, stated flatly, "I think human extinction will probably occur, and technology will likely play a part in this."*

*Before DeepMind was gobbled up by Google, in 2014, as part of its A.I. shopping spree, Musk had been an investor in the company. He told me that his involvement was not about a return on his money but rather to keep a wary eye on the arc of A.I.: "It gave me more visibility into the rate at which things were improving, and I think they're really improving at an accelerating rate, far faster than people realize.*

I could write forever on the many dangers of ASI and the difficulty of reining in a superior intelligence. The arguments used in *Infinity Born*, such as *perverse instantiation*, are all real and have been used by prominent scientists (as have many other arguments that I didn't include). For those of you interested in a very thorough, complex, and scholarly treatment of the subject matter, I would recommend the book *Superintelligence: Paths, Dangers, Strategies* (2014) by Nick Bostrom, a Professor at Oxford.

The book I found most useful in researching this novel is entitled, *Our Final Invention: Artificial Intelligence and the end of the Human Era* (James Barrat, 2013). This described the "God in a box" experiment detailed in the novel, for example, and provided a fascinating, easy-to-read perspective on ASI, at least on the fear-mongering side of the debate. I've included a few quotes from this book that I thought were relevant to *Infinity Born*.

Page 59—First, there are too many players in the AGI sweepstakes. Too many organizations in too many countries are working on AGI and AGI-related technology for them all to agree to mothball their projects until Friendly AI is created, or to include in their code a formal friendliness module, if one could be made.

Page 61—But what if there is some kind of category shift once something becomes a thousand times smarter than we are, and we just can't see it from here? For example, we share a lot of DNA with flatworms. But would we be invested in their goals and morals even if we discovered that many millions of years ago flatworms had created us, and given us their values? After we got over the initial surprise, wouldn't we just do whatever we wanted?

Page 86—Shall we build our robot replacement or not? On this, de Garis is clear. "Humans should not stand in the way of a higher form of evolution. These machines are godlike. It is human destiny to create them."

(Note: This is an example of the faction who believes humanity should step aside and let our new ASI overlords run the show. To give you a sense of who this guy is, here is the first paragraph of his Wikipedia page: **Hugo de Garis** is a retired researcher in the subfield of artificial intelligence (AI) known as evolvable hardware. He became known in the 1990s for his research on the use of genetic algorithms to evolve neural networks using three-dimensional cellular automata inside field programmable gate arrays. He claimed that this approach would enable the creation of what he terms "artificial brains" which would quickly surpass human levels of intelligence).

Page 91—Dr. Shostak (Chief of SETI—the Search for Extraterrestrial Intelligence) argues that SETI should point some of its receivers toward corners of the galaxy that would be inviting to artificial rather than biological alien intelligence.

"Since they can evolve on timescales far, far shorter than biological evolution, it could very well be that the first machines on the scene thoroughly dominate the intelligence of the galaxy. If we build a machine with the intellectual capability of one human, within five years, its successor will be more intelligent than all of humanity combined."

Page 123—"We've got thousands of good people working all over the world in sort of a community effort to create a disaster," Vinge said. (Note: Vernor Vinge is a science fiction writer and the first person to formally use the word "singularity" in a 1993 address to NASA, entitled "The Coming Technological Singularity.")

Page 155—Too many people think the frontiers of AI are delineated by harmless search engines, smart phones, and now Watson. But AGI is much closer to nuclear weapons than to video games.

Page 242—There is no purely technical strategy that is workable in this area because greater intelligence will always find a way to circumvent measures that are the product of a lesser intelligence.

## Mind Uploading/Whole Brain Emulation

The concept of whole brain emulation (WBE) is becoming ever more mainstream and ever more well known. For those interested in learning more, a simple Google search on WBE will return enough reading to keep you busy for a long time. There is even a foundation called Carboncopies (one word), whose mission is to support WBE research.

For those who wish to really drill down into this subject, I recommend two books, "Intelligence Unbound: the Future of Uploaded and Machine Minds" (2014), edited by Russell Blackford and Damien Broderick, and "A Taxonomy and Metaphysics of Mind-Uploading" (2014), by Keith Wiley.

Mind transference has been a science fictional concept for a very long time, but like many science fictional concepts it is quickly moving down the path toward reality.

Every time I think a technology like this is impossible, ridiculous, I'm reminded of when I had to sequence DNA as part of a research project to earn my Master's degree in genetic engineering.

Back then, almost thirty years ago, it took me days to prepare and sequence just a few hundred bases of the virus I was mutating. I had to isolate and extract the DNA, initiate chemical reactions, tag the DNA with radiation, perform electrophoresis, allow the radiation to expose photographic film, and then read the film manually using a light box for illumination.

Today, it is possible to sequence billions of bases in the time it took me to sequence a few hundred. If you had asked me then when I thought a capability this amazing would come about, I would have said *never*. Not in thirty years. Not in *three million* years.

I would have predicted the laws of the universe wouldn't allow this kind of sequencing speed, ever, just like faster-than-light travel.

But I would have been wrong.

So while the perfect transfer of consciousness seems impossible today, you never know what will be possible tomorrow . . .

Anyway, I'll leave you with excerpts from a few articles I thought were particularly relevant to how this subject was presented in *Infinity Born*. The first is from *Stanford News* in 2017, entitled, "Stanford researchers create a high-performance, low-energy artificial synapse for neural network computing."

EXCERPT: *A new organic artificial synapse made by Stanford researchers could support computers that better recreate the way the hu-*

man brain processes information. It could also lead to improvements in brain-machine technologies.

*"It works like a real synapse but it's an organic electronic device that can be engineered," said Alberto Salleo, associate professor of materials science and engineering at Stanford and senior author of the paper."*

The next excerpt is from *Popular Science* (2012) entitled, "Will people alive today have the opportunity to upload their consciousness to a new robotic body?"

EXCERPT: *When Steve Jobs passed away last year, a joke bounced around that the man who had done so much to shape modern technology hadn't really died at all, but rather had figured out how to upload himself into the Mac OS so he could live on with us forever. The notion was ostensibly so far out as to be ridiculous. But not everyone sees it that way.*

*At the recent Global Future 2045 International Congress held in Moscow, 31-year-old media mogul Dmitry Itskov told attendees how he plans to create exactly that kind of immortality, first by creating a robot controlled by the human brain, then by actually transplanting a human brain into a humanoid robot, and then by replacing the surgical transplant with a method for simply uploading a person's consciousness into a surrogate 'bot.*

*He thinks he can get beyond the first phase in just ten years, putting him on course to achieve his ultimate goal—human consciousness completely disembodied and placed within a holographic host—within 30 years' time.*

*Phase one—creating a robot controlled by a human brain—is already well within reach. In fact, DARPA is already working on it via a program called "Avatar" through which the Pentagon hopes to create a brain-machine interface that will allow soldiers to control bipedal human surrogate machines remotely with their minds.*

*And of course there are all the ongoing medical prosthesis projects (DARPA is involved in a few of these as well) that have shown that the human nervous system can interface with prosthetic enhancements, manipulating them via thought. Itskov draws a clear arc from what we have now to the consciousness-containing holograms that he envisions.*

*Theoretically, as long as one could keep his or her gray matter from decaying, he or she could continue to "live" indefinitely. Of course, every attempt we've made at creating a computer that functions just like the brain has come up far short. Still, progress is being made in neural networks, microchips modeled on living brains, and entire computers set up to mimic the brain's functionality.*

Finally, the third excerpt is from *ScienceAlert.com* in 2015, entitled, "A new start-up wants to transfer your consciousness to an artificial body so you can live forever."

EXCERPT: *Death is the one thing that's guaranteed in today's uncertain word, but now a new start-up called Humai thinks it might be able to get rid of that inconvenient problem for us too, by promising to transfer people's consciousness into a new, artificial body.*

*If it sounds like science fiction, that's because it still is, with none of the technology required for Humai's business plan currently up and running. But that's not deterring the company's CEO, Josh Bocanegra, who says his team will resurrect their first human within 30 years.*

*So how do you go about transferring someone's consciousness to another robot body? As Humai explains on their website:*

*"We're using artificial intelligence and nanotechnology to store data of conversational styles, behavioral patterns, thought processes, and information about how your body functions from the inside-out.*

### Bioprinting

Bioprinting is real, as you have probably guessed from the specificity of the experiment discussed in the novel. Here are excerpts of two articles, both published in 2017, that I found fascinating.

The first is from the *Economist*, entitled, "Printed human body parts could be available for human transplants within a few years."

EXCERPT: *Every year about 120,000 organs, mostly kidneys, are transplanted from one human being to another. But a lack of suitable donors means the supply of such organs is limited. Many people therefore die waiting for a transplant. That has led researchers to study the question of how to build organs from scratch.*

*One promising approach is to print them. Lots of things are made these days by three-dimensional printing, and there seems no reason why body parts should not be among them. As yet, such "bioprinting" remains largely experimental. But bioprinted tissue is already being sold for drug testing, and the first transplantable tissues are expected to be ready for use in a few years' time.*

*Researchers have implanted printed ears, bones and muscles into animals, and watched these integrate properly with their hosts. Last year a group at Northwestern University, in Chicago, even printed working prosthetic ovaries for mice. The recipients were able to conceive and give birth with the aid of these artificial organs.*

The second excerpt is from *The Telegraph,* entitled, "The next step: 3D printing the human body."

EXCERPT: *The printing of whole organs, if approved, could be a reality within the next decade. Organovo recently bioprinted its first 3D liver tissue for testing purposes. In 2010 the company also printed the first human blood vessel. In the meantime, Organovo is currently developing bioprinted breast cancer tissues alongside lung and muscle tissues.*

*With the technology advancing at such a rate, entire organs and bodies produced by 3D printers is becoming a concrete reality, rather than a freaky sci-fi concept.*

*Others claim 3D printing human components further blurs the line between man and machine, giving us the right to 'play God' on an unprecedented scale. But there is no denying that bioprinting has the potential to revolutionize medicine and healthcare beyond what seemed possible even 20 years ago.*

### Nanites in the brain

As you've no doubt guessed, scientists really are working on injecting nanites (often called "smart dust") into humans to map their brains and/or to help facilitate a brain/computer interface. I've pasted a few excerpts below.

The first is from an article in *New Scientist* (2015), entitled "Twenty billion nanoparticles talk to the brain using electricity."

EXCERPT: *Nanoparticles can be used to stimulate regions of the brain electrically, opening up new ways to treat brain diseases. It may even one day allow the routine exchange of data between computers and the brain.*

*When "magnetoelectric" nanoparticles (MENs) are stimulated by an external magnetic field, they produce an electric field. If such nanoparticles are placed next to neurons, this electric field should allow them to communicate.*

*Sakhrat Khizroev of Florida International University in Miami and his team inserted 20 billion of these nanoparticles into the brains of mice.*

*Khizroev's goal is to build a system that can both image brain activity and precisely target medical treatments at the same time. "When they are injected in the brain, we can 'see' the brain," says Khizroev.*

The second excerpt is from an article in *MIT Technology Review* in 2013, entitled, "How Smart Dust Could Spy On Your Brain."

EXCERPT: *Intelligent dust particles embedded in the brain could form an entirely new form of brain-machine interface, say engineers.*

*Today, Dongjin Seo and pals at the University of California Berkeley reveal an entirely new way to study and interact with the brain. Their idea is to sprinkle electronic sensors the size of dust particles into the cortex and to interrogate them remotely using ultrasound. The ultrasound also powers this so-called neural dust. Each particle of neural dust consists of standard CMOS circuits and sensors that measure the electrical activity in neurons nearby.*

## The nature of consciousness

This is truly an impossible topic that has been debated for thousands of years, and will continue to be debated for many thousands more. When it comes to the subject of when a computer can be considered sentient, I tried to give a flavor of some of the current thinking, including two common thought experiments (the Chinese room and the woman raised in a black-and-white house, not able to experience the qualia of the color red).

My sense is that most computer scientists now agree that the Turing test is no longer a good indication of AGI, but there is no consensus on what should replace it.

As I was writing the scene in which Jordan Two was suffering through an endless solitary confinement, it occurred to me that perhaps "boredom" would be the simplest test of sentience. I would think that any computer intelligence that could be shown to be losing its mind from boredom would have to be fully conscious. I'm not sure if this is a profound insight or hopelessly off the mark, but for some reason I think this might actually be the case. (Of course, this begs the question of whether boredom is something that can be defined and measured).

In any event, if you have interest in this subject or in speculation about the existence of a soul, you can find extensive material online. But be warned, material on the nature of consciousness can be very deep, so don't be surprised if your brain starts to hurt as you read through it.

### Isaac Jordan's R-Drive fleet (EmDrive Technology)

As mentioned in the novel, Jordan's R-Drive was derived from the electromagnetic drive, or EmDrive. The EmDrive is a real technology that is extraordinarily controversial, namely because if true, it would fly in the face of known physics. I have no idea if it's real or not, but any technology that NASA spends time and effort to test, and which at least one group stands behind, is worth keeping an eye on. I've been following this technology for years and couldn't help but include it in *Infinity Born* (and it fit my needs nicely).

To give you a sense of where things are, I'll provide an excerpt from a 2016 article in *National Geographic* entitled, "NASA team claims impossible space engine works—get the facts," and subtitled, "Scientists just published a paper saying that the controversial EmDrive produces thrust, even though that defies known laws of physics."

EXCERPT: *After years of speculation, a maverick research team at NASA's Johnson Space Center has reached a milestone that many experts thought was impossible. This week, the team formally published their experimental evidence for an electromagnetic propulsion system that could power a spacecraft through the void—without using any kind of propellant. According to the team, the electromagnetic drive, or EmDrive, converts electricity into thrust simply by bouncing around microwaves in a closed cavity. In theory, such a lightweight engine could one day send a spacecraft to Mars in just 70 days.*

*The long-standing catch is that the EmDrive seemingly defies the laws of classical physics, so even if it's doing what the team claims, scientists still aren't sure how the thing actually works. Previous reports about the engine have been met with heaping doses of skepticism, with many physicists relegating the EmDrive to the world of pseudoscience.*

*Now, though, the latest study has passed a level of scrutiny by independent scientists that suggests the EmDrive really does work. What this means, if the EmDrive withstands further scrutiny, is that future vehicles could hurtle through space without needing to carry literal tons of propellant. In space travel, staying light is crucial for fast and cost-effective trips over long distances.*

*It's still unclear that the EmDrive truly generates thrust, a claim that will require further verification.*

### Asteroid mining

The information in the novel about Helium-3 mining on the Moon and the bounty that could be harvested from asteroids is accurate. There are several companies that have been founded for the sole purpose of mining the asteroids in this way, including Planetary Resources and Deep Space Industries.

Here is an excerpt from a 2017 article from *Space Angels Network* entitled, "Asteroid prospects: the facts and future of space mining."

EXCERPT: *The notion of harvesting resources from extraterrestrial sources is not a new one. The lure of untold bounties—orbiting just out of reach—has prompted generations of poets and presidents alike to expound upon the potential applications of space mining. These days, "space mining" is no longer a mere pipe dream. Thanks to recent funding successes, asteroid prospecting is fast becoming a very actionable goal. Commercial prospecting missions are projected to begin as early as 2020.*

*Although it sounds like pure science fiction, asteroid mining is quickly becoming a viable niche industry within the commercial space landscape. While the logistical challenges are not insignificant, early stage ventures are refining the technologies required for commercial deployment. Mining an asteroid for resources would in theory function very much like terrestrial mining—only absent the environmental concerns inherent to Earth-based practices.*

*. . . The advancements in asteroid mining have increased at such a rapid rate—near blinding, actually—that it just might be one of those proverbial "once-in-a-lifetime opportunities" for those who jump in early. Many savvy, early-stage angel investors are already taking the plunge. Why? They understand that we truly are on the threshold of breaking into an opportunity with nearly unlimited potential.*

### Kinetic bombardment (The Rod of God)

It is truly remarkable how much kinetic energy a speeding object carries with it, and until I began doing the math, I never fully appreciated that a spaceship going tens of thousands of miles per second could annihilate an entire planet.

My research suggests that kinetic bombardment from space is probably something the US government has worked on, but most of what is out there is rumor and speculation. I have read that the science fiction writer Jerry Pournelle originated this concept in the 1950s while working at Boeing.

Here is an excerpt from a 2004 article in *Popular Science* entitled, "Rods From God."

EXCERPT: *A pair of satellites orbiting several hundred miles above the Earth would serve as a weapons system. One functions as the targeting and communications platform while the other carries numerous tungsten rods—up to 20 feet in length and a foot in diameter—that can drop on targets with less than 15 minutes' notice.*

*When instructed from the ground, the targeting satellite commands its partner to drop one of its darts. The guided rods enter the atmosphere, protected by a thermal coating, traveling at 22,000 miles per hour—comparable to the speed of a meteor. The result: complete devastation of the target, even if it's buried deep underground.*

*The concept of kinetic-energy weapons has been around ever since the 1950s. Though the Pentagon won't say how far along the research is, or even confirm that any efforts are underway, the concept persists. The "U.S. Air Force Transformation Flight Plan," published by the Air Force in November 2003, references "hypervelocity rod bundles" in its outline of future space-based weapons, and in 2002, another report from RAND, "Space Weapons, Earth Wars," dedicated entire sections to the technology's usefulness.*

Finally, here is an excerpt from *Above Top Secret.com*

EXCERPT: *In the early/mid 1950's there was another program called Project Thor, named after the hammer-wielding Norse god who could rain metal death down as he pleased. It reportedly originated from a U.S.A.F. research project, and is basically summed up as 'an orbiting tungsten telephone pole with small fins and a computer in the back for guidance.'*

*Once given the launch command, a satellite would drop the 'pole,' which would then speed up until going at orbital velocity, around 9 kilometers a second. At this speed, when it hit a ground based target, it would have the explosive equivalent of a small-yield nuclear weapon.*

*This program was the first example of what we now call 'kinetic bombardment,' using dense objects travelling at very high speeds to eliminate targets without the need of explosives.*

*Another program along the same lines initiated in the early 80's, called 'Rods from God', worked on the same principles as the Thor program.*

### The rise of the Internet

We all know just how vast the Internet has become, and that almost every single one of us have contributed to its unprecedented growth. But I never really considered how amazing this really was.

As mentioned in the novel, the Web has grown organically, and really does show what billions of people can accomplish when their creativity can be collectively unleashed.

I never thought about how the Internet changed a paradigm that had been true throughout human history, that a few creators had always produced content for the masses to consume, rather than everyone creating content for everyone else. The statistic I quoted in the novel, that by 2016, more than sixty trillion web pages had been created, almost ten thousand for every living human, is true. I found this statistic, and the insight about how the Internet is being forged by all of us, collectively, in a fascinating book by Kevin Kelly, co-founder of *Wired* magazine, entitled, "The Inevitable: Understanding the 12 Technological Forces That Will Shape Our Future."

### Are our bodies replaced every five years?

According to my research, our bodies *are* replaced every five years. Here is an excerpt from an article in *Time* magazine way back in 1954.

EXCERPT: *About 98% of the atoms in the human body are renewed each year. This surprising fact is discussed by Dr. Paul C. Aebersold of Oak Ridge in the latest Annual Report of the Smithsonian Institution. Dr. Aebersold based his conclusion on experiments with radioisotopes, which trace the movements of chemical elements in and out of the body.*

I'll leave you with one more excerpt, taken from the book, "The Seven Mysteries of Life," (1978), by Guy Murchie.

EXCERPT: *Recent studies at the Oak Ridge Atomic Research Center have revealed that about 98 percent of all the atoms in a human body are replaced every year. You get a new suit of skin every month and a new liver every six weeks. The lining of your stomach lasts only five days before it's replaced. Even your bones are not the solid, stable, concrete-like things you might have thought them to be: They are undergoing constant change. The bones you have today are different from the bones you had a year ago. Experts in this area of research have concluded that there is a complete, 100 percent turn-*

*over of atoms in the body at least every five years. In other words, not one single atom present in your body today was there five years ago.*

## The speed of thought

I probably spent more time researching this than any other topic, trying to pin it down precisely, but I failed miserably. I can tell you how fast nerve impulses travel from the muscles to the brain, and I can provide any number of other parameters, but I could never get comfortable with even a ballpark figure when it came to the speed of thought.

The subject turned out to be much too complex for me to easily sort through. The one reference I found that spoke fairly directly to the speed of thinking was from *Comptons Interactive Encyclopedia* (1997). Based on this resource, the speed I mentioned in the novel, between 200 and 300 MPH, was actually fast. Thinking may be as slow as 50 MPH. Here is the relevant section: "Some actions require split second responses—withdrawing a hand from a hot stove, for example. To relay the information necessary for such a reaction, there are large nerve fibers that can conduct impulses at speeds as high as 220 miles per hour. Other kinds of activities, such as scholarly pursuits, may require a lifetime of thought. For these kinds of activities, other nerve fibers can be used to conduct signals more slowly—50 to 60 miles per hour."

## Are we living in a computer simulation?

Are we living in a computer simulation? The short answer is that a number of scientists much smarter than me think we are. For a fascinating article on this subject, I would point you to a 2016 piece in the *New Yorker* (one that you can readily find online) entitled, "What are the odds we are living in a computer simulation?"

## The Fermi Paradox

I have long found the Fermi Paradox to be fascinating. For those of you who really want to drill down, I can direct you to a book I read three or four years ago by Stephen Webb entitled, "If the Universe Is Teeming with Aliens ... WHERE IS EVERYBODY?: Seventy-Five

Solutions to the Fermi Paradox and the Problem of Extraterrestrial Life."

(Perhaps a longer title than I would have used, but a fun read).

Here is the first paragraph of the book's description on Amazon: *Given the fact that there are perhaps 400 billion stars in our Galaxy alone, and perhaps 400 billion galaxies in the universe, it stands to reason that somewhere out there, in the 14-billion-year-old cosmos, there is or once was a civilization at least as advanced as our own. The sheer enormity of the numbers almost demands that we accept the truth of this hypothesis. Why, then, have we encountered no evidence, no messages, no artifacts of these extraterrestrials?*

### Elon Musk, Mars, tunneling, and brain implants

Like many people, I'm a big fan of Elon Musk. I was one of the first to read Ashlee Vance's biography of the man. When I saw footage of SpaceX's Falcon 9 rocket touching down softly on a landing platform, I was amazed that a private citizen has been able to achieve what Musk has achieved.

It seemed as though everywhere I turned as I wrote this novel, Elon Musk was there. First, it's hard to write a billionaire genius scientist character without thinking of Musk as one prime example. This is especially true since Isaac Jordan's claim to fame was in building a fleet of spacecraft and colonizing Mars, which is exactly what Musk is working toward. In fact, I even pointed out in the novel that Jordan had beat Musk in the race to get to the red planet.

Then I began to research the possible dangers of ASI, and of course Musk was a prominent voice here, as well.

Are we living in a computer simulation? Yep, Musk is perhaps the most prominent of those who have weighed in on this subject, also.

But there was one part of my character's biography that diverged from Elon Musk's. Isaac Jordan happened to have made huge innovations in tunneling technology, which he put to great use in his asteroid mining efforts and his underground lairs.

And then I began reading articles like this one, entitled, "Elon Musk wants to speed up tunneling by ten times, lower costs by ten to a hundred times, and create thirty layers of mostly underground cities." This was on a website called *Next Big Future*, in 2017, and it showed that Jordan's and Musk's biographies didn't diverge in this respect, after all. If you Google *Musk and Tunneling*, or *The Boring Company* (which is what he's naming this new venture) you can find plenty more. I've included a brief excerpt from the *Next Big Future* article below.

EXCERPT: *Tunnel technology is older than rockets, and boring speeds are pretty much what they were fifty years ago. In L.A., plans to extend the subway's Purple Line by 2.6 miles will cost more than $2.4 billion and take almost ten years. "It's basically a billion dollars a mile," Musk says. "That's crazy."*

*Musk says he hopes to build a much faster tunneling machine and use it to dig thousands of miles, eventually creating a vast underground network that includes as many as thirty levels of tunnels for cars and high-speed trains such as the Hyperloop.*

*Objections spring to mind. Such as: Wouldn't having hundreds of feet of hollow tunnels destabilize the ground? Nope, Musk says, the mining industry does it all the time. "The Earth is big, and we are small," he says. "We are so f-ing small you cannot believe it." Not only are these mega-tunnels possible, he argues, they're the only way we can rid ourselves of the scourge of traffic.*

*. . . He plans to use a machine like this to test improvements in tunneling technology. "To make it a little better should be easy," he says. "To make it five times better is not crazy hard. To make it ten times better is hard, but nobody will need to win a Nobel Prize.*

*"We're trying to dramatically increase the tunneling speed," he says. "We want to know what it would take to get to a mile a week? Could it be possible?"*

It was at this point that I realized Elon Musk was reading my mind, knew about Isaac Jordan and his tunneling innovations, and frankly, was jealous of him.

But it gets worse. Today, as I sat down to write this very section, I learned that Musk was starting a company called Neuralink, with the goal of coming up with brain implants that can enhance human mental capabilities and pave the way for human/computer interfaces. I'm not kidding. Just today this was announced.

Many of you may be aware that this is reminiscent of my Nick Hall series (*Mind's Eye*, *BrainWeb*, and *MindWar*), in which the protagonist has electronic implants embedded in his brain that allow him to surf the Web with his thoughts and read minds.

Enough is enough, Elon Musk. Get out of my head. If you're reading this, I'm asking you to back off. It's hard enough for me to come up with science fictional ideas that stay a few steps ahead of reality as it is, without you having to keep inventing things that make it that much harder.

Anyway, I need to hurry up and finish this section before Elon Musk announces his intention of moving to Turlock, California or starting an asteroid mining company.

## Graphene

Graphene has the potential to revolutionize many fields and does have some remarkable properties. I'm not sure it could block the mind-control signals of an Artificial Superintelligence, but if any material was going to do so, it would be graphene. I also chose to feature this material because it's one that would make sense for Isaac Jordan to use in his spacecraft.

Here is an excerpt from a 2015 article entitled, "What is Graphene?" on the website, *ExtremeTech*.

EXCERPT: *The word "super-material" gets thrown around a lot these days, but one super-material overshadows them all, earning its discoverers a Nobel Prize and defining the upper limit for scientific hype and excitement. It has the potential to revolutionize processing, power storage, even space exploration. It's called graphene, and it's the granddaddy of the modern boom in materials science. Graphene has the potential to be one of the most disruptive single inventions of all time—but what is it, really?*

*Scientists have been talking about graphene for the better part of a hundred years, though not always by that name. The idea was easy enough to come up with: what if we could take a diamond and slice it into wafers just one atom thick? This would make it a so-called "two-dimensional" substance, made entirely out of carbon, yet flexible in a way that diamond cannot be. It not only has the incredible physical properties you'd expect from a sheet of crystal, widely cited as the strongest material ever created on a per-weight basis, but it also has incredibly high electrical conductivity. Being atomically small, graphene could allow much, much more tight packing of transistors in a processor, for instance, and allow many electronics industries to take huge steps forward.*

*Yet despite some valiant early attempts, we had to wait until 2004 for anyone to reliably make graphene fragments large enough and quickly enough to be, hypothetically, useful. The incredible physical properties of graphene practically beg to be applied in all sorts of thought experiments. If it could be made in threads at least a meter long, some scientists believe these strands of graphene could be woven together to make a tether both strong enough and flexible enough to be the backbone of a space elevator. This single piece of flexible, woven carbon would stretch all the way from the surface of the Earth to beyond geosynchronous orbit. These are the sorts of sci-fi inventions that will become plausible if graphene manufacturing manages to come into its own.*

## DARPA, the Pentagon, Helen Woodward Animal Center, and smoke alarms

The information in *Infinity Born* about the history of DARPA and the Pentagon is accurate. There really is a Helen Woodward Animal Center in San Diego. I'm quite confident of this because my wife has been a volunteer there for many years. Like Riley, she is an avid dog lover. Unlike Riley, however, her father is not a billionaire (which is really too bad if you ask me—and while I've urged him on, he refuses to come out of retirement to become one).

The Helen Woodward Animal Center is not only well known in San Diego, it has become one of the most influential shelters in the world. In 1999, the Center created a campaign that encouraged pet lovers to adopt rescue animals rather than purchase pets from puppy mills or breeders. While the initiative began locally, by 2009 it had spread to include participants from almost four thousand animal organizations in seventeen countries, and to date has adopted out over nine million animals.

Finally, for those of you who have never had a houseful of smoke alarms malfunction and go off in the middle of the night, I can tell you that no description of the volume of noise they produce could ever do them justice. The alarms in our house have gone off a few times over the years and I really did think my head would explode. Maybe our alarms are set louder than industry standards, but I'm pretty sure they could be heard on the surface of the Moon.

### 3) ESSAY: "Scientific Advances are Ruining Science Fiction!"

For those of you with interest, I've included this essay, which first appeared in Lifeboat Foundation's *Visions of the Future* (2016), a compilation of both fiction and non-fiction written by forty-two authors. I'm one of twenty-one authors named on the cover, and I can't begin to describe what an honor it is to be included alongside some of the absolute greats of science fiction, including Robert Sawyer, James Gunn, Greg Bear, Gregory Benford, David Brin, Joe Haldeman, Ben Bova, and Alan Dean Foster.

Although I can't hold a candle to any of these writers, I gave this essay my best shot, and I hope that you will enjoy it.

### Scientific Advances are Ruining Science Fiction!
### By Douglas E. Richards

I write science fiction thrillers for a living, set five to ten years in the future, an exercise that allows me to indulge my love of science, futurism, and philosophy, and to examine in fine granularity the impact of approaching revolutions in technology.

But here is the problem. I'd love to write pure science fiction, set *hundreds* of years in the future.

Why don't I?

I guess the short answer is that to do so, I'd have to turn a blind eye to everything I believe will be true hundreds of years from now. Because the truth is that books about the future of humanity, such as Kurzweil's *The Singularity is Near,* have *ruined* me.

As a kid, I read nothing but science fiction. This was a genre that existed to examine individuals and societies through the lens of technological and scientific change. The best of this genre always focused on human beings as much as technology, something John W. Campbell insisted upon when he ushered in what is widely known as the Golden Age of Science Fiction.

But for the most part, writers in past generations could feel confident that men and women would always be men and women, at least for many thousands of years to come. We might develop technology that would give us incredible abilities. Go back and forth through time, travel to other dimensions, or travel through the galaxy in great starships. But no matter what, in the end, we would still be Grade A, premium cut, humans. Loving, lusting, and laughing. Scheming and coveting. Crying, shouting, and hating. We would remain ambitious, ruthless, and greedy, but also selfless and heroic. Our intellects and motivations in this far future would not be all that different from what they are now, and if we lost a phaser battle with a Klingon, the Grim Reaper would still be waiting for us.

In short, we would continue to be the kind of human beings a writer could work with, could understand. James T. Kirk might have lived hundreds of years in the future, might have beamed down to planets and engaged warp engines, but viewers still had no trouble relating to him. He was adventurous, loyal, and heroic, and he lusted after life (along with green aliens, androids, and just about anything else that could move).

But what if you believe that in a few hundred years, people will *not* be the same as today? What if you believe they will be so different they will be *unrecognizable* as human?

*Now* how would you write science fiction? You would have to change two variables at the same time: not only addressing dramatic advances in technology, but dramatic changes in the nature of humanity itself (or, more likely, the merger of our technology and ourselves).

In the early days of science fiction, technology changed at a snail's pace. But today, technological change is so furious, so obviously exponential, that it is impossible to ignore. I have no doubt this is why a once fringe, disrespected genre has become so widely popular, has come out of the closet, and is now so all-pervasive in our society. Because we're *living* science fiction every day.

Rapid and transformative technological change isn't hard to imagine anymore. What's hard to imagine is the *lack* of such change.

In 1880, the US asked a group of experts to analyze New York City, one of the fastest-growing cities in North America. They wanted to know what it might be like in a hundred years.

The experts extrapolated the likely growth during this period, and the expected consequences. They then confidently proclaimed that if population growth wasn't halted, by 1980, New York City would require so many horses to stay viable that every inch of it would be knee-deep in manure. Knee-deep! In horse manure!

As someone interested in technology and future trends, I love this story, even if it turns out to be apocryphal, because it does a brilliant job of highlighting the dangers of extrapolating the future, since we aren't capable of foreseeing game-changing technologies that often appear. Even now. Even at our level of sophistication and expectation of change.

But while we can't know what miracles the future will hold, we've now seen too much evidence of exponential progress not to know that Jim Kirk would no longer be relatable to us. Because it seems impossible to me that we will remain as we are. Remain even the least bit recognizable.

This assumes, of course, that we avoid self-destruction, a fate that seems more likely every day as WMDs proliferate and fanaticism grows. But post-apocalyptic science fiction has never been my thing, and if we do reach a *Star Trek* level of technology, we will have avoided self-destruction, by definition. And I prefer to be optimistic, in any case, despite the growing case for pessimism.

So if we do ever advance to the point at which we can travel through hyperspace, beam ourselves down to planets, or wage war in great starships, we can be sure we won't be human anymore.

It is well known that increases in computer power and speed have been exponential. But exponential growth sneaks up on you in a way that isn't intuitive. Start with a penny and double your money every day, and in thirty-nine days you'll have over two billion dollars. But the first day your wealth only increases by a single penny, an amount that's beneath notice. On the *thirty-ninth* day, however, your wealth will increase from one billion to two billion dollars—now *that* is a change impossible to miss. So like a hockey stick, the graph of exponential growth barely rises from the ground for some time, but when it reaches the beginning of the handle, watch out, because you suddenly get an explosive rise that is nearly vertical.

It's becoming crystal clear that we are entering the hockey-stick phase of progress with computers and other technologies. Yes, progress in artificial intelligence has been discouraging. But if we don't self-destruct, does anyone imagine that we won't develop computers within a few hundred years that will make the most advanced supercomputers of today seem like a toddler counting on his or her fingers? Does anyone doubt that at some point a computer could get so powerful it could direct its own future evolution? And given the speed at which such evolution would occur, does anyone doubt that a computer could become self-aware within the next few centuries?

Visionaries like Ray Kurzweil believe this will happen well within this century, but even the most conservative among us must admit the likelihood that by the time the USS *Enterprise* pulls out of space dock, either our computers will have evolved into gods and obsoleted us, or, more likely, we will have merged with our technology to reach almost god-like heights of intelligence ourselves.

And while this bodes well for these far-future beings, it isn't so great for today's science fiction writers. Because what would you rather read about: a swashbuckling starship captain? Or a being as incomprehensible to us as we are to an amoeba?

To be fair, science fiction novels have been written about a future in which this transformation has occurred. And I could write one of these, as well. The problem is that for the most part, people like reading about other people. People who are like them. People who act and think like, you know . . . *people.*

Even if we imagine a future society of omniscient beings, we wouldn't have much of a story without conflict. Without passions and frailties and fear of death. And what kind of a story could an amoeba write about a man, anyway?

I believe that after a few hundred years of riding up this hockey-stick of explosive technological growth, humanity can forge a utopian society whose citizens are nearly-omniscient and nearly-immortal. Governed by pure reason rather than petty human emotions. A society in which unrecognizable beings live in harmony, not driven by current human limitations and motivations.

Wow. A novel about beings we can't possibly relate to, residing on an intellectual plane of existence incomprehensible to us, without conflict or malice. I think I may have just described the most boring novel ever written.

Despite what I believe to be true about the future, however, I have to admit something: I still can't help myself. I *love* space opera. When the next *Star Trek* movie comes out, I'll be the first one in line. Even though I'll still believe that if our technology advances enough for starships, it will have advanced enough for us to have utterly transformed *ourselves*, as well. With apologies to Captain Kirk and his crew, *Star Trek* technology would never coexist with a humanity we can hope to understand, much as dinosaurs and people really didn't roam the earth at the same time. But all of this being said, as a reader and viewer, I find it easy to suspend disbelief. Because I really, really love this stuff.

As a writer, though, it is more difficult for me to turn a blind eye to what I believe will be the truth.

But, hey, I'm only human. A current human. With all kinds of flaws. So maybe I can rationalize ignoring my beliefs long enough to write a rip-roaring science fiction adventure. I mean, it is fiction, right? And maybe dinosaurs and mankind *did* coexist. The *Flintstones* wouldn't lie, would they?

So while the mind-blowing pace of scientific progress has ruined far-future science fiction for me, at least when it comes to the writing of it, I may not be able to help myself. I may love old-school science fiction too much to limit myself to near-future thrillers. One day, I may break down, fall off the wagon, and do what I vowed during my last Futurists Anonymous meeting never to do again: Write far-future science fiction.

And if that day ever comes, all I ask is that you not judge me too harshly.

## 4) About the Author and List of Books

Douglas E. Richards is the *New York Times* and *USA Today* best-selling author of *WIRED* and numerous other novels (see list below). A former biotech executive, Richards earned a BS in microbiology from the Ohio State University, a master's degree in genetic engineering from the University of Wisconsin (where he engineered mutant viruses now named after him), and an MBA from the University of Chicago.

In recognition of his work, Richards was selected to be a "special guest" at San Diego Comic-Con International, along with such icons as Stan Lee and Ray Bradbury. His essays have been featured in National Geographic, the BBC, the Australian Broadcasting Corporation, Earth & Sky, Today's Parent, and many others.

The author has two children and currently lives with his wife and two dogs in San Diego, California.

You can friend Richards on Facebook at Douglas E. Richards Author, visit his website at douglaserichards.com, and write to him at doug@san.rr.com

**Near Future Science Fiction Thrillers by Douglas E. Richards**
WIRED (Wired 1)
AMPED (Wired 2)
MIND'S EYE (Nick Hall 1)
BRAINWEB (Nick Hall 2)
MIND WAR (Nick Hall 3)
QUANTUM LENS
SPLIT SECOND
GAME CHANGER
INFINITY BORN

**Kids Science Fiction Thrillers** (9 and up, enjoyed by kids and adults alike)
TRAPPED (Prometheus Project 1)
CAPTURED (Prometheus Project 2)
STRANDED (Prometheus Project 3)
OUT OF THIS WORLD
THE DEVIL'S SWORD

Made in the USA
Columbia, SC
24 January 2018